10   JUN 1 8 2003

W9-DHM-982

WITHDRAWN

Wild Orchids

ALSO BY JUDE DEVERAUX

Wild Orchids

Jude Deveraux

ATRIA BOOKS

New York   London   Toronto   Sydney   Singapore

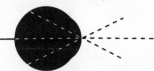

**This Large Print Book carries the
Seal of Approval of N.A.V.H.**

ATRIA BOOKS

1230 Avenue of the Americas
New York, NY 10020

ISBN: 0-7434-6761-2

First Atria Books large-print hardcover edition April 2003

10   9   8   7   6   5   4   3   2   1

ATRIA BOOKS is a trademark of Simon & Schuster, Inc.

For information regarding special discounts for bulk purchases, please contact Simon & Schuster Special Sales at 1-800-456-6798 or business@simonandschuster.com

Printed in the U.S.A.

Wild Orchids

CHAPTER ONE

Ford

Have you ever lost someone who meant more to you than your own soul?

I did. I lost my wife Pat.

It took six long, tortured months for her to die.

I had to stand by and watch my beautiful, perfect wife waste away until there was nothing left. It didn't matter that I have money and success. It didn't matter that I'm called an "important" writer. It didn't matter that Pat and I had finally started building our dream house, an engineering miracle that hung onto a cliff wall and would allow us to sit quietly and look out across the Pacific.

Nothing at all mattered from the moment Pat came home and interrupted me while I was writing—something she never did—to tell me that she had cancer, and that it was in an advanced stage. I thought it was one of her jokes. Pat had a quirky sense of humor; she said I was too serious, too morose, too doom-and-gloom, and too afraid of everything on earth. From the first, she'd made me laugh.

We met at college. Two more different people would be hard to find, and even Pat's family was completely alien to me. I'd seen families like hers on television, but it never occurred to me that they actually existed.

She lived in a pretty little house with a front porch and—I swear this is true—a white picket fence. On summer evenings her parents—Martha and Edwin—would sit on the front porch and wave at the neighbors as they passed by. Her mother would wear an apron and snap green beans or shell peas while she waved and chatted. "How is Tommy today?" she'd ask some passerby. "Is his cold better?"

Pat's father sat just a few feet away from his wife at a wrought iron table, an old floor lamp nearby, and a box of gleaming German tools, all precisely arranged, at his feet. He was—again, I swear this is true—known as Mr. Fix-It around the neighborhood and he repaired broken things for his own family and his neighbors. Free of charge. He said he liked to help people and a smile was enough payment for him.

When I went to Pat's house to pick her up for a date, I'd go early just so I could sit and watch her parents. To me, it was like watching a science fiction movie. As soon as I arrived, Pat's mother—"call me Martha, everyone does"— would get up and get me something to eat and drink. "I know that growing boys need their nourishment," she'd say, then disappear inside her spotlessly clean house.

I'd sit there in silence, watching Pat's father as he worked on a toaster or maybe a broken toy. That big oak box of tools at his feet used to fascinate me. They were all perfectly clean, perfectly matched. And I knew they had to have cost a fortune. One time I was in the city—that ubiquitous "city" that seems to lie within fifty miles of all college towns—and I saw a hardware store across the street. Since hardware stores had only bad memories for me, it took courage on my part to cross the street, open the door, and go inside. But since I'd met Pat, I'd found that I'd become braver. Even way back then her laughter was beginning to echo in my ears, laughter that encouraged me to try things I never would have before, simply because of the painful emotions they stirred up.

As soon as I walked into the store, the air seemed to move from my lungs, up my throat, past the back of my neck, and into my head to form a wide, thick bar between my ears. There was a man in front of me and he was saying something, but that block of air inside my head kept me from hearing him.

After a while he quit talking and gave me one of those looks I'd seen so many times from my uncles and cousins. It was a look that divided men from Men. It usually preceded a fatal pronouncement like: "He don't know which end of a chain saw to use." But then, I'd always played the brain to my relatives' brawn.

After the clerk sized me up, he walked away with a little smile that only moved the left side of his thin lips. Just like my cousins and uncles, he recognized me for what I was: a person who thought about things, who read books without pictures, and liked movies that had no car chases.

I wanted to leave the hardware store. I didn't belong there and it held too many old fears for me. But I could hear Pat's laughter and it gave me courage.

"I want to buy a gift for someone," I said loudly and knew right away that I'd made a mistake. "Gift" was not a word my uncles and cousins would have used. They would have said, "I need a set a socket wrenches for my brother-in-law. What'd'ya got?" But the clerk turned and smiled at me. After all, "gift" meant money. "So what kind of gift?" he asked.

Pat's father's tools had a German name on them that I said to the man—properly pronounced, of course (there are some advantages to an education). I was pleased to see his eyebrows elevate slightly and I felt smug: I'd impressed him.

He went behind a counter that was scarred from years of router blades and drill bits having been dropped on it, and reached below to pull out a catalog. "We don't carry those in the store but we can order whatever you want." I nodded in what I hoped was a truly manly way, trying to imply that I knew exactly what I wanted, and flipped through the catalog. The photos were full color; the paper was expensive. And no wonder since the prices were astronomical.

"Precision," the man said, summing up everything in that one word. I pressed my lower lip against the bottom of my upper teeth in a way I'd seen my uncles do a thousand times, and nodded as though I knew the difference between a "precision" screwdriver and one out of a kid's Home Depot kit. "I wouldn't have anything else," I said in that tight-lipped way my uncles spoke of all things mechanical. The glory of the words "two stroke engine" made them clamp their back teeth together so that the words were almost unintelligible.

"You can take that catalog," the man said, and my face unclenched for a moment. I almost said gleefully, "Yeah? That's kind of you." But I remembered in time to do the bottom lip gesture and mumble "much obliged" from somewhere in the back of my throat. I wished I'd had on a dirty baseball cap with the name of some sports team so I could tug at the brim in a Man's goodbye as I left the store.

When I got back to my tiny, gray apartment off campus later that night, I looked up some of Pat's father's tools in the catalog. Those tools of his were worth thousands. Not hundreds. Thousands.

But he left that oak box out on the porch every night. Unlocked. Unguarded.

The next day when I saw Pat between classes—she was studying chemistry and I was English lit—I mentioned the tools to her as casually as possible. She wasn't fooled; she knew this was important to me. "Why do you always fear the worst?" she asked, smiling. "Possessions don't matter, only people do." "You should tell that to my uncle Reg," I said, trying to make a joke. The smile left her pretty face. "I'd love to," she said.

Pat wasn't afraid of anything. But because I didn't want her to look at me differently, I wouldn't introduce her to my relatives. Instead, I let myself pretend that I was part of her family, the one that had big Thanksgiving dinners, and Christmases with eggnog and gifts under the tree. "Is it me or my family you love?" Pat once asked, smiling, but her eyes were serious. "Is it me or my rotten childhood you love?" I shot back, and we smiled at each other. Then my big toe went up her pants leg and the next moment we were on top of one another.

Pat and I were exotic to each other. Her sweet, loving, trusting family never failed to fascinate me. I was sitting in their living room one day waiting for Pat when her mother came home with her arms pulled down by the weight of four shopping bags. Back then I didn't know that I should have jumped up and helped her with them. Instead, I just stared at her.

"Ford," she said (my father's eldest brother thought he was bestowing a blessing on me when he named me after his favorite pickup), "I didn't see you sitting there. But I'm glad you're here because you're just the person I wanted to see."

What she was saying was ordinary to her. Pat and her parents easily and casually said things to make other people feel good. "That's just your color," Pat's mother would say to an ugly woman. "You should wear that color every day. And who does your hair?" From someone else, the words would have been facetious. But any compliment Pat's mother—I could never call her "Martha" or "Mrs. Pendergast"—gave came out sincere-sounding because it **was** sincere.

She put the shopping bags down by the coffee table, removed the pretty arrangement of fresh flowers she'd cut from her backyard garden, and began pulling little squares of cloth out of the bags. I'd never seen anything like them before and had no idea what they were. But then Pat's parents were always introducing me to new and wondrous things.

When Pat's mother had spread all the pieces of cloth out on the glass-topped coffee table (my cousins would have considered it a matter of pride to break that glass, and my uncles would have dropped their work boot-clad feet on it with malicious little smiles) she looked up at me and said, "Which do you like?"

I wanted to ask why she cared what I thought, but back then I was constantly trying to make Pat's parents believe that I'd grown up in a world like theirs. I looked at the fabric pieces and saw that each one was different. There were pieces with big flowers on them, and some with little flowers. There were stripes, solids, and some with blue line drawings.

When I looked up at Pat's mother, I could see she was expecting me to say something. But what? Was it a trick? If I chose the wrong one would she tell me to leave the house and never see Pat again? It was what I feared every minute I was with them. I was fascinated by their sheer niceness, but at the same time they scared me. What would they do if they found out that inside I was no more like their daughter than a scorpion was like a ladybug?

Pat saved me. When she came into the living room, her hands pulling her thick blonde hair up into a ponytail, she saw me looking at her mother, my eyes wild with the fear of being found out. "Oh, Mother," Pat said. "Ford doesn't know anything about upholstery fabrics. He can recite Chaucer in the original English, so what does he need to know about chintz and toile?"

"Whan that Aprill with his shoures soote," I murmured, smiling at Pat. Two weeks before I'd found out that if I whispered Chaucer while I was biting on her earlobe, it made her wild for sex. Like her father, an accountant, she had a mathematician's brain, and anything poetic excited her.

I looked back at the fabrics. Ah. Upholstery. I made a mental note to look up the words "chintz" and "toile." And later I'd have to ask Pat why being able to recite medieval poetry should exclude knowledge of upholstery fabrics. "What do you plan to upholster?" I asked Pat's mother, hoping I sounded familiar with the subject.

"The whole room," Pat said in exasperation. "She redoes the entire living room every four years. New slipcovers, new curtains, everything. And she sews all of it herself."

"Ah," I said, looking about the room. Every piece of furniture and all the windows were covered in shades of pink and green—or rose and moss as Pat later told me.

"I think I'll go Mediterranean," Pat's mother said. "Terra cotta and brick. I was thinking of trying my hand at leather upholstery with all those little nails around the edge. What do you think of that idea, Ford? Would that look nice?"

I could only blink at her. In the many houses I had lived in, new furniture was bought only when there were holes in the old, and price was the only consideration for purchase. One of my aunts had a whole set of furniture covered in three-inch-long purple acrylic. Everyone thought it was wonderful because all three pieces had cost only twenty-five dollars. Only I minded having to remove long purple fibers from my food.

"Mediterranean is nice," I said, feeling as proud of myself as though I'd just penned the Declaration of Independence.

"There," Pat's mother said to her daughter. "He does know about upholstery."

Pulling the little hair tie out of her mouth, Pat deftly wrapped it around her ponytail, and rolled her eyes. Three weekends before, her parents had visited a sick relative so Pat and I'd spent two nights alone in their house. We'd played at being married, at being our own little family, and that that perfect house was ours. We'd sat at the kitchen table and shucked corn, then we'd eaten dinner at the mahogany dining table—just like grown-ups. I'd told Pat a lot about my childhood, but I'd only told her the deep angst part, the part that was likely to get me sympathy and sex. I'd not told her the mundane, day-to-day things, such as rarely eating meals not in front of a TV, never having used a cloth napkin, and only using candles when the electric bill hadn't been paid. It was odd, but telling her that my father was in prison and that my mother had used me to punish my father's brothers made me seem heroic, while asking her what the hell an artichoke was made me feel like the village idiot.

The second night we spent together in her parents' house, I lit a fire in the fireplace, Pat sat on the floor between my legs, and I brushed her beautiful hair.

So, later, when she looked at me over her mother's head, I knew she was remembering the night we'd made love on the carpet in front of the fire. And from the looks she was giving me, I knew that if we didn't get out of there soon I'd be throwing her down on top of her mother's fabric samples. "You're so **alive**," Pat had said to me. "So primitive. So **real**." I didn't like the "primitive" part but if it turned her on . . .

"You two go on," Pat's mother said, smiling and seeming to intuit what Pat and I were feeling. And, as always, she was unselfish and thinking of others before herself. When the drunk teenager who killed her a few years later was pulled from his car, he said, "What's the big deal? She was just an old woman."

Pat and I were married for twenty-one years before she was taken from me. Twenty-one years sounds like a long time, but it was only minutes. Right after we graduated from college, one of the teaching jobs she was offered paid exceptionally well, but it was in an inner city school. "Hazard pay," the man on the phone who was begging her to take the job said. "It's a rough school, and last year one of our teachers was knifed. She recovered but she wears a colostomy bag now." He waited for this to sink in, waited for Pat to slam down the phone.

But he didn't know my wife, didn't know what her boundless optimism could take on. I wanted to try my hand at a novel, she wanted to give me the chance to write, and the money was excellent so she took the job.

It was difficult for me to understand such selfless love as hers, and I was always trying to figure out the why of it. Sometimes it would run through my head that Pat loved me because of my childhood, not in spite of it. If I were the same man but had grown up in an orderly house like hers, she wouldn't have been interested in me. When I told her that, she'd laughed. "Maybe so. If I'd wanted a clone of myself I'd have married Jimmie Wilkins and spent my life hearing him tell me I was half a woman because I couldn't have kids."

For all that Pat and her family looked like they lived an ideal life, the truth was, there were several tragedies in their past. In my father's family—my mother was an orphan and I was glad of it as my father's eleven brothers were all the family I could handle—a tragedy was a reason to stop life. One of my uncle Clyde's sons drowned when he was twelve. After that Uncle Clyde hit the bottle and stopped going to his night security job. He and his wife and their six other kids ended up living on what she made at McDonald's, and one by one their kids dropped out of school, or ended up in jail or on welfare, or they just wandered away. Everyone in my family seemed to think that this is what should have happened after Ronny's death. Forever after, they talked about Uncle Clyde's great grief over his son's tragic death in mournful whispers.

I was seven when my cousin Ronny drowned and I wasn't sad because I knew that Cousin Ronny had been a brute. He'd drowned while terrorizing a four-year-old girl. He'd grabbed her doll, run into the pond, and proceeded to dismember it, throwing the body parts into the murky water, all while the little girl stood on the bank, crying and begging. But as Cousin Ronny ran into the deep water, he disturbed a snapping turtle that bit his big toe, and he and what was left of the doll went under, where he hit his head on a rock and knocked himself unconscious. By the time anybody realized he wasn't pretending to be dead (Cousin Ronny was a great one for crying wolf) he actually was dead.

When I was told that Cousin Ronny had died—which meant that he'd no longer be around to bully me and the other little kids—all I felt was relief. And I was sure that Uncle Clyde would be glad, too, because he was always yelling at Ronny that he was the worst kid in the world and that he, Uncle Clyde, should have "cut it off" before he'd made such an evil son.

But after Ronny died, Uncle Clyde went into a state of bereavement that lasted the rest of his life. And he wasn't the only full-time mourner in my family. I had three aunts, two uncles, and four cousins who were also in life-long mourning. A miscarriage, a chopped-off limb, a broken engagement, whatever, were all reason enough to put life on hold forever.

I grew up praying hard that nothing truly bad ever happened to me. I didn't want to have to spend decades drinking and crying about the tragedy that had blighted my existence.

When I met Pat's extended family and saw that they were all laughing and happy, I shook my head at the irony of it all. So many tragedies had been thrust on my family, yet here were people who had been blessed—without tragedy—for generations. Was it their church-going ways that had made their lives so free of catastrophe? No, my uncle Horace had gone to church for years, but after his second wife ran off with a deacon, he'd never entered a church again.

About the third time Pat and I were in bed together, back when I still felt superior, as though my hard childhood had taught me more about life than her soft one had taught her, I mentioned this phenomenon, that her family had experienced no tragedies.

"What do you mean?" she asked, so I told her about Uncle Clyde and Cousin Ronny who had drowned. I left out the parts about the doll, the turtle, and Uncle Clyde's drinking. Instead, I used my natural-born gift for storytelling to make him sound like a man who loved deeply.

But Pat said, "What about his other children? Didn't he love them 'deeply'?"

I sighed. "Sure he did, but his love for Cousin Ronny overrode everything else." This last bit was difficult for me. I'm cursed with a clear memory and I could almost hear again the ugly fights that used to rage between Uncle Clyde and his bully of a son. Truthfully, before the boy drowned I never saw any love between Uncle Clyde and Cousin Ronny.

But to Pat I put on my best I'm-older-than-you look (by three months) and I've-seen-more-of-the-world-than-you (by the time Pat was eighteen she'd been to forty-two states on long driving vacations with her parents, while I had been out of my home state only twice) and told her that she and her family couldn't understand my uncle Clyde's feelings because they'd never experienced true tragedy.

That's when she told me she couldn't have children. When she was eight she'd been riding her bike near a construction site and had fallen. A piece of rebar, embedded in concrete, had pierced her lower abdomen and gone through her tiny prepubescent uterus.

She went on to tell me how her mother had lost her first husband and infant son in a train accident. "She and her husband were sitting together and she'd just handed him the baby when a runaway truck hit them," Pat said. "My mother wasn't touched but her husband and baby son were killed instantly. Her husband was decapitated." She looked at me. "His head fell onto her lap."

We lay there in bed, both of us naked, and looked at each other. I was young and in bed with a girl I was in love with, but I didn't see her beautiful bare breasts or the soft, perfect curve of her hip. Her words had shocked me to the core. I felt like a medieval man hearing for the first time that the earth wasn't flat.

I couldn't reconcile that sweet woman who was Pat's mother with the woman who'd had a severed head drop onto her lap. And Pat. If one of my female cousins had had a hysterectomy at eight years old her life would have stopped then and there. Every family gathering would have had everyone clucking in sympathy. "Poooooorrr Pat," they would have called her.

I'd known Pat and her family for months, and I'd met three grandparents, four aunts, two uncles, and an uncountable number of cousins. No one had mentioned Pat's tragedy or her mother's.

"My mother had five miscarriages before she had me and they removed her uterus an hour after I was born," Pat said.

"Why?" I asked, blinking, still in shock.

"I was breech so I was Caesarean and the doctor had been called from a party so . . . so his hand wasn't steady. Her uterus was accidently cut and they couldn't stop the bleeding." Pat got out of bed, picked up my T-shirt off the floor, and pulled it on over her head, where it reached to her knees.

The irony of this matter of uteruses and families flooded my brain. In my family girls got pregnant early and often. So why were my uncles able to reproduce themselves lavishly, but Pat's parents had only one child and no hope of grandchildren?

As I watched Pat dress, I knew there was something else in what she'd just told me about her birth. "A party? Are you saying that the doctor who delivered you was **drunk?**" People like Pat's family didn't have drunken doctors who "accidently" destroyed a woman's uterus.

Pat nodded in answer to my question.

"What about your father?" I whispered, meaning, Did **he** have any tragedy attached to him?

"Macular degeneration. He'll be blind in a few more years."

At that I saw tears form in her eyes. To hide them, she went into the bathroom and closed the door.

That was the turning point. After that day, I changed my attitude toward life. I stopped being smug. I stopped feeling that only my family had experienced "true life." And I relinquished my biggest fear: that if something truly awful happened to me, I'd have to stop living and retreat into myself. You go on, I told myself. No matter what, you go on.

And I thought I'd managed to do that. After that kid ran his car into Pat's mother and killed her, I tried to be an adult. Right after it happened, I thought that maybe if I heard the details of her death I'd feel better, so I went to a young policeman standing by the wreckage and asked him what happened. Maybe he didn't know I was related to the deceased by marriage, or maybe he was just callous. He told me what the kid who'd killed her had said. "She was just an old woman," he'd said, as though Pat's mother had been insignificant.

There was a funeral, a nice Presbyterian funeral, where people politely wept, where Pat leaned on me, and where her father aged by the minute.

Three weeks after the funeral, we all seemed to be back to normal. Pat returned to teaching in her inner city school, I went back to the night school where I taught English to people trying to get their green card, and back to my day job of writing what I hoped would become a great work of literature and give me immortality—and a top slot on the **New York Times** Bestseller List. Pat's father hired a full-time housekeeper and spent his evenings on the porch repairing his neighbor's appliances, something he planned to do as long as his eyesight held out. A year after the funeral, everyone seemed to have accepted the loss of Pat's mother as "God's will." True, there was an empty place that her absence left behind, and she was spoken of often, but her passing was accepted.

I thought it was accepted. But I also thought I was the only one who felt old-fashioned, white-hot rage at the loss of someone so good. I seemed to see things that no one else did. There was a little hole on the arm of the couch where the stitching had come apart. It wasn't more than a half inch long, but I saw it and thought how Pat's mother would have hated that little hole.

At Christmas, everyone except me was jolly and laughing and exclaiming in delight over their gifts. It had been over a year since Pat's mother's needless death and I was still holding the anger inside me. I hadn't told Pat but I hadn't written a word in that year. Not that what I'd written in the previous years had been worth anything, but at least I'd been making an effort. I'd had three agents but none of them could get a publishing house to buy what I wrote. "Beautifully written," I heard over and over. "But not for us."

But "beautiful" or not, my writing wasn't good enough in the eyes of New York editors to be published—and it wasn't good enough in the eyes of my wife. "Not bad," she'd say. "Actually, it's not bad at all." Then she'd ask what I wanted for dinner. She never spoke a word of criticism, but I knew I wasn't reaching her.

That Christmas, the second one after Pat's mother's death, I was sitting on the sofa in front of the fire and running my fingertips over the little hole in the seam. To my left I could hear the women in the kitchen, all of them chattering and quietly laughing. Behind me in the den the TV was blaring and the males were watching some sporting contest. The kids were on the closed-in porch at the back of the house, counting their loot and eating too much candy.

I was worried that I was becoming like my father's relatives. What was wrong with me that I couldn't get over the death of my mother-in-law? Couldn't get over the waste of it? The injustice? The kid who'd killed her turned out to be the son of a rich man; a battalion of lawyers had freed him on a technicality.

I got up and put a log on the fire and while I squatted there, Pat's father came into the room. He didn't see me because his eyesight had deteriorated until he was only able to see in a direct line in front of him.

He was holding a little pink basket with a hinged lid. As he sat down on the end of the couch, just where I'd been sitting, he opened it. It was a sewing basket, the back of the lid padded to make a pincushion that held several pre-threaded needles. I watched him remove a needle, his old hands running down the long thread to check for a knot at the end. His hands were shaking a bit.

He set the sewing basket beside him, and then, using what eyesight he still had and his left hand, he searched along the arm of the couch.

I knew what he was looking for: that little

hole in the couch cover that Pat's mother had made.

But he couldn't find the hole. There were tears blocking his limited vision and his hands were shaking too badly to feel anything. On my knees, I went to the other side of the arm and put my hands over his. He didn't express any surprise when I touched him, and he offered no explanation for what he was doing.

Together, slowly, for my hands were trembling and my eyes, too, were blurred, he and I sewed up the hole. A two-minute job took fifteen minutes, and during that time neither of us spoke. We could hear the other people in the rooms around us, but it was as though they were far away.

When at last the hole was closed, I put my finger on the thread and, bending, Pat's father cut the thread with his teeth. For a second his lips touched my fingertip.

Maybe it was that touch. Or maybe it was what we'd just done together. Or maybe it was just my desperate need for a man in my life who didn't love his truck more than he loved any human. Still on my knees, I dropped my head onto Pat's father's lap, and I began to cry. As he stroked my hair, I felt his silent tears fall onto the side of my face.

I don't know how long we stayed like that. If any of the Pendergasts saw us, no one ever mentioned it to me, not even Pat—but then they were a very polite family.

After a while, my tears began to slow and, as all those women's magazines said, I felt "better." Not good, but there was a knot in my chest that had been loosened. Maybe now it could go away, I thought.

"I'd like to kill that bastard kid," Pat's father said and I don't know how to explain this, but what he said made me laugh. I'd been surrounded for over a year by polite, nonviolent grief, but I couldn't feel that way. Twice, I'd come close to calling one of my uncles. He'd know someone who would "take out" that kid for a fee. I was tempted, but I knew that a revenge killing wouldn't bring Pat's mother back.

"Me, too," I whispered as I got up, wiping my face on the sleeve of my new Christmas shirt. He and I were alone in the room. When a log in the fire burned through and fell, I turned toward it. But then, on impulse, I put my hand on his shoulder, bent, and kissed his forehead. For a moment he held my wrist with both his hands, and I thought his tears were going to start again, but they didn't. Instead, he smiled. "I'm glad my daughter married you," he said, and no praise before or since has ever meant as much to me as those words. They broke something inside of me, something hard and suffocating that had taken up residence in my chest.

An hour later, I was the life of the party. I was Mr. Entertainment. I was laughing and joking and telling stories that had everyone howling. No one, not even Pat, had ever seen me that way. I'd told her that I'd learned to "sing for my supper" when I was a kid, but I hadn't elaborated. The full story was that my mother said that since my father's eleven brothers had been the ones to get her husband thrown into prison, they could take turns being a father to me. For my entire childhood I was moved every three months from one uncle to the next. "Here comes Punishment," my cousins would shout when my mother drove me from one house or trailer to the next. She'd push me toward a door, my one suitcase with all my worldly possessions at my feet, and give my shoulder a little squeeze, the only sign of affection she ever showed me. I'd not see her again until the three months were up and she delivered me to the next uncle. Even if they lived next door to each other, my mother made a point of driving me.

Over the years I'd learned that I couldn't compete with my cousins' fighting skills or their native ability to operate all large machinery that was painted either yellow or green, but I had a talent they didn't have: storytelling. Lord only knows where I got it, although an ancient great-aunt told me that my grandfather was the best liar she'd ever met, so maybe it came from him. In fact, I was so different, one of my uncles said that if I didn't look like a Newcombe he'd swear I wasn't kin to them at all.

Out of necessity, I'd learned to entertain. When tempers got too frayed, someone would poke me and say, "Tell us a story, Ford."

So I learned to tell stories that made people laugh, that scared them, or just enthralled them. The evening after I cried with my head on Pat's father's lap, I turned on like I hadn't done since I'd walked out of my uncle's house, bound for college on a partial scholarship and a student loan.

The next day, in the car, as we started the long drive home from her father's house, Pat said, "Wow. What happened to **you** last night?"

I didn't say much in answer to her question. Actually, I didn't say much on the whole trip back because I was thinking about what Pat's father had said, that he'd like to kill that kid. How could a man who couldn't see well enough to thread a needle kill someone? One thing for sure was that if he could pull it off, no one would suspect him.

And what kind of punishment would a kid like that deserve? Just sneaking up behind him and shooting him wouldn't be enough. He'd need to suffer like the people who'd loved Pat's mother suffered. He'd have to have what he loved most on earth taken away from him. But what did a kid like that love? Booze? His dad who got him off?

And what about Pat's mother? I thought. What about her spirit? Did her spirit, the essence of her, have to be taken off the earth just because her body was gone? What if her husband or daughter needed help? Would she be there? And what was the spirit world like anyway? Was her decapitated first husband there? Her infant son? What about the spirits of the babies she'd miscarried?

Hey! What about the drunken doctor who "accidently" cut up her uterus? Could her bodiless spirit do anything about him?

By the time we got home that night, Pat was looking at me strangely, but then she'd often said that the harder I thought the quieter I got. After I'd had a sandwich and brushed my teeth, I thought I just might go to my typewriter and put a few of my ideas on paper.

Not that I—a **real** writer—would ever, in a million years actually write a crime-slash-ghost-slash-revenge novel. But, still, maybe I could someday use the ideas in one of my good stories. You know, the great literary masterpiece that was going to win me a National Book Award and a Pulitzer. And spend multiple weeks on all the bestseller lists.

When I got to my typewriter, set up in an

alcove off the living room, I was startled to see that I'd left it on. I wasn't usually forgetful. There was a note on the keys. "I put three sandwiches in the 'frig. Don't drink the beer; it'll make you sleepy. If you're still at it by four tomorrow afternoon, I'll call you in sick."

Normally, I might have cried in gratitude to have a wife who understood me so well, but I was all cried out. She'd put clean paper in the machine and all I had to do was start punching in letters.

What's the big deal? She was just an old woman were the first words I typed, and after that, they just seemed to pour out of me. The first time I had the ghost of the murdered woman enter the story, I thought, I can't do this. This isn't literature. But then I remembered something I'd heard a best-selling writer say in a speech. "You can't choose what you write. No one comes down to you, sitting on a pink cloud, and says, 'I'm going to give you the ability to write. So which talent do you want? The Jane Austen model that lives forever, or the kind that makes you lots of money while you're alive but dies when you do?' No one gives you that choice. You just take whatever talent you're given and thank God four times a day for giving you any talent at all."

I had to remind myself of those words several times during the next months. I even typed them on a piece of paper and hung them on the wall above the typewriter. At some point, Pat wrote "Amen!" at the bottom.

I never went back to my classroom full of non-English-speaking students. At first Pat called in sick for me, and for a week she took over the class, but after the third student asked her to marry him so he could stay in the U.S., she quit. And she told them that I quit, too.

The book took me six months to write, and during that time I didn't come up for air. I saw Pat but I didn't see her. As far as I remember, we had no conversations. I didn't think about how she was managing to pay the bills without my income, but I imagine her father helped. I really don't know. My book was all the life I had.

When it was done, I turned to Pat where she was curled up on the end of the couch reading, and said, "I finished it." While I was writing, she'd never asked to read a word of the book and I'd never offered to show it to her. Now, shyly, feeling sheepish, I said, "Would you like to read it?"

Instantly, she said, "No," and I nearly collapsed on the floor. What had I done? Did she hate me? In the seconds before she spoke again, I imagined at least a dozen reasons why she didn't want to read my book—all of them bad.

"Early tomorrow we're driving to Dad's

house and you're going to read the whole book aloud to both of us," she said.

I stared at her for a few silent moments. It was one thing to bare my soul to her but to her father?! I searched for some excuse that would get me out of it. "But what about your job? You can't miss school. Those kids need you."

"It's summer. School's out," she said, without a trace of humor in her voice.

It was a six-hour drive to her father's house, and I was so nervous that after I ran into the left lane the second time, Pat took over driving. By the time we got there, all the blood had left my face, my hands and my feet.

Pat's father was waiting for us with fat turkey sandwiches, but I knew that if I took a bite, I'd choke. Pat seemed to understand. She put her father on the sofa, and me in a chair, then she dropped the first half of my manuscript on my lap. Without a word, she settled herself on the sofa beside her father, full plates on their laps.

"Read," she said as she took a bite.

That manuscript needed a lot of work. It was full of dangling participles, and contained thousands of ambiguous antecedents. I'd been writing so fast that I forgot to put in "he said" and "she said," so sometimes it was difficult to figure out who was talking. And my dates were all mixed up. I had people being born after they were married. I would have a character named

John and twenty pages later I'd call him George. And I don't even want to think about the misspellings and typos.

But for all the errors, the book had something that all my previous work hadn't. At the sixth chapter I looked up and saw that Pat's father had tears running down his cheeks. The book had heart. **My** heart. And in writing about what was inside me, I had at last broken up that huge, hard structure that had been living inside my chest. I had put the ugly thing, molecule by molecule, onto paper.

Night came, Pat put a glass of iced tea by my hand and I kept on reading, and when my voice gave out, she took the pages from me and began to read out loud herself. When the sun came up, I took over again while Pat scrambled eggs and toasted half a loaf of bread. When anyone went to the bathroom, we all went down the hall together and stood outside the door, never breaking in the rhythm of reading.

The housekeeper came at nine A.M., but Pat's father told her to go home and we kept on reading. When Pat finished the book at a little after four that afternoon, she leaned back in the chair and waited for our verdicts as though she were the writer and we the jury.

"Brilliant," Pat's father whispered. "Martha has been avenged."

His opinion was important to me, but it was

the opinion of the love of my life, Pat, that I wanted to hear. But she didn't say a word. Instead, she set the pages on the floor, got up and walked out the front door, taking the car keys and her handbag off the foyer table as she left.

Her behavior was so odd that I wasn't even hurt by it. The book had been about her mother so maybe Pat was upset, I thought. Or maybe—

"Women!" Pat's father said, and that seemed to sum it up.

"Yeah. Women," I said.

"What'd'ya say we get drunk?" my father-in-law asked and I'd never heard a more pleasing suggestion in my life.

By the time Pat returned an hour and a half later, he and I were downing shots of bourbon at an alarming pace, and he was telling me that he thought my book was the best one ever written. "Second only to the Bible," he said.

"You mean it?" I asked, my arm around him. "You really, really **mean** it?"

When Pat walked into the kitchen carrying two big bags with Office Max printed on them, she took one look at us and told us we were disgusting.

"But you didn't like my book," I wailed, the booze having dissolved my manly charade.

"Nonsense!" Pat said, taking the bottle and glasses off the table and placing a huge pizza box before us. She opened it to reveal a giant pizza covered with hot sausage and three colors of peppers—my favorite.

It wasn't until later, after I'd thrown up and shared the pizza with Pat's father, who then went straight to bed to sleep it off, that I realized Pat had taken her other bags and disappeared. I found her in the dining room, the table covered with pens, papers, and my manuscript.

My head ached and my stomach was queasy, and I was beginning to worry because she still hadn't made even one comment about my book. "What are you doing?" I asked, trying to sound everyday and as though I didn't want to jump up and down and scream, "Tell me! Tell me! Tell me!"

"I'm editing," she said, looking up at me. "Ford, it's the best book I've ever read, but even I could hear the errors in it. You and I are going over it sentence by sentence and correct it, and when it's done we're sending it to a publishing house."

"To my agent," I murmured. Best book, she'd said. **Best** book.

"That pompous little windbag?"

I had no idea she didn't like the man.

"No," Pat said. **"I** am going to be your agent."

"You?" I said, and, unfortunately, it came out sounding like I didn't believe that she, a high school chemistry teacher, could, overnight, become a literary agent.

She narrowed her eyes at me. "If you can become a writer, I can become an agent."

"Sure, honey," I said, reaching out to take her hand. I'd call my agent first thing in the morning.

Removing her hand from my grasp, she looked back at the manuscript. "Patronize me all you want, but while you've been writing I've been thinking and I know I can do it. All I ask is that you give me the chance." When she turned to me, her eyes were fierce, determined, almost scary. "I have no talent," she said in a hard tone I'd never heard her use before. "And I'll never have children. I have nothing but you and your talent to thank God for four times a day." She put her hand on the tall two-box stack of typed pages. "You don't know it yet but this is brilliant. And I know that right now, this minute, is my one chance in life. I can step back and become the writer's wife and be stuck at the end of the table with all the other stars' spouses—or I can become your partner. Maybe I can't write, but I'm better with numbers and money than you are, and I can organize anything. You write and I'll take care of the rest of it. I'll take care of contracts and promotion and defined benefit plans and royalties and—"

She stopped talking and looked at me. "Do we have a deal?" she asked softly, but her voice was full of steel. She wanted this as much as I wanted to write.

"Yes," I said, but when she put out her hand to shake mine, I kissed her palm, then her wrist, then I ran my lips all the way up her arm. We ended up making love on her mother's dining room table on top of the manuscript, which slid out of the boxes and spread itself out under us. For the six weeks that it took us to edit and rewrite the book, whenever we came to stuck-together pages, we looked at each other and smiled warmly.

There's no way to describe the twelve years between the publication of my first book and Pat's death.

After we'd edited the book, had it professionally typed, and made six photocopies of it, Pat made appointments with editors in New York and we went there for two days. She went to the meetings alone because she said that I'd turn into a whining baby when people started putting a dollar value to my "blood on a page." I protested that I was never a "whining baby," but I knew she was right. That book was about Pat's mother's life so how could that be worth less than billions?

In the end, I spent the days wandering around Central Park worrying so much that I lost four pounds. "If I'm not around you don't even **eat,**" Pat said, disgusted, but I could tell that she was as nervous as I was. We never talked about the "what if" but it hung in the air. What if she wasn't suited for agenting? What if she couldn't sell the book? And, the worst, what if no one liked the book enough to want to buy it?

At the end of the two days we went home to wait. The people she'd given the book to had to have time to read it. They had to discuss money with their bosses, and they had to—Who knew what they had to do?

I tried to tell myself that this was business, but part of my mind said that if they turned down the book it was as though they were rejecting Pat's mother—which is what I had titled the book: **Pat's Mother.**

Pat pretended she was cool and calm, laughing smugly whenever I jumped at some noise and looked at the telephone. But I got her back. I arranged with a guy I used to work with to call our number, then I hid the two telephones in our house. Pat had forbidden me to answer the phone, so when it rang I remained sitting at the table, the newspaper hiding my face. When the phone rang, Pat went running, and when she couldn't find the phone, she started throwing things around until the house was a jumble.

When she finally got to it and answered, out of breath, the caller hung up.

I kept the newspaper over my face to hide the fact that I was laughing so hard. I thought I'd pulled one over on her until a minute later she refilled my coffee cup. When I took a drink, I sputtered. She'd put dishwashing detergent in it.

As I was hanging over the sink washing out my mouth, Pat gave me a little smile that told me not to mess with her again.

When the phone rang again, I was still at the sink, Pat was rummaging in the refrigerator, and I could see she had no intention of answering it. I grimaced. It was probably Charley asking if he'd done all right.

Slowly, I walked over to the phone, now in plain sight, and when I picked it up I was told to hold for someone at Simon & Schuster publishing house.

I couldn't speak. Holding the phone away from my ear, I looked at the back of Pat. By some sixth sense, she turned, saw my white face, and nearly leaped over the couch to take the phone from me. Sitting down at the table, I took a deep drink of my coffee, and listened. Pat mostly said, "Yes. Yes. I understand," then she hung up and looked at me.

The first thing she did was to take away my cup and pour out the soap-laden coffee. I'd drunk nearly half of it and hadn't noticed. As she handed me a paper towel to wipe out the inside of my mouth, she said, "They're going to auction the book."

I had no idea what that meant but I knew it

was bad. Auctions were for used furniture. If someone died, their furniture was auctioned off.

Seeing that I didn't understand, Pat sat down at the table beside me and took my hand in hers. "Three publishing houses want to buy the book, so they're going to bid on it. Highest bidder gets your book. The auction will go on all day today."

What I didn't know until later was that Pat and I had done everything wrong. We should have presented the book to one publishing house at a time. But she had given the book to three houses and she'd told each house who else was looking at it. Because all three houses liked the book, and because they didn't want to offend the wife of the author, the publishing houses had done the agent's job and arranged the auction themselves.

But on that long ago day, in our innocence, neither Pat nor I knew of anything "wrong." We just settled back and did the only thing we could do: wait. The phone rang every hour as the houses presented their bids to us and asked us about the other bids.

After each call, we called Pat's father to keep him abreast of every bid increment and every development.

It was an exciting, frightening, exhausting day. Pat and I didn't eat a thing and I suspect that her father didn't either. We wouldn't move inches away from the phone for fear we'd miss something.

At five P.M. it was over and I was told I was to receive a cool million from Simon & Schuster.

How do you celebrate something like that? It was more than we could comprehend. Champagne wasn't enough. This was a life change, and it was too big for either of us to grasp.

We sat at the breakfast table in silence, not sure what to do, and having nothing to say. Pat clasped her hands in front of her, then started examining her fingernails. I picked up a pen from the table and began to color in the o's on the front page of the newspaper.

After several minutes of silence, I looked at Pat and she looked at me. I could hear her thoughts as clearly as if she were saying them aloud. "You call your dad," I said, "and I'll . . . Uh . . ." My mind was so blank I couldn't think of what I should do.

"Wait in the car," Pat said, as she called her father to tell him of the deal and that we were on our way to celebrate with him. The thoughts that Pat and I had shared were that there were three of us in this, not just two, and any celebration we had we had to share with him.

When we got to his house, it was nearly midnight, and we had to park three blocks away because there were so many cars parked on the streets.

"What idiot gives a party on a Tuesday night?" Pat asked, annoyed that we had to walk so far.

We were almost there before we realized that the party was in her dad's house and it was for us. Neither Pat nor I could figure out how he'd done it, but in just six hours Edwin Pendergast had put together a party that will live in history. All the doors of his house were open, but so were the doors of the two houses flanking his, and guests and waiters and caterers were swarming all over the three lots and three houses.

What a party it was! In the wide area created by the three front lawns was a live band playing Big Band-era music, the music Pat's parents loved best.

In front of the band were half a dozen professional dancers dressed in forties costumes swinging to a horn player who had to have been a blood relative of Harry James. Neighbors and people I'd never seen before, aged from eight to eighty, were dancing right along with the professionals. They all shouted hellos and congratulations when they saw Pat and me, but they were having too good a time to stop dancing.

As Pat and I got close to the front door, we heard other music coming from the back. I grabbed Pat's hand and we ran down the path at the side of the house and there, just behind Pat's mother's rose garden, was another band, this one playing modern rock and roll, and more people were dancing on the combined lawns of two houses.

The backyard of the house on the left of Pat's father's house was enclosed by a high fence. They had a pool, and when we heard laughter coming from the other side of the fence, Pat shouted, "Give me a boost up." I cupped my hands, she put her foot in them, and looked over the top of the fence.

"What's going on?" I shouted above the music. I saw her eyes widen in shock, but she didn't say anything until she was back on the ground.

"Swimming party," she shouted into my ear.

I looked at her in question, silently asking why a swimming party was cause for her look of shock.

"No suits," she shouted up at me. But when I looked about for something to climb on to look over the fence, she grabbed my hand to pull me into her father's house.

It was chaos inside. There were two live bands outside, one in front and one in the back, and with all the windows and doors open on that hot summer night, it was cacophony.

But it worked. The truth was, the clashing bands were just how I felt. I had hungered after being published for as long as I could remember. I used to write comic books when I was a kid. One time when I was staying with a church-going uncle, I wrote a new book to the Bible. All I'd ever wanted all my life was to write stories and have them published—and now it was going to happen.

But I was also scared to death. Maybe this book was a fluke. A onetime accomplishment. It had been based on the needless death of a woman I had come to love. So what was I to write about for the second book?

My wife punched me in the ribs.

"What are you worried about **now?**" she shouted up at me, obviously disgusted that I couldn't stop even for one night.

"Book two," I yelled back at her. "What do I write about next?"

She knew what I was saying. My success had happened because I'd written about a personal experience. No, I had **exposed** my personal experience. What else did I have to expose?

Shaking her head at me, Pat took my hand, led me into the downstairs bathroom and locked the door. It was quieter in there and I could hear her. "Ford Newcombe, you are an idiot," she said. "You have a mother who used you as a weapon for punishment. You have a father who's in prison, and you have eleven uncles who are, each one, vile and despicable. You've had enough bad in your life to supply you with a thousand books."

"Yeah," I said, beginning to smile. Maybe I could write about Uncle Simon and his seven daughters, I thought. Or about my sweet Cousin Miranda who died young, but for whom no one had ever mourned. Why was it that only the bad ones were missed? Was there a nonfiction book in this?

I was brought out of my thoughts by Pat unzipping my pants. "And what are you doing?" I asked, smiling.

"Going down on a millionaire," she said.

"Oh," was all I could say before I closed my eyes and gave myself to her hands and lips.

It was quite a while later that we left the bathroom, and I was ready to party. No more worries. I'd thought of half a dozen personal experiences that I could write about.

We found Pat's father next door in the master bedroom of the house with the swimming pool, and he was dancing so down and dirty that I stood in the doorway and gaped.

"You should have seen him and Mom together," Pat shouted as she slipped under my arm and went to her father. He stopped dancing, exchanged some sentences, ear to mouth, with his daughter, waved at me, then resumed dancing. She returned to me, smiling. "We're spending the night."

Since it was already nearly two A.M., that seemed redundant information, but I nodded, then let Pat pull me out of the bedroom and back downstairs to the neighbor's living room. All the kitchens of the three houses were full of catering people who were filling the dining rooms and backyards with enormous trays full of food. Since neither Pat nor I had eaten much for days, we made up for lost time. I was on my second plate when she told me she was going to say hello to some people. Nodding, I motioned that I was perfectly content to sit quietly in a corner and eat and drink.

The second I saw her skirt disappear around the corner I was up the stairs in a flash. A suit-less swimming party! I was pretty sure there was a guest bedroom upstairs where I could look down on the pool. Sure enough, there were about a dozen young adults in the back-yard, all beautifully naked, jumping off the div-ing board and swimming in the clear blue water.

"Amazing, isn't it?" said a voice behind me. I had my foot propped on a window seat, food in hand, and was looking out a wide window down onto the pool.

It was Pat's father and he'd shut the bedroom door behind him so we were in relative quiet.

"What's amazing?" I asked.

"Teenagers today. See the one on the diving board? That's little Janie Hughes. She's only fourteen."

I raised my eyebrows. "Didn't I see her on a tricycle last week?"

He chuckled. "She makes me understand why old men marry young girls. And the boys of the same age make me understand why the girls are attracted to older men."

He had a point. Even though several of the girls had removed their clothes, only one of the boys had. For the most part, the boys were skinny, with bad skin, and they looked scared to death of the girls, so they kept their big, baggy swim trunks on. The one boy who was naked had such a beautiful body, I figured he was probably captain of some local high school sports team. He reminded me of one of my cousins who'd been killed in a car wreck the night of the high school prom. Later, I'd thought that it was as though my cousin had known he was going to die early, because by seventeen he'd been a man, not a gangly boy, but a full-grown man.

"He'll probably die before the year's out," I said, nodding toward the nude Adonis standing at the edge of the pool. I looked at my father-in-law. "I thought you were blind, or nearly so."

He smiled. "I have an excellent memory."

Since the day I'd cried on his lap, there'd been a closeness between us. I'd never felt close to a man before and what I felt for Pat's father made me understand "male bonding."

"I'm leaving Pat the house," he said.

I put the food down and turned away. Please don't talk of death today, I thought. Not today. Maybe if I said nothing, he'd stop talking.

But he didn't stop. "I haven't said anything to Pat and I don't want you to, but I know I'm finished here on earth. Did you know that I tried to end my life about a month after she died?"

"No," I said, my head turned away, my eyes squeezed shut. And in my vanity I'd thought I was the only one who was truly and deeply grieving for Pat's mother.

"But Martha wouldn't let me die. I think she knew you were to write your book about her and she wanted that. She wanted it for you, and for Pat, and for herself, too. I think she wanted her life to mean something."

I wanted to say all the usual things, that her life **had** meant something, but hadn't I written a quarter of a million words saying just that? All I could do was nod, still unable to look him in the eyes.

"I know I don't need to tell you this, but I want you to take care of Pat. She pretends that not being able to have kids isn't important to her, but it is. When she was eight, after she got out of the hospital, she gave away all her dolls— and she had a roomful of them—and today she won't so much as touch one."

A lump formed in my throat, a lump of guilt.

I hadn't noticed that about my wife. The truth was I hadn't spent much time thinking about the accident that took away Pat's fertility. Since I had Pat, it never mattered to me whether or not we had kids. And I'd never thought to ask her how she felt about it.

"Let her help you in this writing thing," he said. "Don't shut her out. Don't ever think you've become such a big success that you need to get some glitzy agent with a big name. Understand me?"

I still couldn't look at him. Pat and I had been married for years. Why hadn't I noticed the doll-thing? Was I that unobservant? Or had she been hiding it from me? Did she have other secrets?

Pat's father didn't say any more, just put his hand on my shoulder for a moment, then quietly left the room, closing the door behind him. Minutes later a woman came out of the house downstairs by the pool and I recognized Janie Hughes's mother. She shouted at her daughter so loudly I could hear her over two live bands and what had to be five hundred people partying.

Dutifully, Janie wrapped a towel around her beautiful young body, but I saw her glance over her shoulder at the naked athlete as he stepped into his swim trunks.

When the excitement was over, I sat down on the window seat. The plate beside me was still full but I couldn't eat anymore. In essence, a man I loved had just told me he was about to die.

There was a Raggedy Ann doll stuck in the corner of the window seat and I picked it up, looking at the ridiculous face. No matter how much money I made, how much success I had, there were some things—things I really wanted—that I'd never be able to obtain. Never again would I sit at a table with Pat and her parents. Shaking my head, I remembered how I used to think that they were Chosen People who never had bad things happen to them.

When the bedroom door opened, I looked up. "There you are," Pat said. "I've been looking everywhere for you. This party is for you, you know."

"Can I have little Janie Hughes for my take-home gift?"

"I'll tell her mother you said that."

I put the rag doll in front of my face as though for protection. "No, no, anything but that."

She walked across the room to me. "Come downstairs. People are asking for your autograph."

"Yeah?" I said, pleased and astonished at the same time. I started to put the rag doll back where I found it, but on impulse, I put it against Pat's chest, meaning for her to take it.

Pat jumped back, not touching the doll, and looked as though she might be ill.

Part of me wanted to ask questions, to make her confess. But to confess what? What I already knew? When she walked to the door, she stood there with her back to me, her shoulders heaving as though she'd been running.

I picked the doll up off the floor, put the poor thing back in its corner, walked to my wife, and slid my arm around her shoulders. "What we need is some champagne, and you haven't told me what you want to buy with all the money we are going to get." I put a slight emphasis on the "we."

"A house," she said without hesitation. "Near the sea. Something high up, with a wall of glass so I can look out and see the waves and watch storms at sea."

I drew in my breath. Years of marriage and I'd learned two secrets about my wife in one night.

"Storms at sea, it is," I said, opening the door, my arm still around her.

"And what about you?" she asked. "Other than Jail Bait Janie, that is."

"If I went to jail, I might get to see Dad." I tightened my grip on her shoulders. "I want book number two," I said honestly.

"Don't worry, I'll help you and so will Dad. Now that Mom's gone, your books will give him something to live for."

I was glad when a blast of music hit us in the face and prevented my making a reply to that, for I was now feeling like this huge, noisy party was not for me but was, instead, a farewell to my father-in-law.

And I was right, for seven weeks later, Pat's father died in his sleep. As I stood in the funeral home looking at his slightly smiling corpse, I thought how he'd done just what my melodramatic relatives did and given away his life in grief.

When Pat's mother died, I was the one who was full of anger, but Pat had held me together. When her father died, she was so full of grief and anger that our doctor wanted her to be hospitalized. There was no room for me to give way, too, so I held us both together. The only time I weakened was when the will was read and I was told that Pat's father had left me his set of German tools.

Pat sold her parents' house and all the contents. If it had been my decision, I would have moved in there, as that house had held some of the best times of my life. But Pat kept only the photos—which she put in a safe-deposit box and never looked at—and sold everything else. The only thing we kept was the box of tools.

For the next dozen years, I wrote and Pat wheeled and dealed. As she said, we were a partnership. I wrote and we edited, then she sold.

And she was my first reader. She always told me what she thought of the content of my books, at times being almost brutal. It wasn't easy swallowing my ego, and sometimes we had blazing fights. "Try it my way and see which is better," she once shouted at me. In anger, to show her she was wrong, I rewrote the end of a book to her specification. And she'd been right. Her way was better. After that, I listened more, trusted more.

We didn't buy her house by the sea. For one thing Pat couldn't decide which sea she wanted to live by. And, too, she was fascinated by the idea that as a writer, I could live anywhere in the world, so "we" decided to try out a few places. We ended up moving around a lot.

In all the twelve years, we visited my uncles and where I'd grown up only once. The day before we arrived, I was sick with nerves. Pat tried to laugh me out of it but she couldn't. I was eaten up with wondering how it would be to see all of them again.

"Afraid you'll have to stay?" Pat asked me the night before, and all I could do was gasp, "Yes!"

But I needn't have worried. All my relatives treated me like a celebrity. They showed up with dog-eared copies of my books and asked me for my autograph. And what was really strange was that they collectively seemed to believe that the moment my first book was accepted for publication, a cloud of amnesia had settled on me. Each and every one of them seemed to believe that I didn't remember anything about my childhood.

Years earlier, I'd visited them. It was after I'd graduated from college, but before I was published, and that time no one had acted as though I remembered nothing. They didn't introduce me to relatives who I'd lived with as a kid. They didn't describe places I'd been to a hundred times. And absolutely no one said, "You won't remember this, but ..."

But after I was published, they did. My cousin Noble talked to me as though he'd just met me that morning, and after a couple of hours, I began to wish he'd call me "Buick" as he did when we were kids.

He introduced me to Uncle Clyde as though I'd never met the man. I gave Noble a look he ignored, then made an exaggerated little speech about how I most certainly did remember Uncle Clyde. "Imagine that," the old man said. "Imagine somebody famous like you rememberin' me." I smiled, but I wanted to say, "I have a scar on the back of my calf from where you hit me with your belt buckle so I'm not likely to forget you." But I didn't say that.

Noble put his arm around my shoulders and led me away. "You have to forgive Uncle Clyde," he said quietly. "He lost one of his children a few years back and he ain't been the same since."

Again I looked at Noble as if he were crazy. After Cousin Ronny drowned, Noble and I and four other cousins lit a bonfire in celebration. Noble said he'd had black eyes since he was four years old, all given to him by Cousin Ronny. I—the creative one—had made a big turtle out of rocks, mud, and sticks, and we'd all pretended to worship it in thanks for taking Cousin Ronny out of our lives.

So when Noble told me about Uncle Clyde's great grief as though it were news, I was sure he was joking. "And we've got the turtle god to thank for that," I said under my breath.

Noble looked at me as though he didn't know what I was talking about.

"The turtle god," I said. "Remember? We gave thanks for that turtle that bit Cousin Ronny and—"

Dropping his arm from around my shoulders, Noble straightened his back. "I don't know anything about that."

It was like that all day. By late afternoon, after I'd heard that phrase, "You won't remember this, but—" for the thousandth time, I was pretty fed up. "Why the hell **wouldn't** I remember it?" I snapped at Uncle Reg. "It happened to **me.** I **lived** here, remember? I was the Punishment. Me, Ford. Or Chrysler. Or John Deere. **Me!"**

Pat took my arm and pulled me away from

them, and for a while she and I stood under a
shade tree so I could calm down. I was grateful
that she didn't try to tell me they were just simple country folk who didn't understand.
Truthfully, I felt it was yet another attempt to
exclude me, to make me feel that I didn't
belong. I'd been different when I was a kid and
now I was even more of an outsider.

But even more than that I felt they were
casting me in a role of their making. "He grew
up here but he don't remember us," they'd tell
people. "He got to be a big star and plumb forgot us." I wanted people to say, "Even though
he made it to the top, he never forgot the little
people." Or something like that. But in spite of
the facts, I was being told that now that I was a
"celebrity" I'd become a snob.

Pat stood beside me while I tried to get my
temper under control, then she said, "Too bad
you were such a Goody Two-shoes that you
never learned to give any of it back to them."

"I wasn't—" I began. "And I didn't—" It
took me a full minute of sputtering to understand what she was really saying. I kissed her
forehead and we walked back to where everyone was waiting—and looking concerned about
my inexplicable explosion of bad temper. But I
guess that's how celebrities are, their eyes
seemed to say.

After my talk with Pat, I was in such a good

mood, that I started three fistfights. I knew
where the sore spots were in my relatives so I
dug at them. I asked Noble whatever happened
to that old Pontiac he had and ten minutes later
he and another cousin (who'd stolen the car but
denied it) were into it.

I asked Uncle Clyde about his beloved son
who'd drowned, then I asked him to tell me
wonderful stories about the boy, about what
good deeds he'd performed, and, by the way,
what exactly had Cousin Ronny been doing in
the pond that day?

At one point Pat narrowed her eyes at me,
telling me I was going too far. But I was enjoying myself too much to stop.

When Pat loudly announced that we had to
leave, not one of them suggested that we "come
again." Noble walked me out to the car. "You
ain't changed none, have you?" he said, his eyes
angry as he spit a glob that landed a quarter
inch to the left of my shoe.

"Neither have you," I said, smiling broadly.
The day before I left for college, Noble and three
of his drinking buddies had ridiculed me until I
was caught between homicidal rage and tears. I'd
stalked off into the woods to escape them. When
I went back, just before dark, I found that they'd
run the tractor over my suitcase full of clean,
ironed (by me) new (purchased with money I'd
earned boxing groceries) clothes.

Uncle Cal had lightly smacked Noble across the back of the head for the "prank," but he'd made it clear he didn't think what his son had done was so bad. "Just a little goin' away present," he said, smiling. No one had offered to help me rewash and iron my clothes, so I'd had to stay up all night to do it, finishing just in time to catch the bus the next morning—the bus that took me away from the lot of them.

"It was nice seeing all of you again," I said to Noble, actually meaning it. I'm not sure that getting my first book published had made me feel as good as the second half of that day had. "Listen, Noble," I said in a friendly way, "if any of the kids want to go to college, let me know and I'll help with the expenses."

With that I got into the car and Pat peeled away like she was competing at the local dirt track speedway. When I looked back at Noble, I saw that he was puzzling over my offer. Was I trying to rub it in that he'd told me that only fairy boys went to college? Or was I saying that I was the only one smart enough to get there?

I chuckled on and off for three hours at the consternation on his face. But he must have figured out that I'd been sincere because over the years I sent several of the next generation of my relatives to college. One of them was Noble's oldest daughter, Vanessa, who ended up teaching at the college level.

"One of your ancestors had a brain," Pat said. "That's why intelligence pops out every now and then."

"Recessive gene."

"Real recessive," she said, and we laughed together.

All that ended, all the good times ended, when Pat died. I had grown up without a family, found one, and lost it.

Once again, I was alone in the world.

CHAPTER TWO

Jackie

I think he wanted me because I made him laugh.

No, not **wanted** me. Not like that. He wanted me to work for him.

Of course I said no. After all, many females in town had tried to work for him, but they'd either been fired or quit in tears. Or in anger.

I'd been told how he was great at making people angry. "Pure, unadulterated rage," a friend of mine said while four of us were having lunch together at the local fry place—fried meat, fried onions, fried potatoes. The waitress didn't appreciate my humor when I asked her not to let the cook fry my salad. She walked away in a snit and kept it up for the whole meal.

But I was used to my humor getting me into trouble. My father used to say that I did it so no one would see me cry. That puzzled me because I never cry and I told him so. "That's just what I said," he answered, then walked away.

So, anyway, this big-time, super-duper, best-selling writer asked me to work for him because I made him laugh. And because I told my ghost story. Well, actually, only sort of told my ghost story. As Heather pointed out, I'd told it better. But, gee, it takes a bigger ego than mine to think she can tell a story to a master storyteller. I had visions of his saying that my "syntax" was wrong.

But before the ghost story—or devil story, as Autumn calls it—I made him laugh about the Pulitzer prize.

I was at a party and Autumn—poor dear, lots of hair but no brain—was in tears because her future mother-in-law had yet again been looking down her nose at my friend. We all knew why Cord Handley was marrying the girl, and it certainly wasn't for her intellectual ability. She had a mass of thick auburn hair and a set of knockers that kept her from seeing her feet. Autumn complained that she couldn't find lacy bras in her size. I said, "All I need is lace," and that made everyone laugh.

We knew there was no real future for Autumn and Cord; eventually, his mother would break them up. Cord's family was the closest the town had to "old money." Cord wasn't all that bright himself, but his mother was and she ran things. Unfortunately, her three children had inherited her husband's brain and her looks. It made sense that she was trying to improve the line by getting her three kids to marry brains, but her grown children were having none of it. Her youngest son wanted to marry the beautiful, sweet-tempered, but stupid, Autumn.

Poor Autumn left her future mother-in-law's house every Thursday afternoon in tears because every time Autumn saw her she was quizzed. A sort of verbal SAT test. Tea and stumpers, I called it.

One day when some of my women friends and I were having lunch together, I made the mistake of asking Autumn what she was going to do **after** the wedding. Since she and Cord were moving into the family mansion after they were married, Autumn would be seeing the old battle-ax every day.

Maybe it's because I grew up without a mother, but I seemed to have missed out on some being-a-girl education. I merely pointed out what I thought was an obvious problem and all hell broke loose. Autumn burst into tears, and Heather and Ashley put their arms around her, looking at me in disbelief.

My "What did I do?" look was familiar to them.

"Jackie, how could you?" Jennifer said.

I didn't ask what I'd said that was so horrible. Years before I'd given up trying to answer the question "What have I done **this time?**"

As far as I can tell, women put most things under the category of "being supportive." Pointing out that Autumn was probably going to be crying every day instead of just once a week after she moved in with her mother-in-law was, probably, not "being supportive."

In this instance, I was apparently also being insensitive to the fact that my friend was "in love." As in, Autumn couldn't tell her future mother-in-law to go screw herself because Autumn and Cord were "in love."

"You know about that, don't you, Jackie? You're in love, too."

True, I was engaged and about to be married, but I think I was doing it for some solid reasons. Kirk and I had the same goals and wanted the same things. And, okay, I was sick of living alone since Dad died. Maybe because I'd grown up with only one parent empty houses are not something I've ever liked much. I was always afraid that my beloved father would disappear and I'd be left totally alone.

So, anyway, we were at a party and Autumn was gently, prettily, weeping about the latest hateful thing her future mother-in-law had said to her. Since she couldn't belittle Autumn's looks, it was about her reading matter. "My dear," the old woman had said, "the only fiction worth reading is what has won the Pulitzer prize." I'd learned my lesson and I was trying to "be supportive" so I didn't advise Autumn to tell the old bat to go to hell.

"I don't even know what the Pulitzer prize is," Autumn was saying, sobbing into a lace-edged hanky—no used, frayed tissues for our Autumn!

I knew—bless her pretty little head—that Autumn thought that **Teen People** magazine was intellectual.

"Look," I said, stepping closer to Autumn and getting her attention, "you should learn to defend yourself against her. Tell her you always buy the Pulitzer prize-winning novels, but you, like every one else on earth, can't get through them."

"I know I can't read well, Jackie. I'm not smart like you," Autumn wailed.

The others gave me **that** look. I wasn't "being supportive."

Squatting down in front of Autumn, I took her damp hands in mine. Heaven help me but crying made her prettier. "Autumn, your future mother-in-law is a snob. She thinks that because a book has 'Pulitzer prize winner' on the cover that reading it makes her an intellectual. But it doesn't."

I wanted to cheer her up but I knew I couldn't do that by telling her that I read the fiction winner every year, so I decided to elaborate on a pet theory of mine. "You want me to tell you how to **write** a Pulitzer prize-winning book?" I asked, but didn't give her time to answer. "First you come up with a love story. That's right, just like all the gaudy romance novels in the grocery, Pulitzer prize novels are pretty much all love stories, but they're in disguise. Sort of like buried treasure. And like finding buried treasure, you have to go through a lot of stuff that isn't treasure to find it. Do you know what I mean?"

"Sort of," she said, her tears slowing. She wasn't smart but she was one of the nicest people I ever met.

"Okay, so the author comes up with a teeny, tiny love story, just something as simple as two people meeting and falling in love."

"That's what the books **I** read are about," Autumn said.

"Yes, but we're talking about the ol' prize novels here so those books are different. First of all, the main characters can't be beautiful. In fact, they need to be homely. No smoldering eyes or raven tresses as those traits would disqualify the book."

At that I got a tiny smile from Autumn. "I understand. Ugly people."

"Not ugly and not grotesque. Maybe they have something like big ears. The next thing you have to do is start hiding the treasure. Bury it so the reader can't find it easily. This means you can't have the lovers together very often. They can't be like in a romance novel where the hero and heroine are together on nearly every page. In fact, you can't even call them a hero and heroine. You have to call them 'protagonists.'"

"Why?"

"It's just one of those little rules of literary life. People who think they're smart like to use words other people don't use."

"But Jackie—"she began, but stopped and waited for me to go on.

I didn't believe she'd remember any of this, but I was indeed cheering her up. And besides, even though I didn't look up, I could feel that I was drawing an audience, and I can be an awful ham.

Autumn nodded, still holding my hand, and waited for me to continue.

"Okay," I said, "you start burying your treasure of a love story underneath lots of quirky characters with funny names. You name them Sunshine or Rosehips or Monkeywrench, whatever, just so they get odd names."

"Why would they do that? Who's named Monkeywrench?"

"No one, but that's the point. The judges

probably have names like John and Catherine so they dream of being name Carburetor."

Autumn smiled. "I see. Like Emerald."

I didn't have any idea who Emerald was, but I figured it out and smiled. "Exactly—except the opposite. In romance novels the hero and heroine—"

"Protaga . . ." Autumn said and I grinned.

"Yes. In romances, the protagonists are given beautiful names like Cameo and Briony, and the males are Wolf and Hawk, but those names don't win prizes. Prize-winning protagonists have odd names, but never beautiful ones. So after you get your names for your characters, you make up quirky personalities for them."

"Like what?"

"Well . . ." I thought about it for a moment. "Like Miss Havisham. Heard of her?"

Autumn shook her head. Her crying hadn't even messed up her makeup.

"Miss Havisham was getting dressed to get married when a note was delivered saying the groom wasn't going to show up for the wedding. Miss Havisham decided to stay exactly the way she was for the rest of her life, one shoe on, one off, and in her wedding dress. The author showed her years later as an old woman still in her rotting dress, cobwebs all over a table covered with her wedding feast. Miss Havisham is a celebrated quirky character in literature, and people who award prizes love quirky characters. And they want the treasure—the story—hidden very deep, under lots of people with funny names doing lots of strange things."

"I see," Autumn said.

I knew she probably didn't "see" at all, but I could feel the collectively held breath of my audience so I wasn't about to stop. "In your story you also need to put a shocker, something straight out of a horror novel."

"But I thought this was a romance novel."

"Oh, no! You must never call it that. The people who write these books need for you to believe that they're far above romance writers and horror writers and mystery writers. That's why they bury all those stories deep inside their books; they can't risk association with a genre writer. In fact, prize-winning authors have to bury the story so deep that the judges can barely see them."

Autumn was looking puzzled.

"Okay, let me give you an example. In a romance novel two gorgeous people meet and immediately start thinking about sex, right?"

"Yes . . ."

"That's how it is in real life, too, but if you want to win a prize, your characters must never think about sex except in a self-deprecating way. The judges love characters who think they're unattractive, and who've failed at most things they've tried. And, by the way, the judges also love incomplete sentences."

"But I thought—"

"That sentences need a subject and verb? True, they do. Except in prize-winning novels. In a regular novel—one that's not about to win a prize, that is—the author would write something like 'After she said goodbye, she turned and went up the stairs.' A prizewinner would write 'Said goodbye. Up the stairs. Wished she'd said **au revoir.**' See? It's different. And adding the French helps, too."

"I like the first way better. It would be easier to read."

"But this isn't about 'easy to read.' 'Easy to read' isn't 'intellectual.' This is about reading a mystery, a horror book, and a love story while believing you're a superior being who doesn't read 'those kind' of novels. Oh. And it helps to be a woman whose first name is a variation of Ann. No one named Blanche L'Amour will ever win a literary prize."

When Autumn realized I'd finished, she leaned forward and kissed my cheek. "You're funny," she said. **"You** should marry Cord's brother."

I had to stand up to hide the shiver that ran down my spine. Only in my worst nightmare would I marry into that family. Only if—

My thoughts suddenly stopped because

standing in front of me, just behind Autumn's chair, was Ford Newcombe, one of the best-selling writers in the world. The people who'd been hovering over Autumn when she was crying had pulled back and were squashed together on each side of her chair. They were giving Mr. Newcombe lots of reverential air space around him. As befitted his stature, of course.

He was smiling slightly, his blue eyes focused on mine, as though he'd enjoyed my silly story. He had an interesting face rather than a handsome one, but his body looked soft and unexercised. He'd been writing for as long as I could remember, so I figured he had to be ancient, in his sixties, at least.

Of course I'd known he'd been living in our town for the last two years, but no one knew why. After he fired a friend of a friend of mine, I suggested that he was here because every other town in America had run him out.

I'd heard from everyone in town who could talk, even Mr. Wallace who spoke with a machine at his throat, that Ford Newcombe was impossible to work for. He was always in a bad mood, always grumpy, and nothing anyone did ever pleased him. He'd fired at least three people twenty-four hours after he'd hired them. One of them, a woman my father's age, had told Heather's aunt, who told Heather's mother, who told Heather, who told all of us, that his problem was that he could no longer write. Her theory (taken off the Internet) was that his late wife had written all his books and since she'd died, there could be no more new Ford Newcombe books.

I tried to keep myself from questioning that theory aloud. If his wife wrote the books why weren't they published under her name? This wasn't the eighteenth century where a book needed a male pen name to make it sell, so why would anyone need to go through such a charade? But when my friends went on gossiping, I finally had to ask why. Jennifer looked at me hard and said, "Tax purposes," then gave me silent warning that I was not "being supportive."

So here I was, having made a fool of myself in an overlong, and ridiculous, story about Pulitzer prize-winning books, and he was staring at me. Oh, Lord, had any of his books won the Pulitzer?

Swallowing, I moved away through the people gathered around Autumn (people were **always** gathered around Autumn) and went to the bar to get a drink. It was one thing to make a fool of oneself in front of friends, but quite another to do it in front of a celebrity. Megarich. Megastar. I'd seen a photograph of this man with the president at the White House.

So why was he here in our nothing little town? And at Jennifer's parent's house on a

Saturday night? Didn't he have any presidents to visit? Emperors?

"That was ... entertaining," a voice to my left and above my head said.

I knew who it was so I took a deep breath before looking up at him. "Thanks ... I guess," I said, letting him know I'd caught the little hesitation in his praise. There were lines around his eyes, but I couldn't tell if they were from age or world weariness. His mouth might have been nice, but it was clamped together in a hard line. I'd heard that the first four women he'd fired had been sent packing because they'd made passes at him. But what had he expected? He was a rich widower. Get real.

"Would you like to work for me?" he asked.

I couldn't help it. I burst out laughing. Not a polite, refined laugh, but a real hee haw. "Only if I had two heads," I said before I could get control of myself.

He looked puzzled for a moment, but then he gave a little bit of a smile, so I knew he got it. Back in the sixteenth century, when the duchess of Milan was asked if she'd marry Henry the Eighth, she'd replied, "Only if I had two heads."

"Okay, just thought I'd ask," he said, then walked away.

That sobered me. My father said, "That tongue of yours can make paper cuts seem painless." Now that I'd offended the one and only celebrity I'd ever met, I was sure my father was right.

I turned to the waiter behind the drinks table who'd seen and heard it all. He wasn't local so he didn't know my reputation for putting my foot in my mouth. Instead, he was looking at me with astonishment.

"Rum and Coke," I said.

"Sure you don't want a block and an ax?" he said, showing me that he, too, got my smart aleck remark.

I gave him my best drop dead look, but he just chuckled.

About ten minutes later, Kirk showed up and I breathed a sigh of relief. Kirk was my fiancé and a great guy. He was smart and a good businessman, stable (had lived in one place and one house all his life), and good to look at. He wasn't Autumn's caliber, but he was nice looking. And, best of all, he didn't have a creative bone in his body. In other words, Kirk was everything I wasn't, everything my father hadn't been, and everything I craved.

When he saw me he smiled and held up a finger to let me know he'd be with me in one minute. Kirk was always buying or selling something. He'd buy some dinky little business, like a cardshop from some little old lady, spend twenty grand or so, and make the store into a place that sold music and movies. Then he'd sell the shop for twice what he'd paid for it and buy something else.

Truthfully, I thought Kirk was fascinating. I liked to read and I had a passion for taking photos with my precious Nikon camera that I'd had to take out a loan to buy, but business and numbers bored me as much as they intrigued Kirk. "That's what makes us good together," he said. "Opposites attract."

Since you can't pay the rent by wandering through the woods looking for things to photograph, I had a job that kept me around books all day. I did cataloging and research for a professor at the local university. The university had an unwritten requirement that its professors must publish something every few years, so old Professor Hartshorn had spent years pretending he was working on a book. What he really did was hire young girls to research some subject, then he'd criticize them until they quit. That way he could blame the secretary for the work not being done.

I knew this is what he did when he hired me (everybody in town knew he did this) but I came up with a plan to thwart him. I knew from the gossip among his former secretaries that he waited a month before starting to make their lives hell, so during that month I put together a chapter of a book on President James Buchanan. My father had read everything written about the man and used to tell me about him, so I was somewhat of an expert myself. Buchanan was a lifelong bachelor and even during his lifetime it was hinted that he was gay. The truth was that my father was just pretending interest in this long-dead president. Actually, my father had been half in love with Buchanan's niece who was his White House hostess, the twenty-six-year-old, lush-bosomed Harriet Lane. Nobody else's dad carried a photo in his wallet of a woman born in 1830.

I spent a couple of evenings copying titles, authors, and dates of some of the resource books that were still in my father's bedroom bookcase, made a couple of color copies of Miss Lane (she didn't marry until after her uncle was out of office), and wrote a whopping good chapter from what I remembered of what my father had told me.

Instead of showing the chapter to old Professor Hartshorn and getting it torn apart with criticism, I put his name on it as the author, and mailed it to the university president with a note saying he (Professor Hartshorn) wanted to show him (the prez) what he was working on.

I wasn't prepared for what followed. I'd heard that Hartshorn was a good history teacher and that's why he was allowed to stay at the university. But good as he was, the man hadn't published and it was rumored that at last he was going to be fired.

After the president received the chapter, he was wild with excitement. He came running to Professor Hartshorn's office, chapter in hand, shouting, "This is brilliant. Totally brilliant. You must read this at the next faculty meeting. And here people were saying you weren't actually writing anything."

I was working in the back room, but I have to say that Professor Hartshorn fell into step with it all. He said, "Miss Maxwell, I seem to have misplaced **my** copy of the chapter of **my** book that **I** wrote." If the university president heard anything odd in the word emphasis in that sentence, he didn't let on. I slapped a copy of the twenty-five page chapter on the professor's desk, didn't look at either man, and went back into the other room.

A few minutes later Professor Hartshorn called me back into his office. "Tell me, Miss Maxwell, when did my publishing house say this book must be finished?"

"Three years," I said. I needed a job, and three years was as long as I'd ever stayed anywhere. This was, of course, before I met Kirk and decided to stay in one place for the rest of my life.

"Isn't that a long time?" the president asked, looking at Hartshorn and ignoring that I, a mere student, was standing there.

"Obscure subject," Hartshorn said, frowning at being bothered. "Difficult to research. Now go away, Henry, and let me get back to work."

Smiling, happy that he wasn't going to have to fire an institution like Professor Hartshorn, the president left. I waited for the blast to come from the professor. But it didn't happen. Without looking at me, he picked up my chapter, handed it back to me, and said, "Chapter every three months. And write lots about Harriet Lane's bosom."

"Yes, sir," I said, and went back to work. For the next two years, every three months, I'd go through my father's books and write twenty-five pages about the golden hair, violet eyes, and voluptuous figure of Miss Harriet Lane.

At the end of the second year, as a joke, I got Jennifer's mother to help me make a period costume to Miss Lane's measurements (please don't ask me how my father got hold of her vital statistics, but fanatics have ways) in violet silk with pink piping. I'd bought a dressmaker's dummy at a yard sale and with the help of cotton batting—a **lot** of cotton—Jennifer's mom and I managed to re-create Miss Lane's famous bosom. Jennifer, Heather, and I carried the dressed mannequin into Professor Hartshorn's office at six A.M. one Monday morning so it was there when the professor arrived.

But he said nothing about the headless person that took up the entire corner of his small office. A week went by, and he still said nothing. I was quite disappointed—until Saturday morning, that is. I went through the drive-in at my bank to deposit my paycheck as usual when the teller—a friend of mine—said, "Congratulations."

"On what?" I asked.

"Your raise. And you've made a mistake on the deposit slip. I'll fix it for you but you'll have to initial it."

That's when I found out that the darling old coot had given me a twenty-five percent raise. All for Harriet Lane's magnificent bosom.

But, now, in just three weeks I was going to get married and quit work. For a while, I planned to read, take photos, and have lunch with the girls. I'd had a paying job since I was fourteen years old and now, at twenty-six, I was looking forward to some time off.

But that was all before I went to the party at Jennifer's house and met Ford Newcombe.

Kirk took more than a minute. In fact he took more than thirty minutes. He was deep in conference with the eldest Handley son, the one who handled all the family investments so the father could play golf. Of course everyone in town knew that Mrs. Handley was the one who actually controlled the money, but the sons put on a show.

I was standing by myself, sipping my rum and Coke, and thinking about how I was looking forward to changing my life. I'd become bored by my job with Professor Hartshorn. It wasn't as creative as I'd hoped it would be, and there was no place to advance to. I hadn't yet told Kirk, but I was hoping to eventually open a little business of my own. My dream was to have a small home portrait studio where I could take natural light photos of people, something that I could some-day put into a book. All I needed was some time off so I could use my savings and what my father had left me to set up my business. I wanted a home business so if I had kids . . .

"He's asking for you," Heather whispered into my ear.

I glanced at Kirk, but he was still head to head with the oldest Handley son.

"No, not him," Heather said. **"Him."**

She nodded toward Ford Newcombe who was standing by the window, drink in hand, and listening to Miss Donnelly. Instantly, I felt sorry for him. Miss Donnelly wrote the bulletin for the local Methodist church so she told people she was a "published writer." No doubt she thought she was Ford Newcombe's equal.

"Go on," Heather said, pushing me in the small of my back.

But I didn't move. There isn't much of me, but what there is, is muscle. "Heather," I said calmly, "you've lost your mind. That man is not 'asking' for me."

"Yes, he is. He asked Jennifer's mom about fifty questions about you, who you are, where you work, everything. I think he has the hots for you."

"Better not tell Kirk or there'll be a duel."

Heather didn't laugh. "Look on the bright side. Once he gets to know you, he'll throw you out."

Heather, too, had a sharp tongue.

"Go on," she said, pushing harder. "See what the man wants."

Truthfully, I felt I owed him an apology, and besides, who can pass up time with a celebrity? I could tell my grandkids, et cetera.

When Ford Newcombe saw me, he looked as though I were his life raft. "There you are," he said loudly, over Miss Donnelly's head. "I have those papers you wanted to see, but we need to look at them outside."

That made no sense since it was pitch dark outside. "Sure," I said just as loud. "Let's go." I followed him outside—trailed by Jennifer, Autumn, Heather, and Ashley.

He got all the way to the little waist-high fence that surrounds the big deck behind Jennifer's parents' house before he turned around to look at me, and when he did, his eyes widened.

I knew what he was seeing even before I turned. I had been used. All of them were dying to meet him, and dying to ask him questions he'd probably answered a million times.

Stepping back, I let them have him. After all, for all I knew the man loved having four pretty young women bombard him with questions and shy smiles. I looked back through the glass doors to see if Kirk was finished yet, but he was still yakking away, so I stood to the side and played with the straw in my watery drink.

It wasn't until Ashley asked, "What are you working on now?" that I began to listen. The answer to "Do you write with a typewriter, a computer, or by hand?" held no interest for me.

"It's a true story," he said.

That made me look at him sharply. Okay, so I admit it. I've read every word Ford Newcombe has written and a lot of what's been written about him, so I knew that, more or less, everything he's written has been a "true story." When he said something that was a given, was he just trying not to give out any information?

"A true story about what?" Autumn asked, and I could see Newcombe's face soften. Sometimes I wondered what it would be like to live behind Autumn's face and have people melt whenever they looked at me.

"It's a sort of ghost-witch story," he said, still not giving away anything.

"Ah, like the Blair Witch," Heather said.

"No, not exactly," Newcombe said, and I could tell he was offended by Heather's remark. She made him sound like he was jumping on a bandwagon—or, worse, planning to plagiarize.

"You should tell him your devil story," Autumn said to me, but before I could reply, Jennifer said, "Jackie used to terrify us all with her story about something that happened in North Carolina about a hundred years ago."

Newcombe smiled in what I thought was a patronizing way. "That's when all the good stories took place," he said, looking at me. "Go on, tell me."

I didn't like his smug attitude. It was as though he was bestowing permission on me. "It's just a folktale I heard when I was a kid," I said, smiling over my glass.

But my friends wouldn't let up.

"Go ahead, Jackie, tell it," Ashley said.

Heather poked me in the ribs. "Tell it!"

Jennifer narrowed her eyes at me to let me know that I **should** do this. For my friends. To be "supportive."

"Please," Autumn said softly. "Please."

When I looked up at Newcombe, he was watching me with interest, but I couldn't tell what he was thinking. I couldn't tell if he was just being polite or if he really wanted to hear my story.

Whatever, I didn't want to make a fool of myself again so I said, "It's nothing really, just a story I heard a long time ago."

"It actually happened," Heather said.

"Maybe," I said quickly. "I think it did. Maybe."

"So what's the story?" Newcombe asked, staring at me.

I took a breath. "It's simple, really. A woman loved a man the townspeople said was the devil, so they killed her. They piled stones on her chest until she died." After I finished, I could see that my friends were disappointed.

Heather spoke first. "Jackie usually tells the story so well that she gives us goose bumps."

Autumn said, "I think Jackie should be a writer."

That's when I dropped my glass on the deck, sending shards onto everyone's stocking-clad legs, and we all went rushing inside to assess the damage.

I left the bathroom first and seconds later, Kirk came to tell me that he was sorry but he had to leave. "Business. You understand, don't you, Pumpkin?"

"Sure," I said. "Give me a ride home?"

"Can't," he answered, turning back to the oldest Handley son, and they left the house.

I stood there for a few minutes, not wanting to face the others who were still in the bathroom.

"So why didn't you want me to hear the full version of the story?" asked a voice behind me. Him.

I wasn't going to lie. "It's just that you must get a lot of people telling you they have a story that would make a great book so would you please help them get a publisher?"

"An agent."

I didn't know what he meant.

"People want an agent first. They think that agents can get a writer more money."

"Oh," I said. "I don't know about that because I don't want to write and, even if I did, I'm not the kind of person who would impose myself on you."

He looked down at his drink, which was as iceless as mine had been. "About the devil story, it sounds interesting. Did you really hear it when you were a kid? Or did you make it up?"

"Probably half and half," I answered. "The truth is that I was so young when my mother told me the story that I may have taken poetic license over the years. I don't know what I remember and what I've added to it."

"Your mother told you the story only once?" he asked.

"My parents separated when I was very young and I grew up living with my father. My mother was killed in a car wreck about a year after they separated." I looked away, not wanting to tell him any more about my personal life.

After looking at me for a moment, he drained his glass. "Honestly, I am looking for an assistant. Sure you wouldn't be interested?"

This time I smiled graciously. "Thanks for the offer but no thanks. I'm getting married in three weeks, then I'm going to . . ." I couldn't very well tell my plans to this stranger when I hadn't yet dropped them on my fiancé, so I shrugged.

He gave me a little smile. "Okay, but if you change your mind . . ."

"I'll just follow the Trail of Tears." Oh, Lord. I'd done it again. I clamped my hand over my big mouth and looked at him in horror. I couldn't even get "sorry" to come out.

A couple of times he started to say something, but he didn't. Quietly, he set his drink glass down on a table, then left the house.

I bet he wouldn't be going to any more parties in our small town. And my friends were going to **kill** me.

CHAPTER THREE

Ford

I can't say that I **liked** her very much, but she was the most interesting person I'd met in years. Best of all, I thought she could do the job and that she'd make no emotional demands on me. I needed some way to get back into writing, but since I hadn't found the road yet, I thought Jackie Maxwell and her devil story might send me in the right direction.

I'd read the gossip magazines and the Internet, so I knew people were saying that Pat had written my books. How she would have laughed to hear that! I'd also heard that my writing was linked to her and once she died, I couldn't do it anymore.

That was closer to the truth, because none of

my books were fiction. They were fiction enough that my uncles and cousins couldn't sue me, but, basically, they were the truth. "Distorted truth" as Pat said. As she'd pointed out on that long ago, happy day, I'd had enough bad in my life to write many books. I'd written about every rotten thing that had ever been done to me.

But the truth that no one knew, not anyone at my publishing house or any friend, was that I'd written myself dry long before Pat died. The only book that was left in me was the one about Pat, and I was years and years and years away from being able to write that one.

In the six years since her death, I'd wandered around the country, moving the few belongings I still owned from one house to another. I'd settle into a community, look around and listen to see if anything sparked my appetite, and hope to find a reason to start writing again.

But nothing interested me. Now and then my publishing house would reissue some old book of mine, or put my few novellas into one book so it looked as though I was still publishing, but most people knew I wasn't. When I typed my name onto the Internet, I found three groups that were discussing my death. They listed "facts" that they believed were proof that I'd taken my own life the day my wife died.

The latest town I'd moved to was supposed

to have great weather, but I hadn't seen it. It was also supposed to be "charming," but I didn't find it to be so. I'm not sure why I didn't move out the day after I moved in, except that I was tired. I was tired . . . not tired of living so much as tired of being brain-dead. I felt like those women who go through college, then get married and pop out three kids right away. They went from brain-overuse to not using their brains at all. I guess that's where I was. In six years I'd had a few brief affairs, but since I compared every woman to Pat, I'd found each one wanting.

About a year ago, I'd read something—I was a voracious, eclectic reader in those six years—about a witch that haunted some old house somewhere and it had sparked a tiny interest in me. I began to think about putting together a collection of true stories about ghosts or witches in America. Every state has those poorly-written, locally-printed books about regional ghosts, so I thought about collecting the books, doing masses of research, and publishing an anthology. A sort of **Ghosts of the U.S.** kind of thing.

Anyway, doing the research appealed to me. All I needed was an assistant. But it turned out to be nearly impossible to find someone who was really useful.

Did I have a knack for finding losers? Was it

something in **me** that attracted them? Several of the women seemed to be living in a romantic novel. They seemed to believe that I'd hired them because I wanted to marry them and share all my worldly goods with them. I got rid of those women fast.

Then I went through the ones who wanted everything spelled out for them. They wanted what they called a "job description." I gave in to one of them and spent an hour and a half of my life writing the thing. Two hours later, when I told her I wanted her to go to the grocery for me, she said, "That's not my job," and I fired her.

Some of them I fired and some of them quit. Truthfully, I think that all of them had an ideal in their minds of what it would be like to work for a best-selling author and I didn't live up to what they expected.

From my viewpoint, not one of them could follow an idea. They were like robots and would do what I told them to—as long as it didn't interfere with their "job description"—but they didn't take the initiative. And, too, many of them used their brains only for trying to seduce me to an altar. Free sex I would have taken, but it was "community property" that I saw in their eyes.

Just before I was to move yet again—to where I had no idea—I was having lunch with the president of the local university, and he said, "You ought to get an assistant like ol' Professor

Hartshorn has. She's writing a book for him."

I wasn't much interested in what he was saying because I'd already scheduled the movers for
next week, but I was being polite so I said,
"What kind of book?"

He chuckled. "It's about Harriet Lane, with a
great many passages about her violet eyes and
her magnificent bosom."

I'd never heard of the woman, so he went on to
tell me that she was President James Buchanan's
niece. "I don't know where Hartshorn's assistant
got her information, but I'd be willing to bet it's
accurate. Miss Lane was an equal political partner
to her uncle—who, by the way, was nicknamed
'Old Gurley.' If you know what I mean," he added,
waggling his eyebrows.

Interesting, I thought. I needed an assistant
who could think. "Is she writing the book **with**
the professor?"

The president grimaced. "Hell, no. One time
when I confronted him, he said there was already
too damn much written about everybody, so he
wasn't going to add to the pollution. But the
trustees were on my case to fire him because he
wasn't published, so Hartshorn started using his
students to pretend he was writing." The president waved his hand, meaning he didn't want to
explain that particular story. "Anyway, a couple of
years ago, I received this hilarious chapter of a
book about an obscure president's niece, and it

had Professor Hartshorn's name on it as the author. Right away, I knew he hadn't written it so I gave it to my secretary—who knows everything that goes on in this town—and asked her who was capable of writing such a paper. She started telling me about a man who had a crush on a Victorian woman named Harriet Lane. Had pictures of her all over his office and always wore something violet because Miss Lane had violet eyes."

I was confused. "Hartshorn's assistant is a man?"

The president frowned at me. I knew that look. For a writer, you're not very smart, it said. I'd found out long ago that when you're a writer people expect you to understand everything about everything.

"No," he said, speaking slowly as though to an idiot, "that man was Hartshorn's assistant's father. He's dead. Her father is dead, not Hartshorn. Anyway, Hartshorn's young, female assistant sends me an extremely entertaining chapter every three months. They're too naughty to be published, but the Trustees and I love them. **The Misadventures of Miss Harriet Lane,** we call them."

While he was smiling in memory of Miss Lane's bosom, I was thinking. "If she's so dedicated to Professor Hartshorn she won't want another job."

"Hartshorn is an"—he lowered his voice—

"what is colloquially known as an a-hole. I doubt if he's ever even told her thanks for saving his job. Although I did hear that he gave her a raise for decorating his office with a life-size mannequin of Miss Lane."

This was beginning to sound good. She was creative. And smart. Took the initiative. I needed those things. I didn't find out until after Pat died that I was a person who co-wrote. I need lots of feedback. I've never understood how other authors survived with the two or three words they got from their editors. You could spend a year writing a book and at the end all you'd get was, "It's good."

If I were honest with myself—and I tried not to be—I wanted a partner, someone I could bounce ideas off. I didn't want a fellow writer who was going to be competition, but I wanted . . . Pat. I wanted Pat.

But I had to take what I could get. "So how do I meet her?" I asked. "Through Hartshorn?"

The president snorted. "He'd lie. If he knew you wanted her, he'd drug her before he let you meet her."

"Then how—?"

"Let me think about it and see what I can come up with. A social setting might be best. I'm sure I know someone who knows her. For the next two weeks, accept all invitations." He looked at his watch. "Uh oh. I have a plane to catch."

He stood, I stood, we shook hands, then he left. It was only after he was gone that I remembered I hadn't asked what the assistant's name was. Later, I called Hartshorn's office and asked what his assistant's name was. "Which one?" the young woman on the phone asked. "He has five of them." I couldn't very well say, "The one who's writing the book for him," so I thanked her and hung up. I called the president's office but he'd left town.

"Two weeks," the president had said. I was to accept every invitation for the next two weeks. No one can imagine the number of invitations a celebrity in a small town receives in two weeks. I did a reading of **Bob the Builder** for a local nursery school—and was vociferously told that I had mispronounced Pilchard's name.

I had to give a speech at a ladies' luncheon, (chicken salad, **always** chicken salad) and had to listen to one shirtwaist-clad little old lady after another tell me that I used too many "dirty words" in my books.

I had to give a speech at a local tractor dealership, and ended up talking about the internal combustion engine—something I had to do to keep the attention of my audience.

I also accepted an invitation to a party at someone's house and that's when I finally met Professor Hartshorn's assistant.

At the party, I watched the people and tried

to guess which one might be Hartshorn's assistant.

I noticed a group of girls who seemed to be friends. One of them was so beautiful she made me dizzy. Face, hair, body. Wherever she went in the room, eyes followed her—mine included. But after a while of watching, I began to detect a blankness in her eyes. The proverbial dumb blonde—or Titian red in this case. And her name was Autumn—which made me feel old. Her parents were no doubt former hippies— and my age.

There was a Jennifer who seemed to be angry about something and seemed to have set herself up as the boss of everyone. I knew it was her parents' house, but I'd be willing to bet that she bossed people wherever she was.

Heather and Ashley seemed normal enough, but Heather wasn't very pretty so, to compensate, she wore too much makeup.

The fifth girl was Jackie Maxwell and, instantly, I knew she was "the one." She was short, with a softly curling mass of short dark hair, and she looked like a poster advertising "physically fit." Just looking at her made me stand up straighter and suck in my stomach.

She had a cute face and dark green eyes that seemed to see everything that was going on around her. A couple of times I had to look away so she wouldn't know I was watching her.

After a while, an odd thing happened. In the midst of the party, lovely little Autumn sat down on a chair smack in the middle of the room and began to cry. And cry right prettily, I might add. If Pat had been there she would have made a snide comment about how the girl managed to weep without squinching up her facial muscles.

But the girl going from laughing to tears in a second—and doing it in the middle of the room—wasn't what was odd. What was strange was that when this raving beauty began to cry, all eyes turned toward Jackie.

Even the woman who was blathering on at me about how she was writing a book "not like yours but deep, you know what I mean?" turned and looked at Jackie.

Did I miss something? I wondered. I watched with interest as Jackie went to this girl Autumn, squatted in front of her like some African native, and began to talk to her in the tone of a mother. Jackie had a voice that made me want to curl up with a blankie and have her soothe me. Turning to a man next to me, I started to say something, but he said, "Ssssh, Jackie's gonna tell a story."

Everyone in town—and eventually even the bartenders—tiptoed over to surround the big chair and listen to this girl tell a story.

Okay, I was jealous. No one had ever spontaneously listened to **me** like that. Only if there was a lot of advance publicity and I arrived in a limo did people listen to me with rapt attention.

So what story was she going to tell? I wondered. As all of us waited, she proceeded to cheer up this brainless little beauty queen with a story on how to write a Pulitzer Prize–winning novel.

Since my sales kept me out of the prize-winning circles, ("Money or prizes," my editor told me. "Not both.") I listened. And as she talked, I found myself wanting her to be even more critical than she was. What about the overuse of metaphors and similes? What about emotion? My editor called them "Connecticut books." Not too much emotion in them. Cool. Dignified. Cerebral.

We always want more, don't we? Prize-winners want sales; best-sellers want prizes.

When Jackie finished her story, I expected everyone to burst into applause. Instead, they acted as though they hadn't been listening. Odd, I thought.

She got up (even at her age my knees would have been killing me) looked straight at me, ignored my smile, then went over to the bar to get a drink. I followed her and nearly fell over my tongue trying to give her a compliment. Since the people who knew her hadn't said anything, I thought maybe they knew she hated praise.

Then I **really** messed up because I blurted out that I wanted her to work for me.

Brother! Did she laugh. When she told me that she'd work for me only if she had two heads, it took me a full minute to understand what she was saying. I didn't know exactly where the quote came from but I could guess.

Okay, so I can take a hint. I turned around and walked away.

I would have gone home then and probably forgotten about the whole thing (and would have had to work to not use the woman's "How to Write a Pulitzer Prize–Winning Novel" speech in a book—if I ever wrote again, that is) but Mrs. Lady of the House grabbed my arm and started pulling me from one room to another to introduce me to people. After several minutes of this, she told me that I needed to forgive Jackie, that sometimes she could be, well . . .

"Abrasive?" I asked.

Mrs. Lady looked at me hard. "My cousin worked for you for four and a half weeks and she called me every day to tell me what you put her through. Let's just say that Jackie doesn't have the franchise on abrasive behavior and leave it at that, shall we? Mr. Newcombe, if you're looking for an assistant, I think Jackie Maxwell just might be the **only** woman who could work for you."

When she turned away and left me standing there, if it hadn't been late at night I would have called the moving company and said, "Come and get me **now!**"

A few seconds later, I was trapped by a dreadful little woman who wanted me to personally publish her 481 church bulletins, many of which no one—meaning no congregation—had ever read. "Original source," she kept saying, as though she'd found George Washington's unpublished diaries.

I was rescued by Jackie. I meant to get her alone outside so I could apologize and maybe start over, but when I turned around, I saw she had been followed by an entourage of gawking girls. Within seconds I was bombarded with questions. As the girls took me over, I could see Jackie inching away. I was beginning to adopt the philosophy of "if it was meant to be it will happen" when one of the girls dropped a bombshell on me. She said Jackie knew a true devil story.

Through my limited (mostly assistantless) research I knew that devil stories were rare. Ghost and witch stories were abundant, but devils . . . Rare.

After persuasion, Jackie told the story in a couple of sentences, but she told **all** of it in those two sentences. Someone once told me that if a person was a really good storyteller he could tell the story in one word and that word would be the title of the book. **Exorcist** is an example. Says it all.

Her story intrigued me so much that I thought maybe my ears would start flapping and pull me straight up. Wow! A woman loved a man the townspeople believed was the devil. Why did they believe that? And they killed **her.** Not him. Her. Why didn't they kill the man? Fear? Couldn't find him? He'd gone back to hell? What happened after she was murdered? Any prosecutions?

But before I could ask anything, Jackie dropped her glass—on purpose but I had no idea why—and all the girls turned into squawking hens and ran for the nearest bathroom.

I took a few moments to try to turn myself into their idea of a cool, calm, sophisticated best-selling author, then hightailed it after Jackie.

As soon as she came out of the bathroom some guy went up to her, said he had to leave and called her "Pumpkin." No one on earth looked less like a "Pumpkin" than that curvy little creature.

I didn't like him. He was too slick-looking for my taste. A used-car salesman trying to look like a stockbroker. And he was with a tall young man who looked like someone had turned the lights off inside his head. I'd be willing to bet six figures that those two were up to no good.

But then, maybe it was just that I really was beginning to want this young woman to work for me so I was getting possessive.

I again tried to get into a conversation with her and find out more about the devil story, but she seemed to be embarrassed because her friends had said that she should write a book. First of all, I didn't remember hearing that. It was probably when my ears were twitching and I was floating. Second, I wanted to say, "Honey, **everybody** wants to be a writer."

But as I chatted with her about her not wanting to be a writer, I found out she was getting married in three weeks (I guess to the salesman-broker). Then she more or less told me that she wouldn't work for me if I were the last man . . . Et cetera.

I went home.

Early the next morning I called the moving company and indefinitely postponed my move. I decided I really did need to figure out where I was going before I packed up.

By this time, I didn't have an assistant or a housekeeper, so I lived with dirty clothes and TV dinners—both of which made me think of my childhood. For weeks, I used every resource I had to try to find out about Jackie's story. I went on the Internet. I called Malaprop's in Asheville and had them send me a copy of every book they had on North Carolina legends. I called my publisher and she got me phone numbers of several North Carolina writers and I called them.

No one had heard of the devil story.

I called Mrs. Lady of the House (had to fish her invitation out of the garbage can where it was, of course, stuck to something wet and smelly) and asked her to please, pretty please, find out the name of the town in North Carolina where the story had happened, but not to tell Jackie or any of her friends I'd asked.

By the time I hung up I wanted to ask the woman to negotiate my next book contract—if/when, that is. She said she would get the name of the town, but only if I agreed to talk at one of her women's club lunches ("a reading would be nice and an autographing afterward"). In the end she set me up for three whole hours, and I was to get my publishing house to "donate" thirty-five hardcovers. All this for the name of a town in North Carolina. Of course I agreed.

She called back ten minutes later and said in her best silly-me voice, "Oh, Mr. Newcombe, you're not going to believe this but I don't have to ask anyone anything. I just remembered that I already know the name of the town where Jackie's story happened."

I waited. Pen ready. Breath held.

Silence.

I continued waiting.

"Is the twenty-seventh of this month good for you?" she asked.

I gritted my teeth and clutched the pen. "Yes," I said. "The twenty-seventh is fine."

"And could you possibly donate **forty** books?"

It was my turn to be silent, but I bent the tip of my pen and had to grab another one from the holder.

I guess she knew she'd pushed me to my limit because she said in a normal voice, no ooey-gooey gush, "Cole Creek. It's in the mountains and isolated." Her voice changed back to little-girl. "See you on the twenty-seventh at eleven-thirty A.M. sharp," she said, then hung up. I said the filthiest words I knew—some of them in Old English—before I hung up my end.

Three minutes later I had the number to the Cole Creek, North Carolina, public library and was calling them.

First, in order to impress the librarian, I gave my name. She was indeed properly impressed and gushed suitably.

With all the courtesy that I'd learned from Pat's family, I asked her about the devil story and the pressing.

The librarian said, "That's all a lie," and slammed down the phone.

For a moment I was too stunned to move. I

just sat there holding the phone and blinking. Big deal writers don't have librarians or book-sellers hang up on them. Never has happened; never will.

As I slowly put down the phone, my heart was beating fast. For the first time in years I felt excited about something. I'd hit a nerve in that woman. My editor once said that if I ran out of my own problems to write about, I should write about someone else's. At long last I seemed to have found a "someone else's prob-lem" that interested me.

Five minutes later I called my publisher and asked a favor. "Anything," she said. Anything to get another Ford Newcombe book is what she meant.

Next, I looked on the Internet, found a real-tor who handled Cole Creek, called and asked to rent a house there for the summer.

"Have you ever **been** to Cole Creek?" the woman asked in a heavy Southern accent.

"No."

"There's nothing to do there. In fact, the place is little more than a ghost town."

"It has a library," I said.

The realtor snorted. "There're a few hundred books in a falling-down old house. Now if you want—"

"Do you have any rentals in Cole Creek or not?" I snapped.

She got cool. "There's a local agent there. Maybe you should call him."

Knowing small towns, I figured that by now everyone in Cole Creek was aware that Ford Newcombe had called the library, so the local realtor would be on the alert. I said the magic words: "Money is no object."

There was a hesitation. "You could always buy the old Belcher place. National Register. Two acres. Livable. Barely livable, anyway."

"How far is it from the center of Cole Creek?"

"Spit out the window and you'll hit the courthouse."

"How much?"

"Two fifty for the history. Nice moldings."

"If I sent you a certified check tomorrow how soon can it close?"

I could hear her heart beating across the wire. "Sometimes I almost **like** Yankees," she said. "Sugah, you send me a check tomorrow and I'll get that house for you in forty-eight hours even if I have to throw old Mr. Belcher out into the street, oxygen tank and all."

I was smiling. "I'll send the check and all the particulars," I said, then took down her name and address and hung up. I called my publisher. I was going to buy the house in her name so no one in Cole Creek would know it was me.

I knew I couldn't leave town until after the

twenty-seventh of April when I had to pay the blackmail-reading, so I occupied myself by reading about North Carolina. The realtor called me back and said that old Mr. Belcher would give me the house furnished for another dollar.

That took me aback and I had to think about why he'd do that. "Doesn't want to move all his junk out, does he?"

"You got it," the realtor said. "My advice is not to take the offer. There's a hundred and fifty years of trash inside that house."

"Old newspapers? Crumbling books? Attic full of old trunks?"

She sighed dramatically. "You're one of **those**. Okay. You got a house full of trash. Tell you what, I'll pay the dollar. My gift."

"Thanks," I said.

The twenty-seventh was a Saturday, and I spent three hours answering the same questions at Mrs. Attila's ladies' luncheon (chicken salad) as I had everywhere else. My plan was to leave for Cole Creek early Monday morning. My furniture was to go into storage and I planned to take just a couple of suitcases of clothes, a couple of laptops, plus a gross of my favorite pens (I was terrified that Pilot would discontinue them). I'd already shipped my research books to the realtor to hold for me. And Pat's father's tools were on the floor of the backseat of my car.

At the luncheon Mrs. Hun told me that

Jackie Maxwell was getting married the next day. Smiling—and trying to be gracious and amusing—I asked her to tell Jackie that I'd bought a house in Cole Creek, and was spending the summer there, where I'd be researching my next book, and if Jackie wanted the job, it was still open. I even said she could ride with me when I left on Monday morning.

Mrs. Free Books smiled in a way that let me know I'd missed my chance, but she agreed to relay my message to Jackie.

On Sunday afternoon I was shoving my socks into a duffel bag when there was a hard, fast knock on my door. The urgency of the sound made me hurry to answer it.

What I saw when I opened the door startled me into speechlessness.

Jackie Maxwell stood there in her wedding dress. She had on a veil over what looked to be an acre and a half of long dark hair. The last time I'd seen her her hair had been about ear length. Had it grown that fast? Some genetic thing? And the front of her dress was . . . well, she'd grown there, too.

"Is the research job in Cole Creek still open?" she asked in a tone that dared me to ask even one question.

I said yes, but it came out in a squeak.

When she moved, the dress caught on something on the porch. Angrily, she snatched at the skirt and I heard cloth tearing. The sound made her give an evil little smile.

Let me tell you that I **never** want to make a woman so angry that she smiles when she hears her own wedding dress rip. I'd rather—truthfully, I can't think of anything on earth I wouldn't rather do than be on the receiving end of anger like I saw in Ms. Maxwell's eyes.

Or was this after the ceremony and she was now Mrs. Somebody Else?

Since I wanted to live, I asked no questions.

"What time should I be here tomorrow?"

"Eight A.M. too early for you?"

She opened her mouth to answer but the dress caught again. This time she didn't jerk it. This time her face twisted into a frightening little smirk, and she very, very, **very** slowly pulled on that dress. The ripping sound went on for seconds.

I would have stepped back and shut the door but I was too scared.

"I'll be here," she said, then turned and walked down the sidewalk toward the street. There was no car waiting for her, and since I lived miles from any church, I don't know how she got to my house.

At the street sidewalk, she turned left and kept walking. Not a person or child was in sight. No one had come out to see the woman in the wedding dress walk by. I figured they were as scared as I was.

I watched her until she was out of sight, then I went inside and poured myself a double shot of bourbon.

All I can say is that I was real glad I wasn't the man on the receiving end of that anger.

CHAPTER FOUR

Jackie

I decided I was never going to tell anyone what had passed between Kirk and me just before the wedding ceremony. The organist was playing that march, the one that was my cue to start walking down the aisle, and Jennifer was on the other side of the door, pulling on the knob and hissing at me, but I wasn't moving. I was sitting there with my wedding dress billowing out around me in a life-of-its-own heap (I'd punch it down, then, like bread dough gone wild, it would rise again) and listening to Kirk's tearful story.

The tears were his, not mine. I don't know what he expected from me. Did he actually think I'd do as he asked and "forgive" him? Did he think I'd kiss away his manly tears, tell him I still loved him bunches and heaps, then walk down the aisle and **marry** him?

Yeah, right. As his wife, I'd be legally responsible for half the debt he was telling me that he'd incurred.

No, thanks. The fact that he'd lost all my savings, the tiny inheritance my father had left me, and that now all I owned were my clothes, my camera equipment, and my dad's books, didn't seem to bother him. Kirk held my hands in his and, sobbing, told me that he'd get it all back for me. He swore it. On his mother's grave. On his deep love for me, he swore he'd pay me back.

It's an odd thing about love. When someone you love cries, your heart melts. But when someone you don't love cries, you look at them and think, Why are you telling **me** this?

And that's how I felt at seeing Kirk cry: nothing. I felt nothing at all except rage at his presumption. And rage at how he'd finagled the local bank president (his cousin) into helping clean me out. "It was for you, Pumpkin," he told me. "I did it all for **you.** For **us.**"

Wonder when he'd been planning to tell me? If one coincidence after another hadn't happened, I wouldn't have found out about my empty bank account until after I was his wife. Then what could I have done?

For that matter, what could I do even if I

wasn't married to him? Sue? Now that's a good idea. Kirk's father was a judge. Maybe I'd get my almost father-in-law on the bench in the case. Or one of his father's golfing buddies.

No, I knew that all I could do was cut my losses and get the hell away from him and his relatives as fast as possible. Yesterday, Jennifer's mother had laughingly told me that Ford Newcombe had said the job was still open, that he was leaving on Monday for Cole Creek, and that I could ride with him. At the time, I'd just smiled and shook my head. While watching Kirk cry and beg me to forgive him, I decided to take the job.

There was a backdoor to the little ante-room—the room where brides and bridesmaids are supposed to giggle in happy anticipation—and I walked out of it. Outside, I grabbed one of those tall, steel sprinklers out of the lawn and wedged it through the door handles to give myself a few moments before Kirk ran after me.

By the time I reached Newcombe's house (so ordinary and inexpensive that the townspeople said, "Is he trying to pretend he's poor? That he's just like us?") I hated that big fat white dress. And I hated the hair extensions Ashley and Autumn had talked me into. And I especially hated the padded bra they'd put on me.

When I got to Newcombe's house, I could see that he was dying to ask me a thousand personal questions but I didn't explain anything to him, nor did I plan to. I wanted to keep it on a business level between him and me. And I was glad he wasn't handsome, because the way I was feeling about sexually attractive men, Lorena Bobbitt was my personal hero.

After I left Newcombe's I went back to the little rental house that I'd shared with my dad. Kirk's father owned the house, which is how I met Kirk. As I stripped off that hated dress and pulled on jeans and a T-shirt, I shoved my few clothes and other possessions into some old duffels and a couple of plastic bags, and I packed up my precious camera equipment. I knew I was racing against a clock. It wouldn't take long for my friends to find me, and when they did, I knew they'd be so "supportive" that I might be persuaded into talking to Kirk again.

First they'd do the "men are slime" bit, but then, gradually, like cold chocolate syrup coming down the neck of the bottle, they'd say what a shame it was about the wedding and all. Heather, who owned all the Miss Manners books and studied them as though they were a guide to life, would start talking to me about the disappointment of the guests, and wondering whether or not I was obligated to send hand-written thank-you notes for all the gifts I'd be giving up if I "left" Kirk.

I knew myself well enough to know that I'd

use the f-word to describe my feelings about the gifts—and that would get me looks telling me I'd broken some unwritten girl code. Autumn would, of course, cry. And she would, of course, expect Momma Jackie to hold her hands and fix everything.

I knew that not one of the women would listen to me—I mean, really and truly **listen**—about what an illegal—not to mention despicable—thing Kirk had done to me.

"Oh, well," I could hear Ashley say, "Men are slime. We all know that." But she'd dismiss what Kirk had done.

So I raced. I didn't want to see any of them. I grabbed film out of the 'frig, wrote a note to Jennifer and asked her to please box my father's books and my other personal effects, and said I'd call her later and tell her where I was so she could send them. As an afterthought, I added a paragraph of girl-crap about how I needed to be alone so I could regain my inner peace.

I put all my bags into the back of my old car, stuck the letter in the doorjamb, then drove away. As I turned the corner, I glimpsed Kirk's car careening toward my house and I swear that every one of my friends was in the car with him. The car was still covered in white streamers, with "Just Married" on a piece of poster board on the back.

After I saw Newcombe and was sure I had the

job, I used a made-up name and spent the night at a cheap motel out on the highway, making sure my car was parked out of sight of traffic.

At eight the next morning I was outside Ford Newcombe's house and ready to leave with him. The day before my wedding, I'd been too busy to register my surprise that he was planning to move to Cole Creek—the town of my devil story. At any other time, I'd have been full of questions, especially after I was told that he'd **bought** a house there. And when I saw him on Monday, I was still so upset about Kirk that I didn't say much.

When I got into the passenger side of Ford Newcombe's terrifically expensive BMW—700 series—he asked if I was okay. I said, "Sure. Why shouldn't I be?" Then I said I was sorry for snapping, but he didn't say anything, just backed out of the driveway. He glanced at my old car parked on the street and started to speak but didn't. My car wasn't worth much so I'd left the keys in it and thought that when I called Jennifer later I'd tell her where it was. If I'd told her in the note I left yesterday where the car was going to be, I'm sure she would have been here this morning trying to talk some "sense" into me. That my friends weren't here meant that Jennifer's mother hadn't told them about Newcombe's message she'd relayed to me. I owed that woman one.

I waited until Newcombe and I got on the highway before I spoke. I desperately wanted to forget the past day. "You're interested enough in this devil story that you **bought** a house in Cole Creek?"

He didn't look away from the road when he answered and I liked that. He was settled into that dark blue leather seat like the backside of him was growing from it, his right hand draped over the wheel like he'd grown up using a steering wheel as a teething ring.

Of course I'd read his book **Uncles** and had read how his hero—or protagonist—had uncles who loved any machine that had been built specifically to destroy something, and how the hero had been a misfit. I got the idea that Newcombe had spent his childhood hiding under a tree and reading Balzac. Or ironing his own clothes. He'd made a big deal about having to iron his own clothes. Gee. Maybe **I** could write a bestseller. I'd ironed my clothes **and** my dad's since I was eight. Anyway, if I'd been asked, I would have said that, based on his books, Ford Newcombe didn't know a gearshift from a windshield wiper.

"Yeah, I bought a house," Newcombe said in answer to my question, then closed his mouth.

I wanted to tell him that his silence was going to make it a lllooonnnggg journey, but I didn't. I just put my head back and closed my eyes.

I awoke when he stopped to get gas. I got out to put the gas in the car—after all, I was his assistant—but he got the pump handle before I could.

"Go get us something to eat and drink," he said while watching the numbers on the tank.

That's how all his former secretaries said he was: grumpy and uncommunicative. And no matter how much work they did for him, he didn't consider it enough.

"I have a life, Jackie," one woman I knew said. "He wanted me to stay all night and type what he'd written in his tiny handwriting. And he shouted at me because I said I would bring the papers home." Blowing her nose in an old tissue, she said, "Do you know what's wrong with what I said, Jackie?"

I didn't want to say. I wanted to be "supportive" but to do that I'd have to play dumb. "You take the papers home," I heard myself whisper, unable to stop. "Not bring. Take."

When this made the poor woman cry harder, I looked around the restaurant at the other diners and saw they were frowning at me. Heaven help me but they seemed to think **I** was making her cry. "Men!" I said loudly. Collectively, they turned away, nodding their heads in understanding.

I went into the little convenience store at the gas station and looked around, but I had no idea what he liked to eat and drink. From the look of him, I guessed he probably ate fried things that came in plastic bags, and drank bottles of stuff that didn't have the word "diet" on them.

I got him three bags of cheesy crispy fried things and two colas full of sugar and caffeine. As for me, I got a bottle of still water and two bananas.

When he came inside to pay, I put the items on the counter. He looked at them and didn't complain so I guess I did all right. He added a candy bar to the lot and paid.

Outside, when I asked him if he wanted me to drive, I could see he was about to say no, but then he said, "Sure, why not?" I had an idea he wanted to see how I drove, and from the way he watched me for the first thirty minutes, I knew I was right. But I guess I passed because he finally settled back and began opening his bags and bottles.

"So tell me about this devil story," he said. "The full version of it. Everything you remember."

"With or without sound effects?" I asked.

"Without," he answered. "Most definitely without. Just facts."

So, yet again I told my devil story, but this time I told it, not for drama, but for facts. The truth was that I really didn't know what was fact and what was fiction. The trauma of my mother's telling of the story had so changed my life that I wasn't sure where one began and the other ended.

I was a little awkward at first because no one had ever asked me to tell the facts. Everyone else had wanted spine-tingling drama. I started by telling him that when I was a young child, my mother had read me a Bible story that mentioned the devil and I started to ask questions. I think what I asked was whether or not the devil was real. My mother said that the devil was very real and that he'd been seen in Cole Creek. This answer sparked my interest, and I asked more questions. I wanted to know what the devil looked like, and she said, "He's an extremely handsome man. Before he turns red and goes up in smoke, that is." I asked more questions, such as what color the smoke was and who had seen him. She said the smoke was gray and that a woman who lived in Cole Creek, where we were living then, had loved the devil. "And everyone knows that people who love the devil must die," she said.

As I turned to Newcombe I took a deep breath. Other times I'd told the story, I'd played it for its ability to frighten people. I'd once won a black ribbon at a summer camp for having the best horror story. But to Newcombe, I decided to tell the truth. "They killed her. The story was that there were several people who saw the woman talking to the devil, and when she backed away from them, she tripped and fell. They wouldn't let her get up."

It was just a story but the image in my mind was vivid. "They piled stones on top of her until she was dead."

"And it was your mother who told you the details of this story?"

I glanced at him quickly. "It's not worse than **Hansel and Gretel,**" I said defensively, then calmed. "Actually, I think I've taken my mother's story and embellished it with all the TV shows and books I've read. I told you that I can't remember what she said and what I've made up over the years."

Newcombe was looking at me strangely so I decided to nip this in the bud. "Don't look at me like that. I wasn't involved in some evil coven—and neither was my mother. The truth is that the night I told my father what my mother had said, my parents split up. My parents argued horribly and later my father wrapped me in a blanket, put me in the car and took me away. I never saw my mother again. I think my mother's telling me a forbidden story, one that was too violent for a little kid to hear, was the final straw that made my father leave. And I think the trauma of the separation made the story stick in my mind. Truthfully, I barely remember my mother but I **do** remember that devil story."

Over the years, I'd learned to keep quiet about my parents, but now my father was dead and I was heading toward the town of my childhood. Telling the unembellished truth of what I remembered of what my mother had told me seemed to be making memories come back to me. And maybe it was because Newcombe was such a good listener but I'd just told him things I'd never told anyone else. When I'd calmed myself, I went on to tell him that I remembered that my parents were always arguing, all of it done in quiet whispers that I wasn't supposed to hear. A few days after my mother told me the devil story, my father and I were walking outside and I asked him where the lady had seen the devil. He asked me what I meant. After I'd repeated my mother's story, he picked me up, carried me back to the house and put me in my bedroom and shut the door. But even as an adult, I could still remember the argument they had that night. My mother was crying and saying that they were all going to die anyway, so what did it matter? "And she needs to be told the **truth.**" I remembered that sentence vividly.

I took another breath to quieten the turmoil the memories had raised and glanced at Newcombe. He was frowning, seeming to think about what I'd told him. I didn't see any need to tell him that my father had moved us repeatedly over the years. Sometimes he'd receive a letter or a phone call, his face would turn white, and I knew that within forty-eight hours we'd be on the road again. Over the years I'd lost friends and places I cared about because of my father's constant moving.

As I watched the road ahead, my mind full of my own thoughts, I began to fear that Newcombe was going to try to get me to reveal more than what I had—which, for me, was a tremendous amount. After all, he wrote books about his own life so now maybe he'd want to take mine apart. But he didn't. Instead, he grinned and said, "Okay, now tell me the story with drama and fireworks."

Just weeks before, I'd been embarrassed to find out that he'd heard me tell a story, but things between us were more relaxed now, so I let him have it. I forgot about reality and the involvement of my parents and told him my devil story in the most grisly way possible.

I had never had a more attentive listener. When I glanced away from the road to see if I was boring him, he had the wide-eyed look of a three-year-old sitting at the feet of a storyteller. The telling took me nearly forty-five minutes, and when I finished, we were silent for a while. Newcombe seemed to be thinking about what I'd told him. Finally, he said, "Devil stories are rare. I've read a zillion witch and ghost stories, but I'm not sure I've ever heard one in which someone was believed to have loved the devil. Not just seen him but **loved** him. And a pressing." He went on to tell me that piling rocks on top of a person believed to be a witch was an old form of punishment called a "pressing."

After a moment or two, he lightened the air by telling me what he'd done so far to discover the origins of the devil story. From the moment he told me about a librarian hanging up on him—him, Ford Newcombe—my mouth dropped open and stayed down there. I must say I was impressed when he told me how he'd bought a house over the phone.

Isn't it the dream of every minimum wage person in the U.S. to be able to buy a quarter of a million dollar house just like that? I'd never lived in an "owned" house. My dad and I went from one rental to another, one job after another. He'd managed a bowling alley, sold tires, been night manager at a dozen groceries. It wasn't until I was nine that I realized my dad was moving us around so often because he didn't want to be found.

I must say that it was good to be able to live vicariously through Ford Newcombe's chutzpah and his money. "You bought the house **and** the contents?" I asked.

"Turn south at the next junction," he said as he drained half a bottle of cola. "Yeah, and it's your job to go through all the junk in the house."

I knew he was testing me so I just smiled and said, "Be glad to."

"Unless your husband . . ."

When he trailed off, I knew he wanted to know if I'd left before or after the I do's. "It's still Miss Maxwell," I said. "So you want to tell me about wages, benefits, and hours?"

I don't know what I said that made him angry, but I could see his face start to turn red.

"Job description," he muttered, as though I'd said something vile.

I'd had all I could take from men in the last few days and I really didn't care if he dropped me and my bags at the side of the road. I knew from experience that there were always jobs to be had. "Yeah," I said as I turned south, and there was belligerence in my voice. "Job description."

As he looked out the window for a moment, I could see his reflection in the windshield and damned if he didn't smile a bit. Maybe he was so used to people fawning over his big successful self that he liked it when people didn't bow down to him.

Finally, he said, "I don't know. I haven't written a book since"—he paused and took a deep breath—"for a long time so I don't know what I need in the way of an assistant."

"There are a lot of women who'd agree with

you on that one," I said before I thought, then glanced at him in horror.

But, to my relief, his eyes crinkled up and we both laughed.

"I'm not the monster you've probably heard I am," he said, and explained that most of the women who'd worked for him had marriage, not typing, on their minds.

It was easy to be flippant and think that, of course, he'd be pursued since he was rich and unmarried, but I too well remembered my father in the same situation. Not rich, but unattached. Maybe some of the women Newcombe had fired deserved it. Maybe . . .

For a while he munched on his cheesy things in silence, then I said, "You want to give me a job description?" and that made him laugh again. "And where do **I** live?"

It turned out that—dare I stereotype and say "like a man"?—he hadn't thought of where his assistant was to live. When he said, "I guess you'll live with me," I shot him a look that told him what I thought of that idea.

He tried to get me back by looking me up and down, obviously finding me wanting. "You don't have to worry," he said.

I'm sure he meant to put me down, but it made me laugh instead. He may be rich and famous, but I was the one who was in shape.

Turning away, he shook his head for a moment, as though to say that he'd never before met anyone like me, then he wadded up his empty cheese-poison bag and said he thought the house was big enough for us to live together and not get in each other's way.

"I don't do domestic," I said. "I don't cook or clean anything. I don't do laundry." I almost said that I didn't iron shirts even if they'd been run over by a tractor, but I decided that might be too much.

He shrugged. "If they have a pizza parlor or a diner I'll be fine. You don't look like you eat much anyway."

"Mmmmm," was all I said to let him know that my eating habits were none of his business. It was my experience that if you talked about food to a man he thought you were coming on to him. Men seemed to go from food to body to "you want me, I know you do."

"So what exactly am I to research?" I asked.

"I don't know," he said, honesty in his voice. "I've never done this before. I've spent the last two years reading local ghost stories and trying to put some of them together. And it's been difficult trying to get to primary sources, especially since I've not had a lot of help."

I bit my tongue on his last bit of whining. "So now you want to know about this pressing. Have any idea exactly when it took place?"

At that he gave me a look.

"Right," I said. **"I** am your primary source. But I really have no idea when it happened or even if it did."

"Based on the attitude of the librarian, it did."

"Or maybe she was tired of people asking about it. Maybe it's like Amityville and the residents are sick of people asking about that house. Or maybe she's just afraid that her sweet little mountain town will be overrun by people with swastikas carved onto their foreheads, looking for the devil."

"Mmmmm," he said, giving me the same non-answer I'd given him. He scrunched down in the seat, his long legs looking as though they'd disappeared into the motor, and put his head back. "When you get down to a quarter tank, pull over and I'll drive," he said as he closed his eyes.

I drove in silence for a long time and I enjoyed it. I thought a little about Kirk and what he'd done to me, and thought maybe I'd someday break my vow of silence and ask Newcombe if he knew how I could go about recovering the money Kirk had stolen from me. But mainly I thought about how to research a story no one wanted to discuss.

As the wide interstate stretched before me, I tried to remember everything my mother had told me about the pressing. So very much of my early childhood was a blur, but if I concentrated, I could remember the two incidents that had changed everything. My mother had gone from reading me a bedtime story to telling me that people who loved the devil had to die, and because she'd told me that story, my father had taken me away.

Over the years, I'd often wondered what would have happened if I'd kept my mouth shut and never told my father what my mother said. But now that I was an adult, I knew better than that. Neither my big mouth nor my mother's story had separated my parents. The truth was that they had disliked each other a great deal.

When I looked at the speedometer, I saw I was going too fast, so I slowed down.

As Newcombe dozed, I tried to remember that awful night when my father had taken me away. When he was alive, I wouldn't let myself think about that night for fear I'd become too angry at him, and I knew anger wouldn't have done either of us any good. We only had each other.

The night I'd told my father what my mother said, he'd turned out the lights in my bedroom and closed the door all the way instead of leaving it open a bit as he usually did. But I could have been locked inside a bank vault and I would still have heard the argument he and my mother had. Even though they talked in low, stealthy tones, I could hear them as clearly as though I'd been sitting under the kitchen table.

My father was saying my mother shouldn't have told me the devil story. Suddenly, I remembered what my mother had actually said. She didn't say, as I'd told Newcombe, that we would all die someday. My mother had said, "So how will you explain to her **why** I died?"

I glanced at Newcombe, meaning to tell him, but he was sleeping, his mouth slightly open, his lips softened. With the tension out of his face, he looked much younger. Certainly not in his sixties as I'd thought. Actually, not bad looking at all.

As I looked back at the highway, I remembered that my mother's words had scared me so much that I'd put my hands over my ears and begun to hum loudly. Eventually, I went to sleep, but sometime during the night my father came in and woke me. "We're going on a trip, Jackie," he'd said as he pulled me out of the warm bed and lifted me in his arms. When I shivered, he grabbed a blanket and wrapped it around me. Minutes later we were in the car, there were suitcases on the floor, and my father told me to stretch out and go back to sleep. When I asked about my mother, he said, "She'll come later."

But I never saw my mother again and sometime later my father told me she'd died.

Over the years I came to realize that my father had kidnapped me. Sometimes I'd fantasize that my mother was still alive somewhere and dying of loneliness without me. One day, I said as much to my father. He said that he'd taken me away because my mother was very ill and she didn't want her little girl to see her die. He said he'd taken me away so I'd remember my mother as a healthy, laughing woman who loved me very much. But another time, he told me my mother had died in a car wreck, and that was the story I told when I was asked about her.

My memories of my mother were vague and confused. Sometimes I remembered her as being tall with long, dark hair, smiling and singing, and making me feel good when I was with her. And sometimes I remembered her as being short, with light hair, and always in a bad mood.

I mentioned this dichotomy to my father and he said I was remembering my mother and his sister. I mentally leaped through the ceiling. I had an aunt?!

Quickly, my father said my aunt had been killed in a car wreck when I was very young. Even back then I'd wanted to make a sarcastic remark about so many people in our family dying in car wrecks. But I didn't say anything.

When the tank was down to a quarter full, just as I'd been instructed, I pulled into a gas station.

This time I filled the tank while Newcombe went in to get his own food. He was polite and asked if I wanted anything but I still hadn't eaten my bananas. When he returned to the car with his arms laden with fat and cholesterol, he leaned against the door and watched me doing stretches.

Okay, so I'm limber, but I didn't appreciate being stared at in that way, especially not while he was eating a sandwich that reached from my knee to my ankle. The way he watched me made me feel as though I should hand out popcorn and charge admission.

After we got back in the car, him behind the wheel, we didn't talk for a while. We'd shared some laughter, and we seemed to now share a goal of wanting to find out the truth behind a story, so we were content. At least I was.

As we drove, we watched the landscape change into the drop-dead gorgeous scenery of western North Carolina, with lush, verdant trees covering rolling hills.

He must have memorized the map because he never asked me to look at one for directions. Eventually, we pulled off the major highway and went down a progression of roads that kept growing more narrow with every corner we turned. As the houses grew farther apart, they went from brick with fancy beveled-glass doors and porches too small to use, to the traditional

North Carolina wood frame with porches big enough to live on during the summer.

The beautiful green hills and valleys were salted with barns and houses falling down so picturesquely that my right index finger ached to push a shutter release button.

"What's that look?" Newcombe asked, glancing at me.

"This is beautiful," I said, "and I'd like to take pictures of—" I waved my hand to indicate that I wanted to photograph all of it.

"Is that big black bag full of camera equipment?"

"Yes," I answered, but he didn't ask any more questions. Too bad. I would have loved to talk about my photography. After a while, I had one of those déjà vu feelings. "Are we getting close, because I think I remember having seen some of this area before. There!" I said. "That bridge. I think I remember that." It was an old steel thing with a wooden bottom that had big holes in it.

"Right," he said. "Just a few more miles and we'll be in Cole Creek."

"You're good at remembering directions," I said tentatively.

He gave a little smile at the compliment and said, "Yeah, Pat said—" He stopped and clamped his mouth shut.

He didn't have to tell me who Pat was. Anyone who'd read his books had read the long,

gushy thanks he'd written to her in each one.
Her death had been national news, and I
remembered seeing a photo of him taken at her
funeral. He'd looked like a man who didn't want
to go on living.

"Left," I said suddenly. "Turn left right here."

"This isn't—" he started to say, but he turned
sharply and we took the curve on two wheels.

It made me feel good that he listened to me
instead of relying on his memorized map. The
road we were on followed a creek and was so
narrow he drove down the middle to keep the
overhanging trees from scratching the paint on
his car. Maybe I should have been worried
about oncoming traffic, but I wasn't.

On the banks above our heads we saw houses
that didn't look as though they'd been remodeled
since they were built in the early 1900s or so. It
wasn't unusual to see a patch of land not far from
the house filled with rusting cars, old refrigera-
tors, and washing machines. Porches held an
incongruous assortment of galvanized washtubs
and kids' big plastic cars in gaudy colors that
clashed with the weathered wood and lush green
forest.

Abruptly, the trees ended and before us was
a town that looked like something out of a
book of photographs entitled **Our Forgotten
Heritage.** If this was Cole Creek, and I was
sure it was, then there was nothing modern in

it. The few buildings on each side of the street were old and decaying rapidly. In the few store windows were items that would make a movie set dresser's heart leap in delight.

In the middle of the town was a pretty little square of land with a big white bandstand. The park was perfect for a Saturday afternoon of strolling and listening to the local barbershop quartet. I could almost see women in long skirts, wide belts, and high-necked, long-sleeved blouses with pintucking down the front.

"Wow," I whispered. "Wow."

Newcombe seemed to be equally awestruck. Slowing the car down to a crawl, he was looking at the old buildings as hard as I was. "Think that's the courthouse?"

Across from the perfect little park was a big brick building with huge, two story columns up the front of it.

"'Cole Creek Courthouse,'" I read on the perfect little brass plate beside the door. "'1866.' Right after the war." I pronounced it "wahr" as was proper.

Newcombe slowed the car to a roll. He was looking on both sides of the street by the courthouse. To the left was an alley and next to it was a cute little Victorian house with a curved porch. Was this the house he'd bought?

On the right, across the street from the courthouse, was an impenetrable mass of tall trees which I assumed covered a vacant lot. Further left was another Victorian by the first one. It wasn't in such good shape, but it had an adorable little balcony upstairs.

"There," Newcombe said as he stopped the car.

Yippee! I wanted to say and already I was scheming to get the bedroom upstairs, the one with that balcony. I opened my mouth to start my campaign, but I saw that Newcombe wasn't looking at the little Victorian. He'd driven ahead far enough that we could see into what I'd assumed was a vacant lot on the other side of the street.

I followed his gaze.

Closely planted trees surrounded about two acres of land, enclosing the space so it was private and secluded. In the center was a majestic, noble-looking Queen Anne house that was a wedding cake of balconies and porches and turrets. On the first floor was a porch wrapping around three sides that had—someone catch me, I may faint—big bentwood frames, like parentheses, that ran from the rail to the roof. The second floor had a turret with a porch and curved balusters under a pointed hat of a roof, with a cute little weather vane on the top.

There were windows that had stained glass and some with beveled. There were at least four little pitched roofs that held up tiny porches with big French doors leading out to them.

The whole house had once been painted bright colors, but had faded to pale gray and lavender-blue, with dusty peach brackets here and there.

It was, without a doubt, the most beautiful house I'd ever seen in my whole, entire life.

CHAPTER FIVE

Ford

It was the most hideous house I'd ever seen in my life. It looked like a giant wooden wedding cake made of balconies, porches, and turrets. Everywhere you looked was another little roof and another tiny, useless porch. Skinny, carved posts ran across every edge and surrounded every window. Windows seemed to have the sole purpose of adding more ornamentation to the whole ghastly edifice. The late afternoon sunlight glinted off the edges of beveled glass, highlighting stained-glass windows which depicted various animals and birds.

Even in good repair, the house would have been a monstrosity, but this one was falling apart. Three gutters hung by pieces of twisted wire. A couple of panes of glass were covered by Masonite. I saw cracked balustrades, broken window frames, and porch floorboards that were split and probably rotten.

Then there was the paint—or the lack of it. Whatever color the house was originally had been lost to a hundred-plus years of sun and rain. Everything had faded to dull gray-blue, and the paint was peeling everywhere.

I turned the car into the weed-infested driveway and stared in disbelief. The lawns around the house had been cut, but the old flower beds were knee-high in weeds. There was a broken birdbath and an old arbor that had vines growing through the paved floor. Back against the trees I could see two benches that sat at angles because half their legs were missing.

I really don't care about any story enough to stay in this house, I thought. I turned to Jackie to offer an apology and tell her we'd find a hotel somewhere, but she was already getting out of the car, an unreadable expression on her face. Probably shock, I thought. Or horror. I knew how she felt. One look at this place and I wanted to run away, too.

But Jackie wasn't running away. Instead, she was already up the porch stairs and at the front door. I practically leaped out of the car to run after her. I had to warn her that the place didn't look safe.

She was standing on the porch and looking around, her eyes wide. There had to be fifty pieces of old furniture on that porch. There were beat-up wicker chairs with dirty, faded cushions, and half a dozen dinky little wire tables that weren't big enough to hold more than a teacup—or a glass of sarsaparilla, I thought.

Jackie seemed to be as speechless as I was. She put her hand on top of an old oak cabinet. "It's an icebox," she said and the odd tone of her voice made me look at her more closely.

"What do you think of this place?" I asked.

"It's the most beautiful house I've ever seen," she said softly, and there was so much raw passion in her voice that I groaned.

I'd had some experience with women and houses and knew that a woman could love a house the way a man loved a car. Personally, I couldn't see it. Houses took too much work.

I followed Jackie inside. I'd asked the realtor how I could get the key to my "new" house and she'd just laughed. Now I saw why. No respectable burglar was going to waste his time on this place.

When Jackie opened the unlocked front door, I saw that it was even worse inside. The door opened to a large hallway, with a winding staircase directly in front of us. The staircase might have been impressive if both sides of each step weren't covered with foot-high stacks of old magazines. The trail up the stairs was no more than eighteen inches wide.

In the entrance hall was an oak hall tree: big, ugly, with six moth-eaten hats hanging from hooks. On both sides of the hall were three-foot-tall stacks of yellowing and brittle news-papers. On the floor was a rug so threadbare there was no pile left.

"There's an Oriental rug under that, and it's made out of tile," Jackie said as she disappeared between double doors of a room on the left.

Kneeling, I lifted up the corner of the dusty rug and saw that beneath it was, indeed, an Oriental "rug" made of mosaic tiles. It was the work of a master craftsman and if it weren't so dirty, it would have been beautiful.

I followed Jackie into the next room. "How did you know about . . ." I began, but couldn't finish the sentence. She was standing in the middle of the parlor, better known as the living room. I'd been told that the house had been continuously occupied for over a hundred years, and when I looked about that room, I was willing to bet that every occupant had bought at least six pieces of furniture—and each one was still there. To walk between the furniture, even skinny Jackie had to turn side-ways. In a far corner were three frighteningly ugly walnut-trimmed Victorian chairs covered in worn-out red velvet. Next to them was a 1960s flourescent green sofa that had pillows on it printed with big lips. In the opposite corner was a square couch that looked Art Deco. Along the walls were old oak bookcases, new white bookcases, and a cheap pine cabinet with doors hanging by one hinge. Every souvenir anyone had bought over the course of a hundred years was in that room. Above the bookcases were framed prints, dirty oil paintings, and what looked to be a hundred or more old photographs in frames of varying degrees of dilapidation.

"They've moved all the furniture into here. Wonder why?" Jackie said as she left the parlor and went into the room across the hall.

I started to follow her but I tripped over a stuffed duck. Not like a kid's stuffed toy duck, but a real bird, something that had once flown through the air and was now sitting on my living room floor, feathers and all.

As I untangled myself from the duck, three more fell off a shelf and pelted me. It was a mother duck and her ducklings, preserved forever in lifelessness. After I'd conquered my urge to scream, I ran out the door and into the room across the hall.

Jackie was standing in what I assumed was the library. Three walls were covered with grand old bookcases and the ceiling was magnificently coffered. The bookcases were filled with old leather-bound volumes that made me itch with wanting to look at them. But it would take a forklift to make a path to those books because in front of them were cardboard shelves—the kind with wood-grained wallpaper on them (as though that would fool anyone)—filled with thirty years of best-sellers. Everything Harold Robbins and Louis L'Amour had written was in those shelves.

"It's the same," Jackie said, her eyes still glazed over, as though she were in a trance.

As she turned to leave the room, I made a lunge to grab her arm, but I missed because my foot caught on an old coal bucket that was filled with paperbacks. Four copies of Frank Yerby fell on my foot. I stepped out of the books and started forward, but when I saw a copy of **Fanny Hill,** I picked it up, put it in my back pocket, and went after Jackie.

I found her in the room behind the library, the dining room. Tall windows ate up one wall and would have let in light if two-thirds of them hadn't been swathed in dark purple velvet draperies. I started to speak but was distracted by what I was sure was a bird's nest at the top of the curtains.

"It's fake," Jackie said, seeing where I was looking. "It has tiny porcelain eggs in it." With that she left the room.

I started to run after her but three of the

eighteen or so mismatched chairs in the room stuck out their legs and tried to trip me.

It was too much! I knocked the chairs over— after all, they were mine now—and ran into the hallway. No Jackie. I stood there for a moment, then I let out a bellow that sounded as though it were coming from the moose head I'd seen somewhere.

Jackie appeared instantly. "What in the world is wrong with you?" she asked.

Where do I begin? I wondered, then got hold of myself. "How do you know so much about this place?"

"I don't know," she answered. "My father said we lived in Cole Creek for only a few months when I was very young, but for all I know we lived in **this** house. Maybe my parents were housekeeper and handyman, that sort of thing."

"If you remember so much, you must have been older than 'very young.'"

"I think you may be right," she said as she entered the big room across from the dining room. I followed her, but stopped short. It was a smaller room than the others and it was clean and neat. Even the windows had been washed. The ceiling was exquisitely painted with vines and flowers, and the floor was blond oak inlaid with a border of walnut. What was really good was that there wasn't one piece of furniture in the room.

Jackie stood in the doorway looking around, but I walked in to sit down on a cushionless window seat.

"I think Mr. Belcher moved everything out of here and into the other rooms," she said as she walked to a corner of the room and picked up a small brown prescription bottle. "I think this was his sick room, and he probably lived in here."

"Hey!" I said. "Is that an outlet for cable TV?"

Looking at me, she shook her head in disgust. "You're not much of an intellectual, are you?" she said over her shoulder as she left the room.

The thing I liked most about Jackie Maxwell was that she treated me as a man, not a best-seller, but a **man.** The thing I liked least about Jackie Maxwell was that she treated me like an ordinary human being and not with the deference that my success deserved.

I found her in the kitchen. It was a big room with white metal cabinets over worn and dented stainless steel countertops. The height of 1930s elegance. Truthfully, I was surprised to see that the house had been touched since it had been built in 1896. In the middle of the room was an oak table that had thousands upon thousands of knife cuts in it.

Jackie looked inside the cabinets while I opened the doors to the left. First was a big walk-in pantry, every inch of shelf space crammed full of boxes and cans of food. Reaching to the back of the highest shelf, I pulled down a box of cereal with a photo of a man in a football uniform from about 1915. I was tempted to look inside the box, but thought better of it and put it back.

Two other doors revealed a powder room with a pull chain toilet and a maid's room with a narrow, hard-looking brass bed.

When I walked back into the kitchen I was hit by a smell so awful I put my hand over my nose. Jackie had opened the round-cornered refrigerator.

She sneezed a couple of times and I coughed. "I got the contents of the 'frig in the deal?" I asked.

"Seems so. You ready to go look at the upstairs?"

"Only if I have to," I muttered as I followed her out of the kitchen back to the front staircase. I'd been looking at the endless spiral of old magazines and hadn't noticed the little brass dragon on the top of the newel post.

"Wonder if it still works?" Jackie said under her breath, then gave a sharp twist to the pointed tip of the dragon's tail.

I jumped back as a four-inch-long blue flame shot out of the dragon's mouth.

She twisted the tail tip again and the flame stopped.

"Cool," I said. It was the first thing I'd seen in the house that I really liked.

Jackie ran up the stairs, having no trouble stepping between the piles, while I stayed downstairs to investigate the dragon. It was amazing that the thing was still hooked up to a gas line after all these years, and even more amazing that it still worked. The tail tip could use a little oil, I thought as I turned it again.

"Can I have the mistress's bedroom?" Jackie called from above.

I was looking down the dragon's mouth, trying to see the gas pipe inside. "Yeah," I said, "but who gets the wife's bedroom?"

"Very funny," she said. "Could you stop playing with that and look up at where I am?"

She was at the very top of the stair spiral, third floor. A huge, round, stained-glass window was in the ceiling above her head.

"Stairs like these were air-conditioning," she said. "Hot air rises."

"Straight up to the servants' bedrooms?" I was kneeling to see where the gas line entered the newel post.

"The heat up here would keep them downstairs so they could work," Jackie called down, then her voice lowered. "My goodness, the old nursery has been converted to an office. I bet they stored that big old train set in the attic."

Train set? I quit looking at the dragon and decided to mosey on upstairs.

Jackie met me on the landing of the second floor, and dutifully, I looked at four bedrooms, three bathrooms straight out of a BBC set of Edwardian England, and a storage room so full of boxes we couldn't open the door all the way.

At the front of the house was a master and "mistress" suite. Two big bedrooms, each with a private bath, had a sitting room between them that opened onto the spiral staircase. The bedroom Jackie wanted so much that I could see her heart beating in her throat, had doors opening onto a deep, round porch that was filled with delicate white furniture. It was no hardship on my part to say she could have the room.

As with the downstairs, the second floor rooms were full of furniture and semi-antique junk. The wallpaper was enough to give a person nightmares. The flowers on it could swallow a person whole. Jackie's bedroom had roses on the wallpaper—complete with needle-pointed serrated leaves and stems with thorns a quarter inch long. It was creepy.

The only room I truly liked was my bathroom. It had wallpaper of dark green leaves interspersed now and then with small oranges. ("William Morris," Jackie said.) All the original mahogany bathroom fixtures were in the room and they all worked. There was no shower but there was a bathtub—

"William Taft could get in that tub," Jackie said.

"With the first lady," I said, looking at her to see if she was going to accuse me of making a sex joke. When she laughed, I was glad. None of my other assistants had laughed at my jokes.

I was getting hungry so I suggested we find a grocery before it got too late. Jackie gave a longing look upward and I knew she wanted to rummage around in the rooms on the top floor. Part of me said I should tell her to stay in the house and I'd go to the grocery alone, but I didn't want to do that.

The truth was, the long drive down together had been pleasant. I was glad to see that she wasn't one of those women who talks nonstop. And she seemed to already know something about me because at the first gas station she had instinctively chosen my favorite snacks.

I felt only relief after we got outside the house again. It would be dark in another hour, so I thought we should go. But Jackie got within three feet of the car door, then floated off toward the broken birdbath. I went to her, put my hands on both her elbows, ushered her into the car, and backed out of the driveway. Since we'd entered the little town from the east, I drove west, this time staying on a numbered highway.

Once we were out of the town, Jackie seemed to come to herself. "I know you bought a furnished house, but—"

"Yes?" I asked.

"The truth is, there are some things missing."

"Besides parts of the roof, the railings, and the windows?"

Jackie waved her hand in dismissal. "You didn't happen to see the pots and pans in the kitchen, did you? Or lift up the quilts on the beds? Or touch the pillows?"

The answer was no to all her questions so she filled me in. It seemed that in terms of livability, the house might as well have been vacant. There were probably sixty-one Statue of Liberty souvenirs in the living room, but no bed linens, and I could just imagine the pillows: hard, damp, and moldy.

About twenty miles out of town, around twisty mountain roads, was a Wal-Mart. I didn't say a word to Jackie, just turned into the parking lot. I must say that she was an efficient little thing. She grabbed a cart, I got another one, and thirty minutes later they were packed so full she couldn't see over the top of hers. I had to grab the front of her cart and lead it to the register.

"It's a good thing you're rich," she said, looking at our hoard of kitchen paraphernalia—clean, new kitchen equipment—plus sheets, towels, and paper products.

The first few times she'd made these offhand remarks I'd wanted to tell her where to get off, but now I was beginning to get used to them. This time I smiled. "Yeah. It **is** good I'm rich. With a house like that one, I might as well paper the walls with twenties. How in the world will I be able to **sell** it?"

"Sell?" Jackie asked, her face falling, and looking like a kid who'd just been told her pet rabbit was going to be eaten. "How could you **sell** a house like that?"

"I doubt if I'll be able to. I'll probably die owning the place."

She started to say something, but it was our turn at the register so she started unloading.

After Wal-Mart, we went to a grocery store and again filled two carts. At the checkout counter I was selecting candy bars when she said, "Are you planning to eat those things before or after dinner?" The way she said it made me put half the candy back.

When we got back Jackie said that she'd cook dinner "this once" if I'd bring in the groceries. I agreed quickly. Cooking was not something I was good at. By the time the groceries were in and put away (one shelf of the pantry cleaned off, refrigerated food in the iced-down cooler we'd bought) she'd set the table with candles and plates that even to my untrained eye looked expensive.

She saw me looking at them. "Limoges," she said. "The cabinet in the dining room has three sets for twelve."

"Wonder why Belcher didn't take them with him?"

"And do what with them?" Jackie asked, stirring something on the old gas stove. There was a single bare bulb over the cooking surface and it was so low wattage it made a little spotlight around Jackie, highlighting her and the cooktop in the dark room. "You told me the realtor said he's over ninety, heirless, and an invalid. He probably eats off those suction plates made for babies. And if he sells the dishes, who does he leave the money to? However . . ."

I ate a cracker she'd spread with cheese and put half an olive on top of, and waited for her to finish.

"He did take the silver."

We laughed together. So much for old age and no heirs. I ate four more of the cracker things. "You almost seem to know the man personally."

"True," she said, spatula paused in midair. "I feel like I almost know what he looks like. And I seem to know a lot about this house. I'm beginning to think my father told me a few little white lies." She paused a moment. "And maybe one or two whoppers."

I thought about what she was saying. Her father had said they'd lived in Cole Creek for only a short time when Jackie was "very young," but she seemed to remember too much for that to be true. And what "whoppers" was she referring to? Yeow! Her mother? "You think your mother could be alive?" I asked, trying to sound causal.

She took a moment before answering, but I could tell that she was working hard to get her emotions under control. "I don't know. I do remember that they fought a lot. I think maybe he kidnapped me, and that maybe the reason we spent our lives moving from one town to another was so she and the law wouldn't find us. He didn't have a copy of my birth certificate and whenever I asked for facts, he became vague."

"Interesting," I said, trying to sound light-hearted. I had an idea she'd just told me more than she'd ever told anyone else. "Maybe my next book will be about a young woman who finds her origins."

"That's **my** book," she said quickly. "You're here to find the devil so you can talk to him about your wife."

Damn! but she could cut! I had a cracker at my lips when she said that, and it was as though my heart stopped beating. Not even in my own mind had I let myself think of the truth of what she'd just said.

She was standing absolutely still at the stove,

her back to me, spatula paused. I couldn't see her face, but the back of her neck had become three shades darker than normal.

I knew that what I replied would set the tone for our future relationship. About two-thirds of me wanted to tell her she was fired and to get the hell out of my life. But I looked at that candlelit table and the last thing I wanted was yet another evening alone.

"Only God would know anything about Pat," I said at last. "The devil would say, 'Never heard of her.'"

Slowly, she turned to look at me, and there was such gratitude on her face that I had to look away. "I'm sorry," she said. "Sometimes I say things that—"

"Are the truth as you see it?" I asked, not wanting to hear her apology. Truthfully, I think that my first idea about the project had been about Pat. Maybe I'd thought that if I could find out how one became a ghost, I could figure out how to bring Pat back in spirit form. Or maybe a witch could cast a spell to bring her back.

But as I started reading, the project itself had begun to interest me. For one thing, several states claimed the same stories. Did that make them folklore rather than truth?

We were quiet for a while as Jackie served some kind of chicken casserole that was quite good. She seemed to be a vegetable fanatic because she put three kinds of vegetables on the table, plus potatoes, plus more vegetables in the casserole.

At first we ate in silence, then I started telling her how close she'd been in her assessment of why I'd started on the ghosts and witches, but that I'd changed.

"Maybe I'm being romantic, but I'd like to find out if there's any truth in those old stories. Or maybe I'd just like to give the readers a bloody good read."

"Better to want a good story than to ask the devil for anything," she said as she began to clear the table.

Since there was no dishwasher, I washed and she dried. After the kitchen was cleaned up (except for the mold growing over most surfaces) we went upstairs and started on the bedrooms. She laughed when I complained about the hideous wallpaper in my bedroom. It was dark green, magenta, and black. The bed was dark walnut, as were the other thirty or so pieces of furniture in the room. Between the wallpaper and the furniture, the room was as light as a tunnel at midnight.

"How about if tomorrow I call an auction house and get rid of the excess furniture?" she asked. "Actually, you could get rid of all of it, then buy new."

When I looked at that ugly old bed, the

thought of buying something new made me smile. White maybe.

But then I caught myself. I was **not** going to be living in this tiny throwback of a town. I was going to do some research here then move on to—Well, I had no idea where I was going, but it would be far away from this horror-movie house.

Jackie and I put new, but unwashed sheets (an ancient washer and dryer were in the pantry, harvest gold, sixties vintage) on my bed, then we went to her room to do the same.

"You know," she said slowly, "I saw a Lowe's just down the hill from the grocery." She stopped tucking in her side of the sheet and looked at me as though I was supposed to read her mind. When I said nothing, she told me that if you buy new appliances at Lowe's, they take your old ones away. When I realized what she was saying, we looked at each other and laughed. Some poor, unsuspecting appliance movers would take away that refrigerator whose smell could pollute outer space.

"What time do they open?" I asked, and we laughed some more.

An hour later, as I snuggled down in bed (and vowed to get a new mattress) I felt better than I had in a long time, and I finally allowed myself to think about the devil story that Jackie had told me in the car. I don't think she had any idea how unusual her story was. For the last couple of years I'd been reading regional ghost stories, and for the most part, they were quite mild—so mild that I couldn't remember any of them an hour after I'd finished the book. There was so little meat in the stories that the writers had had to embellish them with long phrases about the beauty of the people, or add some sinister aspect that had nothing to do with the real story. You could feel that the writer was just trying to fill up pages.

But Jackie's story was different. The first version, the so-called "factual" story, the one she said her mother had told her, was interesting, but it sounded like several small town legends I'd read.

I didn't want Jackie to know it, but it was her second story that interested me. I'd already seen that she was a good storyteller, but her dramatic telling of the devil story had given me the creeps.

Jackie started by describing the woman who'd been murdered. She told of a woman who was kind to everyone, who loved children, and who always wore a smile.

Jackie said that the woman used to take long walks in the woods, and, one day, she came to a beautiful house made of stone and a man was there. Jackie described him as "nice looking, like Santa Claus, without the beard." I wanted to ask her how she knew this, but there was something so odd about the way she was telling the story that I didn't interrupt her.

She said the woman had gone often to the house, and Jackie told about food the nice man and nice woman had shared, how they'd laughed and talked together. She told about the pretty flowers that grew all around the house and how the inside smelled like gingerbread.

After a few moments, I realized what was odd about her storytelling. There were two things. One was that Jackie related it as though she'd been an eyewitness, and the second was that she told it in the manner of a very young child. When she came to the part where the towns-people saw the couple, she said, "You could see all the people through the bushes . . ." "How many people?" I wanted to ask, but didn't, and as she spoke, it occurred to me that the child who saw this may have been too young to know how to count. If I'd asked Jackie how many people were there, I wouldn't have been surprised if she'd said, "Eleventy-seven."

She said some "grown-ups" had seen the woman but they couldn't see the man because he was invisible. Jackie said the townspeople had shouted at the woman but Jackie didn't seem to know what they'd said, just that they were "shouting." When the woman had backed up, she'd fallen, and her ankle had been caught between some rocks. "She couldn't get out," Jackie said in what seemed to me to be a child's voice. "So they piled more rocks on top of her."

When Jackie told the rest of the story, the hairs on the back of my neck stood up. It seemed that after the townspeople left, the woman hadn't died right away. Jackie said she'd "cried for a long time." What really got to me was when Jackie told of "someone trying to get her out" but "she" couldn't lift the stones.

I didn't say anything then and I tried not to think about it, but I couldn't help speculating. From the first I'd been told that this pressing happened many years ago. But after hearing what Jackie said was a "made-up version" of the story, I couldn't help but wonder if it had happened in recent times. And was it possible that Jackie had seen this horrible thing? Had Jackie been a child and seen some adults put stones on a woman, then leave her to die a slow, agonizing death? Had Jackie the child crawled out of her hiding place and tried to get the rocks off the woman but failed?

Jackie told me that her father had taken her away from her mother on the night he'd found out that his wife had told the devil story. Looking at it from an adult point of view, I wondered if her father knew his young daughter had witnessed the murder, and when his wife told their daughter about the murder and said it was "right," the man had been driven over the edge.

When Jackie finished her story, I'd been quiet, thinking about it all. I wanted to ask questions, but at the same time, I didn't want to ask them. It was my guess that Jackie had been much more involved than she knew—or wanted to know.

As I settled myself more snugly under the sheets, I wondered if I really wanted to write about this story. If my theory was correct, maybe I should find something else to write about. Something that wasn't recent and didn't involve living people.

As I fell asleep, I knew I was being torn in half. I didn't want to hurt anyone, but at the same time, for the first time in years, I was excited by a story. A true story. What I was good at.

The next morning, I was awakened by sounds over my head. When I opened my eyes and saw that wallpaper, I jumped, but then I remembered where I was, and sighed. House of Horrors. I lay there for a while, listening. My watch, on the heavy marble-topped table beside the bed, said it wasn't even six yet and I could see that it was barely daylight out. It could be robbers making the noise upstairs, I thought, hope buoying my spirits. Maybe they were looking for hidden jewels in the attic. Maybe in their search they'd take away some of the trash in this house.

I heard a loud sneeze. No such luck. Little

Miss High Energy was already upstairs moving boxes around.

Reluctantly getting out of bed, I shivered. The mountains of western North Carolina were quite cool in the morning. I took my time taking a bath (at least the hot water tank worked well) and getting dressed before I went upstairs to see what was going on.

Opening doors, I looked around before going to the room where I heard the noise. There were a couple of bedrooms and a bath that I was sure had been servants' quarters. The bleakness of the rooms was depressing; they were lightless, airless, and colorless.

At the front of the house was a fairly large room with a big window. I can write in here, I thought as I looked out the window. I could see over the shorter houses across the road to the mountains beyond. The mountains were in the distance, blue and misty, and so beautiful they made me draw in my breath and hold it.

I stayed that way for a while, then looked at the giant oak desk that set at an angle to the window. I could sit there and write and, when I needed to think, I could turn and look out at those mountains. In the far corner of the room, where there was now some hard little sofa that looked as though it was covered in horsehair, I could put a real couch, something soft, with wide arms that could hold papers.

A loud noise from down the corridor brought me out of my reverie, so I went to see what my industrious little assistant was doing.

She was in a big room that looked like the quintessential attic from every old movie ever made. I looked around for the discarded dressmaker's dummy. There was always a discarded dressmaker's dummy.

"So **now** you show up to help," Jackie said, sounding angry.

I started to snap back at her, but then I saw her face. She looked awful. Her eyes were sunken, with dark circles beneath them. At my age I looked like that every morning, but at her age, she was supposed to look dewy-fresh. "So what's wrong with you?" I asked in the same tone she'd used with me. "Ghosts in your room?"

To my horror, she sat down on an old trunk, put her hands over her face, and began to cry.

My first impulse was to run away. Second was to rent an apartment in New York and stay away from females forever.

Instead, I sat down on the trunk next to her and said, "What's wrong?"

She took a couple of minutes to get herself together. I didn't have any tissues nor did she, and the only cloth in that room would be so full of dust it would probably have suffocated her. So she sniffed a lot.

"I'm sorry," she said at last. "You'll never

believe this, but my dad said I never cry. Not even as a child. It was a joke between us. He used to say, 'What kind of tragedy would it take to make you cry?' Of course I bawled my head off at his funeral but—"

When she looked up at me, she saw that this was more than I wanted to hear. I had enough grief inside me. I didn't need to add anyone else's.

"I had a dream," she said.

I looked toward the door. Had I been insane to invite this stranger to live with me? Was I now condemned to daily recitations of her dreams? Was she prone to nightmares? Was she going to wake me in the middle of the night screaming?

Then I'd have to comfort her and—I looked at her. She was more cute than pretty and she seemed to fluctuate, at random, from being nice to having a tongue like a razor blade. However, she also had a beautiful voice and a round little fanny that was quite nice. And yesterday at a pit stop she'd started doing some contortions worthy of a performer at Cirque du Soleil.

"What was your dream?" I heard myself ask, which annoyed me because I hated dreams so much that when I was reading novels that told of the hero's, er, ah, protagonist's, dream, I'd skip the passage.

"It was—" she began, then stopped. Getting

up, she opened an old box that had ancient, dried-out tape on it.

I think she meant not to tell me, but she couldn't stop herself. Turning, she sat down on the box and I heard something inside rustle, like old leaves crunching.

"It was just so real," she said softly, "and I was so helpless." When she looked up at me, her eyes were hollow-looking, and I was silent. I'd never had a dream I could remember past breakfast, much less one that upset me this much.

"You and I were in your car," she said, "driving along a mountain road, and when we rounded a sharp curve we saw an overturned car. Four teenagers were standing by it, and they were laughing. You and I could see that they were happy because, even though they'd just been in a wreck, they were safe and unhurt. But the next second the car exploded and pieces of it flew everywhere."

Putting her hands over her face for a moment, Jackie looked back at me. "You and I were safe in your car, but those kids were . . . They were cut apart by the flying pieces of steel. Arms, legs, a . . . a head went flying through the air." She took a breath. "What was so horrible was that we could do nothing to save them. Absolutely nothing."

It did seem like an odd dream. Weren't most people's nightmares about something that was trying to get **them?** But Jackie had been perfectly safe in her dream. Sure, flying body parts were horrible, but she'd been upset because we could do nothing to help those poor dismembered kids.

I don't know why but it pleased me that she'd said "we." It was as though she believed that I would have helped if I could. In her dream she didn't think I was the kind of person who'd see an exploding car and think only of getting myself to safety.

I'm sure it was awful of me, but her dream kind of made me feel good.

I smiled at her. "How about if we have breakfast, then go buy some appliances? Refrigerator, washer, dryer, microwave. You want a new stove? Hey! How about some air conditioners?"

Sniffing, she looked at me with an expression that made me think I'd said something wrong. **"Window** air conditioners?" she asked.

I played dumb. "Sure. We'll stick them out the windows and paint them purple to match the house."

Her eyes widened for a second, as though she believed me, then she relaxed. "Why don't we tear out that big colored-glass skylight over the stairs and put in an air conditioner up there?"

"Great idea," I said enthusiastically. "Think they carry them that size locally?"

"The Victorian Historical Society carries

them," she said, smiling. "You just tell them what you plan to do and they take care of you." She made her hand into a gun as though some Victorian-loving zealot would shoot me.

When we laughed together, I was glad I'd been able to take her mind off her bad dream.

"Come on," I said, "I'll make you an omelet."

I didn't cook, but I set the table and cut up some fruit per Jackie's directions, and she told me about what she'd seen in the attic. There were old clothes and boxes of broken toys, and costume jewelry from the fifties plus lots of old phonograph records.

"There are some nice things up there," Jackie said, "and someone, somewhere, would like to have them. Even those old magazines in the hall are of interest to somebody."

"EBay," I said, my mouth full of an omelet filled with green and red peppers. No ham. At the grocery, Jackie had made such a fuss about the high fat content of ham—all while glancing down at my stomach—that I'd not bought any. "Hey!" I said. "You take photos, so why don't you photograph all this"—I waved my hand—"and auction it over eBay?"

"Before or after I research a book for you?" She put two potato pancakes (cooked in some no-calorie spray) on my plate. "Before or after I get an auctioneer to clean the excess furniture out of this house? Before or after I cook three meals a day for you?"

"I'll have to get back to you on that," I said as I bent my head and filled my mouth with food.

After breakfast, I suggested we also buy a dishwasher and hire someone to install it.

"Good idea," Jackie said, drying her hands on a paper towel. "And when do we start trying to find out about the devil story?"

"Let's talk about it in the car," I said, and minutes later we were driving.

I must say that buying things with Jackie made me remember my childhood. She was as in awe of spending money as I had been when I was a kid—or I was at her age, before my books were published.

Jackie's delight at being able to buy several major appliances at once was infectious. She made me understand how good dirty old men felt at buying their young mistresses bags full of jewelry. We bought vacuum cleaners (one for each floor), lots of knobs for the kitchen cabinets, and enough cleaning supplies and equipment for a hospital. I was getting bored until we got to the gardening and tool section where I felt more comfortable.

"I thought you hated machines," she said, leaning against a shelf and flipping through a book on landscaping.

I didn't answer but just smiled.

"What?!" she said.

"I never said that so you must have read my books."

"Never said I didn't," she replied, wedging the book into the already-full cart. "Who's going to do the cleaning and the gardening? And don't look at **me.** And, by the way, you still haven't told me how much you're paying me or what my hours are."

"Twenty-four/seven. And what's the minimum wage now?" I said, just to see her sputter.

But she didn't sputter. Instead, she turned around and started walking toward the front door of the store. She was moving so fast the big glass entrance doors had slid open before I caught her arm. "Okay, so what do you want?"

"Nine to five, twenty dollars an hour."

"Okay," I said. "But are you on or off the clock at breakfast and dinner?"

After a look of disgust, she shrugged. "Who knows? I can't figure out anything about this job."

"Excuse me," said a woman loudly.

Jackie and I were blocking the exit and the woman wanted out, so we stepped aside.

"Okay," I said quietly. "How about a grand a week and we play the hours by ear? If you want time off I'll stay home and take care of the furniture."

I got a tiny smile out of her at my joke, and we went back to our overloaded cart.

I couldn't for the life of me figure out why I was putting up with her cantankerousness. I hadn't put up with **anything** from the other women who'd worked for me. One second of bad temper and they were out of there.

But each time Jackie bit my head off, I remembered her story about the Pulitzer prize. That had been insightful and creative. And I remembered the way that lovely little Autumn had sat down in the middle of the room and cried—and I wondered if she'd done it just to get Jackie to tell a story. If so, what other stories had Jackie told?

As I looked at weed whackers, I thought, Jackie can research the devil story and I'll research Jackie.

We had lunch at a fast-food place, where Jackie had a salad and I had about four pounds of sandwich and curly fries. Through the whole meal, I could tell she was dying to lecture me on fat and cholesterol.

By two, we were on our way back to that monstrosity of a house, the car loaded nearly to the ceiling, appliances to be delivered tomorrow, when I couldn't resist telling her she should eat more. It was like I'd turned the crank and the jack-in-the-box sprang out. She started in on arteries and saturated fat until I was yawning and wished I'd not said anything.

But we both came alert when I drove around

a hairpin curve and there before us was an overturned car. In front of it were four laughing
teenagers, obviously laughing in relief that they
hadn't been hurt in the accident.

For a second both Jackie and I sat frozen to
our seats; we were seeing her dream come to
life. The next second we had thrown open the
car doors and were screaming, "Get away from
the car!"

The four teenagers turned to look at us,
dazed from having just been tumbled about, but
they didn't move.

When Jackie started to run toward the kids, I
ran after her. What the hell was she going to do?
Get torn apart **with** them?

I don't think it occurred to me to doubt that,
any second, that car was going to blow up, and
anything near it was going to be sliced into
pieces. When I reached Jackie, I grabbed her by
the waist and held her on my hip like a sack of
cornmeal. Even in that position, she didn't stop
screaming at the kids, nor did I, but I wasn't
going to let her get any closer to that belly-up
vehicle.

Maybe it was that I wouldn't get closer to the
car or that I wouldn't let Jackie run toward
them, that finally got through to one of the
kids. A big, good-looking boy with lots of black
hair finally seemed to understand what Jackie
and I were saying and moved into action.

Grabbing one of the girls, he nearly threw her across the road, where she began rolling down the steep hillside. The other boy grabbed the hand of the girl beside him and started running.

Like something in a movie, the three kids leaped toward the far side of the road just as the car exploded.

I got behind the safety of a big rock, holding Jackie's trim little body against mine, and covering her head with my arms. I bent my head and ducked under an overhang of tree roots.

The sound of the explosion was terrifying, and the brilliance of the light made me close my eyes so tight they hurt.

It was all over in seconds, then we heard pieces of steel falling onto the road, and the car began to burn. Still holding Jackie, I waited to see if it was really over.

"I can't breathe," she said, struggling to lift her head.

It was finally hitting me that she'd **seen** all of this. And her prophetic dream had just saved the lives of four kids.

She seemed to know what I was thinking because when she pushed away and looked at me, her face was beseeching. "I didn't know the dream was real. I've never had anything like this happen to me before. I—"

She cut off when one of the boys came over to say thanks for saving their lives. It was the boy whose fast actions had saved all of them. "How did you know?" he asked.

I could feel Jackie looking at me. Did she think I was going to betray her? "I saw a spark," I said. "By the gas tank."

"I sure do thank you," he said, putting out his hand to shake as he introduced himself as Nathaniel Weaver.

"Let's call the police from your cell phone," Jackie said. There was so much gratitude in her voice that I didn't dare look at her or I would have turned red in embarrassment.

In the end, it took the rest of the day to straighten everything out. The girl Nate had thrown—"Like a football," she said, looking up at the boy with eyes full of hero worship—had a broken arm so I drove her to the hospital while Jackie stayed with the other three kids until the police arrived. The police gave her and the kids a ride home.

After the girl's parents arrived at the hospital, I drove back to the scene of the explosion and looked around. The wrecked car had been towed away, but I picked up a piece of metal from the side of the road and sat down by the rock that had protected Jackie and me from flying metal.

For the last two years I'd been reading ghost and witch stories that were littered with tales of fortune-tellers and people who could see the future. This morning Jackie had told me of a dream of something that was going to happen. Yet she said she'd never glimpsed the future before.

Was it just my writer's imagination or was there a connection between the fact that Jackie had returned to a place she seemed to remember and her dream of the future?

A pickup truck going by brought me out of my thoughts. My car was still loaded with mops and brooms and a microwave, and tomorrow a truckload of appliances was to be delivered. I had to leave.

CHAPTER SIX

Jackie

I was determined to forget the whole dream thing. I've never really liked the occult and I certainly didn't want to participate in it. Yes, I used to scare the wits out of people with my highly-embellished devil story, but I still didn't like anything occult. One time when we were at a fair, my friends went to a tarot card reader, but I refused to go. It wasn't my future I didn't want to see but my past.

Of course I didn't tell my friends the truth. I told them I didn't believe in fortune-telling so I didn't want to waste my money. Only Jennifer looked at me hard and seemed to realize I was lying.

As I grew older, it became second nature to

me to tell people as little as possible about myself. The only person I really remembered living with was my father, and since he made such an effort to keep secrets, he had respect for mine. If I came home late, he never asked me where I'd been or what I'd been doing. If he'd yelled at me, I could have rebelled like a normal teenager, but my father had a way of silently telling me that I had only one life and it was up to me whether or not I screwed up.

I guess that's why I grew up so "old." The other kids in my class were always being punished for spending too much, "borrowing" the car, staying out too late, or doing any number of childish things. But I never got into trouble. I didn't spend too much money because I'd balanced the bank account since I was ten years old. My childish handwriting was on all the checks and my father signed them. I always knew how little there was in the bank and how much went for bills. I was amazed when I heard my classmates talk about money as though it just appeared. They actually had no idea how much the family water bill was. They'd make two-hour long-distance calls, then get yelled at by their parents and "grounded." The kids would laugh about it and plan their next long-distance call. I often thought their parents should turn the bank account over to them for a few months and let the kids see how much it cost to live.

Anyway, maybe because my situation at home was so different from everyone else's, I learned to keep my mouth shut. And maybe because my father seemed to be hiding so much, I learned to ask few questions, and answer even fewer.

By the time I was a teenager, I'd learned that it was useless to ask my father about my mother and why he'd left. If he did answer, he'd contradict himself. For years I lived in a romantic dream that he and I were in the government's Witness Protection Program. I made up a long, complicated story in which my mother had been killed by bad guys, my father had seen it, and to protect us, we were moved from one state to another.

But, gradually, I came to realize that the truth was known only by my father, and no outside agencies were involved. Eventually, I decided that whatever the truth about my mother was, it was probably better that I didn't know it, so I avoided psychics who might be able to tell me about my past.

However, secrets have a way of revealing themselves, whether you want them to or not. From about twenty miles outside the little town of Cole Creek, I began to recognize the area. At first I didn't say anything to Newcombe, but then I began to point out things that seemed vaguely familiar. The first time I said anything, I held my breath. If I'd said such a thing to my friends they would have squealed and started prying. Kirk would have ignored me as he had no curiosity whatever.

Newcombe seemed interested, but he didn't pretend to be a psychoanalyst and try to get me to tell him more. He listened and made comments, but he didn't act as though he was dying to find out everything about my life—and as a result, I ended up telling him more than I'd told any other person.

And he could get to the heart of a matter in seconds! The first night we were in the house, I nearly fainted when he asked me if I thought maybe my mother was still alive. It's what I'd been thinking since I saw the old bridge a few miles out of town. I could almost see myself as a little kid walking across that bridge, holding the hand of a tall, dark-haired woman. Was she my mother? My father had told a couple of stories about how she'd died, so maybe the fact of her death was a lie.

The good thing about Newcombe was that he didn't judge. Jennifer would have told me my father was a bad man since he'd kidnapped me and taken me away from my mother. But Jennifer's mother was loving and kind, so Jennifer couldn't comprehend that not all mothers were like hers.

All I knew for sure was that whatever my father had done, he'd done it for good reasons.

And he'd done it for me. I knew he was intelligent and educated, and that he could have had better jobs than selling shoes at a discount store. But how could he get a better class of job if he couldn't provide a résumé and a transcript of his schooling? Yet to do so would have left a paper trail so he—and I—could have been found.

It was after I had the dream about the kids and the car that I began to wonder if maybe my father had been running away from something evil. And I began to wonder if Cole Creek was someplace I should never have returned to.

But twenty-four hours after the incident happened, I managed to calm down enough to conclude that, obviously, I'd lived in Cole Creek longer than my father said we had, which is why I remembered things. As for the dream, lots of people'd had dreams of the future, hadn't they? It was no big deal. Someday it would make a great dinner party story.

Instead of obsessing, I threw myself into making that wonderful old house livable. I'm not sure why I made the effort because Newcombe hated the place. Every other sentence out of his mouth was a complaint about the house and its contents. He hated the wallpaper, the furniture, and all the little knickknacks the Belchers had accumulated in over a hundred years of living. He even hated the porches! The only things he really liked were his giant bathtub and the little flame-spitting

dragon on top of the newel post. I think I would
have liked the dragon, too, but the fact that I
remembered it so well made me uneasy.

I didn't tell Newcombe but I knew every
inch of that house. And what's more, I knew
how it had once looked. I didn't say so, but I
knew that all the good furniture had been
removed. There'd been some cabinets in the living room that weren't there now, and the "small
parlor," as I knew it was called, had been cleaned
out of some very elegant pieces.

Newcombe had laughingly told me that Mr.
Belcher had offered him the entire contents of
the house for a dollar and the realtor had paid
the fee. After viewing what was left, I wanted to
say, "You should have asked for change." But
Newcombe was bellyaching so much that I put
on a happy face and told him that everything
was great. Besides, on that first day, he was playing with a bunch of stuffed ducks, moving the
dining room chairs around, and turning the
dragon on and off until I wanted to scream, so I
said nothing about the missing furniture. And,
too, I knew that if I could get his permission to
have some repairs done, I'd be able to make that
house into the beauty it had once been.

I've always been a "good worker" as my
teachers used to write on my report cards, but I
must say that the day after Newcombe saved
those kids, I went into overtime.

Maybe my work frenzy was caused by my deep embarrassment. I was embarrassed about my vision, and embarrassed about the way I'd sat there in front of my employer that morning and bawled. But I think I was mostly embarrassed about the way I'd reacted when I saw my dream come true. When I saw that car and those kids, exactly like it was in my dream, I was unable to move.

It was Newcombe who reacted. He leaped out of the car and started yelling. It was his action that made me realize I wasn't having the dream again, that this was reality, and that those four kids were about to be cut into pieces. I went blind. A split second after he reacted, I jumped out of the car and ran screaming toward the kids. Thank heaven that Newcombe caught me before I got to the overturned car.

He was a hero. That's the only way I can describe him. He acted in a heroic manner and saved all of us. And later, he didn't give me away by saying I'd had a dream and "seen" the future.

That night when he got back from taking one of the girls to the hospital, he didn't ask me a single question about the dream. I'll go to my grave being grateful to him for not asking me questions that were guaranteed to make me feel like a freak.

The next morning I awoke early, vowing that I was going to make that house livable as soon

as humanly possible. At breakfast I had a brief
discussion with Newcombe about money—
which, for some unfathomable reason, made
him shake his head at me in wonder—then I set
to work.

The old black telephones in the house had
been disconnected, but I found a telephone
directory that was only two years old, so I used
Newcombe's cell phone to call people and
make appointments. If a workman couldn't
come that week, I called someone else. I knew I
was taking a chance on hiring unknowns and
that I'd probably get some scalawags, but I didn't
have time to meet the locals and ask who the
best tradesmen in the area were.

After the appointments had been made, I
knew I needed to get Newcombe out of the
way, so I gave him the address of a nearby electronics store and he was out of the house in a
flash. He'd investigated and, yes, the little round
silver thing in the wall of the small parlor was a
hookup for satellite—no cable in town—TV.

Newcombe didn't return until eight that
night and we had a very pleasant dinner in
which we competed to see who had accom-
plished more.

While I had arranged for a nearby auction
house to come with a truck and haul away three
loads of cheap, hideous furniture, Newcombe
had bought computer, stereo, TV, and video

equipment—and a pickup truck to carry it all home in.

We shared a bottle of wine, and laughed about it all while he cooked steaks on a new stainless-steel gas grill, complete with rotisserie. All while we played our game of one-upmanship. Personally, I think I won because I hadn't spent money but was going to earn it from the sale of the furniture. And I'd worked out a sort of trade—all based on photos—with the auctioneer that I was rather proud of. But I didn't tell Newcombe about that. I thought I'd just let him be surprised on Friday morning.

The next day was chaos. I didn't count them, but I think there had to be at least fifty men in and out of the house that day. I had three strong men from a moving company rearrange what furniture was still in the house after the auctioneer's trucks left, and I had plumbers, carpenters, and a wallpaper hanger for Newcombe's bedroom. While we'd been at Lowe's I'd jotted down the name and number of a plain blue-on-blue wallpaper that had big urns and flower garlands on it. It looked masculine and simple, although to my eye a bit funereal, but I thought Newcombe would like it. The wallpaper hanger measured, picked up the in-stock rolls, and hung it over the old wallpaper. I knew this wasn't the proper way to do it—the old paper should have been steamed off first—but this was an emergency. I was afraid Newcombe was going to have a heart attack in that bedroom. Or give me one from hearing his constant complaining.

While repairs were being made, I had three crews with their steamers cleaning the curtains, rugs and upholstery, plus removing the mold from the kitchen.

While all this was going on, Newcombe locked himself and his new electronic equipment in the library and said he was going to put it all together. The two times I looked in on him, he was sitting inside a deep circle of books and reading. He looked divinely happy.

At about three an extraordinarily handsome young man came to the back door and started talking to me, but I was so busy directing workmen that I didn't at first recognize him. He was Nathaniel Weaver, the boy from the overturned car.

I got a pitcher of lemonade and some cookies out of the new refrigerator and we went outside to talk. He'd come to thank Newcombe, but I said he was busy. Actually, I didn't want the two males to talk about what had happened because I was afraid my premonition might come up.

Nate kept looking around the two acres of weeds and broken garden ornaments in a nervous way. I thought that being near a celebrity like Newcombe was what was making him jittery, and I was about to tell him that Newcombe was a normal, ordinary person when Nate blurted out, "Do you need someone to clean this place up for you?"

I didn't grab his hands and kiss them—nor did I put my hands on his face and kiss his lovely full-lipped mouth—but my gratitude made me want to. The child—all nearly six feet of him—wanted a weekend job and he seemed to think that clearing out two acres of weeds was something he could do.

I don't know what made me do it—heavens but I hope it wasn't some "second sight" lunacy—but I made one of my lame jokes. I said that now all I needed was someone to sell the hundred-plus—I'd started to count them, but quit at one fifty—Statues of Liberty in the house and I'd be in Nirvana.

That dear, beautiful boy told me that he lived with his grandmother (parents dead) and Granny went to flea markets in the area and sold things over the Internet on eBay.

That's when I **did** kiss him. It was a sisterly sort of kiss—on his lips, true, but it was a light, quick kiss of gratitude—and from the look on his face I think he was used to females of all ages kissing him. By six P.M. he and I'd filled Newcombe's new pickup with boxes full of the accumulation of years of souvenir hunts, and Nate and I shook hands—no more kissing—on the deal.

But that night I almost got into a fight with Newcombe because I'd allowed someone to borrow his brand-new 4 x 4.

That surprised me. "I thought you were a writer," I said. "I thought that all those books of yours were against men who loved trucks."

"Control, not trucks," he said, and I pretended I didn't know what he meant. Of course I did know but I just didn't want to lose a fight.

Men are such strange creatures. He didn't mind that I was spending thousands of his money to fix up a house he hated, but when I lent his new pickup to a kid whose life he'd saved, he got angry.

I guess males understand each other, though, because at ten-thirty that night Nate returned Newcombe's pickup, and the two of them disappeared into the library until two A.M. I went to bed, but about four times I was jolted alert by wall-shaking blasts of music. Obviously, they were putting together the new stereo equipment.

At two A.M., I heard a car outside and from the chug-chug sound of it I was sure it was Nate's rusty old Chevy Impala. Minutes later, I heard Newcombe come up the creaky stairs and go into his bedroom. I'd been in bed for hours, but only when I knew he was safely in his bed one room away from me did I allow myself to fall into a deep sleep.

On Thursday morning a boy knocked on the

door and handed me a thick envelope. It was addressed to Newcombe in a beautiful old-fashioned handwriting that could have been done with a quill. I took the envelope to the kitchen, where he was eating his usual stevedore breakfast and reading a stack of instruction manuals, and handed it to him. I was pretending to pay no attention to the letter, but I was actually watching him intently.

He wiped his hands before touching the envelope. "I haven't seen stationery like this outside a museum."

I quit rinsing dishes and sat down by him, curiosity eating at me. "Look at that handwriting. Do you think you've been invited to a cotillion?"

"Hmmm," he said as he started to stick his finger in the side and tear the envelope open.

Paper like that deserved to be slit, not torn. I handed him a knife.

He cut the top off the envelope, started to open it, but, instead, put the envelope down on the table and picked up his fork.

"You don't want to see who sent you what?!" I asked.

"Maybe," he said as he put a bite of waffle in his mouth. "And I might even want to share the information with you—but on one condition."

Here it comes, I thought. Sex. I gave him a dirty look and started to return to the sink.

"Stop calling me Mr. Newcombe," he said. "Start calling me Ford and we'll open this together."

"Done," I said as I sat back down at the table.

The cream-colored envelope was lined with light blue tissue paper and inside was an engraved invitation. Engraved, not thermograph, that imitation engraving. Someone had used one of those tiny engraving tools and carved into brass that there was to be a party on the lawn of the town square on Friday afternoon.

"Tomorrow?" I asked, looking at him. What in the world did I own that was good enough to wear to an engraved-invitation party? On the other hand, it was Ford's name alone on the envelope. "Nice," I said, getting up and going back to the sink. "You'll have to tell me about everything that happens," I said in my absolute best I-didn't-want-to-go-anyway voice.

When Ford didn't say anything, I looked back at him and saw that he was staring at me as though he was trying to figure out a puzzle. But he didn't say anything. After he finished eating, he put his dishes in the dishwasher and went upstairs to the room he'd said he wanted for his office.

Since he'd left the invitation on the table, I looked at it. "The Cole Creek Annual Tea" it was called, and I could imagine ladies in pretty summer dresses and picture book hats—just what I'd imagined when I'd first seen that lovely little square with the white bandstand in the middle of it.

As I picked up the invitation, a piece of paper fell out. It was the same heavy cream paper as the rest of the invitation, and written in the same beautiful copperplate handwriting that was on the outside. The note said "Please bring your houseguest with you." It was signed Miss Essie Lee Shaver.

I loaded the dishwasher in a split second, shoved the door closed, and, even though I had workmen everywhere, I ran upstairs to my bedroom to look inside my closet. I'd never owned many clothes, but when I was near my friends I didn't need to. Autumn delighted in dressing me as though I were one of the fifty or so dolls she kept on her bed. I owned only one dress, an old, flowery cotton thing that had a rip in the skirt.

Taking the dress out of the closet, I sat down on the bed. Could I repair the tear?

"Didn't you tell me there were boxes of old clothes in the attic?"

I looked up to see Newcombe—Ford—standing in the doorway and it took me a moment to comprehend what he was saying. When I did understand, I dropped my old dress to the floor, ran under his arm and up the stairs to the attic. He was right. I'd seen some lace blouses in a box somewhere. I opened three

boxes before Ford said, "This what you're looking for?"

He was holding up an exquisite creation of
white linen, with white lace panels running
from shoulders to waist. The long sleeves were
inset with more lace and the high, boned, stand-
up collar was all lace.

"Ooooh," I said as I went toward him, arms
outstretched.

"Think it'll fit?" he asked.

I could tell by his tone that he was laughing
at me, but I didn't care. I was holding the blouse
by the shoulders. Of course I couldn't **wear**
something like that, I thought. It belonged in a
museum.

"Try it on," he said, smiling.

Sometimes, when the light was dim, I
thought, he didn't look half bad.

"Use this." Grabbing a couple of old curtains,
he hooked them to some nails in the rafters to
make a screen.

I went behind the curtains, quickly removed
my T-shirt, and put on the beautiful linen
blouse. It fit perfectly. I was glad to see that the
original owner hadn't been some Buxom
Bertha like Autumn had tried to make me into
at my almost-wedding.

There were forty-some buttons up the back
and I did enough of them to hold the blouse
together but I couldn't get all of them. I stepped

out from the curtain, feeling a little nervous, and said, "Is it okay?"

When Ford just stared at me, I thought, If he says something that's a come-on, I'll leave his employment this minute.

"Who would have thought," he said at last, "that there have been **two** such skinny, flat-chested girls on this earth?"

"You!" I said, looking around for something to throw at him. I grabbed an ugly satin pillow with four inch long fringe, "Atlantic Beach" written across it, and tossed it at his head.

He ducked, and the pillow hit the wall behind him, where it gave a bang as it went down.

Ford and I looked at each other and said, "Treasure!" in unison, then we went for the pillow. As befit his background, Ford had a little folding knife in his pocket and he used it to cut open a seam. When out tumbled half a dozen more Statues of Liberty, we both went into spasms of laughter.

"Who would hide them when there are hundreds more downstairs?" I asked.

"Maybe these are made of gold," he said as he used his knife to scrape off the painted finish at the bottom of one of them. But they were all just plastic—which made us laugh more.

After that it was as though we'd broken through some barrier of reticence. For all that we'd been in the same house together for nearly a week, we'd seen little of each other. Ford had been locked away with his truckload of electronics and I'd spent my days with workmen. But finding those silly souvenirs sealed away in a pillow as though they were great treasures—or "Forbidden," as Ford said—made both of us loosen up.

I put my T-shirt back on and we started going through the boxes. I was looking for something to wear on the bottom half of me; I don't know what he was looking for. Ford told me I'd done a great job with the house and now he almost liked his bedroom. "Almost," he said, eyes twinkling.

When he found the boxes holding the turn-of-the-century train set, he started putting it together in the hallway just outside the door, while I continued searching. I needed something to wear with the blouse besides blue jeans. And hadn't I seen some costume jewelry somewhere?

When I asked Ford about the hours he and Nate had spent locked in the library together, I opened a floodgate. It seems that the boy was very poor and had to work weekends and after school. But his lack of free time hadn't hurt him socially as he was a candidate for prom king.

"No wonder," I said, looking inside a box of old handbags. The leather had dried out and cracked on most of them. "The boy is gorgeous.

That hair. Those eyes. Those **lips.** I can tell you
that he made me—" I stopped because I'd forgotten where I was and that I was talking to my
boss instead of a girlfriend. Pulling my head out
of the box, I looked at Ford. He'd stopped
putting his train together and was staring at me,
waiting for me to continue. I hid my red face
inside the box. "So what else did Nate tell you?"

"How grateful he is to you for helping his
grandmother. You know, Jackie, he's only seventeen."

At that I gave Ford Newcombe a look that
let him know how likely I was to have a fling
with a seventeen-year-old.

With a little smile, he went back to his train
set. "His grandmother is partially disabled and
walks with two canes, so it's difficult for her to
get out. The boy didn't say so but I think it's a
pretty hard existence for them. And I think he's
worried about what will happen to her after he
graduates and starts working full-time."

I pulled a little white beaded bag from the
bottom of a box and held it up. "Isn't he going
to college? If he can't afford it, maybe he could
get a scholarship."

When Ford didn't reply I looked at him. He
wore a look of . . . what? I wasn't sure, but I
think it was a look of fear. What in the world
about a boy going to college could cause such a
look?

"Oh, Lord," I said. "Writing. Young Nathaniel Weaver wants to be a writer."

"Right," Ford said.

I opened another box. "You know, this invitation said it was the 'annual' tea party, but it didn't say which annual. It could be the first one. You don't think it was concocted just so a whole town full of would-be writers could ask you questions, do you?"

When I glanced at Ford, he'd turned so white that a devil entered me. As I went toward him, I rubbed my hands and made noises like a talkies villain. "And so, Mr. Newcombe, I'd like to tell you the plot of my book so you can write it for me and we'll split the money."

By the time I'd finished, I was inches in front of him. He threw his arms over his face as though I was about to attack him with an ax.

"No! No!" he said, and began scooting backward along the floor.

"And an agent," I said, leaning over him and following. "You have to get me an agent who'll get me lots and lots of money for my story and if you don't I'll—"

He peeped up at me through his arms. "You'll what?"

"I'll put your home address on the Internet and tell people you want them to send you all their manuscripts. Handwritten manuscripts and you'll type them yourself."

"No, no," he moaned, and began sinking into the floor as though he were the Wicked Witch and starting to melt.

I leaned over him. "And furthermore—"

"Uh, excuse me," came a voice from the head of the stairs. It was one of the workmen. "Could one of you come look at the kitchen sink drain and make a decision?"

Ford and I looked at each other like two kids whose mother had called them in to dinner. Shrugging, I went downstairs. One thing I'd already learned about Ford Newcombe was that he did **not** look at drainpipes.

CHAPTER SEVEN

Ford

No wonder she's so skinny, I thought. She worked like a dozen demons on speed. She ran up and down stairs all day long, answered questions from countless workmen, and cleaned up messes. Part of me said I should help, but the larger part of me said I wanted no part of the chaos. Instead, I took on the job of connecting that old house to the twenty-first century. After I got Jackie to find an electronics store nearby, I spent a day purchasing equipment to set up an office with a computer system and music—which I needed for inspiration. I also went through some of the volumes in the library: Nothing valuable, no first editions, but there were some excellent books on North Carolina history, flora, and fauna.

However, as far as I could find, not one book in that home library mentioned Cole Creek. Either those books had been purposely left out or removed—or the town was too small to warrant anyone making a record of its history. I discarded that theory, though. It was my observation that people loved their small towns and wrote lots about them.

On Thursday morning an invitation came to attend an afternoon tea party in the local park. I probably wouldn't have attended, but Jackie was about to come apart with wanting to go so I said I'd go, too.

Five minutes after I left the kitchen she was thundering up the stairs, almost knocking a painter down. Curious, I followed her. I found her sitting on her bed holding a dress that should have been consigned to a ragbag. Ah, clothes for the party, I thought, that was her concern. Jackie'd told me she'd seen some old clothes in the attic so I mentioned them.

If I'd been blocking the doorway, I'm sure she would have knocked me down and walked over me on her way up to the attic. As it was, she ran under my arm so fast I was nearly spinning.

We searched through some old boxes, found her clothes, and had about forty minutes off before one of her workmen came and got her.

After she left, I sat there for a few minutes and felt kind of good. I'm not sure what it was about Jackie, but when I was around her I didn't feel that deep sense of grief that I'd had since Pat died.

When I thought about that, I decided I needed to start dating. Jackie was beginning to look too good to me. When she put on that lacy blouse, she'd looked like a woman. In her T-shirts and jeans, she was resistible, but in that lacy, feminine garment she looked . . . Well, she looked too damned good. And since she'd made it clear that she wasn't interested in me in any way except to write her paychecks, my pride wasn't going to allow me to make overtures to my cute little assistant.

By Friday afternoon, the house didn't look half bad. I'd been so busy setting up my office and sorting out the library that I'd paid little attention to what Jackie was doing. Maybe she'd told me she and the auctioneer had worked out some deal, but I didn't hear her, so early Friday when the trucks pulled up in front of the house and I saw them moving furniture **in,** I protested. But it seemed that some rich old lady had died in the next county over and her adult kids had wanted all the contents of their mother's house sold. So Jackie had used the proceeds from the auction of the Belcher goods to buy the woman's furniture. And when it arrived, Jackie ran around like an insane person, directing four men about where to put couches, chairs, and tables.

During that chaos, I locked myself in the library and refreshed my mind on what had made Frank Yerby's books sell so well back in his day.

At one, she knocked on the door and handed me a tray full of food, and at three she knocked again, this time dressed for the party. She had on that white blouse that I'd found for her, and a pair of black trousers with big legs, like something from a Carole Lombard movie, and she looked good.

"Go get dressed," she ordered me in the same tone she'd used on the movers.

I laughed at her, but I also went upstairs and put on a clean shirt and trousers.

We walked down the street together, saying not a word, and after we rounded the corner of the house next door to the park, we had only seconds to look at the scene before people descended on us. There were picnic tables loaded with food, and probably about fifty people milling about. Musicians were in the bandstand tuning up and getting ready to play. Children, in their Sunday best, were sedately walking about, looking for the second when they could escape their parents' eagle eyes and do the things they'd been warned not to do. All in all, it looked like a pleasant gathering, and

Jackie and I headed straight for the food tables.

I tried to stay with Jackie because, basically, I don't like strangers, but she was Little Miss Gregarious and disappeared within seconds.

I was left to be "welcomed." This consisted of being overtaken by the mayor of Cole Creek and the head librarian, Miss Essie Lee Shaver.

Just looking at the two of them made me blink in wonder. The mayor—I'm not sure he had a name but was always referred to as "Mayor"—had on a green coat and a gold brocade vest. He had a huge reddish blond mustache and a body like Humpty Dumpty. His belt must have been fifty inches around, but his legs were as thin as a whooping crane's, and his tiny, shiny, black shoes would have fit a toddler. He also had a high-pitched voice that I had difficulty understanding.

I was standing there listening to him, trying to keep my eyes on his and not look him up and down in amazement, when Jackie came by, a full plate of food in her hands, and said under her breath, "Follow the yellow brick road. Follow the yellow brick road."

After that I had a hard time keeping a straight face, for the mayor did indeed look like a tall Munchkin.

It was a long time before the mayor wound down, finished his speech of welcome, and Miss Essie Lee took over. She was tall, thin, even flatter chested than Jackie, and she had on an old blouse very much like the one Jackie was wearing. I kept waiting for the mayor to take a breath so I could tell Miss Essie Lee that I liked her blouse—and thereby maybe be forgiven for our disastrous telephone conversation—but the mayor kept talking.

Jackie was near the two picnic tables that looked as though a couple of cornucopias had been working all night, and she was laughing with about a dozen people. I was torn between jealousy and annoyance. I'd like food and laughter, too, so why wasn't she rescuing me?

I was so distracted by the matter of food that I missed what the mayor was saying.

"So you can see that it was all a mistake," he was saying. "The kids made up a story to explain what they'd found. And Miss Essie Lee thought you were someone pretending to be the illustrious writer you are and that's why she hung up on you."

There was a woman standing to one side of the picnic tables. She was quite handsome in a way that I liked. She had an oval face and dark eyes, and long, straight chestnut hair that hung to her waist. She was wearing a black T-shirt dress and little sandals. She was listening to something Jackie was saying, and when she turned and glanced at me, I smiled at her. She didn't smile back but she didn't break eye contact either. I was about to excuse myself from Mayor Munchkin, when Miss Essie Lee took my arm and led me away. With regret I glanced back at the dark woman by the picnic tables, but she was gone.

With a sigh, I gave my attention to Miss Essie Lee. She and I were alone now, half hidden from the others by overhanging trees, and she was telling me something she seemed to think I should know.

It took me several moments before I realized that my worst nightmare was coming true. Miss Essie Lee Shaver was telling me some story she thought I should write. Since this woman ran the local library, the place where I hoped to do some research, I couldn't be rude and walk away. I had to listen.

She seemed to think that because I'd bought "dear old Mr. Belcher's house" that I was dying to hear about the great romantic tragedy of Mr. Belcher's only child, Edward. She was going into detail about how Edward Belcher was a saint of a man and when he was fifty-three years old, he'd asked the beautiful Harriet Cole, twenty-seven years his junior, to marry him.

The name "Cole" perked up my ears. I said, "As in Cole Creek?" and that's when I was told that the town was founded by seven families and, yes, Harriet Cole was a descendant of a founding father.

As Miss Essie Lee chattered on, a man carrying a plastic cup full of liquid strolled by. I was tempted to offer him a hundred bucks to get me something to drink. Instead, I looked back at the librarian.

She was saying that the dreadful Harriet Cole had wanted nothing to do with the "lovely" Edward.

I refrained from making a comment about age and youth not mixing, something I was seeing every day in my own house.

Seems the beauteous and **young** Ms. Cole had eloped with a handsome young man who'd come to town to manage the local pottery.

I stood there waiting for the rest of the story, but that seemed to be all of it. Miss Essie Lee closed her mouth and said not another word. As I looked at her, I thought, Why has she told me this long-winded story about true love thwarted? The word "distraction" came into my mind. Maybe she was using the unrequited love story to entice me away from the devil story.

If she was, it wasn't going to work. My assistant had told a murder story as though she'd been there, and days after she entered this town she'd had a vision of the future. No, I don't think a story of lost love was going to pull me away.

When Miss Essie Lee stopped talking, I thought, now I can get away. I can go get food and drink and seek out the woman with all that hair.

But I couldn't move. I'd heard that writers were cursed with a need to write so, like I had to breathe, I **had** to hear the end of this story. "What happened to them?" I heard myself ask.

"Died young, of course," Miss Essie Lee said, as though she were disappointed that I, a best-selling writer, had to ask. "Love like that can't live long." She said this as though it were a given, like water being wet.

I wanted to ask which love, the love between the two who eloped, or old Edward and young Harriet? But the look on Miss Essie Lee's face didn't allow me to ask questions. "Perhaps I could visit your library and you could tell me more," I said, then was rewarded with a brilliant smile from her. Nice teeth, I thought.

"Yes, you do that," she said, then, abruptly, she turned and walked away.

Freedom! I made a beeline for the food table.

By the time I got there, most of the food was gone and some people were already leaving. Three five-year-olds were under the bandstand and wouldn't come out no matter what their parents threatened them with.

Jackie was talking to two women, but they moved away when they saw me. Being "famous" was like that. Either people pushed and shoved to get near me or they ran away at first sight.

"It's a nice group," Jackie said, lifting up a cloth on a bench to reveal a full plate of food. "I saved this for you. So what did ol' Starch and Vinegar want with you?"

Smiling, I took the food. "To distract me with another story."

"Let me guess. About the seven—"

"Founding families," I said, letting her know that I'd learned something.

"What was she telling you?" Jackie asked, nodding toward Miss Essie Lee. "She seemed to be very serious."

"Old love story," I said. "I'll tell you later. Who was the—"

"The woman with the long hair? The one you were making ga-ga eyes at?"

"I wasn't—" I began, but decided not to let Jackie get to me. "Yeah, that one," I said. "Married?"

"Twice," Jackie answered, looking at me hard but I wouldn't meet her eyes. "But divorced both times. No kids. She's forty-two and she's a personal assistant to D. L. Hazel."

From her tone of voice, I knew I was supposed to have heard that name before but my mouth was full of some barbequed chicken that was so delicious I couldn't think. Years ago I'd heard something that had stayed with me. "No Northerner ever ate anything he could sell and no Southerner ever sold anything he could eat." The food on my plate verified that, so I didn't pause in eating to try to guess who D. L. Hazel was.

"Sculptor," Jackie said. "Pieces in some of the major galleries in the U.S. and in lots of museums."

"Did you know that before today?" I asked, biting into corn bread with whole pieces of corn in it.

Jackie smiled. "Naw. Rebecca Cutshaw told me. She's the woman you were hyperventilating over."

I looked at Jackie. Was she teasing me or was she jealous? She was smiling in a way that I couldn't read.

"See the blonde woman over there?" Jackie asked.

I looked to see a small, sweet-looking dumpling of a woman who was talking earnestly to a little girl in a white dress with a big mud stain on the skirt. The two of them made me smile. It was obvious that they were mother and daughter, but they seemed to be exact opposites. In spite of the dress with a big blue sash (left over from a wedding?) I was sure the girl was a tomboy. She had red hair in pigtails, freckles, and feet that, even in patent leather Mary Janes, looked made for climbing trees. But her mother looked as though she were made for bubble baths and clinging helplessly to some man's arm.

"I like her," Jackie said firmly. "Her name's Allie and she's nice." She was looking at me as though I was expected to understand something.

I paused with a chicken leg to my mouth. "You mean you **like** her?"

"Would you get your mind off sex for ten seconds? I mean she's nice and she has a sense of humor and it's your house but do you mind if I have friends over?" she said in one breath.

I was so relieved I ate the chicken leg in two bites. It didn't matter to me what my assistant's sexual inclinations were, of course, but—Jackie was staring at me. "What?" I asked.

"Baby-sitting. I told Allie that Tessa, that's her daughter, could stay at our house—your house—on Thursday afternoons. Is that all right?"

"I guess so," I said tentatively. How was I going to work with women giggling in the parlor and kids screaming in the backyard? But then I hadn't worked in the peace and quiet of the last six years, so maybe noise would help.

Before I could say any more, Nate came up to us. He reminded me of myself. He'd had a hard time in his life, with his parents dying when he was four, and afterward having to live with his half-crippled grandmother. All his life he'd had to work for anything he had.

The evening we'd spent hooking up the electronic equipment had been enjoyable, and I'd vowed to help him all I could. But it had been Jackie who'd helped him the most when she'd given him about a ton and a half of junk.

"Granny says thanks," Nate said, looking embarrassed, but my eyes were on Jackie. She'd said some pretty lascivious things about this boy, so I was wondering if she really would try to seduce him. "She asked me if there was anything she could do to repay you."

"She was doing us a favor by taking that stuff off our hands," I said. Jackie and I hadn't talked about it, but I was glad she hadn't asked Nate for a share of the proceeds of the sales. "There's more in the attic. Maybe next week you could stop by and take another load away." Hard as I tried, I couldn't see that Jackie was looking at the boy with lust in her eyes.

"Didn't Jackie tell you?" Nate asked, enthusiasm in his voice. "I'm going to be working at your house all summer. I'm your new gardener. Oh! There's—" He cut off and I turned to see what he was gaping at. The girl I'd taken to the hospital, her arm in a cast, had just arrived.

"Go," I said and the boy was away in a flash. I looked at Jackie. "Don't you think you could have informed me about who I was hiring?"

"And interrupt **Mandingo?**" she asked. "Besides, I only hired him so I can seduce him—when I'm not in bed with Allie, that is. Look! There's Rebecca, your heartthrob," she said, as she walked away.

I wasn't going to let Jackie's remarks bother

me, so I sauntered over to introduce myself to Rebecca. "Hello," I said. "I'm—"

"Ford Newcombe." She was even prettier up close. "We all know who you are: our resident celebrity. So, tell me, Mr. Newcombe, how do you like our little town?"

"Actually, I haven't seen much of it." I was hinting that she might give me a tour.

When she sipped at her drink, I caught a whiff of bourbon and wondered where they were serving booze. "If you walked from your house to here then you saw the whole town."

There was some underlying tone of anger in her voice that was turning me off. "True," I said, still smiling, "but there's the surrounding countryside that I haven't seen."

When she drank more and didn't say anything, I tried again. "I bought a big gas grill and I need help in breaking it in," I said in what I hoped was a charming way. "Maybe next Friday you could come for dinner."

"Can't," she said. No excuse. No regret. Just "can't."

"Saturday?" I asked.

"Can't," she repeated, then drained her glass and walked away.

So much for being the town "celebrity," I thought. I couldn't even get a date.

"Struck out, huh?" Jackie said, coming up behind me.

"No, I . . . She . . ."

"Don't get too upset about it. Allie says Rebecca has a problem." Jackie made a motion of drinking. "Come on," she said, "let's go talk to Allie."

I'm not sure exactly what happened after that, but four hours later we were having a dinner party at my house. After I bombed out with the tipsy Rebecca, people began coming up to me to ask for my autograph and I was kept busy for a while.

Eventually, though, the band put away their instruments, the party was over, and Jackie came and got me. She wrapped both her arms around one of mine and pulled me away from the people surrounding us.

"Really!" she said. "I've never seen anyone like you. Why are you so rude to people who work for you, but so nice to the ones who act like you're their ticket to stardom?"

"It's a matter of money," I said, suddenly happy because the party was over. "I can take all my frustrations out on people I pay, but I have to be nice to people who pay me. You know, the people who buy my books."

"You and money," she said, but I could see she was laughing. "I hope it's okay, but I invited a few people over so we need to go."

The very last thing I wanted was more company. I wanted to go back to my library and—

"Don't give me that look," Jackie said. "I invited **nice** people."

I have to say that she did. Allie came with her nine-year-old daughter, who turned out to be quite self-sufficient. She disappeared into my weedy garden and we rarely saw her again. "Probably inventing something," her mother said.

A couple my age, Chuck and DeeAnne Fogle, also came. They didn't live in Cole Creek, but had been driving through town, seen the party, "And crashed it," Chuck said. He was an engineer, so he was interested in the equipment I'd bought, and we spent some time together inside the house exploring what it could do.

When Nate and his injured girlfriend arrived, Jackie sent them off in my new truck to pick up pizzas while she and Allie and DeeAnne went for beer and wine. An hour later we were all outside, eating and laughing. Except for the two teenagers, that is. They disappeared into the house as soon as it was dark. I was a bit uncomfortable with whatever they were doing but not so Jackie. She stood in the entrance hall and shouted upward, "No clothes are to be removed. Got it?" After a few seconds' pause, Nate's voice came from upstairs. "Yes, ma'am," he said meekly.

It was a nice evening. When Tessa stretched out on an old-fashioned metal glider and went to sleep, Jackie covered her with a blanket and the adults kept on laughing and talking.

"So what was Miss Essie Lee on at you about?" Allie asked me.

Allie had a sharper brain than I'd thought when I first met her. Earlier, she'd told us that she'd grown up in Cole Creek and met her husband while he was in the area doing some soil testing for a mineral company. But when he'd been transferred to Nevada, Allie and Tessa hadn't gone with him. Jackie asked, "Why not?" but Allie had shrugged in answer, revealing nothing.

"Edward Belcher," I said. "Miss Essie Lee was telling me about Edward Belcher and The Great Love Story."

At that Allie snorted in a way that made me sure there was a story there.

"You're in for it now," Jackie said. "You'll have to tell him every word of the story or he'll never let you go home."

"Is that where you get your ideas?" DeeAnne asked. "From real life stories?"

"He gets them from reading everything," Jackie said before I could answer. "If it has printing on it, he reads it. He spends whole days locked in the library reading, then he goes upstairs to his bedroom and reads. If I want to ask him a question, I have to make sure there's nothing to read within fifty feet or he doesn't hear a word I say."

Chuck put his head back, closed one eye, and

said, "Me thinks thou art trying to escape from something."

"Yeah," Jackie said. "Work."

Everyone, including me, laughed, and I noticed both Allie and DeeAnne looking from Jackie to me speculatively. Before they started matchmaking, I said to Allie, "So tell us about old man Belcher's saintly son."

"Saintly, ha!" Allie said, sipping her wine. "Edward Belcher wanted to marry Harriet Cole only because the town was named after her family. He seemed to think that uniting the descendants of two of the seven founding families would raise his status. He had his eye on the governorship."

I was thinking of this in writer terms. "Those seven families seem to be important here in Cole Creek," I said. "Besides old man Belcher and Miss Essie Lee, are many of them left in town?"

"Yes," Allie said softly. "Tessa and me." She looked at me. "And Rebecca is from one of the families."

DeeAnne looked at Allie. "It's amazing that any of you are still here."

The smile left Allie's face. For a moment she hid her face behind the big balloon wineglass, and when she set it down, she was solemn. "There's a blood descendant of every family still in Cole Creek. Except for the Coles, that is. The most important family is missing."

Her tone seemed to take the joviality out of the party, and I started to ask what was going on, but Jackie nudged me under the table.

"So tell us about this great love story," Jackie said brightly.

"There's nothing to tell. Sometime in the 1970s, fat old Edward decided he was going to merge his family name with the Coles' through marriage, and rename the town Heritage. But Harriet eloped with a handsome young man and had a baby. The end."

"What happened to them?" I asked, watching Allie closely and wondering if she'd give the same answer as Miss Essie Lee had.

"I don't really know."

She's lying, I thought. But what was she lying about? And why?

"Edward died not long afterward, and I think Harriet did, too," Allie said at last. "And I think Harriet's handsome young husband left her."

"What happened to their child?" Jackie asked quietly and I hoped I was the only one who heard the odd tone in her voice.

Allie finished her glass of wine. "I have no idea. She didn't grow up in Cole Creek, that's for sure. No more direct descendants of the Coles live here, and I'd stake my **life** on that!" She said the last so emphatically that the rest of us looked at each other as though to say, What was that all about?

Except for Jackie. She was sitting very still and I was willing to bet that she was doing some subtraction in her head. Seventies, Allie had said. Harriet Cole had had a baby, a "she," in the 1970s and her young husband had left her.

Jackie had been born in the seventies and her father had left her mother. And they had lived in Cole Creek when Jackie was very young.

CHAPTER EIGHT

Jackie

I didn't want to tell Ford but there was a big part of me that wanted to run to the nearest bus station and get as far away from Cole Creek as I possibly could. There were too many strange things happening to me, too many things that I seemed to remember.

On Sunday I put on a 1940s dress and walked to church. It was about three miles from the house but I "knew" a shortcut through the woods. When I got there, I saw the charred stone foundation and brick chimney of what had once been a large building, and I felt sad that "my" church had burned down.

When I got back to Ford's house, he asked me if I'd enjoyed the service, but I just mumbled

a response and went up to my room. I changed
clothes and cooked a big dinner, but I couldn't
eat much. How had I known my way through
the woods? When had I been in this town
before? Oh, Lord, what had happened to me
here?

"Want to talk about whatever's bothering
you?" Ford asked.

He was being sweet but I didn't want to tell
him anything. What could I say? That I had a
"feeling?" Kirk had laughed at me the one time
I'd said I'd a "feeling" about something.

In the afternoon I puttered in the garden
while Ford watched some long movie on TV,
and I wished I'd invited Allie and Tessa over.
Long ago I'd found that sticking my nose into
other people's business made me stop contemplating my own problems. I could have spent
the afternoon asking Allie why she didn't leave
Cole Creek when her husband was transferred.
And in spite of my vow never to speak of it to
anyone, maybe I could tell her what Kirk had
done to me. But then, I was ready to talk about
anything except how I was feeling in this little
town.

When Ford spoke from behind me, I jumped.

"You scared me," I said, jamming the little
trowel into the dirt around the roses.

"Why don't you call your old friends?" he
asked as he sat down. "Have a few laughs."

"Maybe I will," I said. "Here, move your foot. You're on my glove."

He moved his foot the smallest distance possible to get it off my glove, then looked up at the sky through the trees. "It's nice here."

I stopped gouging out weeds and sat down on the ground. "Yeah, it is." Mountain climate had always been my favorite: The sun was warm, but the altitude made it cool in the shade.

"What happened at church today?" he asked, making me look at him.

He had really intense eyes that could bore into a person. "Same ol', same ol'," I said. "You know what church services are like. Or do you?"

"I know enough to know that no preacher ever let out early. So what happened that you didn't stay for the whole service?"

I opened my mouth to emit some quickly-made-up lie, but I stopped when something big and heavy came sailing through the trees. As it whistled through the air, we both ducked for cover.

Actually, I ducked and Ford sort of did a swan dive out of his chair to land on top of me. I'll give it to him that he was protective of women.

"Sorry," he said as he rolled off of me. "I heard—Then I—" He looked embarrassed.

When I got up, I had to take a couple of breaths. He's tall and he's heavy, but, worse, my trowel had been under me. I felt my ribs. I didn't think they were cracked, but I was going to have a beaut of a bruise there tomorrow.

Ford was searching through a thorny tangle of shrubbery as he looked for the projectile that had come sailing toward us. Wincing at my bruised ribs, I got up to help him look.

We saw it at the same time: a big rock wrapped in two-inch-wide clear tape so we could see the note underneath. Using his pocketknife, he cut the tape away.

Both of us held our breaths as we looked at the note. "Time Magazine," it read, "in July 1992."

For a moment he and I looked at each other in puzzlement, our thoughts reflected in each other's eyes. Who had thrown this rock at us? Why? Should we have gone after the perpetrator before we searched for the rock? And what did this date mean?

"Too bad it's Sunday," Ford said. "The library is closed today or we could—"

The same idea hit us both at the same time. There had been hundreds of old magazines—**Time** included—stacked in the entrance to the house when we moved in.

Ford looked at me in horror. "You didn't—?" he whispered, meaning, Did I throw them away?

No, I hadn't. I'd planned to give them to Nate's grandmother to sell over the Internet but hadn't yet. "Servant's bedroom. Attic," I said over my shoulder as I started running for the nearest door into the house.

Ford, with his longer legs, got there at the same time in spite of my head start. "Ow!" I yelled as he tried to push into the house first. "My ribs." Immediately, he stopped pushing, so I slipped under his arm to reach the stairs before he did, but he took them three at a time.

"Didn't anyone ever teach you not to cheat?" he called down to me when he reached the top first.

But I beat him into the room anyway because he was out of breath and had to lean against the wall. I stuck my finger in his belly as I ran past him and into the Room of Magazines. There were so many of them and so little space to maneuver that it took us nearly an hour to find the four issues of July, 1992. And by the time we found them, we were both dirty and sweaty. I wanted to sit down on the stacks and go through the magazines instantly, but Ford had to have liquid, so we went downstairs, where I got us lemonade before we went outside where it was cooler. However, this time I suggested we sit on the round porch outside my second-floor bedroom, and Ford agreed readily. We didn't want any more missiles lobbed at us from above.

We split the magazines and I was the one to find the article. After I'd scanned it, I handed the issue to Ford as I didn't trust my voice to read it aloud.

The small article had been written as though it were a joke. "A Ghostly Cry for Vengeance?" the title read. It seems that in July, 1992, a group of young people had been hiking through the mountains near the small town of Cole Creek, North Carolina. They'd made their camp near the site of a fallen-down cabin and had used the chimney to make their fire.

But during the night one of the campers, a young woman, had started screaming. She said she'd heard moaning, "a sad, deep moaning of a woman in great pain" coming from the old stone foundation of the cabin. No one had been able to quieten her, so when the sun came up, all the campers were tired and short tempered. One young man, in an effort to make his fellow camper stop crying, began to toss stones around to show her that nothing was there.

"And that's when they discovered a skeleton," Ford read, glancing up at me. "Her long, dark hair could still be seen, and bits of her clothing remained."

I pulled my knees up to my chest and buried my face. It looked as though my devil story— the crushing part of it anyway—was probably true.

And I had an idea that I was here in Cole Creek as a young child and since my recall was so vivid, I'd probably seen it happen. That's why my father got so angry when he found out my mother had told—or, I guess, reminded—me of the story.

"You okay?" Ford asked.

I didn't lift my face when I shook my head no.

Ford didn't ask any more questions. He went on to read the rest of the article that said the police had been called and the skeleton taken away to a lab, where later testing revealed that the woman had probably died in 1979.

"'So who was she?'" Ford read. "'A hiker who took refuge in an old house during a storm only to have a wall collapse on her? Or was it more sinister and she was murdered? Whatever caused the woman's death, according to the camper who "heard" her moans, the woman didn't die instantly, but lived long enough to cry from the pain.'"

When Ford put down the magazine, I could feel him watching me. "Long, dark hair," he said after a while. "The woman on the bridge."

I lifted my head and looked at him. I'd forgotten I'd told him about that—and I wished I hadn't. Right now what I wanted to do was crawl onto my father's lap and have him comfort me. But my father wasn't there.

"Listen to me," Ford said softly. "I'm beginning not to like this. Things are happening in this town that I don't like. I think you should leave."

I agreed with him. In fact I decided to get up, pack my clothes, and leave Cole Creek right that instant.

But I didn't move. Instead, I sat there with my knees drawn up and stared at the porch floor. I didn't say the words but we both knew that I didn't want to leave. I liked it there. And, besides, all we knew for sure was that I remembered things. And I'd had a vision of the future. The rest was speculation.

After a while, he gave a great, melodramatic sigh. "Okay," he said, "tell me everything you've told everyone about your connection to this town."

Scenes raced through my head like a video on rewind. I went over everything and everyone. "You," I whispered. "Everyone wants to know about **you.** No one asks much about me."

"Allie," he said. "What have you told her?"

"That I'm your assistant and you're working on ghost stories."

"Devil or ghost?" he asked.

I narrowed my eyes at him. "You called the librarian, asked about the devil and she hung up on you, remember? I wasn't about to have the same thing happen to me."

Ford stared out over the porch rail for a few moments. I didn't interrupt him because it seemed as though he was in a trance. When he looked like that, I would have thought he was in the preliminary stage of a petit mal, but I'd learned that he was "thinking."

After a while, he looked back at me.

"The kids made something up," he said, his mouth a grimace. "I was so P. O.'d that I was stuck with the mayor and Miss Essie Lee that I didn't hear all of it. The mayor said the kids had—" Pausing, his eyes widened. "The kids had made up a story to **explain what they'd found.** That's what the mayor said."

He was looking at me in triumph for having remembered this, but I still couldn't move. "So you think the townspeople are saying that a woman, some tourist maybe, was accidently killed, and, later, the local kids made up a devil story around the accident?"

"I think so," Ford said. "That would explain why the story is in no books about local legends. Maybe no one could verify it."

He was obviously trying to calm me down. Or maybe he was trying to make himself believe that there'd never been a murder. "That makes sense," I said and saw him smile a bit. What an ego he had! He thought he could say something totally stupid and I'd believe him. "I'm sure no one has ever written a word that isn't true. And I'm sure that if some writer heard a whopping good tale about the townspeople getting together and crushing some woman because they believed she loved the devil, that the writer would never tell such a story unless he could 'verify' it."

Ford gave a little one-sided smile. "Okay, you win. We writers do tend to stretch the truth. Whatever, I do think this town is keeping one very big secret. And I think Miss Essie Lee has been trying to distract me with the Edward and Harriet story."

"But who cares about love when there's horror, right? Is the best-selling writer in the world a romance writer? Or does he write about horror?"

After a few moments of silence, Ford spoke. "So what do we do now?" he asked softly. "I thought this was a hundred-year-old devil story, but I think it may be a twenty-some-year-old murder story that several people in this town know about. In fact, I'm beginning to think that someone—or more than one—may have killed a woman and the murder was hushed up."

"And the murderers went unpunished," I said, holding on to my legs tighter.

"Which means that he, she, or they are probably walking around free—and would probably kill again to keep from being found out."

I took a deep breath at that. I'd slipped out of my shoes so I concentrated on my bare toes. Anything rather than think seriously about what he was saying.

"Jackie," he said softly, making me look up at him. "Before we came here, I searched fairly thoroughly for any mention of this story any- where, and I found nothing. The only place the full story seems to exist is in your head. When you add the detail you know to the way your father absconded with you . . ." He motioned toward the old **Time** magazine on the little wrought-iron table. "I think maybe you were a child in this town and you saw something truly horrible."

I didn't know what to say to him. I tried to imagine myself on a bus, and the bus was mov- ing. Moving to where? I wondered. All I'd ever had in my life was my father. After he died I'd stayed in the town where I'd lived with him. I'd even said yes when a man I didn't really love asked me to marry him. I'd said yes to roots and to belonging somewhere.

But now here I was in this house that I knew so very well, with this man I had grown to like, and I was going to have to leave and go some- where "else," a place where I knew no one.

"You think I saw that woman killed?" I asked.

"I'd say there's a good chance that that's what happened," he said as he took both my hands in his, and his touch was comforting. "It seems to me that you have a couple of choices now. You could stay here and maybe find out the truth of something awful that happened to you, or—"

"Or I could run as fast and as far as I can and get away from here," I said, trying to smile. "If I did see some woman . . . crushed to death, I don't think I want to remember it. I think God made me forget because I'm supposed to forget."

"I think that's a wise decision," he said softly, leaning back in his chair.

After that we sat in silence, listening to the sounds of the approaching night. All that went through my head was, Last night. Last night. This was my last night here with this funny, generous man in this beautiful old house.

CHAPTER NINE

Ford

Okay, so I was curious. Occupational hazard. Murder wasn't something I knew much about. Manslaughter, yes. I'd had a cousin or two who'd gone berserk with a shotgun, but there'd been lots of booze and lots of passion involved.

I couldn't imagine what would make someone—or a group of people—pile rocks on a woman until she was dead. If it had happened in the 1700s I could almost understand. I once saw a special on TV about the Salem witch debacle and scientists now believe the grain in that year had a kind of mold on it that was, basically, LSD. The theory proposed was that those little girls who accused people of witchcraft were on a major hallucinogenic trip.

That explained the past, but what about something that happened in the seventies? If the woman's death had been an accident, why wasn't it reported? Or maybe the woman had been alone when a wall had fallen on her. But if that was the case, how did Jackie know so much about it? But Jackie said she didn't know what was truth and what she'd added.

As always, the why of it plagued me.

When I awoke on Monday morning, I half expected Jackie to be gone. It would fit her independent nature to up and leave, a note on the refrigerator. For a while I lay there imagining what the note would say. Would it be sweet? Or acid? Or just practical? She'd contact me and tell me where to send her paycheck, that sort of thing.

When the unmistakable smell of ham sizzling in a skillet wafted up to me, I pulled on yesterday's clothes so fast I put my shoes on the wrong feet and had to switch them.

In the kitchen, Jackie had her back to me. She had on her usual teeny, tiny clothes that hugged her curvy little body, and I was so glad to see her I nearly hugged her.

Instead, I got myself under control and said gruffly, "I thought you were leaving town."

"And good morning to you, too," she said, pulling a ham steak out of a big skillet.

"Jackie, I thought we agreed that you were going to leave town."

She set a plate full of ham, fried eggs, and whole wheat toast on the table. I assumed the food was for me so I sat down in front of it.

"I was thinking," she said as she poured herself a bowl of what looked like sawdust. "Since no one knows I remember Cole Creek, then no one here will know that I may have seen a murder when I was a kid. Right?"

"I guess not," I said, mouth full. She'd cooked the eggs exactly the way I liked them.

"So maybe if no one tells anyone that I remember this town, no one will know I was here. That way, we can research and ask questions, and if the murderer is still alive he'll—" Breaking off, she looked up at me with wide eyes.

"Will only want to kill **me** when **I** find out too much," I finished.

"Yeah, I guess so," she said, looking down at her bowl of ground-up twigs. "Not such a good idea, huh?"

Not really, I thought. A truly bad idea. But then that old curiosity popped up again. Why? Why? Why?

"Your eyes are going round and round like pinwheels," Jackie said. "Do you think smoke is going to start coming out of your ears?"

"Only if I set your tail on fire," I shot back at her.

I'd meant my remark as a reference to a devil's tail, but Jackie cocked an eyebrow at me as though I'd made a sex joke, and to my disgust I felt my face turning red. Smiling, she returned to her carpenter's special.

"So what's your plan?" she asked and I could tell she was laughing at me. Why, oh, why, did each generation think it had been the one to discover sex?

"I don't know," I said, flat-out lying. "I have some writing to do that'll take me a couple of days so why don't you—" I waved my hand.

"Keep busy?" she asked. "Stay out of your hair? Go play with the other children?"

"More or less."

"Great," she said, taking her empty bowl to the sink.

I knew from the way she said it that she was up to something, but I also knew that if I got her to tell me, I'd then have to tell her what I was planning to do.

We parted, and I went up to my office to start calling people. There was a famous true crime writer with my publishing house and, through my editor, I got her phone number and we had a long talk. I had no idea how to investigate an old murder, so she gave me some tips— and some of her private phone numbers.

Without giving too much away, I told her about the skeleton that had been found and that the police had taken away. She asked for dates and said she'd call me back. A few minutes later she called and gave me the name and number of a man in Charlotte she said knew about the case.

I called him, introduced myself, promised him six autographed books (I took down the names to be inscribed in the books) and he started telling me what he knew.

"We never found out who she was," the man said. "We concluded she was a hiker and an old wall fell on her."

"So you never found out who did—? I mean, you think it was an accident?"

"You think she was murdered?" he asked.

"I don't know," I said. "But I heard that the kids around here made up a story about—"

"The devil," the man said. "Yeah, one of the cops told me that. Somebody said she'd been 'consorting with the devil' so the townspeople dropped a pile of rocks on her."

I drew in my breath and let it out slowly so my voice wouldn't squeak. Here at last was someone else who'd heard Jackie's story. "That's kind of unusual, isn't it? I mean, a devil story like that."

"Hell no. Nearly every long-dead body we get in here has some story attached to it. And this one was found by a hysterical girl who said she'd heard the dead woman crying."

"You have a great memory," I said with admiration.

"Naw. Bess called me earlier and I pulled the file. She was a pretty woman."

"Bess?" I asked, referring to the true crime writer. I'd seen photos of her and "pretty" didn't come to mind.

"No," the man said, chuckling. "The woman who was buried under all that rock. We had one of those clay heads made of her."

As Jackie'd said, my eyes began to whirl. "If I give you my FedEx number could you send me a copy of everything you have?"

"I don't see why not. We showed copies of her face all over that little town of—What's its name?"

"Cole Creek," I said.

"Yeah, that's right."

I could hear someone speaking in the background and the man gave his attention to the voice. When he came back on the line, he said, "Look, I gotta go. I'll send this stuff out to you ASAP."

I gave him my FedEx number, hung up, then leaned back in my chair and looked up at the ceiling. Why was I doing this? I wondered. I was no sleuth. I had no desire to meet a murderer on some dark and stormy night.

I just wanted—

And that's where the problem was, I thought. I had no goal in life. I had enough money to live well forever, but a man needed more than that.

Closing my eyes, I remembered those first years with Pat and how wonderful they'd been.

Nothing on earth could match the excitement of having a book accepted for publication. It was satisfying in a deep, soul-gratifying way.

I remember thinking, Someone wants to read what **I** wrote. I'd only been able to come to terms with that thought when I told myself that people wanted to read about Pat's mother, not me. Somewhere along the way, though, I'd realized that I was selling myself and it felt good to be wanted. But I'd lost it all, lost that driving force even before Pat died, and nothing had felt as good since.

Until now, that is. Every day I could feel a little bit of myself returning. I could feel the old Ford coming back, the one who'd fight to the death for a cause. As a kid I'd been determined not to be like my relatives, so I'd fought like a pit bull to go to college. Nothing my backward, iron-headed relatives said or did made me lose sight of my goal.

But since Pat died, I'd done nothing. I hadn't felt the need to write, hadn't felt the **need** to do anything. Even before she'd died, I'd achieved every goal I'd ever set myself and then some.

But now . . . Now things were changing. Was it Jackie? Was it she who was bringing me back to life? Only indirectly, I thought. Truthfully, it seemed to be all of it: the house, the town, the . . . The story, I thought. The story that would answer that ageless "Why?"

With every step I took into this mystery, I seemed to prove that Jackie's original story was true. But the best news I'd heard was today's. Maybe kids had made up a horror story about the woman's death. This meant that if Jackie lived in Cole Creek as a child she could have heard the story from some sadistic kids who got their thrills from frightening a small child.

On the other hand, maybe the kids had just told what they knew. Since the body wasn't found until '92, did that mean the devil story started then? If so, Jackie would have been old enough to remember if she heard or saw or—

I put my hands to my head. This whole thing was getting to be too much for me. Besides, my stomach was beginning to rumble so I headed downstairs. Wonder if there was any ham left? And, by the way, why had Jackie changed from being adamant about "no ham" to frying me a big steak? Was she trying to give me a heart attack? What would be her motive? Hmmm. Was there a story in this?

I'd gone down just two steps when I was met by Jackie running full speed up the stairs. Two flights and as far as I could tell she wasn't even winded.

"You'll never believe what we found in the garden," she said, her eyes so wide they nearly ate up her face.

"A dead body," I said.

"Have you ever had therapy?"

"Considering the last few days—" I began, defending myself, but Jackie didn't listen. Turning, she ran down the stairs.

I followed her and found my heart pounding by the time I met her at the side door. She didn't say anything but she took note of my out-of-breath state. Maybe I should lay off the ham for a while.

"Come on," she said, excitement radiating from her like sunbeams.

I'm not sure what I expected, but not what she showed me. It was an old building that had been hidden behind a mass of what looked to be unpruned grape vines and pubescent trees. All I could see was double glass doors, peeling white paint, and broken panes of glass.

Nate was standing there, his shirt off and sweating, a ringer for one of those models in a Calvin Klein ad, and all I could think was that he and Jackie had been out here alone all morning.

"Isn't it wonderful?" Jackie was saying. "Tessa found it. Remember when she disappeared on Friday night and Allie said she was probably inventing something?"

For the life of me I couldn't remember who Tessa was.

"Allie's daughter," Jackie said, frowning. "Remember?"

I looked at the old building, looked back at Jackie, and I knew she wanted something. No one on earth could get that excited about a standing pile of termites without a reason. "All right," I said, "how much is this gonna cost me?"

Nate gave a kind of laugh, then said he thought he'd go work on the front yard for a while. After he was gone, I looked at Jackie. "What's this all about?"

"A . . . a summerhouse," she said. "You could write out here."

She knew very well that I liked being at the top of the house and looking out at the mountains, so I didn't bother to reply to that statement.

After a while she gave a sigh and pulled open one of the doors to the building. I was surprised the hinges held. I followed her inside. It was two rooms and had probably been built to be a garden house with attached storage. There was one fairly large room with floor to ceiling windows on two sides. A wide doorway in one solid wall led into a storage room that was also quite spacious. My main thought was disgust at the state of a property that could hide a building this size.

Jackie was chattering nonstop, pointing out the big galvanized sink in one corner of the second room, and talking about the light coming through the cracked and broken windows in the main room.

My stomach gave a loud rumble. It was nearly two o'clock and I was hungry, but I was having to listen to this build-up to a punch line that didn't seem to be coming any time soon.

"You're hungry!" Jackie said in a loving and kind tone. "Come on and I'll make you some lunch."

Fifty grand, I thought. That's what this great concern for the state of my belly was going to cost me. Never mind that I was under the illusion that this young woman was my employee and was therefore to do what I wanted her to. I'd been married. I knew what that sweeter-than-nectar voice meant. Jackie wanted something big from me.

I didn't say anything as I followed her into the kitchen. And I sat in silence as I watched her scurry about making me a sandwich Dagwood would envy, and a cup of soup. It was some kind of expensive soup with one of those labels meant to make it look like it came from Aunt Rhoda's kitchen, but it still wasn't homemade.

Heaven help me, but I began to tell Jackie about this wonderful bean soup that Pat used to make from scratch. The truth was that Pat had found out she could empty four different cans into a pot and it came out tasting pretty good. Pat's mother was a cook; Pat was not.

It was interesting to watch Jackie's face fall when I mentioned "homemade soup." She stopped in the middle of the kitchen, her eyes wide in horror.

It was difficult for me not to laugh, but I was willing to bet that I got homemade soup tomorrow. Obviously, whatever Jackie wanted with that old building was important to her.

Throughout lunch, she chatted in a way that was meant to amuse me. Geishas weren't as charming as she was.

I ate in silence and waited to see when she was going to drop the stone on my head.

By four she'd maneuvered us into the newly-furnished small parlor, and I was beginning to get sleepy. I'd been charmed all I could take. All in all, I liked the tart-tongued Jackie better.

Gradually, the words "business deal" came through to me and I realized she was at last getting to the heart of the matter. Since I'd been dozing, I'd missed a lot of what she was saying, but it seemed that she wanted me to back her in some kind of business venture.

Here. In Cole Creek.

I blinked a few times to clear the sleep out of my eyes and said, "Yesterday we were talking about your getting out of Cole Creek as fast as possible because you may have witnessed a murder, but today you want to open a business here?"

"Yeah. Well," she said. "I—" Lifting her hands helplessly, she looked up at me, her eyes pleading. "Couldn't you write about something else?"

"So now it's **my** fault," I said. "Did it occur to you that if I write about something besides the devil story there's no reason for me to be in this dead town?"

"Oh," she said, her eyes downcast, but then she looked up at me brightly. "You'll never be able to sell this house so maybe I can stay here and be the caretaker."

"And run your business," I said.

Jackie looked at me as though I'd won the prize.

I leaned toward her. "In all your buttering-up of me, did you ever tell me **what** business you want to open?"

She opened her mouth as though she meant to say she hadn't been "buttering me up," but the next second she jumped up, leaped over an ottoman, and I heard her running up the stairs. I leaned back in the chair—a nice one. In fact I liked all the furniture Jackie had bought—and closed my eyes. Maybe twenty winks would do me good. Help me to think.

But Jackie was back in about three minutes and she dropped two books on my lap. On top was a big, color, trade paperback on photographing children, and she opened it to the last few pages. There were some truly exquisite black-and-white photos of children by a man named Charles Edward Georges.

Jackie sat down on the ottoman at my feet.

"Taken with all natural light," she said quietly.

It didn't take a genius to put two and two together. There were six double-page photos made by this man and in the background could be seen windowsills with peeling paint.

I flipped through the book. Wonderful photos of children. Black and white. Color. Sepia. Studio portraits, candids. Several had been taken in a lush garden. A garden like the one around my old house could be.

I put that book down and picked up the other one. It was a smaller paperback, published by the University of North Carolina, and it was on orchids in the southern Appalachians.

I looked at Jackie. "Hobby," she said, meaning the portraits were to make money, the flower photos were to be a hobby.

Putting the books down, I leaned back in the chair, and said, "Tell me everything."

It took some questioning on my part, but I was finally able to figure out why she'd called off her wedding and why she'd been so angry at her former fiancé. Seems the jerk had stolen her life savings, money she'd planned to use to open a small photography studio.

I pointed out that she could prosecute, but she said her former fiancé's father was a judge and his cousin was president of the bank. I'd not grown up in a circle of judges or presidents of anything, but I sure did know about the "ol' boy system."

As I listened to her, I thought I might call a lawyer I knew and see what could be done about this. While I was thinking, Jackie said something that caught my attention.

"What?" I asked.

"It was the name Harriet that did it," she said. "And the dates, of course."

"What was?"

I could see that she was itching to say something snarly to me because of my inattention, but since she was hitting me up for investment money, she didn't dare. Brother! It was tempting to see how much she'd take and still pretend to be sweet-tempered.

"Harriet Cole," she said with exaggerated patience. "It was the name that got me. See, my father had a . . . Well, a bit of a fetish about Harriet Lane. She was—"

"The niece of President James Buchanan," I said. "Magnificent . . ." I held my hands out in front of my chest.

It was quite gratifying to see Jackie's eyes widen in surprise. How many people knew such an obscure piece of information? "Right," she said slowly, looking at me out of the corner of her eye. "Anyway, I think I got scared because when I heard the name 'Harriet' I associated it with my father and thought maybe she'd been my mother."

She hadn't told me this, but I'd guessed

something of the sort that night at the party. I couldn't imagine what it would feel like to not know who your parents were. I'd never met my father, but I certainly knew where he was. Hell, I even knew the number on his shirt.

"So now you've decided you're safe," I said. "And that you saw nothing, and you have no connection to anyone in town. All because you found a rotten old building buried under half a ton of overgrown grapevines."

She gave a little smile. "More or less."

I wasn't going to tell her so, but the man inside me was jumping up and down and shouting, "Hallelujah!" I don't know what it was about that empty little town, but I was beginning to like it there.

"Okay," I said, and I could see that it took her a moment to understand that I was saying yes to her project.

She jumped up, threw her arms around my neck, and began kissing my face as though I were her father.

Maybe she felt daughterly toward me, but I certainly didn't feel fatherly toward her. Rather than make a fool of myself by showing her this, I kept my arms at my side and my lips closed—and moved them away when she got too near.

After this moment of childish exuberance, she pulled her face away, but her arms were still around my neck. "I'm sorry about Rebecca," she said softly.

Part of me wanted her to get far away from me, and part of me wanted her to get much closer. If she didn't move away soon, the closer part was going to win.

"And your wife," she said.

That did it. I put my hands on her shoulders, moved her away, and got up. "Fix up the old building," I said, "and give me the bill."

CHAPTER TEN

Jackie

He was great about the building. Of course I had to work hard to lead him up to my idea, but it was worth it.

It seemed that all my life I'd had an affinity for cameras, and my father once said that I was taking pictures by the time I was three. I'd taken some courses in photography, but with the way we moved around, I never got to complete any of them. And I'd never been able to take all the pictures I wanted because film and processing cost too much. Over the years I'd been tempted to apply for a job in a photography studio, but my vanity wouldn't allow it. I was afraid that if I learned to take pictures from someone commercial I'd never develop my own style.

That, and the fact that the only photography studio in the last three towns my dad and I lived in had been in the local mall.

My plan had been to let Kirk support me while I used my savings and my inheritance to open a small photography studio. When I told Ford about Kirk, he was certainly interested! Ford asked me about fifty questions about who, where, and how much. I told him I never wanted anything to do with Kirk again, but Ford kept asking me questions, and since I was trying to get him to finance my new business, I couldn't very well snap that it was none of his business.

In the end Ford came through and said he'd pay for fixing up the building so I could use it. I didn't mention that I would, of course, have to add a small powder room onto the back of the house. When kids have to go, they have to go, so you have to have a WC nearby. There was water in the house, but I'd have to hook onto the city sewage and that would cost.

Nor did I mention that I'd also need money to buy equipment. I had my camera and a wonderful lens, but I'd also need lights and soft boxes, reflectors, tripods, flash brackets, a few backgrounds, and, well, some darkroom equipment and supplies, as I hadn't—ha ha—seen a super photo processing shop in or around Cole Creek. And I'd need another lens or two. Or three.

During our long conversation about my opening a business, he asked me why I'd changed my mind and no longer wanted to get out of Cole Creek as fast as possible. I think I lied well. Actually, it was more that I left out some things. I told the truth when I said the name "Harriet" had rung a big gong in my head—and Ford nearly knocked me over when he knew who Harriet Lane was.

During the night, I'd decided that my overactive imagination had made me believe I knew more than I did about what did or did not happen in Cole Creek. By dinner—candlelight, seafood, chocolate cake—I was calmer since Ford had agreed to renovate the building, so we talked in depth about what we both knew and had found out. It was our first real heart-to-heart in days.

I told him about my several déjà vu instances in Cole Creek, and about how I knew the house so well.

"But you didn't know that building was out there," he said.

"Maybe I did," I answered, because I'd gone straight to it on the first morning I started cleaning up the garden.

As always, he was an attentive listener. I told him I remembered so many things about the house that I even knew where the hidden room was—and until that moment I hadn't remembered there even was a secret room. At that, we looked at each other in complete understanding.

"Second floor," I said. "Behind all those boxes."

We jumped up so quickly that both our chairs hit the floor, and we took off running, reaching the doorway at the same time. I was going to push ahead of him, but I remembered the camera equipment I wanted, so I stepped back. "You first," I said politely.

Ford looked at me as though he was going to be a gentleman and let me go ahead, but then he said, "Beat you up the stairs," and took off running.

What could I do after a challenge like that? What he didn't know was that a little door in the kitchen, which looked like a broom closet, actually opened to a set of stairs so narrow I doubt if Ford could have climbed them. As he ran for the big front stairs, I slipped up the back and was waiting for him when he arrived.

The look on his face! If I'd had my camera that photo would have won every prize given.

I knew he was dying to ask me how I'd beaten him to the top, but he didn't. Instead, we ran to the storage room and began flinging boxes into the hallway.

It wasn't much of a secret room. It was just a part of a room that had been made into a closet, then sealed off. Someone (me as a child?) had pulled the old wallpaper off so the door could open a few inches. We had to pull hard to open it wide enough to allow Ford to get inside.

"Why would someone seal off a closet?" Ford asked.

We were together inside the small space and it was absolutely dark.

Ford rummaged around inside his pockets and withdrew a book of matches—the contents of his pockets rivaled a nine-year-old boy's— and lit one. When he held the flame up, all I saw was old wallpaper behind him.

But Ford's eyes widened until I could see the whites. He blew out the match, then said in a voice of such exaggerated calm that it put fear into me, "Get out. Open the door and get out."

I did as he said—one obeys that tone—and left the closet, Ford close behind me. Once he was out, he closed the door and leaned against it.

"What was it?" I whispered, and the word "devil" went through me. Was the devil in this house? Maybe as a kid I'd found this closet and I'd seen—

"Bees," he said.

"What?"

"The biggest beehive I've ever seen was behind you. The bees probably built in that closet, and instead of getting rid of it, some lazy so-and-so sealed the door shut."

"I thought—" I began, then started to laugh,

and when I told Ford about my devil thoughts, he laughed, too.

We laughed together but we didn't touch. I'd decided to do no more touching of him. Earlier I'd spontaneously thrown my arms around his neck and kissed him, just as I would have done with my father. But suddenly I didn't feel like I was with my father.

When I'd pulled back from him, I thought that he didn't look old at all. In fact, those lines at his eyes were more like character lines than old age wrinkles. And he had a very nice mouth. In fact, the more time I spent with him, the better looking he got. John Travolta, I thought. Even as out of shape as he was, Travolta was still sexy. And so was Ford.

Abruptly, I'd dropped my arms from around his neck. First I was lusting after a gorgeous seventeen-year-old, and now I was drooling over a man old enough to be my . . . Well, too old for me, anyway.

I decided I needed to start dating.

CHAPTER ELEVEN

Ford

Considering everything, I decided that the wisest thing to do was to change my priorities. I would stamp down my desperate need to know why and redirect my mind to something other than Jackie's devil story. And Jackie's passion for her photographic studio gave me my new direction. I'm sure that, long ago, I must have looked as she did. When I first started writing, I was driven, and writing was all I could think of—just as Jackie was driven to get her photography studio set up and find out whether or not she could make it in that world.

We had over a week of peace and quiet, and, in spite of my intentions, I thought about things. Facts were piling up in a way that made me feel sure that when she was a child, Jackie had seen something she shouldn't have, namely, a murder. And I suspected that her mother had been one of the people who'd helped kill that poor woman, and her lack of remorse was part of what had driven Jackie's father to abduct their child and run away.

I wasn't a psychiatrist or I would probably have wanted Jackie to "get it out." But, personally, I've always thought that releasing great pain was overrated as a cure. What good would it do if I brought all that to the surface again? Would it help Jackie to remember that she actually saw—and heard—a woman's slow, agonizing death? And if we did find out who killed her, would it bring her back to life? And what would the murderer—or murderers—do to an eyewitness?

Whatever my excuse, I decided not to continue my pursuit of the devil story. I hoped that whoever had tossed that rock over the wall and given us information wouldn't contact us again. And when the package from the forensics man in Charlotte didn't arrive, I didn't call and remind him.

Okay, so the truth was, I'd had an idea for a book that had no devil in it. It was a book about loneliness, about a man who'd lost faith in himself and others, but who, eventually, finds something to believe in. I hadn't worked out the details of the novel yet, such as exactly what the man came to believe in, but I felt that it would come to me.

And the deeper truth was that I was beginning to enjoy myself. I wasn't such a fool that I didn't know that I was once again in some semblance of a marriage, the time when my life had been happy. And I wasn't so dumb that I didn't know I must have been looking for that from the many secretaries I'd hired and fired. I hadn't wanted a research assistant, I'd wanted someone like me, someone who had no life and wanted to join in my life. I used to yell at them that they were incompetent, when the truth was that I was angry—or maybe jealous—when they went home to their friends and relatives. I wanted to scream that I'd once had a family, people to share Thanksgiving and Christmas with.

But I couldn't do that. For one thing, no one would have believed me. The world thinks that if you're a person who gives out autographs, you don't need what "ordinary people" need.

Right. Lonely at the top. Cry all the way to the bank. I'd heard it all before. But whatever my problem was, I found that I was happier than I'd been since Pat died, and I didn't want to mess it up. I was writing down ideas in the mornings, but in the afternoons I found myself sitting in the garden that Jackie was wrestling from the weeds, sipping lemonade, and talking with whomever stopped by to visit.

For all that she was often as sharp as an artichoke leaf, people liked Jackie and her enthusiasm for her new studio was infectious. Every
afternoon someone came by to see how the
work was going. And I must say that the excitement made me want to be part of it all. At dinner I'd go through the thick B & H catalog that
the photography company in New York had
sent Jackie and we'd talk about all the gewgaws
that are available for a photographer. I read all
the books she had on photography, a grand total
of three, then ordered seventeen more books
from Amazon.com, and after they arrived, we
spent the evenings going over them.

One afternoon Tessa, Allie's daughter, came to
stay with us. I don't know if her mother was
working or if she just wanted a break—or if
Jackie wanted the girl to visit. Whatever, I ended
up enjoying the child's company.

At first I was annoyed by her presence. My
experience with children was limited, and
mostly, I wanted them to go away. So I wasn't
happy when I went down for my lemonade and
cookies and found Jackie sitting there with a
nine-year-old girl. I felt that my time was being
intruded on and, besides, how was I supposed to
deal with her? Should I ignore the child and
talk of adult things? Or was it better to ask the
kid about her school and heap praise on a
bunch of stick figure drawings?

Since the girl didn't say anything, I decided
to ignore her and talk to Jackie. But when the
phone rang, Jackie ran to answer it, and I was
left alone with the girl. She didn't seem to be
any more interested in me than I was in her so
we sat there and drank lemonade in silence.

After a while it seemed that Jackie was going
to stay on the phone forever so I said to the kid,
"What were you inventing?"

One thing I like about kids is that they have
no idea of rules. They don't have their minds full
of what a person should and shouldn't do. For
instance, a kid doesn't know that you shouldn't
celebrate the death of a bully of a cousin. So,
based on the little I knew, I guessed that I
wouldn't need to make small talk about the
weather before leading up to the more interesting things. And besides, I'd never yet met a kid
who paid any attention to the weather.

"Things," she said, and looked at me sideways
in a way that I recognized as an invitation.

I didn't answer, but just held my hand up in a
gesture that said, You lead the way.

I followed her into the bush. The jungle,
really. Way back in the corner of my property,
where no cutting implement had been for many
years, she showed me an opening against the
ground that a rabbit would have loved. She
looked at the size of me and said, "You can't get
through there."

I'd had all I could take of females telling me I was too big. I gave her a look and said, "Try me."

I don't know what got into me, but I ended up slithering through the brush on my belly like a snake chasing a rat. Of course I enlarged the hole as I moved, which took its toll on my clothes and whatever skin was exposed, but I finally made it into the interior.

Inside, the girl had formed a green igloo. "This is great," I said and really meant it. Sitting down on the ground, I looked up at the way she'd twisted and woven the vines and tree branches together. I wasn't sure but I thought the place might be tight enough to repel water.

She was a homely little girl, but when I looked at her smile of pride I could almost see her someday running a corporation. She was smart, determined, and an individual. She wasn't a run-of-the-mill kid who colored in the lines and did everything to please her teachers.

"Shown this to anyone else?" I asked.

When she shook her head no, she made me feel good. Reaching behind her, she picked up a little green thing and handed it to me. It was an assemblage of leaves, sticks, moss, bits of mud, a rock here and there, and acorns—and it was fantastic. "I like it," I said, and again she grinned.

When she didn't say anything more, I realized she wanted us to leave, maybe so Jackie wouldn't see the hideout. Stretching out on my belly, I slithered back through the now-larger tunnel and out into the sunlight. When Jackie at last got off the telephone, Tessa and I were back in our chairs, looking for all the world as though we'd never left them. When Jackie turned away to say something to Nate, I winked at Tessa and she grinned at me before ducking her head and looking back at her lemonade.

For days, I made notes for my book about the lonely man and spent the afternoons enjoying the social life Jackie was carving out for the two of us. We had a second barbeque dinner with Allie, Tessa, and some people from Asheville who were staying in the area. Since Jackie had met them in the grocery, she and I almost had a fight about her inviting strangers to dinner. But they turned out to be nice people and we had a good time.

One afternoon I went downstairs but found no lemonade, no cookies, no Nate working, and no Jackie. After searching, I found her in the kitchen laughing with a good-looking woman who seemed vaguely familiar. Jackie introduced her as D. L. Hazel.

"Ah," I said, "the sculptor." I was proud of myself for having remembered that, but still, it didn't explain why she looked familiar.

She was about my age or maybe a bit older, and I could see that she'd once been beautiful. She still was, but she'd faded somewhat. And maybe I imagined it, but I thought I saw something unhappy in her eyes. When I caught Jackie looking at me, I knew she had something to tell me later.

Sure enough, after Dessie, as she told us to call her, left, Jackie told me that the woman had once been an actress on a soap opera. "Ah," I said. I didn't say so but I knew which one. It was the one Pat's mother had watched and I'd seen it often when I sat by her peeling potatoes for dinner.

"She quit?" I asked. "To live here?"

Jackie shrugged to tell me that she couldn't understand it either. "The story is that she grew up in Cole Creek, but left when she was quite young to go to L.A. She got a job on a soap right away and was a big hit. But when she returned here for her best friend's wedding, she remained in Cole Creek and never went back to L.A. They killed off her character on the soap and Dessie started sculpting. D. L. Hazel is her professional name. Her real name is Dessie Mason."

"Who was the friend?" I asked, thinking it was male.

"The love of your life," Jackie said, and it took me almost a minute to figure out who she was talking about.

"Rebecca?"

"The very one."

"She's not the—" I began, but closed my

mouth. Why bother? I thought. But I wondered if the entire town thought I was having it off with a woman I'd barely spoken to.

I came to like Dessie. In fact, I liked her a lot. She came to dinner at our house on Friday and invited me—not Jackie—to lunch at her house on Sunday.

The first time I met Dessie, she'd been rather quiet, subdued even, and she'd spent most of her time talking to Jackie. She caught me staring at her a couple of times and I'd looked away, feeling guilty. But I'd been trying hard to place her and having no luck.

Besides, the more I looked at her, the better she looked. She was a mature woman with a grown-up body, grown-up clothes, and she knew about grown-up things. I looked at Jackie and Dessie standing side by side in front of the kitchen sink and I thought, It's like looking at Sophia Loren and Calista Flockhart.

Dessie didn't stay long that first visit, but when she came for dinner on Friday, she looked fabulous. She had on a dress, something with a wide belt and a V-neck that showed off her great bosom.

And then she did something that nearly made me burst into tears in front of our guests.

She was the last one to arrive. I was filling plates with corn on the cob and barbequed chicken when she came in, looking and smelling like a woman, and I can tell you that it was a relief to see a female in something besides blue jeans and a T-shirt. She had her hair all fluffed out and she wore big gold earrings and tiny sandals, with her toenails painted pink.

She was holding a wooden box in front of her as though it contained something fragile. I assumed it was a cake and held out my hands to take it from her, but I heard Allie whisper, "Oh, Lord," then Nate's grandmother said, "Heaven be merciful," so I put my hands to my side and looked at Jackie. She just shrugged to say that she had no idea what was going on.

Tessa, the kid who usually stayed on the outskirts, ran forward, stopped in front of Dessie, and said, "May I open it? Please? Please?"

I didn't know what was going on but my curiosity meter just about broke its dial.

When Allie began to grab the plates and glasses on the round iron table, I thought she might throw them on the ground, but Jackie took them from her. Dessie stood there waiting, holding the box until the table was clear, and only then did she set the box down in the center of the table.

Dessie stepped back, smiled at Tessa, and nodded.

After a smile of triumph sent to her mother, Tessa stepped forward and put her hands on the box. The bottom of the box was a flat piece of wood, about a foot square, and the top, a fourteen-inch cube, was set over it.

Jackie came to stand beside me. The box had the word **front** on it and that word was facing me. I watched with wide eyes as Tessa slowly lifted the wooden cube straight up.

I had, of course, figured out by now that since Dessie was a sculptor, one of her pieces was probably inside. And since she was so famous it was no surprise that people were in awe of her work.

But nothing on earth could have prepared me for what I saw when Tessa lifted up that lid. Before me was a small clay sculpture of the head and shoulders of two women. The younger one was smiling and looking down at something, while the older woman was looking at the younger one, love in her eyes.

They were Pat and her mother, their likenesses and expressions perfectly captured.

If Jackie hadn't shoved a chair into the back of me, I would have collapsed. No one said a word. I think maybe even the birds held their breaths as I looked at that piece of clay. It was them; it was the two women I had loved more than my own soul.

I reached out to touch it, to feel their warm skin.

"Careful," Dessie said. "It's still wet."

Drawing my hand back, I had to take a few

breaths to calm myself. Jackie was standing behind my chair with one hand on my shoulder, her fingers pressing on me, giving me strength.

I managed to recover enough to look up at Dessie. "How . . . ?" I got out of my dry mouth.

She smiled. "Internet. You're a famous man so you're all over the Net. I ran off copies of photos of your late wife and mother-in-law and . . ." She glanced back at the sculpture. "Do you like it?"

My throat was swelling up and I could feel tears behind my eyes. I was going to make a fool of myself!

"He **loves** it!" Jackie said, sparing me. "He's mad about it, aren't you?"

All I could do was nod and swallow repeatedly as I looked at that beautiful piece of art.

"I'd say this calls for champagne," Jackie said, "and I need everyone's help in getting it out of the 'frig."

I was grateful to Jackie for taking all those people away. She got all the guests, about a dozen of them, to follow her into the kitchen, and left me alone with Dessie. Moving a chair beside mine, she sat down, her hands on the table.

"I hope it's okay," she said softly. "It was presumptuous of me but **Pat's Mother** was one of the best books I ever read. I think I cried from page two to the last page. You made a heroine

out of a woman who would otherwise have
been forgotten. After I met you, I wanted to
give you something to say thanks for what you
gave me with that book."

I couldn't speak. I knew that if I did, I'd start
bawling. Reaching across the table, I took her
hand in mine and squeezed. All I could do was
nod.

"Good," she said. "It means everything to me
that you like it. But this is just the clay so I can
change anything you want to."

"No!" I choked out. "It's perfect."

I could feel her smiling at me, but I couldn't
take my eyes off the sculpture. I'd seen Pat smile
just like that when she was reading my manuscripts. And I'd seen her mother secretly look at
her husband and daughter with that face full of
love. Had she ever looked at me like that? I
wondered.

But I knew the answer. Yes, she had, I
thought, and I squeezed Dessie's hand tighter.

"Here they come," she said, "so pull yourself
together."

I smiled at that, wiped my eyes, sniffed a couple of times, then watched Dessie slip the top
back over the sculpture. "Why don't you come
to lunch at my house on Sunday and let's talk
about casting it in bronze?"

I nodded, feeling better, but not yet secure
enough to talk.

"You," she said quietly. "Alone. One o'clock?"

Turning, I looked at her and saw that this was more than just an invitation to a meal. She was telling me that if I was interested, she was. Yeah, I thought, I was, so I nodded, we smiled at each other, and stayed separate for the rest of the evening.

But our physical separation didn't fool Jackie. Approximately three and a half seconds after the last guest left, she informed me that my behavior toward Dessie had been "indecent."

"And what does someone of your generation know about decency?" I shot at her. "You run around in shirts the size of my socks, with your belly button exposed, and you think you know about decency?"

To my extreme annoyance, Jackie gave me a cold little smile and walked out of the room.

I didn't see her again until the next morning, and I expected her to be slamming pots and pans around in the kitchen in a jealous fit. Why were women so jealous? I wondered.

But Jackie wasn't in the kitchen. Worse, there was no breakfast in the kitchen. I had to search that oversize house for twenty minutes before I found her. She was on the front porch and she was packing camera equipment into a big, padded backpack. She had on high-topped, thick-soled shoes that looked like they weighed twelve pounds each.

"Going somewhere?" I asked.

"Yes," she said. "It's Saturday and I'm taking the day off. It's a gorgeous day and I'm going to photograph flowers."

I didn't want to spend the day alone in that cavernous house. I'd had six years alone and a few weeks of being around people, and now I couldn't seem to bear solitude. "I'll go with you," I said.

Jackie gave a snort of derision and looked me up and down. I had on an old T-shirt and a baggy pair of shorts—my sleeping attire. And, okay, I'd put on a few pounds in the last years, but I knew there was muscle under there.

"I'm going to be climbing," she said, as though that excluded me. "And, besides, you don't have the proper shoes or even something to carry water in."

She had me there. I'd never been much of a hiking-climbing person. Climb all day, look at some fabulous view for ten minutes, climb down. I'd rather stay home and look at a book. "Wasn't there a store next to Wal-Mart called mountain something?"

"Yes," Jackie said, slipping her arms into her backpack. "But I'm sure the store doesn't open until nine, it's seven now and I'm ready to go." With a little smile, she turned toward the steps.

I gave a great sigh. "Okay, I'll call Dessie and see what she's doing."

Jackie stopped and turned back, looking as though she wanted to murder me. "Get dressed," she said through clamped-shut teeth. "Blue jeans, T-shirt, long-sleeved shirt."

I gave her a mock salute and went up the stairs.

The sports store didn't open until ten, but by the time I'd eaten enough breakfast to fortify me for the strenuous day ahead, and we'd stopped in the big Barnes and Noble where I'd picked up $156 of books I needed, the sporting goods store was open. By that time, Jackie's temper was a little frayed. She'd explained about light levels and the position of the sun three times, all to let me know that she was missing the best daylight, so I think she took delight in outfitting me with enough gear to attempt Mount Everest.

Oh, well, I thought, as I handed the clerk my credit card, Tessa and I could probably set up the tent in the backyard and have some fun with it. At least I wouldn't have to slither to get into it.

One day last week Tessa told me she and her mother had been to a big antiques warehouse just off the interstate and she'd seen some fencing for sale. It took me three whole minutes to figure out what she was really telling me, and after I did, we jumped in my new 4 x 4 and went to the warehouse. We came back with enough Victorian fencing, complete with a fancy gate, to surround her secret house and keep Nate and his bushwhacker from destroying it.

Tessa and I also bought some of those poured concrete statues of various creatures—two rabbits, four frogs, one dragon, two painted geese, fourteen ladybug stepping-stones (they were on sale) and a little boy fishing. Jackie hadn't looked too pleased when she saw them, but all she said was, "What? No gnomes?" Tessa and I'd laughed because we'd spent thirty minutes debating whether or not to get gnomes. But, in the end, I was able to persuade Tessa against them.

Anyway, by the time Jackie and I had run all the errands and purchased all my hiking gear, it was after eleven o'clock. When Jackie saw me look at my watch, she said, "I swear by all that's holy that if you so much as mention lunch, I'll make you sorry you were born."

I was curious to know what she thought of doing, but I decided not to ask. In my backpack I had several packages of those high energy bars and a few pounds of those nut and seed mixtures, so I could make do. Grinning to show I was a good sport, I said, "I'm ready to go."

Jackie turned away without a word, but I think I heard her say, "There is a God."

We got into the truck and she gave me directions. I wanted to ask how she'd planned to get to the trailhead if I hadn't come with her, but she didn't look in the mood to answer questions.

She had me drive down one country lane after another until we came to a dirt track that had weeds growing down the middle. The road didn't look as though it had been used in years. "I take it you didn't find this on a map," I said. She'd lost her look of anger and was looking at the beautiful countryside around her.

"No," she said. "It's just something I knew."

That again, I thought, and part of me wished we hadn't come. But I was glad I was with her, as I didn't want her wandering around alone. I wasn't so much afraid of what might happen to her as I was afraid of what she might see. A fallen-down cabin maybe? A place where a woman had been buried alive?

I pulled the truck into a clearing, but when Jackie started to get out, I caught her arm. "This isn't the place where . . . You know."

"Where a woman talked to the devil?" she asked, smiling at me, and I smiled back, relieved to see that she was no longer angry at me. "No," she said. "I'm not sure, but my intuition tells me that that place is on the other side of Cole Creek."

Again she started to get out, but I held her arm. "Look, if you've made a mistake and we do see an old cabin . . ."

"I'll turn around and run so fast even the devil won't be able to catch me."

"Promise?" I asked, serious.

"Hope to die."

"Not the answer I wanted," I said, and we laughed as we got out of the truck.

Two hours later I was cursing my stupid idea of going with her. What had I been afraid of back at the house? Loneliness? Time to sit down in the quiet and read a book? Maybe sit in my giant bathtub, drink a beer, and read? Take a nap on the sofa? Were those the things I'd not wanted to do?

I followed Jackie up the mountain on a trail so narrow my little toes were hanging over the edge. Every step was a test of balance as I tripped over sticks, rocks, holes hidden by moss, slick plants, anthills, and black mud that Jackie called "boggy places." My feet hurt, my back ached and I was wet. Even though the sun was high and hot overhead, it didn't reach the floor of the forest, so everything dripped. And things fell on our heads: yellow things, white things, millions of green things. And every spider in the state had played leapfrog across that trail so invisible, sticky strands of web were constantly hitting me in the face. And when, no matter how much I tried, I couldn't get all of them off, I began to feel that I was a fly being readied for dinner.

"Isn't this the most beautiful place you've ever seen in your life?" Jackie said, turning toward me, walking backward on the treacherous trail.

I pulled six long, sticky strands off my tongue.

I would have kept my mouth shut while walking, but the air was so full of water that I had to take two breaths to get any oxygen. "Yeah, beautiful," I said, swatting at some bug. I was discovering species that had never been seen by another human being.

Ten minutes later Jackie went into some kind of ecstasy because she saw these big pink flowers that she said were orchids and she wanted to photograph them. I started to collapse on a log, but she yelled at me to stop. Seems she wanted to inspect the area for—and I quote—"water moccasins, copperheads, or rattlers."

By the time she told me it was safe for me to sit down, I was thinking kind thoughts about my cousin Noble. If he'd wanted pictures of orchids (which I couldn't imagine but that's neither here nor there) he would have driven back here in one of those four-wheel drive John Deere Gators, ecology be damned, and the noise of the diesel engine would have made any self-respecting snake run away in fear.

But I was with Jackie so we "respected" all flora and fauna, including deadly poisonous vipers.

She spread out a big shiny piece of plastic on the ground and told me to stay far away from her while she worked. I didn't protest her attitude, but I did take off my heavy pack—so what if she was carrying the camera equipment and all I had was those little packages of food and some water, it was still heavy—and lay down. I was too tired to even sit up.

I would have fallen asleep, but the tree over my head started dropping yellow and green missiles on me. "Tulip tree," Jackie said, glancing up from her camera.

I got out some food and drink, then turned over on my side and watched her for a while. She'd set her camera on a heavy tripod and was taking pictures from every possible angle. Plus, she spent a lot of time manicuring the area around the flowers, removing microscopic bits of debris so her flowers could be seen easily. She put another shiny sheet down, then lay on it as she shot the flowers looking up.

After a while I got used to being pelted by foliage, and I turned on my back and began to doze.

I awoke when someone poured a bucket of icy water on me. Or so it seemed.

"Let's go!" Jackie shouted.

She had on a long yellow poncho that covered her big backpack, making her look like a hunchback, and she was shoving the gear I'd taken out into my pack. "Put this on," she said as she tossed a blue poncho at me.

The thing was still in its package so I used my teeth to tear it open.

"Don't use your—Oh, never mind," Jackie

said as she grabbed the empty plastic package I'd dropped on the ground. I put the poncho on over my head, then Jackie disappeared under it to put my pack on my back. The resulting situation was too much for me to resist. Sticking my head inside the poncho, I looked down at her. Rain was pelting all around us. "Jackie, darling," I said, "if all you wanted was to get inside my clothes, you didn't have to go to all this trouble."

I expected her to laugh, but instead, she pulled the waist strap so tight I yelped in pain. "Save it for Dessie," she said, then got out from under the poncho.

I assumed we'd hightail it back through the mud and webs to the truck, but Jackie yelled, "Follow me," and we went the other way. Sure enough, about a hundred yards down the trail was a huge outcropping of rock that formed a floor and a roof. The ceiling was black from a thousand campfires so we clearly weren't the first to use the place as a shelter.

Once we were inside, we removed our ponchos and packs and sat there looking at the rain. It didn't look as though it intended to let up, and I thought with dread about walking back in that deluge to my nice, warm truck. Again I asked myself why I'd not wanted to stay home.

But I wasn't going to let Jackie know of my

discomfort so I didn't complain. "How's your equipment? Anything get wet?"

"No," she said, putting her pack on the rock floor. "It's fine. At the first drops I felt—"

She put her hand to her head.

"What is it?"

"Pain," she whispered. "I suddenly—"

If I hadn't shot out my arm to catch her, her head would have hit the rock. But I caught her and pulled her to me. "Jackie, Jackie," I said, my hand on her cheek as I pulled her head onto my lap. I didn't like the look of her; her skin had gone very pale and it felt cold and clammy to my touch.

Hypothermia, I thought. What was it that you did to help the victims? Something warm and high energy had to be put inside them.

Moving Jackie to the driest part under the overhang, I put my pack under her head. There was dry firewood stacked in a corner, no doubt there through some unwritten camper's law that said you must replace what you took. Thanks to Uncle Clyde's many warnings, I always carried a book of matches, so in minutes I had a fire going. I was glad Jackie had made me buy a couple of tin cups. I heated bottled water in one, and when it was hot, I used a stick to lift it and pour the hot water into the cool cup.

When I took the water to Jackie, she was sitting up, ghostly pale, but at least she no longer looked as though she was going to die. I handed her the cool-handled cup of hot water, and while she sipped it, I got a protein bar out of my pack, opened it, broke off a piece, and put it in her mouth.

"What happened?" she whispered.

Her hands were shaking so much that I took the cup from her, and when she looked as though she was going to fall over, I leaned against the rock and drew her to me, her back to my front. "You passed out," I said, and thought about all the doctors I was going to take her to. **Diabetic coma** came to mind.

She sipped the water from the cup as I held it to her lips. "It was like I went to sleep and had a dream," she said. "Fire. I saw a fire. It was in a kitchen. There was a pan on the stove and it caught a towel on fire, then the wall caught and everything went up in flame. There was a woman nearby, but she was on the phone and didn't see the fire until it was too late. There were two little children asleep in the next room, and the fire burned the kitchen and the bedroom. The children were . . ." Jackie put her hands over her face. "The children died. It was horrible. And so very vivid. So **real!** I could see everything."

Maybe it's because I live a good part of my life in a place of fantasy, but I knew instantly what had happened. Jackie had had another vision. Only this time she'd been awake, not asleep, and I knew she wasn't going to like that. "This is like your dream," I said slowly, preparing to start persuading her. "This is something that hasn't happened yet, so I think we should try to prevent it."

But I underestimated her because she understood instantly. Weak as she was, Jackie made an effort to stand up. "We have to find the place. We have to go **now.**"

I knew she was right. Since she wasn't in a condition to carry anything, I grabbed it all, put her heavy pack on my back and my lighter one on my front. Jackie filled the cups with rainwater and doused the fire, then we put on our ponchos, went out into the rain, and started back to the truck. This time I led and this time our pace was at a jog. I was driven by remembering Nate and what a great kid he was and how Jackie's vision had saved his life.

"Tell me every detail," I called back to her as we half ran down the slippery trail. Her face was unnaturally white, surrounded by her bright yellow poncho.

"I saw the children screaming for their mother, but she—"

"No!" I said. "Don't tell me what happened, tell me the details of the place. We have to identify the **place,**" I said over the rain, walking backward, looking at her. "What color was the house? Did you see the street? Give me facts!"

"A pink flamingo," Jackie said, nearly running to keep up with me. "There was a pink flamingo in the backyard. You know, one of those plastic things. And a fence. The whole yard was fenced."

"Wooden? Chain-link?" I called over my shoulder.

"Honeysuckle. It was covered with honeysuckle. I don't know what was under the vines."

"The house? What did you see inside and outside?"

"I didn't see the outside of the house. There was a white stove in the kitchen. And green cabinets. Old cabinets."

"The kids!" I yelled. How far away was the truck?! "How old were the kids? What color skin? Hair?"

"White skin, both with blond hair. About six, maybe younger." When she paused, I knew she was thinking. "There was a baby, less than a year old. I don't think she was walking yet."

"She?" I asked.

"Yes! She was wearing pink pajamas. And the older child had on cowboy pajamas. A boy."

All the saints be praised, I saw the truck. I got the keys out of my pocket, pushed the button to unlock the doors, and helped Jackie tumble inside. I pulled off the packs, got out my cell phone, handed it to Jackie, then dumped the packs in the compartment behind the seat. Seconds later, I had the truck turned around and we were heading back to town.

"Who would know this place if you described it to them?" I asked Jackie.

"Anyone who'd lived in this town all their life," she said, and I looked at her.

"Yeah, but if we call them and explain, they'll think you're . . ."

"Crazy?"

We didn't have time to go into that right now. "We need someone we can trust." I was going so fast over the ruts and holes that my truck tires were hardly touching ground. I had someone in mind but I didn't think Jackie would agree. I was sure she'd want to call Allie, but something about Allie made me think she lacked a calmness that we needed right now.

"Dessie," Jackie said, then began pushing buttons on my cell phone. I'd saved Dessie's number in the directory. When Dessie answered, Jackie held the phone to my ear so I could drive.

"Dessie," I said, "this is Ford Newcombe. I don't have time to go into details now but I need to find someone really fast. She's a woman with two blond kids, a boy about six, and a girl who isn't walking yet. The backyard of the house has a pink flamingo and a fence that's covered in honeysuckle."

"And a swing set," Jackie said.

"And a swing set," I said into the phone.

Dessie didn't bother me with questions. She hesitated a moment as she thought, then said, "Oak. At the end of Maple Street."

We were finally on paved roads, the rain had nearly stopped, and I looked at a sign. "We're on the corner of Sweeten Lane and Grove Hollow right now. Which way do we go?"

"Turn right onto Sweeten toward the Shell station," Dessie said. "Do you see a stop sign?"

"Yes."

"Take a left, go two blocks. Are you at Pine-wood now?"

"Yes."

"Turn right and it's the house at the end of the street on the left."

"I see it!" Jackie said, her window down, her head stuck out in the drizzle. "I can see the swing set and the flamingo. And . . . and the honeysuckle-covered fence."

"Dessie," I said, "I'll see you tomorrow." I didn't say I'd explain; I just hung up. I stopped the truck in front of the house on the end. Jackie and I looked at each other and **What do we do now?** hung between us.

"Maybe we should . . ." Jackie said.

I got out of the truck, but I had no idea what I was going to do. I walked to the front door, Jackie close behind me, and hoped some inspiration would come to me. When I reached the door, I looked at her for courage, took a breath, then rang the bell. We heard footsteps from inside, but then we heard a phone ringing and a woman's voice yelled, "Just a minute."

"The phone," Jackie whispered.

I turned the knob, but the door was locked.

In the next second, Jackie started running to the back of the house and I was close on her heels. The backdoor was unlocked and we tip-toed inside. We could hear the woman laughing and as we stepped further into the kitchen, we could see the side of her through a door that led into the front room. On the stove was the pot with a tea towel beside it. And the towel was ablaze, the flames licking upward to a shelf that contained pot holders and dried flower arrange-ments, all highly flammable.

I grabbed the towel, threw it in the sink, and ran water over it.

When I turned around, there was a little boy, wearing cowboy pajamas, standing in the door-way, rubbing his eyes, and looking at Jackie and me. Jackie put her finger to her lips for the child to be quiet, then we backed out of the kitchen and ran around the house to the truck.

CHAPTER TWELVE

Jackie

Maybe I was jealous of Dessie, but I didn't think so. First of all, why would I be jealous? If I were madly in love with Ford Newcombe and some woman was about to take him away, I would, yes, be very jealous. Or if Dessie were the type of woman who wanted to "do" for a man, that old Southern term that meant wait on him hand and foot, and I thought my job was in jeopardy, I'd probably try to break them up.

But Dessie Mason wasn't like that. True, I could imagine her marrying Ford and assuming that I was to be her slave. And of course she'd move me out of the best bedroom and into the servants' quarters at the top of the house, but I couldn't see her firing me. No, I did too much work to be fired. I ran the house, was Ford's social secretary, was cook and purchasing agent. I did everything except have sex with him—and I was sure that Dessie would take over that job.

So why would I be jealous, as Ford constantly let me know he thought I was? He smirked at me so much I was afraid his face was going to shift to one side.

The problem I saw on that first day was that Dessie was setting her cap for him and she meant to have him. And if she got him, I was sure she'd make him miserable.

Yes, Dessie was beautiful. Actually, she was more than beautiful. She was luscious. I could imagine that over the years thousands of men had declared undying love for her. My personal opinion was that she'd probably left L.A. because there were too many beautiful women there. Her beauty combined with her formidable talent as a sculptor made her the Queen of Cole Creek. The residents mentioned her name in whispers.

So now Dessie had decided she wanted my boss and I had no doubt she'd get him. Ford was smart when it came to books, but he didn't seem too smart about women. On the night Dessie came to dinner, Ford was after her like she was in heat. Truthfully, I thought it was disgusting.

First of all, Dessie made a big production of

showing Ford a sculpture she'd created. It was good, true, and maybe I was being petty when I thought she was presuming too much, but I didn't think a sculpture of Ford's late wife and mother-in-law was something she should have made without asking his permission.

But since she did make it, why hadn't she shown it to him in private? Why did she have to make a big production in front of other people and make Ford cry like a baby? That poor man had tears rolling down his cheeks from the moment he saw the sculpture until the lid was put back on.

I'm sure I'm just being cynical, but I bet she'd never made an uncommissioned sculpture for a **poor** man. It was all too much of a coincidence that Ford was rich and she'd made a 3-D portrait of two women he'd written millions of love words about.

When he told me he was going to her house on Sunday to discuss casting the sculpture in bronze, I was anxious to see how many other pieces he'd order from her. Ford and Tessa had already littered the garden with about fifty hideous little concrete statues, and I'd seen Dessie looking at them with calculating eyes. She's probably planning to replace them with something of hers that she'll charge Ford six figures for, I thought.

I told myself that none of it was my business.

Ford had a right to have an affair with or marry any woman he wanted to. My job was to— Well, the truth of the matter was that I was beginning to wonder exactly what my job was.

For the last week, any time I mentioned research, Ford changed the subject. He said he was working on something else and he'd get to the devil story "later."

But I felt that the truth was, he was afraid for me. Since we'd both decided that my devil story was probably based on something I may have seen when I was a kid, I wasn't unhappy when he didn't pursue it.

Besides, I was happy working on my photography studio. And, okay, I was happy living with Ford. He could be very funny sometimes, and if anything had to do with books, he was a great companion. Every night while I fixed dinner, he read to me from one of the many books on photography he'd ordered, and both of us were learning a lot.

And his generosity was boundless. I made out an order for the bare essentials of photography equipment I'd need, but Ford added to the list and upgraded it until the total price was something that made me sick to my stomach.

"I can never pay this back," I said, handing the list back to him.

Ford shrugged. "We'll work out something."

Earlier, I would have thought that meant sex,

but I'd come to realize that Ford didn't think of me in that way. Actually, I was beginning to think he thought of me as the daughter he'd never had. And, truthfully, that was beginning to depress me. So, okay, maybe I'd been pretty adamant about there being no sex between us when I first met him. But at the time I'd been engaged to Kirk, and when I left for Cole Creek with Ford, I'd just been ripped off by a man. My distrust of men was understandable. But since then . . . Well, since then, I'd come to find Ford rather attractive. But ever since we'd arrived in Cole Creek he'd been lusting after other women, first Rebecca and now Dessie. All I could do was be his assistant and his business partner.

On Saturday our little household was shaken. First of all, I was in a bad mood about the way Ford had made a fool of himself over Dessie the night before. I didn't mind his crying in front of everyone—that was kind of sweet—but I did mind the way he couldn't stop looking at her. She had on a dress that showed her enormous breasts about as much as was legal, a wide belt that cinched in her spreading waist, and a full skirt that attempted to camouflage a rear end that had to be forty-five inches around. Dessie talked and laughed all night, but Ford just sat there nursing a beer and looking at her. He stared at her little pink toenails until I moved the chair she had her feet propped on, so she had to put her lacquered toes out of sight under the table.

But no, I don't think I was jealous. I think that if Dessie had acted like a woman on the verge of falling in love, I would have been happy. Or even if I'd seen that she was in lust with Ford it would have been okay. But Allie told me that everyone in Cole Creek knew that Dessie was sleeping with her twenty-five-year-old gardener. One time I saw her looking at Nate, and both Nate's grandmother and I stepped between her and the beautiful boy. When Dessie laughed, it was the only honest emotion I saw on her face all evening.

Anyway, Saturday morning I wasn't in a good mood, so I decided to take my camera and go shoot some flowers. But just as I was leaving, Ford showed up and insisted he go with me.

He has some good points, but he can also be the most infuriating man on earth. By the time I got him outfitted, the sun was high in the sky, which meant I wouldn't get interesting shadows on the flowers, and I wished with all my might I'd let him spend the day with Dessie. Let her do whatever she wanted to with him.

Worse, when we finally got on the trail, he complained every step of the way. We didn't go more than a mile, if that, but to hear Ford's grumbling, you would have thought we'd hiked thirty miles on a survival trek. He ate and drank every step of the way, grunted and groaned over every twig in his path, and even whined about cobwebs across the trail. I felt like smacking him!

In the end, though, it was good he went with me because I had another one of those disaster-dreams. Only this time I was fully awake. Sort of awake. I think I blacked out for a few minutes. When I came to myself, Ford had a fire going and had heated water in a cup, and he started feeding me one of those pseudo-nutritional bars he eats by the dozen.

He was the one who figured out that I'd had another vision, and the second he said it, I knew he was right. Thirty minutes before, he'd been lying down, with all the energy of a dead slug, but suddenly he was a jet engine. He grabbed both packs, put one on his back, one on his front, and started running back to the truck. Yes, **running.**

When he got behind the wheel of the truck, I had to hold on for dear life. He was asking me a million questions about my dream-vision, but I could hardly concentrate for fear he was going to turn the truck over. What really amazed me was that he drove like that with one hand on the wheel and didn't seem to think it was at all unusual. All his books ran it home that he (in a fictional guise) wasn't like his redneck relatives, but all he needed that day was a cigarette in his mouth and a rifle across the back window, and I would have put him up against any Billy Joe Bob in the U.S.

In spite of my head repeatedly hitting the roof of the truck, I managed to get Dessie on his cell phone. I called her because I felt sure she wouldn't care about anything outside herself. Allie would have asked me a hundred questions, none of which I wanted to answer.

Thanks to Dessie, we found the house of my dream-vision in record time, then slipped in the backdoor and put out the fire before the house went up in flames.

I must say that the whole thing was exhilarating. The wild ride, then accomplishing a task that saved the lives of two children . . . Well, truthfully, it turned me on. I wanted to get naked, pour champagne over my body, and make love until the sun came up. With Ford. Yeah, that shocked me a bit, but when we were laughing on the way home, it seemed possible that we could end up fooling around. Maybe not all night with a man his age and in his physical condition, but still . . .

At my suggestion, we stopped and got pizza and beer and took it home, and I was contemplating the best way to suggest that we could . . . Well . . .

But when we arrived at that beautiful house, Dessie was on our front porch with a basketful of champagne and smoked oysters, and she was saying how she'd been so worried about Ford that she'd just been sick. Her accent had deepened into Classic Southern Belle, and she'd even managed to pull in her belt another notch. I wondered if she'd had a colonic.

Ford gave me an I'm-helpless-to-do-anything-about-this look, so I said I was tired and wanted to go to bed. He started to get all fatherly on me, but I pushed his hand away from my forehead, and went upstairs. I had to close all my windows to keep from hearing Dessie's exaggerated laugh as she and Ford sat in the garden talking for most of the night.

Even if I wasn't jealous, I was certainly lonely on Sunday. Because he'd stayed up so late, Ford didn't get out of bed until noon, and even then I could see that his mind was elsewhere. I made him a big cheesy omelet, put it on the plate in front of him, then went outside to the garden to reread one of the new books on photography. I'd meant to go to church, but the truth was that I was feeling so lazy I couldn't seem to work up any interest in going. At twelve-thirty I called Allie but no one answered the phone.

It was while the phone was ringing that I heard Ford's car and looked out the window to see him driving away. He hadn't even said good-bye!

I sat down on the little upholstered chair by the telephone and suddenly felt bereft. No, actually, for the first time, I felt like an employee. Yes, I know he gave me a paycheck, but still . . .

It was absurd of me and I knew I was acting like a kid, but it was the first time Ford and I had been apart since we'd arrived. Would Dessie cook something divine for him? Would she wear black toreador pants and a red blouse? Would she show a cleavage four and a half feet long?

I gave a great sigh of disgust at myself. For someone who wasn't jealous, I was certainly acting like I was.

Maybe I was just bored. I called Nate's house. Maybe he and his grandmother would like to come over for lunch, or invite me to their house. She was a nice woman and I'd enjoyed telling Ford that the grandmother was his age. Ford had replied that he wasn't going to marry her and that Nate wasn't going to be forced to bunk with me so I might as well stop trying. As always, we'd laughed together.

There was no answer at Nate's house.

"Where is everyone?" I said aloud. Was there another tea party and I hadn't been invited? Maybe that's where Ford was now, I thought. Maybe he and Dessie were going to the party without me.

I told myself that I needed to get a grip. And I needed to find something to do with myself that didn't involve other people. Which, of course, meant taking pictures.

For a moment I hesitated and had to work to stamp down a feeling of panic. What if I went into the woods and had another vision? Who would be there to help me if I blacked out again? And even more important, who would help me undo the horror of what I saw?

Sitting there for a second, I lectured myself on codependency. I'd had twenty-six years before I met Ford Newcombe, so I could certainly spend an afternoon without him.

I got up from the chair and went upstairs to my bedroom. Empty, the house seemed too big, too old, and too creaky. And it seemed that I heard sounds from every corner. The exterminators had rid the house of the bees, but now I wondered if there were wasps in the attic. Or birds.

I checked my big camera backpack for film and batteries, picked it up and went downstairs. I didn't know where I was going, but I certainly needed to get out of that vacant house.

As it turned out, I only walked about a mile down a narrow road when I came to a little sign that said "trail." It was one of those signs that looked hand carved—and maybe was for all I knew—and made a person feel as though she was about to embark on an adventure.

The trail was wide and worn down, the bare earth hard packed, the tree roots exposed and worn smooth by many feet. Why don't I remember this trail? I thought, then laughed at myself. I felt eerie when I did remember things and confused when I didn't remember them.

It didn't take me but minutes to find flowers worth preserving forever. I mounted my F100 on the tripod, used Fuji Velvia ISO 50, and shot some Downy Rattlesnake Plantain standing in a tiny spot of sunlight. I clicked the cable release and held my breath that no wind would move a leaf and blur the picture. But it was dead still at the moment so I had hopes that the photo would come out sharp-edged.

I really loved to photograph flowers. Their colors were so gaudy that I could satisfy the child in me who still loved the brightest crayons in the box. I could look at pictures of brilliant reds and pinks and greens and still feel I was doing something "natural."

When I photographed people, I liked just the opposite. The expressions on people's faces and the emotions they showed were, to me, the pyrotechnic "color" of the picture. But I'd found that color film too often drew attention to skin that was too red, or blotched with age spots, and so hid the emotion I wanted to show. And with a child, how could you look at a face when it was competing with a shirt that had four orange rhinos dancing across it?

Over the years I'd learned to satisfy my color lust with photos of brilliant flowers taken with film of the finest grain. I could blow up a stamen to 9 x 12 and still have it crystal clear. And I indulged my love of seeing the insides of people by using black-and-white film—true black-and-white, the kind that had to be developed by hand instead of churned out by some giant machine.

I shot four rolls of Velvia and two of Ektachrome, then packed up and headed back toward the house. It was nearly four o'clock and I was hungry and thirsty, but I'd brought nothing to eat with me. I guess that in the last weeks I'd grown used to being with Ford because wherever he went food and drink followed close behind.

I allowed myself a great, self-pitying sigh as I shouldered my pack and headed back down the trail. But the truth was, I was feeling better. I wasn't feeling lonely anymore, and I was no longer angry at Ford. I'd had a nice afternoon and I felt sure I'd taken some good photos. Maybe I could start a line of greeting cards and sell them to tourists passing through the Appalachians, I thought. Maybe I could—

Suddenly, I halted and looked around me because I didn't recognize where I was. There was a narrow stream in front of me, but I knew I hadn't crossed a stream on my way in. Turning back, I looked for the trail I'd come in on—all the while imagining how very sorry Ford Newcombe was going to be when the National Guard had to be called out to look for me. "I shouldn't have left her alone," he'd say.

I walked for about twenty minutes, but still saw nothing I remembered. I was beginning to be concerned when I looked to my left and saw the sunlight flash off something that was moving.

Curious, but also a little frightened because I didn't know where I was, I stepped off the path and into the forest. I tried to move as quietly as possible on the soft earth and succeeded in making little noise. The forest was quite dark; there was a great deal of underbrush, but I could see the sunlight ahead. I saw the flash again and my heart leaped into my throat. What was I going to see? Thoughts of Jack the Ripper and a flashing knife went through my mind.

When I got to the edge and could see through the trees, I nearly laughed out loud. I was looking at someone's backyard. On the far side was an old fence nearly broken by the weight of the pink roses that covered it. When a slight breeze came up, rose petals fluttered softly to the ground.

The grass had been recently mowed and I

closed my eyes for a moment at the heavenly smell. The forest I was in was on one side, the fence on two sides. The fourth side, to my right, had shade trees so dense that I couldn't see the house that I assumed was farther up the hill.

But the truth was that the White House could have been up there and I wouldn't have seen it, because I was distracted.

Under a huge shade tree was a wooden park bench and sitting on it was a man. A very, very handsome man. He was tall and slim, his neck resting on the back of the bench, his long legs stretched out in front of him. He was wearing blue jeans, gray hiking boots, and a dark blue denim shirt, the kind with snaps down the front. His thick hair was as black as a crow's wing and it didn't look as though it had been dyed. The silver flash I'd seen was a cup. He was drinking something hot and steamy out of the top of a tall aluminum Thermos that stood on the ground by his feet.

Also on the ground was a blue canvas bag with a loaf of long, skinny French bread sticking out of it. Beside the bag was—I drew in my breath and my eyes widened until they hurt—a Billingham camera bag. Billingham bags were made in England and they looked like something the duke of somewhere would carry, something handed down from his ancestors. Prince Charles once said he didn't think anyone actually bought tweeds, that tweeds were just something people had. That's the way Billingham bags looked: as though they'd always been there. They were made of canvas and leather, with brass buckles. Prince Charles aside, the truth was that Billingham bags could be bought, but, like tweeds, they cost dearly.

I was standing there, skulking in the trees like a voyeur, lusting after his big camera bag, when I felt the man looking at me. Sure enough, when I looked up, he was staring directly at me, a faint smile on his lips, his dark eyes warm.

I turned at least four shades of red and wanted to flee into the forest. Like a unicorn, I thought. But then, unicorns probably knew how to find their way out of the forest.

Taking a deep breath, I tried to pretend I was an adult as I walked toward him. "I didn't mean to spy on you," I said. "I just—"

"Wanted to make sure I wasn't the local mass murderer?"

Full face, he was even better looking, and he had a beautiful voice: rich and creamy. Oh, no, I thought. I'm in trouble.

Moving to one side of the bench, he motioned for me to sit down beside him. He was so beautiful in such a sophisticated, elegant way, that as I removed my pack, I made myself keep my eyes on the roses. "Beautiful, aren't they?"

"Yes," he said, turning to look at them. "I

knew they'd be blooming now so I made a point of coming today."

I put my vinyl and canvas camera bag on the ground beside the Billingham and they seemed to make a New World versus Olde Worlde statement.

As I sat down on the far end of the bench, I kept looking at the roses, but the man was between them and my eyes, so my vision strayed.

He turned toward me, eyes twinkling, the sweetest smile on his face. As I'd come to know Ford, I'd grown used to his looks, but this man made me feel like a nerdy teenager alone with the captain of the football team.

"You must be Jackie Maxwell," he said.

I groaned. "Small town."

"Oh, yes. Very small. I'm Russell Dunne," he said, holding out his hand to shake mine.

I gave his hand a little shake then released it. That's my self-discipline for the year, I thought. Releasing that big, warm hand had not been easy to do.

"Is that your house up there?" I asked, looking back through the trees, but all I could see was more trees.

"No," he said. "At least not anymore."

I wanted to ask what he meant but didn't. I was so attracted to the man that I seemed to have electricity running through me.

"You aren't possibly hungry, are you? I

brought too much food and either it gets eaten or I have to haul it back." He looked at me through long, spiky lashes. "It's heavy so you'd be helping me out if you shared it with me."

What could I do? Refuse to help him? Ha ha.

"Sure," I said, and the next minute he was standing before me and stretching. Oh, yeah, sure, I knew he was showing off his drop-dead gorgeous, hunky body, but well . . .

I made myself stop looking as he picked up the canvas bag and pulled out a red and white checked tablecloth. I knew that pattern was a little hokey but, still, it looked perfect spread on the dark green grass.

"Help me?" he asked as he sat on one side of the cloth.

In an embarrassingly short time I was sitting on the tablecloth, both of us facing the splendid view of the roses, and I was arranging the items he pulled out of the bag.

I must say that he'd been able to pack a great deal in that bag. There was a bottle of cold white wine and two crystal glasses—the kind that ping when you tap them—and plates from Villeroy and Boch. The food was wonderful: cheeses, pâtés, olives, meats in little cold packs, three kinds of salad.

"This is like the loaves and fishes," I said.

He stopped unloading and looked at me, puzzled. "What do you mean?"

He hadn't spent a lot of time in church, I thought. I told him of Jesus feeding the multitudes with a few fish sandwiches.

The story seemed to amuse him and he smiled. "Nothing Biblical, just an experienced packer."

Had it been anyone else, I would have thought my joke had fallen flat, but his smile was so warm that I returned it. He poured us glasses of wine, broke bread from the loaf, and handed me a plate of cheese and olives. It was my absolute favorite kind of meal.

After we'd eaten some, I leaned back on one arm, sipped my delicious wine, and looked at the roses. "So tell me everything about yourself," I said.

When he laughed, the sound was as rich and creamy as the Brie. "I'd much rather that you tell me what all of Cole Creek is dying to know. What's going on between you and Ford Newcombe?"

Startled, I turned to look at him. "Why would anyone care to know that?"

"Same reason you want to know all about me."

"Touché," I said, smiling and beginning to relax. My physical attraction to him was so strong that I didn't trust myself to behave, but I was beginning to calm down enough to think and talk. "So who goes first?"

"How about scissors, paper, rock?" he said,

and I laughed again. That had been the way my
father and I often settled who was going to have
to do the more onerous chores.

I won. "Who are you? Why weren't you at
the Annual Cole Creek Tea and what happened
to your house up there?" I squinted into the
deep shade of the forest at the last question.

"Okay," he said, chewing, swallowing, dusting
his hands off. Then he got up, bowed to me, and
put his right index finger to his temple. I knew
he was imitating Jack Haley, the tin man in **The
Wizard of Oz**—one of my favorite movies.

"Russell Dunne," he said. "Thirty-four years
old. Associate professor of art history at the
University of North Carolina in Raleigh. I lived
in Cole Creek until I was nine, and after we
moved, we sometimes returned to visit relatives.
My mother grew up in the house that used to
be there, but it burned down about ten years
ago. I was married but I'm a widower now, no
children, no real attachments, actually. I wasn't at
the party because I don't live here and am not
considered part of the town." He looked at me,
eyes laughing. "What else?"

"What's in the Billingham?"

His laughter turned to mock seriousness. "So
now we get down to your **real** interest in me.
And here I thought it was my charisma. Or at
least the cheese."

"Nope," I said, glad to pretend that I wasn't

already thinking about my bridesmaids. "What equipment is in there?"

Stepping over to the bench, he picked up the big bag, set it on the edge of the tablecloth and withdrew a camera I'd only seen in catalogs: a Nikon D1-X.

"Digital?" I asked and I could hear the sneer in my voice. I like automatic focus on my cameras but that's as modern as I got. I hated zoom lenses as I didn't feel they gave me as clear a photo as a fixed lens. As for digital, that was for Mr. and Mrs. Homeowner. Even though I knew that his camera body, no lens, cost thousands wholesale, still, in my view, it wasn't a "real" camera.

Turning the camera toward the sunlit roses, Russell fired off a couple of shots, then opened a door and removed a plastic card from the side. As I drank wine, he looked inside his bag and withdrew a little machine—two of them could have fit in a shoe box. At first I thought it was a portable DVD player and wondered what movie he was planning to show me. I hoped it wasn't too sexy or I'd never be able to keep my hands off of him.

When he stuck the card in the machine, I paused, glass frozen to my lips, and I don't think I breathed until I saw a photograph come out. When he handed the photo to me, I set my glass down and marveled at a 4 x 6 photo of perfect color and clarity. I could see the thorns on the rose stems.

"Oh," was all I could say. "Oh."

"Of course you can put the photos on a computer and manipulate them, and there are much better printers than this gadget, but you get the idea."

Oh, yeah, I thought. I could see uses for this. A sort of New Age Polaroid.

"But I also use this," he said as he pulled a big Nikon F5 out of his bag. Take my camera, add some features and a couple of pounds, and you have an F5.

I love a heavy camera. I really do. I said that to Jennifer once and she said, "Yeah, like a heavy **man.**"

Maybe it was as sexual as she was implying, but there was something so fundamentally solid about a camera that weighed a lot that I could never get interested in the little ones.

I was impressed by what he'd shown me, but I didn't want to gush. "So what else do you have in there?"

Lifting the top flap, he peered inside. "A scanner, a 6 x 6. Couple of lights. A backdrop or two. A motorcycle to get home on." When he looked back at me, we laughed together.

Maybe he'd been joking about the motorcycle, but as he sat down, he pulled out a palm size Nikon digital that I knew was new on the market and touted as tops.

"Last one, I promise," he said. "Go on, shoot."

But as I lifted the camera and pointed it toward him, he put his hands over his face. "Anything but me."

I aimed the camera at the roses. Had I been sitting there with Ford I would have clicked off a dozen photos of him, hands or not, but I didn't feel secure enough with this man to go against his wishes. Or maybe I was in that girl mode where I didn't want to displease him.

"Your turn to tell all," he said as I played with the camera, pushing its many buttons to see what would happen.

"Absolutely nothing between Ford Newcombe and me," I said emphatically. "In fact, today he's out on a date with Cole Creek's most illustrious citizen."

"Ah," Russell said, and his tone made me look at him. He had a striking profile, his features sharp and clear, as though they were carved from stone. I bet Dessie would like to sculpt him, I thought, then it hit me what that tone in his voice was.

"Do you know Dessie?" I asked quietly.

"Oh, yes. But, then, don't all men know the Dessies of the world?"

Yeow! I thought. There was a condemnation if I ever heard one. I vowed then and there not to make a pass at beautiful Russell Dunne. I didn't ever want him, or any man, to refer to me like that. "She's . . . ?" I wasn't sure how to phrase my question. How much danger was my innocent, naive boss in?

When Russell turned to me, all humor was gone from his face. His dark eyes were intense—and I thought I might wilt under his gaze. "Look, do me a favor, will you?"

"Anything," I said, and, unfortunately, I meant it.

"Don't mention meeting me to anyone in Cole Creek, especially not to Newcombe. He might tell Dessie and she'd tell others and it could get, well, unpleasant. I'm not welcome in Cole Creek."

"Why ever not?" I asked, aghast. A man with his manners and elegance not welcome? This man made James Bond seem like a redneck.

Russell smiled at me in a way that made me want to lie down on my back and open my arms to him.

"You're good for my ego, Miss Maxwell."

"Jackie," I said, trying to stay upright. I made myself look back at the camera. "Okay, I'll keep your secrets but I need to know all of them." I was trying to be lighthearted, sophisticated even. I fiddled with the zoom lens, making it go in and out, then flipped the switch to screen view and looked at the few photos he'd taken. All landscapes, all perfect.

After a while he looked back at the roses and I relaxed.

"I wrote a bad review of one of Dessie's shows," he said. "I earn a little money on the side from writing reviews, and I wrote an honest opinion, but no one in Cole Creek has ever forgiven me."

I didn't do a little dance of joy, but I wanted to. It was, of course, downright mean-spirited of me to want Dessie to get a bad review, but still . . .

"That's it? The town dislikes you because you gave a bad review to one of its citizens?" I asked, looking up at him.

He gave me a little one-sided smile that nearly made my socks curl off my feet. If I were in a Disney film, bluebirds would have flown down and plucked at my silk gown.

"That and the fact that I'm an outsider who knows they crushed a woman to death," he said.

I nearly dropped the camera. If I'd fallen off a cliff I probably would have held whatever camera I had protectively to me, but what Russell said nearly made me drop that beautiful instrument.

"Shocked?" he asked, looking at me hard, but all I could do was nod. "Shocked at what I said or shocked that I know?"

"Know," I said, and my voice was so hoarse I had to clear it.

He seemed to study me for a moment before he finally looked away. "Let me guess. Newcombe got wind of the story somehow, but when he asked questions, no one in Cole Creek knew anything about it."

I was ready to run away with this man, certainly to have a mad affair with him, but I wasn't ready to reveal what I'd found out since I'd arrived in this town. If I did that, I might slip and start telling him about my visions and that I remembered too many things. I decided to say as little as possible about what I knew.

"Exactly," I said. "Miss Essie Lee."

Russell smiled. "Ah, yes. The inimitable Miss Essie Lee. She was there, you know. She heaped stones on that poor woman."

I tried to stay calm. I'd read newspaper accounts of horrible things happening, hadn't I? But my stomach lurched at the thought of having been near someone who had done such a vile thing. "Was anyone prosecuted?" I managed to ask.

"No. Everything was hushed up."

I asked the question that Ford loved so much: "Why? Why would they do such a thing?"

Russell shrugged. "Jealousy would be my guess. Amarisa was loved by many people—and hated by a few."

"Amarisa?" I asked.

"The woman who was crushed. I met her when I was just a kid and I thought she was very nice. She . . . Are you sure you want to hear this?"

"Yes," I said. I set down the camera, drew my knees to my chest, and prepared to listen.

"Amarisa's brother, Reece Landreth, came to Cole Creek to run a small factory that made pottery. There's a lot of good clay around here and tourists were coming into the area so I guess the owners thought it would be a good business to get into. Reece opened the factory and hired some locals to work in it. The trouble came about because the prettiest girl in town was a Cole—"

"One of the founding families."

"Yes," Russell said. "Harriet Cole. She was young and beautiful, and Edward Belcher wanted to marry her. I remember him, too. He was a pompous bore. But Ms. Cole wanted to get out of Cole Creek, so she latched onto a man who was free to move around."

"The young and handsome potter."

He was silent for a moment. "Did I mention 'young and handsome'?"

"Must have heard it somewhere," I mumbled, cursing myself for giving too much away.

"Anyway," he said, "the problem was that after Harriet and Reece were married, he found out she was the town bitch, and she made his life hell. The irony was that she'd married him to get away from Cole Creek, but afterward she refused to leave her parents. By the time poor Reece found out his wife wouldn't leave the town, they had a daughter he was mad about, so he was trapped."

I didn't say anything. There was no reason whatever for me to believe that **I** was that daughter. Because my memories fit the story exactly wasn't enough evidence. "How did Reece's sister, Amarisa, fit into all this?" I asked.

"Her husband had died and left her well off, but she was alone, so when her brother asked her to move to Cole Creek, she gladly accepted. I remember hearing my mother—who despised Harriet Cole—say that Amarisa knew her brother was in trouble so his rich sister came to Cole Creek to bail him out. And it was true that by the time Amarisa got here, the pottery works had gone out of business and Reece was working for his father-in-law. My mother used to say that Reece worked fourteen hours a day, but old Abraham Cole stole all the profits."

"So Amarisa saved her brother," I said.

"Yes. Amarisa supported her brother and his little family." Pausing for a moment, Russell looked at me. "But the problem wasn't money. The problem was that everyone in town liked Amarisa. She was a lovely woman. She listened to people and, as a result, they told her their secrets."

When he didn't say any more, I looked at him. "Do you think she knew too many secrets?"

Russell began to clear away the food. "I don't

know exactly what happened, but I do remember hearing my mother say that people in Cole Creek were jealous of Amarisa and it was causing problems."

"So they killed her out of jealousy," I said. Even if I didn't know the details, I could imagine the strong emotions.

"That's what my mother said," Russell said. "One night she was crying hysterically, 'They killed her! They killed her!' I was in bed pretending to be asleep but I heard it all. The next day my father put my mother and me in the car and we left our home, never to return."

I felt a tightening of my skin. I had a kinship with this man. I, too, had been bundled up and taken away from my home. Only I had also been taken away from my mother. Had she been Harriet Cole, the "town bitch"?

"But you came back to Cole Creek for visits."

"After my mother died when I was eleven," Russell said softly, "my dad and I returned here for visits. Not often and we never stayed in the old house. I don't know why. Maybe it had too many memories for him. I do know that my mother was never the same after that night when she came home crying." He was silent for a moment, and when he looked at me, his eyes were dark with pain. "I think that on that night they killed my mother as well as Amarisa. It just took my mother longer to die."

We sat in an intimate silence for a while, and I'm not sure what would have happened if it hadn't started raining. Never in my life had I met anyone who'd been through what I had. I'd been younger than Russell when I'd "lost" my mother, but we shared the trauma of having been whisked away from everything we knew.

But perhaps what really bound us together was that maybe we had been through the same tragedy. Maybe Amarisa's death—murder—had disrupted both our lives.

We sat on the tablecloth, watching the fading light on the roses, saying nothing, thinking our own thoughts, but when the first raindrops fell, we went into action. **Protect the equipment!** was an unspoken command. I grabbed my yellow poncho out of my bag as Russell grabbed a blue one out of his. We tossed the big ponchos over our heads and clutched our precious equipment to our bosoms.

When we looked out the head holes and saw each other, we began to laugh. The canvas bag containing what was left of the food (not much) was in the rain, and Russell had a jacket slung across the bench—but our camera equipment was safe and dry.

Scooting over to me, he raised the front end of his poncho, then lifted mine so that we were sitting under a little tent, our bags of equipment between us. The rain was coming down hard, pelting the plastic over the top of us, but it was cozy and dry inside our little tent. Too cozy, actually.

"I want you to take these and play with them," Russell said, holding out the little camera and the tiny printer. The camera had five million pixels. Gee. Funny how your scruples disappear when something becomes free. Had I been disdainful of digital photography merely because I couldn't afford a digital camera?

"I couldn't. Really," I began, but he was slipping both items into my bag.

"It's just a loan." He was smiling, and at this close range I could smell his breath. Flowers would be jealous. "Besides, to get them back I'll have to see you again."

Looking down at my bag of camera equipment, I tried to smile demurely. What I really wanted to do was tattoo my address and phone number across his upper thigh. "Okay," I said after what I hoped was a suitable interval.

"That is, if you're sure there's nothing going on between you and Newcombe."

"Nothing whatever," I said, grinning. I didn't add that there might have been, but Ford had dropped me the second he saw Miss Dessie's cleavage. And her talent, I thought. I didn't want to be fair, but I was cursed with the ability to see both sides of a problem.

Russell peeked out of the ponchos. The rain

didn't seem to be letting up. "I think we better go or we'll be caught in the dark."

Wouldn't that be a tragedy? I wanted to say, but didn't. I was feeling a bit frantic that we hadn't exchanged telephone numbers, but I didn't want to appear anxious.

Russell solved the problem by opening a pocket on the side of his bag and removing a couple of cards and a pen. "Could I possibly persuade you to give me your telephone number?" he asked.

I would have said that I'd give him the number of my bank account, but I'd done that with Kirk and look what had happened. Oh, well, that was water under the bridge. I wrote the phone number for the house I shared with Ford on the back of one of the cards, but before I handed it to him, I turned the card over and looked at it. "Russell Dunne" and a telephone number in the lower left corner was all that was on the card. I looked up at him in puzzlement.

He understood my unspoken question. "When I had them printed, I was about to move and I couldn't decide whether to put my new address or my old one on it." He shrugged in a way that I found endearing. "Ready?" he asked. "I think we should try to get out of here while we can."

If we couldn't spend the night together, I guess I'd have to follow him to wherever he was going. Minutes later we were on the trail, heads down against the driving rain, camera equipment safe under our ponchos, mud clinging to our shoes. Somewhere along the way, I told myself that I needed to ask him what his address now was. Was he staying nearby? Or had he driven here all the way from Raleigh? When would he return to his job and his real life?

But the rain and our fast pace kept me from asking anything. I just kept my head down and followed him, watching his heels, not looking ahead, and having no idea of the direction he was taking to get us out of there.

After a while we came to pavement, but it was still raining too hard for me to look up. It was odd that even though I'd just met this man, I had complete faith that he knew where he was going. I followed him as though I were a child with its father, unquestioning.

When he halted, I almost ran into the back of him, and when I did look up, I was surprised to see that we were in front of Ford's house. The rain was making such a racket that I knew we couldn't talk. I looked up at Russell and made a gesture for him to come inside for something warm to drink.

Lifting his poncho-covered arm, he pointed to where a wristwatch went, and shook his head. Then he used his finger to do a pantomime of tears running down his cheeks and sniffed. Like most people, I hated mimes, but he was making me change my opinion.

Turning the corners of my mouth down, I imitated great sadness. Pretended to imitate. Actually, I wanted to take him inside, tell Ford I'd found him in the forest, and could I keep him? Pretty please?

Smiling, Russell leaned forward, put his beautiful face inside the hood of my poncho and kissed my cheek. Then he turned and was gone from my sight in seconds.

For a moment I stood there looking into the mist of the rain and sighing. What an extraordinary day, I thought. What a truly extraordinary day.

Turning, I went down the path, up the porch stairs, and into the house. Like something in a 1950s teen movie, I floated up the stairs. I just wanted to take a hot bath, put on dry clothes, and dream about Russell Dunne.

CHAPTER THIRTEEN

Ford

I'm sure a psychic experience in which you see a couple of little kids go up in flame wasn't what a normal person would label as "fun." But saving those children had been.

Sometimes Jackie had a way of looking at me that made me feel like I could solve all the world's problems. At other times, she made me feel old and decrepit. Whatever she thought of me as a physical specimen, she certainly looked surprised when I grabbed her backpack and mine and headed back down the trail. It was easier going on the return because, if nothing else, the cobwebs had been cleared away.

Then there was the ride in the truck. As we bounced along the trail, the look on her face reminded me of something my cousin Noble liked to do. He was blessed—or cursed as one of my female cousins said—by not having the Newcombe looks. In other words, Noble had a face girls love. He'd go into town, do his "shy-little-me act" as a cousin called it, and a girl would inevitably sashay over to him. Noble would eventually treat her to a "Newcombe special" which was a fast pickup ride across deep ruts. Afterward, he'd come home and entertain us all with vivid accounts of the indignation and fear of the girls.

Back then I never appreciated the humor or the appeal in what Noble did. I'd always wanted to spend time with a town girl—namely, one who wasn't likely to give birth at sixteen—but my looks and my shyness didn't attract those twinset-clad girls with their perfect pageboy hair and single strands of pearls. It wasn't until I was at college and away from the stigma of the Newcombe family that one of those girls paid any attention to me. When I met Pat she was wearing a sky blue twinset, a darker blue skirt, and a strand of creamy white pearls. "Fake," she told me later, laughing when I asked her to leave the pearls on while we made love.

On that day when I was driving the truck across the ruts, I finally understood why Noble had so loved scaring those town girls. Jackie's face bore a combination of fear and excitement that did things to me in a sexual way. She looked at me in horror, true, but she also looked at me as though I were a magician, a race car driver, and a rescuing hero all in one.

After the exhilarating experience of saving the kids was added to the thrill of the drive, I don't know what would have happened if Dessie hadn't shown up. While Jackie and I had bought pizza and beer, my mind was tumbling all over itself with images of a naked Jackie with little rings of black olives scattered over her nude body. I could imagine myself drinking beer and trying to decide which delectable little ring I was going to eat next.

I was trying to figure out how I was going to make this vision a reality when we arrived home and Dessie was standing there waiting.

Since the last time I'd seen her and she'd unveiled the sculptures, I'd had some time to think and— Well, okay, Jackie's sarcastic, albeit painfully true, remarks had dimmed some of the stars in my eyes. Maybe it hadn't been so tasteful of Dessie to unveil a statue of a man's beloved, deceased wife in front of guests. And, yes, Jackie was right that that sort of thing pretty much always produced tears. I didn't, however, agree when Jackie said, "Especially in someone as soft and sentimental as you are." That didn't sound very masculine, so I protested. Then she pointed out that I had written some books that were "pretty weepy."

Okay, so she had me. Jackie had a way of seeing to the heart of a matter, which was a good thing. But, sometimes, I really wished she'd keep her mouth shut about what she saw.

By the time I was to leave for Dessie's house on Sunday, I wanted to call her and tell her I wouldn't be able to make it. At breakfast Jackie made a remark about which of the little statues that Tessa and I had bought Dessie would replace first. I was determined not to let Jackie see what was in my mind, so I began reading the nutritional content on the back of the box of that cereal she eats. "Amazing," I said. "This stuff has more vitamins and minerals than three of those green pills you take." I'd read the label on those, too.

When Jackie narrowed her eyes at me, I knew she knew I was avoiding her comment.

The night before, Dessie had stayed until a little after midnight. I'd had to give a couple of huge yawns to get her to leave. Of course I knew what she wanted. She was after a trip to my bedroom.

But I couldn't do it. A couple of hours before I'd been lusting after Jackie, and I wasn't the kind of man who could change from one woman to another in the course of an evening.

Besides, Jackie made me laugh. Her sarcasm and black humor nearly always amused me.

When I was around Jackie I felt alert, and as though something exciting was about to happen. Jackie was interested in things in the same way I had been before Pat died. I was finding Jackie's photography fascinating, and I had a good time when she invited people over.

So I sat there that night and tried my best to talk to Dessie, but I couldn't seem to get into it. For one thing, the conversation always seemed to go back to her and her sculpture. If I mentioned a movie, that would lead to her remembering some movie that was the inspiration for a bronze she'd made for some really famous man. "Not as famous as you are," she said as she looked over her wineglass at me.

Of course I knew she was hinting that I buy a bronze from her. But that didn't bother me. What bothered me was that she didn't ask a word about what Jackie and I had been doing when we'd called and asked for her help. Wasn't she curious about why we'd needed to find a specific house, and why we'd had to find it **fast?** But Dessie never mentioned the incident.

After Dessie left Saturday night—or, actually, it was early Sunday—I fell into bed and slept hard.

The next morning I studied the back of the cereal box and made no comment on Jackie's snide remark about the little frogs and other beasties that Tessa and I had scattered about the garden. I didn't even comment when Jackie said that maybe Dessie could make a frog with a mouth big enough that Tessa and I could hide inside it. I started to say that that was a great idea, but I knew Jackie was baiting me and trying to get me to—to what? I wondered. Not go to Dessie's house that afternoon? Did Jackie want me to stay home and try out some of the new camera equipment we'd ordered together?

Jackie and I had talked about how to open her business and we'd decided she needed to photograph some·kids for free. We could use those pictures to publicize her work. She'd be able to get some people to drive to Cole Creek, but she was also going to need to do a lot of location shooting.

We'd decided that Jackie could start her photography career by taking photos of Tessa. "And Nate," Jackie said. "Don't forget that he's a kid, too. And pictures of him would certainly sell a lot of portraits." As I was supposed to, I grimaced and pretended I thought Jackie was after young Nate. But, actually, I thought photographing him was a good idea. The art director of my publishing house knew some photographers in the fashion industry. Maybe they'd like to see pictures of beautiful Nate. If the camera loved him, he had a chance at a career that would support him and his arthritis-crippled grandmother.

His grandmother had done well at selling the

junk from the house. It seemed that there were people in the U.S.—and Europe, which surprised me—who wanted old Statues of Liberty, and they were willing to pay for them. When Nate returned from a day of hacking away at the man-eating jungle around my house, he packaged what his grandmother had sold and took them to the post office.

On Sunday morning I was thinking of helping Jackie photograph both Tessa and Nate, and I knew I'd rather do that than spend the day with Dessie and be hit up for some giant bronze statue. Of what? Truthfully, after hearing Dessie's descriptions of her previous sculptures, I liked Jackie's big-mouthed frog idea the best.

When it was time to go to Dessie's, I just left. I started to say goodbye to Jackie, but I didn't. What was I supposed to say? "Bye, hon, see you later"? And, also, I didn't want to hear any more sarcastic remarks. I especially didn't want to hear Jackie tell me about whatever I was going to miss that afternoon. Part of me wanted to tell her that if she had a vision to be sure and call me. But that was like telling an epileptic that if he had a seizure he should call.

I took the car, leaving Jackie with the truck. It wasn't until I got to Dessie's that I realized I had the truck keys. I flipped open my cell phone to tell Jackie I had them, but then I closed the phone. I knew it was wrong of me to leave her with no transportation. I even knew I was being a throwback to a caveman for doing it. On the other hand, who could fight centuries of tradition?

I dredged up a smile and knocked on Dessie's door. She had a pretty house, even if it was a little artsy for my taste. All those wind chimes on the porch would drive me mad.

When Dessie opened the door, I let out my breath. I hadn't been aware of it, but I'd been dreading what she'd wear. Would it be cut down to her belt buckle? But she had on tan pants, fairly loose, and a big pink sweater with a high neck.

"Hi," I said, handing her the bottle of wine Jackie told me I was to take, and following her into the house.

Right away I saw that Dessie seemed nervous about something. She had a table set up in her small dining room that was off her kitchen, with big double glass doors leading onto a brick-floored, covered patio. It was a beautiful day and I wondered why we didn't eat outside.

"Mosquitoes," Dessie said quickly when I asked.

"But I thought—" I began, but stopped. There were so few mosquitoes in the Appalachians that they weren't a problem.

She seated me with my back to the glass door, which made me feel jittery. As a kid, I'd learned to sit with my back to the wall because cousins tended to leap in through windows. All too often I'd been jolted when frogs, snakes, and various colors and textures of pond slime were dropped down my back through the open window behind me.

We had just sat down to eat when a lawn mower was started just outside the door. The resulting noise made it impossible to speak.

"Gardener!" Dessie shouted across the table.

"On Sunday?" I shouted back.

As she started to answer, she looked to the left of my head and out the glass doors, her eyes widening in horror.

I twisted around just in time to see a young man push a mower across a bed of tulips. When he got to the end, the grass littered with chopped-up tulips, he turned to look straight at Dessie and smiled. A malicious smile. A jealous, angry-lover smile.

It was that smile that made me relax. Maybe I should have been angry to realize that Dessie had been flirting with me because she was having a fight with her boyfriend, but I wasn't. When I saw that she was attached, more or less, to a guy who was obviously quite jealous, all I felt was relief.

I pressed the napkin to my lips, said, "Excuse me," then went outside and spoke to the young man. I didn't take time for small talk. I just told him that I wasn't a rival, that it was business only between Dessie and me, and that he could stop razing the tulips.

When he didn't seem to believe that I wasn't insane with lust and love for Dessie, I understood. To me, Pat had been the most beautiful woman on earth, and I never understood why other people didn't think so, too. But Dessie's gardener was young and I wasn't, so he eventually believed me and pushed the mower back into the little shed at the end of the garden. I stayed outside for a few moments while he went inside. After a while, an embarrassed-looking Dessie opened the glass door. I noticed that her lipstick was gone so I guess she and the Lawn Mower Man had made up.

"You can come in now," she said and I smiled. Gone was the aggressive-salesman tone in her voice and gone was the flirt.

I said, **"Now** can we eat outside?" and she laughed.

"You're a nice man," she said and that made me feel good.

We moved food and dishes outside, and we both relaxed and enjoyed each other's company. Unfortunately for me, she'd read all my books so there was nothing new I could tell her about myself. But Dessie was full of stories about her life, both in L.A. and in Cole Creek. She made me laugh about what she'd been through when she was on a soap because the viewers thought she was the tramp she portrayed.

I sipped beer, munched on little puffy, cheesy things she seemed to have an unlimited supply of, and watched her as I listened. The stories she told were hilarious, but they had an often-repeated quality to them, and there was a sadness in her eyes that I couldn't figure out. I'd heard that she'd decided to stay in Cole Creek to pursue her real love, sculpture.

I'm not sure what it was, but something wasn't ringing true. There was a look of longing in her eyes that I couldn't figure out. From the sound of her voice as she told the stories, she'd loved L.A., and loved her job. So why did she give it up? Couldn't she have combined sculpting and acting?

When I asked her that, she just offered me more of the little cheesy things. I said no, but she still jumped up to go get them. When she returned, she told me another funny soap opera story. By three I was getting bored and wondered if it was too early to leave. She must have sensed my restlessness because she suggested I see her studio. It was a separate building, big, modern, beautiful. Through a carved wooden door, we entered a small office, and on the desk was a photograph of two teenage girls laughing and hugging each other. They were Dessie and Rebecca.

I'd almost forgotten that Rebecca worked for Dessie. I started to ask about her, but Dessie opened two wide doors and we went into a marvelous room. It was the size and height of a six stall barn, with light everywhere. Windows ran along one long wall, enormous cabinets along the other. The ceiling had rows of sky-lights, and at both ends of the building were tall, wide, sliding doors.

Dessie had several big projects going, and in one cabinet were a dozen small clays of projects she hadn't yet made. Most of her sculptures were of people. She had a nice one of old men sitting on a park bench that appealed to me. Life-size, I thought, it could be kind of interest-ing in my garden. Tessa and I could play check-ers with the old men.

But before I could ask about it, she reached behind a cabinet frame, withdrew a key, and unlocked a cabinet door. "I only show these to very special people," she said, her eyes twin-kling.

Uh oh, I thought. The erotica. The "collec-tion" of porno.

But when Dessie opened the cabinet and the automatic light came on, I laughed. Actually, I snorted at first, then I let out a real laugh. I looked at Dessie. Could I pick them up? Eyes twinkling even brighter, she nodded yes.

Inside the cabinet were small bronzes of

nearly everyone I'd met in Cole Creek. But they weren't exact likenesses; they were caricatures. They looked like the people, but they also showed their personalities.

The one my hand went to first was a six-inch-tall Mayor. Dessie had exaggerated his strange body and facial features. "Pompous windbag" were the words that came to mind. Dessie had shown him rocking back on his heels, his belly stuck out, his hands clasped behind his back. "You should name it 'Little Emperor,'" I said, and Dessie agreed.

Next I picked up Miss Essie Lee and gave a low whistle. Dessie had shown her as a skeleton. Not a real skeleton, but it was as though Dessie had covered a figure with skin—no muscle or fat—and put Miss Essie Lee's vintage clothes on her.

There were several other statues of people I didn't know, but I could guess their personalities. She told me one was of a former client, an odious man who'd wanted a fawning, self-loving sculpture made of himself. She'd done it, but she'd also made a small one that showed the man with long, narrow teeth and eyes that exuded greed.

"Remind me never to ask you to do a portrait of me," I said.

Dessie was about to close the door when her cell phone rang. She grabbed it out of her belt holster so fast she reminded me of an Old West gunslinger. When she looked at the caller ID, her face lit up, so I was sure it was Lawn Mower Man.

"Go on," I said, giving her permission to leave her guest alone.

After she was out of the room, I shut the cabinet door, but then I saw that below it was another cabinet door that was also locked. On a hunch, I reached behind the door frame where the other key had been hidden and, sure enough, another key was there.

I knew I was snooping, but I could no more have stopped myself than if I were an alcoholic locked overnight in a liquor store. Quickly, I inserted the key and opened the door.

Inside were two items. One was a small bronze of seven people standing in a line: five men and two women. These weren't caricatures; they were realistic. Three of the men were older, one of them quite old, while one was a kid who didn't look too smart. He looked like someone who if you said, "Let's go rob a bank," he'd say, "Sure, why not?"

The two women were both young, but one was as ugly as the other was beautiful. The women stood in the middle of the group, side by side, but not touching. It was easy to see that these two women were not friends.

And what was easier to see was that the ugly

one was either a younger version of Miss Essie Lee or a close relative of hers.

When I heard Dessie laugh in the other room, I started to close the cabinet door. But there was another item in the cabinet with a cloth covering over it.

Maybe it was the writer in me that made me jump to conclusions, but I was sure the seven people in the bronze were the ones who put stones on that poor woman back in 1979. And my writer's mind was spinning with the thought that under that cloth was a casting of the woman who'd been crushed.

As I heard Dessie's returning footsteps, I yanked off the cover—only to reveal a little bronze of Rebecca. She was young and smiling, but it was indeed Rebecca.

Superman would have envied the speed with which I closed those cabinet doors and put the key back in its hiding place. When Dessie returned, I was placidly looking out the glass doors at the shattered tulips.

After her phone call, she got rid of me pretty quickly, so I guessed she and her jealous boyfriend were ready to finish making up. I was glad to go. Maybe Jackie and I could still do something today, I thought.

But as I pulled out of Dessie's driveway, it began to rain and by the time I got home, it was a downpour. I can't describe my disappointment when I found the house was empty. Jackie's big camera bag was gone from the hall closet so I knew where she'd gone.

Without me, I thought. She went on a hike without me.

Or with someone? I thought, and that annoyed me even more. I called Nate's house and his grandmother told me Jackie had called and left a message, but that Jackie wasn't there. I called Allie, but Jackie wasn't there either.

I didn't know who else in Cole Creek to call, so I sat down to wait. When I got hungry, I started making spaghetti—which consisted of dumping a jar of sauce into a pan and turning on the gas.

The pasta was done and the rain was coming down hard, but, still, there was no Jackie. A couple of times the lights flickered in the house, so I got out candles and two flashlights, then made myself a small plate of spaghetti. I'd eat more when Jackie got back and we could eat together and tell each other about our day—as we usually did.

Finally, when it was nearly dark outside, I heard the front door open. I jumped up from the table and ran to the door. When I saw Jackie— and registered that she was safe and unhurt—I put on my best angry-father look and prepared to dump an ocean liner full of guilt on her. How dare she not let me know where she was? She could have been hurt or had a vision. Obviously, I needed to know where she was at all times.

But Jackie never even looked at me. She was covered in her giant yellow poncho, her big pack on her back, just her face peeping out, and her eyes were . . . Well, if I were writing a bad novel, I would have said her eyes were "full of stars."

Whatever her eyes were full of, they certainly were blind. She looked straight ahead, without seeing me, and I'm certainly no small item easily missed. She went toward the stairs—dare I say "as though she were floating"—then up the stairs to her room.

Standing at the bottom, I looked up in wonder. Jackie didn't usually "float." No, she ran and she jumped, and she had an unnatural inclination to climb on rocks and ladders, but she never, ever "floated."

I went up the stairs and stood outside her door for a few moments, contemplating knocking and telling her I'd cooked something. For a moment I allowed myself the pleasure of imagining Jackie's remarks about my cooking, and my ensuing witty replies. And for a few seconds I let myself remember my little fantasy about the black rings of olives on Jackie's pale skin.

I raised my hand to knock, but when I heard her humming and the bathwater running, I put my hand down and went back downstairs. I tried to watch TV, but I was restless and went into the library to search for something fabulous to read instead. Nothing interested me so I went upstairs to my office and turned on my computer.

I'm not sure why I did it, but I logged onto the Internet and went to a search service to see what I could find out about the people who had been alive in Cole Creek in 1979.

I typed in the names of anyone in Cole Creek I could think of, including Miss Essie Lee, and all the names of the seven founding families that I could remember.

What came up on the screen were obituaries—and what I saw shocked me. The head of the Cole family, Abraham, had died in 1980 in a freak accident. He'd been on the highway just outside Cole Creek and had a flat tire. A man driving a truck carrying a load of gravel had stopped to help the old man. But the mechanism that made the bed dump had malfunctioned and the entire load of gravel had dropped onto Abraham Cole and killed him.

I leaned back from the screen, trying to comprehend what I was seeing. Abraham Cole had been crushed to death. By rocks.

Edward Belcher had also died in 1980, when a Wells Fargo truck went around a corner too fast. They had just picked up a load of gold and the weight, combined with the nervousness of the driver, had made him misjudge the angle of the curve. Edward had been waiting for the light to change, and the truck had toppled over on him.

In other words, he'd been crushed to death.

"By money," I said aloud. "As he lived."

I found an article describing the death of Harriet Cole Landreth in a car wreck. Before I read the newspaper account about what had happened, I made a little prediction, and, unfortunately, I was right. She'd been trapped under the weight of her automobile when it tumbled down the side of a mountain. The car wasn't found for two days so Harriet had had a long, slow, lingering death.

Getting up, I walked away from the computer. Revenge? I wondered. Had some relative of the crushed woman taken revenge and seen to it that her murderers died as she had? But how had he done it? I wondered. How could a person arrange for a dump truck to discharge its load? A truck full of gold to tip over? A car to plunge down a mountain and not burn but to crush its passenger?

I went back to the computer and read the end of the article on Harriet Cole's car wreck. She was survived by her husband, her daughter, and her mother, who had been in the car with her. "Mrs. Abraham Cole is in the hospital in critical condition," it said.

Taking a deep breath, I pulled up Harriet Cole's obituary. She'd been only twenty-six years old when she'd died. There were four paragraphs about her family being one of the founders of Cole Creek, and it said that her father had predeceased her. Her mother's name was Mary Hattalene Cole, but there was nothing about her condition at the time of her daughter's funeral. Harriet's husband was listed as Reece Landreth, and her daughter was—

When I saw the name I drew in my breath. Jacquelane Amarisa Cole Landreth. Jacque-LANE. As in Harriet Lane, the president's lovely niece.

Leaving my office in a rush, I went down the stairs so fast I nearly slid. Jackie's bedroom door was still closed, so I tiptoed down to the entrance hall. There on the little table by the door was Jackie's handbag. Every man on earth knows that the ultimate taboo is looking inside a woman's handbag. It ranked right up there with cannibalism. A woman might have her purse stolen, but everyone knew that only a real sicko would actually **go through it.**

I had to take a couple of breaths before I slid the zipper open. As much as Pat and I had shared, I'd never gone through her handbag.

Considering what I was doing, I used as much courtesy as I could muster and pulled her wallet out with just my thumb and forefinger. I told myself I wasn't really snooping. I only wanted one thing: her driver's license.

It was on top, in the little see-through compartment of her wallet. I held it up to the light and looked. Jackie's whole name was Jacquelane Violet Maxwell. JacqueLANE. As in Harriet Lane, the woman her father had a crush on. And Violet was, no doubt, for Miss Lane's violet eyes.

I sat down hard on the chair by the hall table. Congratulations, Newcombe, I told myself. You just found out what you didn't want to know. The woman you hired was almost certainly an eyewitness to a murder. And worse, she probably saw her own mother, as well as her grandfather, commit that murder.

I sat there for a long time, holding Jackie's driver's license, glancing at it now and then, and trying to think about what I may have done. My snooping may have put someone's life in danger. Jackie may have been very young when she saw the murder, but it was obvious that she could remember a lot from the time she was in Cole Creek.

She remembered every inch of the old house I'd bought. Two days ago I'd found her tapping on a wall in the kitchen. I didn't bother to ask what she was doing, but stood in the doorway and watched. After a moment, her tap sounded hollow and she said, "Found it!" She often knew where I was, so I wasn't surprised when she turned and looked at me.

"I went to put the olive oil on the shelf but the shelf wasn't there," she said as she picked up one of the knives I'd bought. It had a serrated blade and the ad said it could cut aluminum cans in half. (It could, too, because Tessa and I had cut through six cans before Jackie made us stop.)

I watched as Jackie felt along the old wallpaper, then began to cut. After about ten minutes of feeling and cutting, she peeled down a big square of wallpaper to reveal a mouse palace. Insulation (probably illegal asbestos), dirt, globbed-up paper, threads, lint, and hair of what looked to be four shades, were all matted together with many years of mouse pee and millions of little black droppings.

Behind the nest were boards so greasy they made my uncle Reg's car repair shop look clean. That's why the shelves were covered over. If it'd been me, and I'd been given a choice between cleaning those shelves and wallpapering over them, I would have definitely wallpapered.

"A good place for food storage," I said.

Turning to me, Jackie made a wicked face while rubbing her hands together. "Mr. Hoover will now do his work," she said as she ran to get the vacuum.

By the time I came down to lunch, the shelves were clean and shiny, and the kitchen smelled like the bleach Jackie had used to clean them.

I didn't bother to ask Jackie how she'd known the shelves were there. And she seemed to take her knowledge for granted. As she dished up some kind of shrimp thing and four steamed vegetables, she ranted on and on about what kind of lazy idiot would board up a closet rather than remove a beehive, and who would cover over shelves just because they had about a hundred years of grease on them.

I put my head closer to my plate.

So, anyway, I knew that Jackie's memories of the time she was in Cole Creek, no matter what her age, were clear. I doubt if any court would convict people for murder based on what Jackie remembered, but then I'd never thought that murderers were logical people who would stop to reason out what they were going to do.

On the other hand, based on what I'd seen on the Internet, everyone who had been involved—or who I thought was probably involved—seemed to have died soon after the woman did.

I put Jackie's license back in her wallet and her wallet back in her handbag just where I'd found it, then zipped her bag closed and went back upstairs.

The search service had found one more name. Miss Essie Lee was the sister of, and the sole surviving relative of, Icie Lee Shaver who had died in yet another "freak" accident. Seems Icie Lee had been walking in the woods and fallen into an old well. She'd been buried to her neck, but the rotten timbers of the old well had held enough that she'd been able to breathe. Eventually, after a day or two, her struggles to free herself had caused the walls to collapse on her.

"Crushed," I said aloud. As they had all murdered, so they had died.

I shut down my computer and went to bed, but I didn't sleep much. The images from the words that had come up on my computer screen haunted me. The words "as they lived" kept running through my head.

At three A.M. I gave up trying to sleep, put my hands behind my head, and stared up at the fan on the ceiling. It was going full speed and I stared at the little wooden end of the chain as though it were a hypnotist's sphere.

As the first ray of sun came in through my window, I thought that if I wanted to know who had crushed that woman, I should read all the obituaries for the year after her death. Based on what I'd found so far, whoever had died by being crushed had probably participated.

When I had things sorted out a bit in my

mind, I began to relax and finally fell asleep. I didn't wake up until noon. When I saw the clock, I felt a sense of panic. Where was Jackie? She was so industrious that I could always hear where she was, but the house was absolutely silent.

I found Jackie sitting at the kitchen table playing with one of the neatest gadgets I'd ever seen in my life. It was a tiny Hewlett-Packard color printer, and beside it was a little camera with a door open on its side.

I'm ashamed to say that, as I sat down at the table and watched that little machine make a perfect print, I forgot all about who got crushed and why. When I started playing with the two pieces of equipment, Jackie didn't say a word, just got up from the table and began scrambling eggs.

The printer was very simple to use, and by the time Jackie put the eggs in front of me, I'd made two 4 x 6 enlargements. One was of roses on a fence, and the other was a photo of a red and white tablecloth, a wine bottle, and half a loaf of bread.

"This what you did yesterday?" I asked, smiling. A picnic by herself?

But my question seemed to disturb Jackie because she snatched the little disk out of the printer, stuck it back in the camera, pushed some buttons, then put the camera back on the table. I knew without a doubt that she'd just erased the two photos of the picnic. As for the photos I'd printed, she burned them in the flame on the stove.

Of course I was dying to ask questions, but I didn't. Besides, Jackie gave me a look that said that if I asked anything, she'd make me sorry.

That was okay, I had my own secrets. I never even considered telling Jackie what I'd found out on the Internet. I also wasn't going to tell her that Harriet Cole's daughter had the same unique spelling of her name that Jackie did.

For the next two days, all I can say about Jackie's behavior is that it was odd. She didn't act like herself. Not that I'd spent masses of time with her, but after the Sunday I spent with Dessie, Jackie seemed to change. It was as though her mind was elsewhere. She cooked three meals a day for me, and she answered the telephone, and she even told Nate what to do in the garden, but there was something different. For one thing, she was quiet, hardly ever saying a word. And for another, she wasn't moving around much. Three times I looked out my office window and saw her just standing there, staring into space. It was like seeing a humming-bird with its wings still, motionless.

Of course I asked her what was wrong, but she just looked off into the distance and said, "Mmmm."

I tried to get a reaction out of her. I told her Dessie and I'd had a fabulous time together on Sunday. No comment from Jackie. I told her Dessie and I'd had great sex together. "Mmmm," was all Jackie said as she kept staring into space. I told her I was running away with Dessie to Mexico and we were taking Tessa with us. No comment. I told Jackie I was in love with a green-eyed grizzly bear and she was heavy with my child. Jackie said, "That's nice," then wandered outside.

On Wednesday, she took some snapshots of Nate with that new camera of hers—I didn't say so but I was a little hurt that she'd bought that and the tiny printer without letting me help choose them. When we saw the photos, Nate looked like something out of a fashion magazine. And that was without a bath.

When I tried to talk to him about the possibility of a future in the fashion world, he wouldn't consider it. I understood. What self-respecting male wanted a job being photographed? On the other hand, the money could be very good. I wanted Jackie to talk to him, but she stood at the far end of the garden and wouldn't get involved.

On Thursday morning the FedEx package from the man in Charlotte finally arrived. Part of me wanted to open it and part of me wanted to burn it instead.

I'd had a couple of days to think about the situation now. I'd decided that some very angry people had piled rocks on a woman back in 1979, and that Jackie, as a child, had seen it all. After the murder, I think someone played vigilante and somehow, one by one, killed all the people who had committed the murder.

If my theory was correct, then Jackie was in no danger. And as far as I could tell, she knew nothing about the later vendetta killings. She knew only about the crushing.

Jackie also knew the reason her mother, who was probably one of the murderers, gave to justify killing the woman. She'd said that people who loved the devil **had** to die.

The devil made me do it, I thought. Isn't that the reason that's been given for so many murders over the centuries? "It wasn't my fault," I heard people on news programs say. "The devil controlled my mind." When I first met Jackie she'd told me that the townspeople believed a woman had been in love with the devil.

I put my hand over my eyes. If Jackie was safe, then we could stay. But if we stayed, I knew myself well enough to know that I'd dig until I found out the truth about why that woman had been killed. What **human** emotion had driven them to murder? And I deeply wanted to know who had avenged her death.

With shaking hands, I opened the FedEx

package. The top page was a letter of apology. The man had been ill so he was late in sending the material, but he hoped I'd still send the autographed books. That's one for him, I thought. I hadn't been ill, I'd just forgotten to send the books.

The photograph of the remade skeleton was what I wanted to see, and it was at the bottom of the stack. When I pulled it out, I saw the face of a pretty woman, probably late thirties, and I had no doubt she was a relative of Jackie's. When Jackie was the same age, she was going to look a lot like this woman.

As I stood there looking at the picture, I tried to figure out who she was—other than the woman on the bridge, that is. She wasn't Jackie's mother because I was pretty sure her mom had been crushed by a car.

I flipped through the papers the man had sent me. "Unknown" was everywhere. She was an unknown woman and it was unknown whether her death was an accident or a murder. The police might have been able to figure it out by the way the stones were on top of her, but by the time the police had arrived, the kids who'd found the body had removed them all. It seems the girl who'd "heard" the crying during the night had been screaming hysterically that they needed to "let the poor woman out," so **all** the stones had been taken off the skeleton.

The police had interviewed the kids and each of them had been positive about the way the stones had been arranged. But half had been positive one way, and the other half were sure of another way. In the end, the evidence had been "inconclusive."

I looked at the names of the kids and wondered what I'd find out if I put them through a search service. Even as I was telling myself I shouldn't do such a thing, I turned toward the stairs to go up to my office.

But I was stopped when Tessa threw open the front door, and, running full speed, leaped up on me, her legs around my waist, her arms tight around my neck.

"Thank you, thank you, thank you," she said, kissing me all over my face.

I had no idea what she meant but it was nice. She wasn't old enough to have developed pretenses, so whatever she was feeling came out honestly and openly.

"What?" I asked, smiling. The whole packet about the murdered woman had been knocked out of my hands and was now spread on the floor under my feet. I wanted to leave it there and hoped it fell through the cracks.

I pulled Tessa's arms from around my neck so I could breathe. "Thanks for what?"

"The gnome."

I didn't know what she was talking about.

When we'd bought the garden statues, we'd spent quite a bit of time debating about gnomes, but I was pretty much against them. When I was in the first grade, Johnnie Foster and I'd had a fight when he'd said I looked like a gnome. I'd never heard the word before so I asked the school librarian and she'd handed me a book. I didn't like what I saw.

Truthfully, I was afraid Tessa wanted gnomes in the garden because she liked **me.**

I peeled Tessa off my body, stood her on the floor, and began picking up the papers.

"Who's that?" she asked, looking down at the photo of the recreated face. As with most kids, Tessa conserved her energy and didn't help me pick up the papers.

"Just somebody," I said, shoving all the papers back into the cardboard envelope. I didn't want Jackie to see anything inside the packet, so I put it in plain sight on the hall table. I figured that if I hid it inside a book in the library on the top shelf, she'd find it in about three seconds.

"Okay," I said to Tessa. "What's this all about?"

"You bought the biggest gnome statue in the whole world and put him in the garden. He's wonderful and I love him. Thank you."

For a nanosecond it flashed through my mind that Jackie had got together with Dessie and commissioned a gnome statue. Sure. And a frog was coming next week.

I put my hand out for Tessa to take and we walked out to the garden together.

She was right.

Sitting in the shade on one of the old park benches Nate had repaired was what looked to be a gnome. Standing, it would have been about five foot four, with a big head, a powerful torso and short, strong limbs. The eyes were wide open, but sightless, the mouth slightly open. It had big eyes with thick lashes, a wide nose with a horizontal end, full lips, huge ears flat to the head, and long black and gray hair pulled back into a braid.

"Ssssh," Tessa said, pulling me by the hand. "He looks real, doesn't he?"

I let her lead me around the bushes to see the rest of the "gnome." He had on dark green pants, a worn yellow shirt, and a purple vest that was covered with hundreds of little enameled pins of insects. An entomologist's dream.

While Tessa went forward to get closer to the creature, I stood back and stared. He wasn't a statue, but a man. And he was sound asleep. He was sitting upright on a bench, his eyes wide open, but he was asleep.

Way inside my mind I knew I should be telling Tessa he was real and that she should get away from him, but I couldn't seem to move. Of course I knew who he was. It was just that I'd never seen him in person before.

Reaching out, Tessa touched the man's cheek. He didn't so much as move an eyelash, but I saw that he instantly went from asleep to awake. A light came into his eyes and he was looking at me.

"Hello, son," said my father.

"Hello, cousin," said my cousin Noble as he stepped out of the bushes.

Both of them were smiling at me.

CHAPTER FOURTEEN

Jackie

All I wanted was to be with Russell. He made me feel good in a way I'd never felt before.

All my life I'd been accused of being angry. So many women I'd met had decided to play therapist and tell me that my sarcastic remarks stemmed from a deep anger inside me.

I could agree with that, but what I didn't agree with was when they said I should "let it all out." They weren't happy when I refused to tell them my deepest secrets. I think they thought I wasn't playing the girl-game by the girl-rules, which clearly state that everybody has to tell everybody else everything.

The truth was that I had no reason for my anger. The bad that had happened to me wasn't all that bad and in fact, I felt guilty for having any anger at all. In one town my dad and I'd lived in for a couple of years while I was in high school, my best friend confessed to me that her father got into bed with her at night and "did it" to her. She swore me to secrecy before she told me, but I didn't keep my word. I told my dad.

When the dust settled from the turmoil my father raised, he and I left that town.

No, I had nothing deep-seated to be angry over. It was just that for most of my childhood I'd felt torn in half. I loved my dad a lot, but I was also angry at him for not telling me about myself. As I'd grown up and seen and read about what went on in the world, I realized that something awful must have happened to make my father take me away in the middle of the night. All I wanted was for him to tell me what it was.

But whenever I hinted at wanting to know about my mother, or the aunt he'd mentioned, my dad would either mumble something that contradicted what he'd said before or he'd clam up. It used to make me furious! It was especially infuriating because I could talk to him about anything else in the world. As I grew up, we girls would loftily inform each other about the birds and the bees. Then I'd go home and tell my dad every word, and he'd tell me what was true or not. Later, the girls would say, "You asked your **dad** that?!"

But my dad wasn't embarrassed by anything. One time he said, "I used to be normal. Long ago I was like your girlfriends' fathers and was embarrassed by sex and other private matters. But when you go through what I did, it puts life in perspective."

Of course I asked him what he was talking about. What had he been through? But he wouldn't tell me.

So I had to control my anger over my father's refusal to tell me about our past. And I had to conceal my resentment over the fact that my father and I seemed to belong nowhere and to no one. How much I envied my friends' families. I used to fantasize about huge Christmas dinners with fifty relatives at the table. I would listen avidly to my friends describing the "horror" of their holidays. They told how this cousin had done that dreadful thing, and that uncle had made their mother cry, and that aunt had worn a dress that shocked everyone.

It all sounded wonderful to me.

My father was a real loner. He and Ford would have been great friends. They could have hidden inside books together. My father had his love for Harriet Lane who was long dead, and Ford had his late wife to love. That a sculpture of her could reduce him to tears showed how much he still loved her.

Oh, well. Ford's problems had bothered me

until the Sunday I met Russell Dunne. With Russell, I felt a kinship that I'd never felt with another man. Physically, he was just my type: dark, elegant, and refined in a way that reminded me of my father. And Russell and I had so much in common, like photography and our love of nature. And we both liked the same kind of food. I hated the term "soul mate," but that's what flashed through my mind when I thought of Russell.

After I got home on Sunday night, I spent about an hour in the tub. When the water grew cold, I got out, put on my best nightgown and robe, and sat on the little porch off my bedroom for a while. The night seemed especially warm and fragrant, and the fireflies looked like little jewels sparkling in the velvet air.

Just having such sappy thoughts almost made me sick. When other females had said dopey things like that about some guy, I'd nearly barfed. I even refused to read novels that were about falling in love with a man. "Check his references," I'd say, then close the book.

Of course I'd done all the logical things with Kirk and had planned everything carefully, yet I'd still been hornswoggled. But at least I'd never rhapsodized about the color of his eyes or the "cute little way his nose crinkles." Gag me with a spoon.

I could have gone on and on about Russell

Dunne, though. His eyes had little flecks of gold in them that caught the sunlight when he moved his head. His skin was the color of honey warmed in the sun. His beautiful hands looked as though they could play the music of angels.

Et cetera. I could go on—and did in my thoughts—but I tried to force myself to stop. I really tried to get my mind off of Russell and put it on my work—whatever my work was. I was still waiting for Ford to tell me how he wanted me to help him with his writing, but he never said anything. Instead, I was a sort of housekeeper cum hostess. Basically, if Ford didn't want to do it, it was my job.

On Monday, the day after I met Russell, I had a hard time keeping my mind on anything. There was a lot to do outside, and I still hadn't tackled the library and gone through the books in there. And of course I needed to go to the grocery. Also, I wanted to call Allie and set up a time for Tessa to come and pose for me so I could get my photography studio started.

On Saturday my mind had been full of all the things I wanted to do, but after Sunday, I couldn't seem to remember any of them. Instead, I sat at the kitchen table and spent what seemed to be hours looking at the little printer Russell had lent me. He'd slipped a pack of photo paper in my bag, and after fiddling with the machine, I managed to produce an index print showing tiny, numbered pictures of every photo on the disk. I sat there staring at the pictures until I'd memorized them. Maybe I was hoping that a photo of Russell would appear on the disk, but it didn't.

Ford came thundering downstairs sometime during the day—I hadn't even put on my watch—and took over the printer. He had a real knack with machines so he figured out how to operate it in seconds. He punched buttons and out came a big photo of the picnic Russell had laid out on the sweet grass.

I don't know what got into me, but I shoved that disk back into the camera and pushed the little garbage can icon as fast as I could. There was something so private about that scene that I didn't want anyone else to see it. And I knew that if I let him, Ford would make derogatory comments about our lovely picnic. Where was the fried chicken? he'd ask, thinking he was being amusing. The cooler full of beer? What kind of picnic was it with just a bunch of cheese and crackers?

No, I didn't want to hear his comments.

In my haste, what I didn't realize was that I was spiting myself. After I erased them from the disk, and burned the photos, including the index print, I had nothing for **me** to look at.

But such was my euphoria that I didn't get upset over my stupidity. Oh, well, I thought, I had my memories. And that thought nearly made me burst into song.

I carried Russell's card with his name and telephone number inside my bra, on the left over my heart. There wasn't a minute of the day that I didn't want to call him. But I had an iron-clad rule: I didn't call men.

Of course I called Ford. I called him from the grocery on the cell phone he'd given me and asked if he wanted roast beef or pork roast. (He said, "I thought pork was cooked in a skillet.") I called him from the fruit stand to ask if he liked yellow squash. ("This is a joke, right?") And I called him from the service station to ask what kind of oil to put in the car. ("Don't let those monkeys touch my car. **I** will change the oil.")

I could call Ford because I wasn't trying to impress him. Long ago I'd learned that you never called men you really, really wanted. Not for any reason. If you saw smoke coming out of his house, you called his neighbors and got them to save him. But you don't call a man.

I'd learned this lesson from years of living with a handsome, single man: my father. Sometimes I thought he moved from one place to another just to escape the women who pursued him. I was eleven before I knew what a kitchen was. My dad and I never had to use one because single women gave us food. "I had this left over and I thought you and your adorable little girl would like some," they'd say. One time I looked at the perfectly cooked casserole and asked how it could be "left over" when none of it was missing. My dad, who sometimes had a wicked sense of humor, had stood there and let the poor woman flounder about in her attempt to answer me.

Truthfully, they didn't care about feeding my dad as much as they wanted a reason to call and ask after their "favorite dish." Always, but always, the women delivered food to my dad in their "favorite dish," as doing so gave them a reason to come back. Or call. Then call again. When we moved into a town, it wasn't unusual for my dad to change his telephone number four times in three months.

So, anyway, when I was growing up, I made a sacred promise to myself to never call a man I was interested in. I was sure that a man as beautiful as Russell Dunne had calls all night long, so I wanted to be different, unique.

I needn't have worried because Russell stopped by the house on Tuesday afternoon. I quickly maneuvered him into my studio because I didn't want Ford to see him. I couldn't imagine Ford being gracious about another man being around "his" assistant.

"I hope I didn't interrupt you," Russell said in that soft, silky voice of his.

Why hadn't I done something with my hair? I asked myself. "No, not at all," I managed to say. I wanted to offer him food. Actually, I wanted to offer him my whole life, but I thought I should start with lemonade. But Ford's meanderings were unpredictable so he could possibly wander into the kitchen while Russell was there.

"So where are your photos?" he asked, smiling at me in a way that made my heart flutter.

"You'll be my first," I said as I grabbed my dear F100, aimed and snapped. Isn't automatic focus great? I thought.

But I knew from the sound of the click that the picture hadn't taken. I glanced down at the LCD panel. No film.

No, I didn't burst into tears.

Russell was shaking his head at me and smiling. "You are truly naughty," he said in a way that made me blush. If Ford had said those same words I would have said something about dirty old men, but when they came out of Russell's mouth they were sexy.

"I want to see everything," Russell said and I started talking.

I showed him the equipment Ford and I had chosen, and I told him Ford's idea of putting retractable awnings over the windows. I told him about the afternoon Ford and I had painted the interior of the storage room, and how Ford and Nate had put the shelves up for me.

"You seem pretty attached to this man," Russell said.

I nearly fell for that trick, but since I'd seen my father use it a thousand times with a thousand women, I caught myself. I used to look away in embarrassment when a woman would turn verbal somersaults as she tried to make my father believe that there was no other man in her life.

"Yeah, I am," I said, looking at the floor as though Russell had pried some great secret out of me. I tilted my head up to see how he was taking this news. I was pleased to see that he was looking a little surprised. Good, I thought, since I didn't want him to know how I felt about him.

"I guess I'll just have to try harder, won't I?" he said, smiling.

I took a tiny step toward him, but Russell looked at his watch.

"I have to go," he said, and was at the door before I could reach him. Pausing, he stood there for a moment, a ray of sunlight on his cheek. "Jackie," he said softly. "I think I said too much the other day about . . . You know."

I did know. About the woman who was crushed. "That's all right," I said. "I don't mind."

"It was all long ago and—" Breaking off, he gave me a grin that made me weak-kneed. "Besides, who knows? The woman may actually have been in cahoots with the devil. I heard she used to have visions."

"Visions?" I said, blinking fast and not trusting my voice. He was trying to be lighthearted, but I wasn't feeling very light. In fact, I wanted to sit down.

"Yeah. She had visions of evil deeds. No one in town could do anything bad because she saw what they were going to do **before** they did it."

I swallowed. "But wouldn't visions like that be a gift from God? To be able to stop evil would be from God, wouldn't it?"

"Perhaps," he said. "I think it started out that way, but her visions got stronger until she began to see the evil in people's minds. It was said that she—" Breaking off, he waved his hand, as though he meant to say no more.

"What?" I whispered. "What did she do?"

"My father said she started **preventing** people from doing what she saw in their minds."

I didn't like to think about what that meant. I put my hands to my temples.

"I've upset you," Russell said. "I knew I shouldn't have told you about what happened. It's just that I've carried these secrets so long and you seem so caring. It's as though . . ." He didn't finish his sentence.

"I am," I said. "It's just—" I didn't want to say what was in my head. I couldn't very well tell him that I'd had two visions, a car wreck and a fire. What if I next saw that someone was plotting to kill someone else? How would I stop it?

Russell looked at his watch again. "I really must go. Are you sure you're okay?"

"Yes, I'm fine," I said, trying to smile.

"How about lunch this weekend?" he asked. "Another picnic? And **no** ghost stories."

"Promise?" I said.

"Sacred honor. I'll call you to set up time and place." Then, with one more brilliant flash of a smile, he was gone.

Leaning back against the wall, I tried to still my pounding heart. The first vision had upset me a lot, and when I'd seen it in reality, I'd been shocked into immobility. The second time, Ford had been there and the whole thing had been almost fun.

But what would happen if—?

"Who were you talking to?"

I turned to see Tessa standing in the doorway. She was a funny little kid who talked little. Except to Ford. The two of them seemed to be on the same circuit board so they agreed on everything. Allie said she'd never seen anything like it. She'd always bemoaned the fact that her daughter was antisocial and wouldn't talk to adults or her peers. But Ford and Tessa were often together, doing things like looking inside some hole in the ground and speculating as to what was inside it.

"A man," I said to Tessa.

She didn't ask any more questions, but during the day I saw her looking at me oddly a couple of times. I ignored her. I knew from experience that to ask Tessa anything would only get me silence and a blank stare.

One time Allie was watching Ford's feet disappear as he slithered on his belly into some dungeon of greenery he and Tessa had made, and she gave a huge sigh. "My daughter is hungry for male companionship."

I leaped on the chance to find out about her former marriage. After all, I'd told Allie about Kirk. Truthfully, Allie was the only woman I'd revealed more to than I'd learned from. "Does Tessa see her father often?" I asked.

"Rarely," Allie said quickly, then turned and walked away. And that was all the info I could get out of her.

So I ignored Tessa's funny looks at me on Tuesday and got her to pose. At least I got her to pose after Ford told her she should do it.

I wish I could describe how good my photos of Tessa came out. It was one of those cosmic things that happens now and then. I think that if I'd been myself that day the pictures wouldn't have been half as good. Usually, I tend to be a bit anal about depth-of-field and light meter readings, but that day I was so distracted that I didn't think about adjusting every knob on my camera.

My camera had a depth-of-field preview button, so I just pushed that, and when Tessa and the background looked okay, I pushed the remote cord and took the shot.

Maybe Tessa caught my mood that day. Usually, she was impatient to be off and doing her own thing, so I'd thought of what I could use to bribe her to get her to sit in front of a camera. A gift certificate to that garden store where she and Ford had bought the truckload of ugly little statues?

But I didn't have to bribe her that afternoon because Tessa seemed to be as much in a dream-like state as I was. My attention wandered as I thought about Russell Dunne. I imagined wearing a ball gown—not that I owned one or had ever worn one—and waltzing in the moonlight with him.

I sat Tessa in an old chair by the window, gave her a book to read, then snapped pictures. Not too many pictures and not too quickly because my mind wasn't moving that fast. Instead of scurrying around and adjusting hair and reflectors as I usually did, I just let things be.

Tessa and I hardly said a word in the three hours that I took pictures of her. Usually, I'd take an hour and six times the photos I took that day, but I was so dreamy that I moved in slow motion, and the result was more time but fewer photos.

After a while, Tessa and I moved outside. She stretched out on the grass in the dappled shade of a tree and looked up at the overhead leaves. Had I been myself that day I would have straddled her and given her a thousand directions about how to look, where to look, and even what to think. But since I wasn't my usual bossy self, I just let Tessa do whatever she wanted and trusted my camera to perform.

That night Ford stayed in his office late, so I went to my studio and started developing my black-and-whites of Tessa. When that first photo came into focus I knew I had something. With a capital S: Something.

I was still moving at half speed, but I was awake enough to see that I'd finally done what I'd always dreamed of doing: I'd captured a mood. I'd put a personality on paper. Not just a face, but a whole person.

As I stood there looking at those wet pictures, I learned a lot in an instant. Whenever I'd photographed kids previously, I'd done it fast because they move a lot and get bored quickly. "Look at me! Look at me!" I was always saying, then snapping rolls of film as fast as I could push the button.

Maybe a photographer had to do that with some kids, but there were also children like Tessa. She was an introverted, moody child, and today, purely by accident, I'd been in the same state, so I'd caught it on film.

The photos were good. Very, very good. Maybe even, win-a-prize good. I had some close-ups of Tessa that were so beautiful they brought tears to my eyes. And as I looked at those pictures, I saw why Allie and I got silence from Tessa, while Ford got invited into the secret house.

Allie and I were alike. We were doers and movers. Ford could sit in the same chair for twelve hours, but I couldn't sit in one place for more than thirty minutes. For me, reading was easiest when I was on a treadmill. There was a world going on inside Tessa's head and Ford saw it. Today, I had captured Tessa's inner world on film.

I left the photos hanging in the studio, wandered into the house, and up to bed, smiling all the way. Obviously, Russell was good for me. Being around him had put me in this state where I could be quiet long enough to listen to Tessa with my camera.

It wasn't until I was getting ready for bed that I remembered what Russell had said about Amarisa having visions. I remembered my fright when he'd told me about her seeing evil in a person's mind. Again, I wondered what I'd do if that happened to me.

As I slipped on my nightgown, I thought that if I had another vision maybe I'd tell Russell about it. Maybe I'd break my ironclad rule and call him and tell him what I'd seen. Maybe he'd understand. Maybe that would be a way Russell and I could form a bond. A forever bond.

Smiling, I climbed into bed and went to sleep.

On Wednesday, I was still wandering about in a daze. I'm not sure what I did all day, but everything seemed to take twice as long as usual. Ford said, "What the hell is wrong with you?" and I had enough presence of mind to say, "PMS." I guessed correctly that that statement would make him back off. He didn't comment on my mood again.

I didn't show Ford the pictures I'd taken of Tessa. When they were dry, I slipped them inside a big portfolio because I wanted to show them to Russell first. After all, he and I shared a love of photography, didn't we?

In the afternoon, I used the little digital to snap some photos of Nate in the garden. He was sweaty, had flecks of grass on his face, and he was squinting at the sun, so I was sure the pictures would be awful. While I cooked dinner, Ford ran the photos off on Russell's little printer.

I was removing a dish of sweet potatoes from the oven (coated in brown sugar, swimming in marshmallows, the only way Ford would eat them) when he held a photo in front of my face. It was impossible to believe, but Nate was better looking on film than he was in person. He was only seventeen, but on film he looked about thirty, and he was handsome in a way that made your breath catch.

I put the potatoes on top of the stove and looked at the photo while Ford ran off more. When he had a stack of them—and each one was gorgeous—he said he'd send them to the art director at his publishing house.

But the next morning when Ford showed the photos to Nate and said he might have a modeling career ahead of him, Nate said he couldn't leave Cole Creek. He said it as though it were an unchangeable fact, then he turned on the lawn mower and began to cut.

Standing to one side, I watched Ford turn the mower off and start talking to Nate in a fatherly way. I was too far away to hear all of it, but I caught phrases like "deciding your future" and "this is your chance" and "don't throw this away." Nate looked at Ford with an unreadable face, listened politely, and said, "Sorry, I can't," then turned on the mower again.

Ford looked at me as though to ask if I knew what was going on, but I just shrugged. I figured Nate was really saying that he couldn't leave his grandmother. She'd raised him and she'd be alone if Nate left town. But my impression of his grandmother was that the last thing she'd want was a grandson who'd sacrificed his future for her.

I decided to let Ford handle it. He was pretty good at talking to people, so I figured he'd eventually get Nate to come around. Besides, I didn't have time to get involved. I needed to go to the grocery to buy food for Ford—and for the picnic with Russell. He hadn't called yet, but when he did, I wanted to be ready. I planned to take enough food that Russell and I could stay out all day long. Just the two of us. Alone in the woods.

So I left Ford to talk to Nate while I went to the grocery. When I returned hours later, the house was empty. There was an open FedEx envelope on the hall table and I figured it was "maintenance," as Ford called it. His publishing house often sent him paperwork that he had to approve or disapprove about his books, which were all still selling after all these years.

As usual, I lugged all the groceries in by myself. After a glare at my cell phone because it still hadn't given me a call from Russell, I put away all the groceries, then went to the sink to get myself a glass of delicious well water.

When I turned the handle, it came off in my hand, and water came shooting up, hitting me in the face. I threw open the doors below the sink and tried to turn the water off, but I couldn't budge the rusty old knobs.

I ran out of the house shouting for Ford, but when I reached the garden, I was drawn up short by the most extraordinary sight. Ford and Tessa were standing side by side, looking at two men I'd never seen before.

One man was standing behind the old bench Nate had repaired. He was tall and ruggedly handsome in that country-and-western way that made some women swoon.

Sitting on the bench in front of him was a little man who looked like Ford—if you saw him in a fun house mirror, that is. Every one of Ford's features was exaggerated. On this little man, Ford's thick eyelashes were like one of those sleepy-eyed dolls. And Ford's rather nice lips were like a nursing baby's. And his nose! Yes, Ford's nose was a bit unusual, but it was small enough that no one noticed it. But this man's nose looked as though a miniature hot dog had been placed crosswise on the end of it, then smoothed out.

When I first saw the man sitting there, my face and hair wet, water dripping into my eyes, I thought he wasn't real. I wanted to say crossly to Ford and Tessa that they had to take that huge statue back to the store and get a full refund.

But as I wiped water out of my eyes, the stout little creature turned his head and blinked at me.

It was then that I knew who the men were. The handsome one, the one with the face that looked as if he could write songs about his "honky-tonk life," was called "King" in Ford's books. As in "King Cobra." Ford had described him well enough that I recognized him—and I remembered that he hadn't been portrayed as a good guy.

As for the little man, he was Ford's father. In his books, Ford called him "81462"—which was the number on his shirt in the prison where he'd been since before the hero's birth.

The man in back, the country-and-western singer, said to me, "Is something wrong?" He had a voice that was filled with every cigarette he'd ever smoked and every smoky bar he'd ever been in. And he had an accent so thick I could hardly understand him.

"Sink," I said, suddenly remembering that the kitchen of my beautiful house was being flooded. "The sink!" Days of lethargy left me; I was myself again. I sprinted back toward the kitchen, four people close behind me.

"You got a monkey wrench?" the younger man said to Ford as soon as all of us were in the kitchen. There was contempt in his voice: a blue-collar worker's contempt for a white-collar worker. The water was shooting up to the ceiling and these two men were about to get into a socialist war.

The little man, 81462, grabbed a cookie sheet off the countertop and directed the spray of water out the open window over the sink. Smart, I thought. Why hadn't **I** thought of that?

"Course he's got tools. He's a Newcombe," Number 81462 said.

At least I think that's what he said. I could have understood Gullah more easily than his twang.

Ford disappeared into the pantry for a moment and returned with a heavy, rusty wrench that was probably new when the house was built. I'd never seen it before and wondered where he'd found it.

Two minutes later, the water was stopped and the five of us stood there on the flooded floor, staring at each other and having no idea of what to say.

Tessa spoke first. She seemed to be fascinated with 81462, couldn't take her eyes off him. "Praying mantis?" she asked, and I wondered what she was talking about.

81462's eyes started twinkling in a way that made him as cute as a . . . Well, as cute as a garden gnome. Or a bug's ear. Or a—

Turning slightly, he said, "Halfway down."

I was trying to understand his dialect—it was too strong to be called an accent—when I noticed his vest for the first time. It was covered with hundreds of little enameled pins of insects. They were all about the same size and as far as I could see, there were no two alike.

"Centipede," Tessa said, and 81462 lifted his left arm to show a centipede.

I couldn't believe it, but out of my mouth came "Japanese beetle"—the bane of my gardening life.

When Number 81462 looked at me, smiling, I couldn't help smiling back. He was just so cute!

"Right here." He lifted up the tip of his vest. "Where I can see that he don't eat nothin' good."

I don't know why, but I kind of melted. Maybe it was because of all the drippy-movie hormones that Russell had released in me. "Are you two hungry?" I asked. "I just went to the grocery and—"

"They're not staying," Ford said. Or, actually, grunted.

When I looked at him, his face was as hard as the steel in his truck, and his eyes were flashing angrily. But you know what I'd learned about Ford Newcombe? He had a heart made out of marshmallow cream. He complained and he bellyached about a lot of things, but his actions never fit his words. I'd seen him risk his life to save a bunch of teenagers who were strangers. And I well knew he wasn't researching his devil story because he feared I was involved.

"Nonsense," I said. "Of course they're staying. They're **family.**" I wanted a family more than life, and I was damned if I was going to stand aside and watch Ford throw his out because of some silly childhood arguments.

"Lightning bug," Tessa said, ignoring the adult drama playing around her.

81462 crooked one of his short fingers at her and Tessa waded through the water on the floor to stand before the man. Bending so the upper part of his vest was right before her eyes, he reached inside, pushed something, and the tail of a lightning bug lit up.

Tessa looked at it in awe for a moment, then turned to Ford. I didn't have a mirror in the kitchen, but my guess was that she and I were wearing identical expressions. Of course they'd stay.

When he saw Tessa's face, Ford's marshmallow cream heart turned to liquid. Throwing up his hands in defeat, he left the kitchen.

For a moment the four of us stood there in silence, then Country-and-western said, "Ma'am, do you have a mop?"

"Sure," I said, blinking at being called "ma'am."

Tessa took 81462's hand and pulled him outside, leaving Country-and-western and me alone. He took one of the two mops I got out of the closet, and from the efficient way he used it, I could tell he'd done it before. We worked in silence, with him doing most of the work.

"Noble," he said as he wrung out the mop into the bucket.

"I beg your pardon?"

"My name is Noble."

"Ah," I said, thinking that that's why Ford had named his character "King."

"When my mother was carryin' me she heard somethin' that was in a book. 'The nobles of the land were new come to God.' Since my daddy's name was Newcombe, she called me Noble."

I stopped mopping. "I like that. It's sort of a prayer."

"I never thought of it that way, but I guess it is." He stopped mopping for a moment to look at me. "And I take it you're Ford's new wife?"

I smiled at that. "No. His assistant."

"Assistant?" Noble asked, his voice full of disbelief.

Isn't marriage strange? I thought. In front of this man I'd snapped at Ford and ordered him around. Therefore, it was assumed we were married. So where was "love and honor" in that formula?

"Yes. His assistant," I said firmly. "Jackie Maxwell."

"Nice to meet you, Miss Maxwell," he said, wiping off his hand on his jeans before he held it out for me to shake.

I did the same thing and shook his hand. Now that Ford was no longer in the room, the arrogance and hostility were gone from his eyes and he seemed nice.

"So . . . ?" I began. "You and Mr. Newcombe are . . . ?"

"Toodles just got released from—" He looked up at me to see how my pure, easily-shocked, middle-class morals were going to take the coming revelation.

"Prison," I said. "I know." Truthfully, the name "Toodles" shocked me more than the idea of prison.

"Yeah, prison," Noble said. "And the truth is, he ain't got no home."

Oh, dear, I thought. Ford wasn't going to like this. His father to **live** with him? "And you?" I asked.

Noble shrugged in a self-deprecating way. "I take care of myself. Tumble about the country. Do odd jobs."

"I see," I said, wringing out my mop. "You're dead broke so you volunteered to take, uh . . . Toodles to his rich son in hopes you'd get a . . . what? A loan? Or do you want a place to stay?"

When Noble looked up at me, I could see the "King" Ford had written about, a man who "could charm the pants off any female."

But I was in no danger. Between liking Ford so much and living in a daydream over a handsome stranger, my psyche didn't have room for another man.

"You **sure** you ain't married to my cousin?" Noble asked.

"Double sure. So tell me what you're after and if I like it I might help you." I didn't say so, but it was my opinion that Ford needed family as much as I did. To hear him talk, he despised his family. On the other hand, Ford was so deeply involved with his relatives that he'd written books about them.

I could see that Noble was debating whether or not to tell me the truth. I had a feeling that "truth" and "women" weren't two words he thought of as belonging together.

After a while he sighed as though his decision had been made. "I need a place to live. I've had a little trouble at home, and, well, I ain't exactly welcome there right now."

I lifted my eyebrows and made a guess. "Nine months kind of trouble?"

Looking down at the floor, Noble gave a little smile. "Yes, ma'am. One of my uncles has a new wife, and she's real young and real pretty, and reeaaaal lonely and . . ." Breaking off, he looked up and gave me a little what-could-I-do? kind of grin.

I thought about what he'd just revealed and wondered why I'd ever craved a family.

"Ford won't like this," I said.

"I understand," Noble said, then, slowly, dramatically, he leaned his mop against the kitchen cabinet. When he turned away, his shoulders were slumped and his head was down so low he looked like a turtle retracting into its shell.

"You ought to go on the stage," I said to his back. "I haven't seen such bad acting since I was in the fourth grade. Okay, what can you do to earn your keep?"

When he turned around to look at me, I saw what I was sure was the **real** Noble. Gone was the slump; he was standing up straight and proud.

"I could put this rat trap of a house back together," he said. Also gone was his meek attitude—and so was half his accent. "In one stint in the poky I worked in the bakery."

I wasn't going to be so uncool as to say, "And what did you do to get put into jail?" I decided to test him. I said, "Tell me how to make a croissant."

With a little smile he described—accurately— how to make a croissant with the butter between the layers.

I hated to be redundant even in my own mind, but all I could think was, Ford isn't going to like this.

"Look," I said after a while, "you rummage around, find what you need, and start baking. The richer and more gooey the things you make, the better. This plan calls for some sweetening-up of the boss."

And exchange of information, I thought. If there was anything Ford liked better than high-fat food, it was information. I knew he was aware that I'd been withholding info from him lately, so if I wanted to coax him into letting

Noble and . . . uh, Toodles, stay, I was going to have to bargain.

As I went up the stairs to Ford's office—where I was sure he was hiding—I thought of the absurdity of it all. I was going to have to reveal private information about myself in an attempt to get Ford to allow his own family to live with him. It didn't make sense.

But as I reached his door, I thought, Who are you kidding? I was dying to tell somebody about Russell. And since Ford was becoming the best friend I ever had, he was the one I wanted to tell. And I didn't agree with Russell that Ford would tell Dessie. It had been days since his date with her and, as far as I knew, there'd been no contact between them since then. And, yes, I did push the button on the phone that shows all the incoming calls for the last month. Not one from Ms. Mason.

Lifting my hand, I knocked.

CHAPTER FIFTEEN

Ford

I wanted to tell them to get out. I wanted to tell Noble that I'd never liked him, that he'd always been my enemy, and that I was done with that part of my life, so he could get into his rusted-out old Chrysler and leave. I wanted to tell my father to get out, too. He was nothing to me.

But I couldn't do it. Even though I knew what they wanted from me, I still couldn't kick them out.

I could tell myself I was being heroic in allowing them to stay, but the truth was, I was curious about my father, and I . . . well, I had kind of missed Noble. Maybe it was because I was getting older, or because I no longer had Pat's family as mine, but in the last couple of years I'd been thinking of visiting my relatives again. Then I would remember that, "You won't remember this . . ." crap and cancel the plans I'd been making.

So now here was this man I'd only seen in pictures and the cousin I'd spent my childhood being tortured by, and I knew they needed a place to stay. No one had told me my father was going to be released years before the end of his sentence (Good behavior? Got a Ph.D. in ento-mology?) but Noble's eldest daughter had e-mailed me about what her father had done. Vanessa had been furious and ready to disown her father, but, to tell the truth, the story had made me laugh. Uncle Zeb had married some girl a third his age, then left the poor thing to cry in loneliness. Vanessa told me her dad had just been released from the local hoosegow where he'd been thrown for thirty days for threatening to shoot some man's eternally-barking dog. Noble might not have received jail if he hadn't been caught inside the man's alarmed fence, loaded shotgun aimed. Worse, Noble'd had to be wrestled to the ground to keep him from shoot-ing the dog **after** the sheriff arrived. He said that if he was going to be sent to jail anyway, he wanted it to be for an actual crime, not for something he'd just thought about doing.

So, anyway, Noble had been in jail for thirty days, and presumably celibate during that time, then he'd been confronted with a nubile and extremely neglected young wife. Vanessa was saying she never wanted to see her father again, but it all didn't seem too bad to me.

It was my guess that Noble had found out that my father was being released from prison, kept the knowledge to himself, and on his way out of town, had picked the old man up. So now they were here, two ex-cons, with no job, no cash, and no place to stay.

Oh, yeah, I knew what they wanted. I was sure Noble wanted a grubstake and the second I gave him money enough to open some business somewhere, he'd be off. And he'd leave the old man with me.

So what would **I** do with a geriatric gnome?

I didn't get any further in my thoughts because Jackie knocked on the door, and when I told her to come in, right away, I saw that she wanted something from me. Let's see. What could it be?

When she started to speak, I wanted to tell her to spare me the lecture, that I'd just get out my checkbook. I'd buy Noble some business far away from the angry relatives (if I knew them, only the younger generation was angry; Uncle Clyde's generation was probably laughing their heads off) and I'd send the old man to a nursing home.

But as soon as I saw Jackie's face, I decided to

use her guilt to get her to tell me why she'd been so weird lately. First, though, I had to listen to what she was saying about family. She was saying how everyone needed one and how as a person got older, family meant more to him, and someday I'd regret not getting to know my father, and I should let bygones be bygones and—

I'd seen my father sitting upright, eyes wide open, but sound asleep. After he'd unnecessarily told me who he was and before Jackie made her dramatic wet-dog entrance, Tessa had asked him how he could do that. He said that where he'd been he'd learned that he had to look as though he were alert at all times. He said that a man with his fine physical looks couldn't let down his guard ever. Tessa had giggled because she thought he was joking about his "fine physical looks," but I could see that he was serious.

While Jackie was going on at me about family, I tried to see if I'd inherited this ability to sleep with my eyes open while sitting up. When I'd about decided I was going to be able to do it, Jackie stopped talking and looked down at her hands. Uh oh, I thought. She'd gone off family and was on to something else, but I hadn't been listening. I searched my mind to remember what she'd been saying. Oh, yes. Camera. Something about a camera. Her new digital maybe? Or that fantastic little printer she'd bought?

"Where'd you get it?" I asked. That seemed a safe question.

"I . . ." she began. "I met this man and he lent me—"

She couldn't have woken me up more completely if she'd shot at me. "A man?" I asked.

"You . . ." She looked hard at me. "He doesn't want me to tell you about him because he said you'd tell Dessie. But I think you're a better person than that. You **are** a better person than that, aren't you?"

"Much better," I said. I saw no need to tell Jackie that Dessie's mad passion for me had only been an attempt to make her jug-eared lawn boy jealous.

Instantly, Jackie gave me so much information that I had trouble understanding it all. Of course my hearing may have been clogged by the fact that my temperature had risen approximately twelve and a half degrees. What kind of town was this? I'm a rich bachelor. Where were the women who were dying to have me? Women who would do **anything** to get me? Dessie wanted some kid who only knew how to push a lawn mower, and now Jackie had—my temperature went up two degrees more—"met a man."

"Wait a minute," I said, "let's backtrack. His name is—?"

"Russell Dunne."

"And he is—?"

"An associate professor of art history at the University of North Carolina."

"Right. And he gave you—?"

"**Lent** me the digital camera and the printer. They're his, not mine. At the picnic he took a photo, printed it out, and I thought it was—"

"The printer isn't battery-operated so how'd he use it out in the woods?"

"I don't know. Maybe he had a battery pack. He had so much stuff in his bag it was almost magic."

I think she was trying to make me laugh, but laughter was the furthest thing from my mind. "Magic," I said.

"If you're going to be nasty, I'm not going to tell you anything."

I apologized, but I was dying to ask her to spell the guy's name. When I searched out his credentials on the Internet I wanted to be sure I had the name right.

I listened politely as she told me how "nice" he was, but my mind was racing. She had to have met him on Sunday. While I was at Dessie's, solving her love life and being a great friend to a woman I hardly knew, Jackie had been picking up men . . . Where?

"Where did you meet him?" I asked. "**Exactly** where?" I added, in case she'd already told me.

She waved her hand. "That doesn't matter. I'd been taking photos of flowers and—"

"You picked up a man on a trail somewhere?" I asked, truly shocked. "I didn't think you were that kind of woman. But then, you're not from my generation, are you?"

Jackie didn't take my bait. "He grew up in Cole Creek, but he—" She looked down at her hands. "He asked me not to tell you about him because of your relationship with Dessie."

Again with Dessie. Was I tied forever to her because I'd had dinner with her? First Rebecca and now Dessie. "What's Dessie got to do with this?" I asked more sharply than I'd intended to.

"Russell wrote a bad review of her work and since then the town has considered him a pariah."

That took me so aback I couldn't prevent a smile. What an old-fashioned word. "A pariah, huh?" I stopped smiling. This thing needed some logic applied to it. "Why would the town care whether or not Dessie Mason gets good reviews?"

"She's the town celebrity so they don't want her hurt."

"Really? It's my opinion that this town pays no attention to celebrities. Take me, for example. In that town where I met you, they were all over me, but here, we've had one invitation to an afternoon in the park and since then, zilch."

"What does that mean?" Jackie asked, frowning.

"Just that something isn't ringing true." I could see she was getting angry, so I smiled to soften what I wanted to say. "Are you sure this guy didn't ask you not to tell me about him because I might stop him from getting what he wants?"

Jackie narrowed her eyes at me. "And just what is it that you think he wants?"

"You. In bed."

"Is that supposed to shock me? You just said that I'm from a different generation than you are. Women today aren't eternally-virgin Doris Days. I **hope** he wants me in bed. I really, really, hope he does. But, so far, no luck."

I didn't want Jackie to see my shock. Or was it shock? Was it, maybe, red-hot jealousy?

"Let's not fight, okay?" she said softly. "I really came up here to talk to you about your relatives. They don't have any place to stay."

Sorry, but I couldn't move my mind around that quickly. Some man had written a bad review of Dessie Mason's work and now an entire **town** hated him for it? Did that include Miss Essie Lee? She was as dried-up as Dessie was luscious, and human nature told me that the Miss Essie Lees of the world did **not** defend the Dessies.

I wanted to ask Jackie more questions about

this man. Top of my list was to ask for his social security number so I could run a major search on him. But when I looked at Jackie, I could tell that she'd just asked me a question. Ah, yes. Toodles. My dear old dad.

"You didn't put it in your book," Jackie said.

That startled me. Had I ever had a thought that I hadn't put in one of my books? She spoke again. Oh, yes, why had my dad been in prison? True, that particular story had not been put into any book. I had, of course, written the story, but that manuscript had been a thousand pages long, so Pat had done some cutting. She said it was better to leave out the reason the hero's father was in prison because the missing story lent some mystery to the book. She didn't say that I was revealing too much, but then Pat could sometimes be as polite as her mother.

"When he was a baby," I said, "my father was dropped on his head and afterward, he was always slow. Not retarded, but . . ." I thought. "Simple. Childlike. My mother told me he took everything literally."

I settled back in my chair. I'd told this story only once before, and that was to Pat. Right now, part of me didn't want to accord Jackie the honor of being the second person to hear it. After all, while I'd been patching up someone's broken romance, Jackie had been picking up a strange man in a forest, believing every word he said, and lusting over him. I couldn't make myself think about what she'd said, that she **wanted** to go to bed with this stranger. Had I misjudged her character? Was she after **all** men? Would Noble have to fend her off? My funny-looking father?

I made a vow to never again eat black olives that had been sliced into little rings.

"My uncles," I said, "decided to rob a bank. They were all young and full of themselves and they saw it as a way to make themselves rich. Of course they didn't think how they were later going to explain the fact that even though half of them were unemployed, they could suddenly afford houses and cars. But anyway, they came up with what they thought was a foolproof plan: They'd use Toodles as a decoy. He—"

"Why's he called 'Toodles'?"

I looked at her. "I'll tell you the details if you want to hear them, but it might be better just to say that one of the results of my father's injury was a very long delay in toilet training."

"Oh," Jackie said. "So how were your uncles going to use a poor, innocent man like your father to help them commit a crime?"

"Tootles was to sit outside the bank with the motor running in the getaway car, thinking he was going to drive away when they came running out. But my uncles double-crossed him. They planned to rob the bank, then go out the backdoor where another car was waiting. They figured that by the time the police came, they'd be long gone. When the police stopped to arrest Toodles, that would give them time to escape."

"They **wanted** your father to be arrested?"

"Yes. As a diversion. They knew Toodles hadn't done anything wrong, so what could the police charge him with? Sitting outside the bank in a car with the engine running? My uncles figured the police would let him go after a few hours, then the lot of them would share the money and live happily ever after."

"And the police wouldn't search for the bank robbers? Wouldn't they suspect your uncles?" Jackie asked, eyes wide.

"The police could find them for all they cared, because my uncles believed they had iron-clad alibis: each other. Who could fight eleven men swearing that they'd all been together?"

"Okay, so what went wrong?"

"My uncles didn't know that Toodles had been seeing a girl."

"Your mother."

"Yes. She'd been raised in an orphanage and she was pretty much alone in the world. And she had such a bad temper that she didn't have a lot of dates, plus she was past thirty, so maybe when little Toodles came along, she was ready to try anything." I shrugged. Who knew what went on in my mother's head? The woman had certainly never shared any of her inner feelings with **me.**

"Anyway, my uncles didn't know that the night before the robbery, my parents had crossed the state line and been married by a justice of the peace. Three days before, my mother had told Toodles she was going to have me. I believe her exact words were, 'Look what you did to me, you little cretin.' But, as I said, my father doesn't seem to see things as other people do, so he was very happy that his girl-friend was going to have his baby, and he asked her to marry him. One of my aunts told me that my mother said she'd rather let a train run over her feet than marry him, but then my father told her he was going to buy her a house and a car and that she'd never again have to milk a cow."

"He was under a bit of pressure, wasn't he?" Jackie said. "He had a wife, a child on the way, and no way to provide for his new family. So there he was, sitting in the car waiting for his brothers to show up with the loot, but, instead, the police arrived. He must have been frantic."

"Yeah. By the time the police arrived, my uncles had already run out the backdoor, but my father didn't know that. And what my brothers didn't know is that Toodles had a gun. They never did find out where he got it, but between you and me, I think my mother gave it to him. She told the police she didn't know anything, but I think my dad had told her about the bank job. My mother wasn't one for taking someone's word for anything, so if Toodles told her he was going to buy her a house and a car, she'd want to know where he was going to get the money. I think Toodles told her what he and his brothers were going to do, and I think my mother had some suspicions about his brothers, so she gave him an old revolver she'd got from somewhere. She was going to see that she got what she wanted."

Jackie gave me one of "those" looks. "And what she wanted was a home for her child." When I didn't say anything to that, she said, "Did your father shoot someone?"

"Three people, two of them policemen. When the police went charging into the bank, guns drawn, Toodles thought his beloved brothers were still inside, so he went in shooting."

"In other words, your father risked his life to save his no-good, lying, double-crossing, rat fink brothers."

"That's the way my mother saw it, too. Toodles didn't kill anyone, but he wounded the two policemen and grazed a hysterical bank teller. Took off her left earlobe."

Jackie leaned back in the chair. "So your father went to jail, and after you were born, your mother gave you to your uncles to raise." Her head came up. "What happened to the money from the bank job?"

I smiled. "They didn't get a dime. One of the tellers, not the one who got shot, but another one, recognized my uncle Cal's voice and called out his name. They all panicked and ran out the backdoor."

Jackie got up and walked over to one of the bookcases along the wall. I knew she wasn't looking at the books, but was thinking about my family. They did that to people. Hadn't that been proven when people bought the books I'd written about them?

I decided to change the subject. "Had any visions lately?" My intention was purely malicious. I wanted her to remember the fun she and I'd had when I'd been around to save the lives of the people she saw. Would this Russell Dunne have done that? Or would he have hesitated and told her that she'd just had a dream? Or would he have taken her to a doctor to be examined?

Jackie took a long time before she answered. "What would happen if I started seeing evil inside a person's head?"

Wow! Where had that come from? And what an intriguing question. It was one of those questions that could inspire an entire novel.

I started to answer, but then I sat upright. Was this question from the guy she'd picked up in the forest? If it was, then that meant Jackie had told him about her visions. Having sex with someone else was one thing, but this . . . this sharing of what was private between her and me was betrayal. When I didn't—couldn't—say a word, she kept on talking. It was a good thing her back was to me because if she'd seen my face, she would have run from the room.

"What if we were having dinner with two couples and I had a vision that one man and one woman, not married to each other, were having an affair and were going to kill her husband and his wife? How would you—or I—stop it?"

I liked the way that question made my mind work so I put aside Jackie's betrayal and thought about it. "Warn the victims," I said.

She turned to look at me. "Oh, yeah, sure, and people believe that their spouse is going to kill them. Don't you think that if a man was plotting to kill his wife that he'd be really nice to her? And he'd make sure that others saw how much he loved her, and that she was the most important person in his life? If you told her this darling man was going to kill her, she'd never believe you."

"You've done some thinking about this, haven't you?"

"Yeah," she said, plopping down onto the chair across from my desk. She hit the seat so hard that if it hadn't been padded, she would have broken her tailbone. "I, uh . . . I think I know why Amarisa was killed."

If someone had held a gun to my head, I wouldn't have let her know that I'd never heard the name "Amarisa" before, although it took only about a second to figure out who she was.

"Why was she killed?" I asked in a whisper and couldn't help a glance at the door. Please don't let anyone knock and disturb us.

"She had visions. At first they were like mine, but, gradually, they got stronger until she began to see what was inside people's heads. And she started to . . . to prevent the evil from happening."

Prevent, I thought. Was she hinting that this woman, Amarisa, murdered people before they did what they were just thinking about doing? But how could she be **sure** they were going to carry through? Didn't everyone at some time think of killing someone else? "This Russell Dunne tell you about her?" I asked, and hated the jealousy that was in my voice.

"Yes. I shouldn't be telling you this, but—"

"Why shouldn't you tell me?" I snapped. When had **I** become the enemy? The outsider?

Jackie shrugged. "I don't know. Russell was telling me these things in confidence, but maybe if this story were brought out in the open, people would tell what they know. Maybe then this evil wouldn't hang over Cole Creek."

"I can't think of anything it would solve if this story were made public," I said firmly, my jaw rigid.

Jackie looked at me. "Do you think the people who killed that woman are still alive?"

"No."

"What makes you say that?"

It was my turn to reveal secrets. "I looked up some of the people from this town on the Internet. Several people died in freak accidents the year after the woman was crushed."

"How freaky?" she asked.

"You ready for this? Crushed. In one way or another, they were all crushed."

"So who did it?"

"That's just what I wondered. Think Russell would know?" I was being facetious, so I expected Jackie to rein me in as she usually did, but, instead, she got up and walked back to the bookcase.

"I think he probably knows a lot more about this than he's told me. It changed his life—just as it did mine. I really think that . . . that . . ."

"Your mother was one of the people who put rocks on . . . Amarisa?" The name sounded strange, but it fit her. Part of me wanted to show Jackie the photo of the woman's reconstructed face, but I couldn't bring myself to do it. First of all, I was sure that Jackie would see the resemblance to herself. And I was just as sure that she'd

remember the woman. She remembered everything else in town, so why not her own relative?
I'd heard that we never forget traumatic events in
our lives, so I doubted if Jackie could look at that
photo and not recall what she'd seen.

But I couldn't get past my hurt. I'd been
honest with Jackie since the day I met her. I'd
told her everything about my life. Well, okay,
actually, I'd written my life story, sold it, and
made a lot of money off it, but still, Jackie knew
all about me. Maybe it was true that I'd not told
her much about my dinner with Dessie, but
then I'd not found out anything that I could
share with Jackie. Except about the sculptures
in Dessie's locked cupboard. And the fact that I
thought one of the women in the sculpture was
Jackie's mother. But still, I wasn't hiding anything as big as what Jackie was keeping from
me. Except maybe the photo in the FedEx
envelope.

"Jackie," I said softly, "if you had another
vision, you'd tell me, wouldn't you? Me. Not
someone you hardly know."

When she looked at me, she seemed to be
trying to decide whether or not to answer me.
And whether or not she should tell me first—or
him.

What had this man done to win her loyalty
so completely? I wondered. She couldn't have
spent too much time with him because she'd

been with me nearly every minute for the last few days. Yet she was contemplating telling him and not me about something that I'd come to think of as a secret between us.

"Yeah, I'll tell you," she said after a while, and gave me a small smile. "But what do I do if—"

"You see evil inside a person's head?" I had no idea. That was a question that would take a philosopher a lifetime to answer. I wanted to lighten the mood between us. "Look into my eyes and tell me what I'm thinking about Russell Dunne," I said, leaning across the desk and staring at her hard.

"That you want him to move in here with us, along with your father and cousin," she said instantly, without a hint of a smile.

Groaning, I leaned back in my chair. "Very funny. You should have been a comedian."

"I have to be around this house. What are we going to do with your family?"

"Why don't we ask Russell?" I said.

"Before or after we ask Dessie?"

I clamped my mouth closed before I let it out of the bag that there was nothing between Dessie and me. Right now I wished I'd not been such a great guy and smoothed things out between Dessie and her young boyfriend. I should have grabbed Dessie in front of the windows and kissed her. At least now I'd have a girlfriend to balance out Jackie's boyfriend.

I forced myself not to ask Jackie if she could repair her last wedding dress, and instead said that my father and Noble absolutely, positively could not, under any circumstances in the world, live in this house with me. As I hoped it would, that set Jackie off and took her mind off Russell Dunne.

I got to practice my sleeping-while-sitting-up-with-my-eyes-wide-open again, and was on the verge of mastering it, when a delightful smell wafted up through the old floorboards. "What's that?" I asked and knew by Jackie's sly look that she was up to something.

"Did you know that your cousin can bake?"

I just blinked at that. It was certainly my day for shocks. If Jackie had said that Noble was secretly Spiderman I couldn't have been more surprised.

"It smells like he's taken something out of the oven. Shall we go down and sample the wares?"

I wanted to be aloof. I wanted to tell Jackie that I had work to do and couldn't be bothered with something as lowly as doughnuts. Or cinnamon rolls. Or whatever was making that divine smell.

But I followed her like a dog on a leash all the way down to the kitchen. The table in the middle of the room was loaded with baked goods, and from the sheer quantity of it all, it wasn't difficult to figure out where Noble got his training.

I was sure he was used to cooking for many men at a time, maybe a whole jail full of them.

Toodles and Tessa were already seated at the table, both of them with big glasses of milk and wearing white mustaches. Once again, my jealousy flared. First some stranger takes away the loyalty of my assistant, and now my own father was taking away my sidekick.

As Noble dumped a bunch of fat, and extremely sticky, cinnamon buns onto a plate about four inches below my nose, he punched my shoulder and said, "It looks like it's just you and me."

The real trouble with relatives is that they know you too well. If you've grown up with them, they knew you when you were too young to have developed disguises. Maybe I could hide my feelings from Jackie, who hadn't known me very long, but I couldn't hide anything from Noble. He knew that I was jealous as I watched my former buddy, Tessa, practically sitting on my father's lap.

Once I'd eaten one or two of Noble's baked goods—certainly not enough to warrant Jackie's remarks about Henry the Eighth being alive and well—I decided to keep my mouth shut and think about things for a while. I needed to see what was going on around me and make some decisions. And, no, I wasn't "sulking" as Jackie said I was.

I got a book, stretched out in the hammock in the garden, and watched the lot of them as they interacted. Okay, so what I really wanted was a reason to send my father to an old-age home, and to tell Noble that he definitely had to make his own way in life. I'd willingly given Noble's kids a start in life, but I didn't owe anything to my cousin.

But, oh, hell, why did it all have to be so damned **pleasant?**

It seemed that my father had a thousand ways to sit in one place and occupy himself. I watched with fascination while he showed Tessa how to weave a cat's cradle with a loop of string. I'd seen that done in books but not in real life. With a twist of his wrists, he could make a swing dangle from the loop, then he'd twist again and make a rowboat.

What really fascinated me was when he said that my mother used to send him books that showed him how to do things. I knew my mother had never visited my father in prison. In fact, she didn't go to the trial, or, to my knowledge, had she ever seen him after their wedding night. To say that she'd discouraged me from wanting to visit him was an understatement. Pat had tried to get me to visit my father, but I hadn't even bothered to answer her.

But I heard Toodles say that his wife—and he said the name with great affection—had sent him how-to books, so he'd learned to do a lot of really interesting things. "She sent him kids' books," Noble said softly when he saw me staring. "Get him to do some magic tricks."

I looked down at my book and pretended I wasn't observing the lot of them.

Noble had always been one of those really useful men. From an early age, he'd taken to tools the way I'd taken to words. As pre-schoolers, I'd imagined things and he'd built them.

First, Noble tore into the grapevines that had overgrown a rotting covered seat. Within minutes, he'd pruned the vines in what I was sure was a professional manner. Nate was there and he stood back in awe. "Where'd you learn to do that?"

"Worked for a landscape company for a few years," Noble said as he wiggled the old wood that supported the vines.

"I'll help you tear it out," Nate said, but Noble stopped him.

"There's good in it yet. You got any wood around here, something I could use to repair this?"

"Sure," Nate said. "There's a pile of boards behind Jackie's house."

"Jackie's house" turned out to be her studio. Looking over my book, I watched as Nate and Noble disappeared behind the studio to look for wood that I didn't know was there. Meanwhile, my jealousy flared up again when I saw my father disappear into the tunnel that led into Tessa's "secret" house. It wasn't very secret if she let everyone in the neighborhood in, was it?

Minutes later, Jackie came out of the kitchen with a tray holding tall glasses of lemonade and more things that Noble had baked, this time savory, topped with cheese, onions, and rings of black olives. She handed me a plateful, and I had begun picking the olives off the third one when I heard a loud whoop that almost made me drop everything.

Noble came out from behind the studio holding a big black portfolio and flipping through what looked to be photographs. "These are great!" he was saying, looking at Jackie. "These are the best pictures I've ever seen in my life."

Jackie told Noble he had no right to look at something that she considered private.

But Noble rattled off some long story about how he'd "accidently" opened a window in her studio when he'd picked up a board, then "accidently" dropped the board inside. When he'd climbed through the window to get the board, he'd "accidently" knocked the portfolio down and "accidently" seen the pictures. Two seconds after he finished this B.S., Jackie was asking him for praise. Begging for it.

Noble couldn't stop himself from glancing at me, and under his skin, darkened from years in the sun, I saw a blush. We both knew he was lying. How many windows had Noble and I climbed through when we were kids? Between my rampant curiosity and his inclination toward criminality, no one in our family could hide anything.

Nate called to Toodles and Tessa to come out of the house that I had heretofore thought was mine and Tessa's, to look at the pictures and have some food. I stayed in my hammock, the book in front of my face, as the lot of them oohed and aahed over photographs that Jackie hadn't shown me. Were they of Russell Dunne? I wondered.

But after a while Toodles held one up beside Tessa, facing me, and I saw a knockout picture of the kid. I was several feet away, but even at that distance I could see that it was good. Jackie had shown Tessa as she really was: not a cute kid, but one who lived on another plane than the rest of us live on.

After the lot of them had run out of words to praise the photos, Jackie took the pictures out of everyone's hands, put them back into the portfolio and brought them over to me. Pulling up a chair beside the hammock, she handed me the portfolio as though it were an offering.

With great solemnity, I took it from her, and went through the photos one by one. Man, oh, man, were they good! I was really and truly and **deeply** impressed.

Even though I'm a writer, I couldn't think of anything adequate to say to convey what I thought of those pictures. I knew Tessa so I could tell how perfectly Jackie had captured her, but even if I hadn't known her, I could have written an essay about the child.

Closing the portfolio, I tried to think of how to tell Jackie what I thought. But there were no words in any language to explain how amazed I was. So I turned and pressed my lips to hers; it was the only thing that seemed appropriate.

However, what was meant to be a kiss to tell her that I thought her pictures were fabulous, turned into something more. I didn't touch her except with my lips, but for a moment I thought I heard bells ringing. Or maybe it was stars tinkling like little silver bells. When I pulled away, I looked at her in shock. It was one more shock in a day that could have put an earthquake to shame. And she seemed to be feeling the same way because she just sat there staring at me with her eyes wide.

"I don't know about anybody else, but I'm hungry," Noble said, and broke the spell that was on Jackie and me.

Turning, I looked at the four of them standing there, and had to blink a couple of times to clear my vision. Noble had an I-told-you-so expression on his face and Nate looked embarrassed. Tessa was frowning, while Toodles was looking at me, well, kind of fondly, like a father might look at his son. I turned away and studied the façade of Jackie's studio.

A minute later, everyone was back to normal, except that I thought I'd had enough of lying in the hammock and watching, so I got up and, after we'd eaten all of Noble's cheese-things, I helped him put that old frame over the broken seat back together. I got out Pat's father's toolbox and we used the tools. Noble didn't comment when he first saw the tools, but when he got one dirty, he apologized. I said it was okay, and a minute later, he mumbled, "Sorry about your wife."

I didn't say anything, but his words meant a lot to me. They were of sympathy, yes, but the words also showed that he'd been interested enough to learn about the contents of my books.

In the late afternoon, Nate went home, and when Allie came to pick up Tessa, I thought Toodles was going to cry. Allie kept looking at Toodles, trying not to, but he was indeed an odd-looking little man. Since Toodles and Tessa were holding hands and looking at Allie as though she were an evil social worker about to take Tessa away from her beloved grandfather, Jackie asked if Tessa could have a sleep-over.

Allie said, "You mean I could have an evening to myself? Take a long, hot bath? Watch a movie on TV that has sex in it? Drink wine? Naw, I don't deserve such happiness." She practically ran through the garden gate before anyone changed his mind.

Eventually, Noble and Jackie went into the kitchen to fix dinner, while Toodles, Tessa, and I stayed outside. Tessa ran around chasing fireflies while I sat on a chair next to my dad.

What a strange thought: my dad. All my life he'd been nothing but a head in group photo shots. I don't think there was one picture of him alone. And none of my uncles spoke about him. It was hard to believe in a family like mine, but I think they felt guilty. At least one good thing had come of my dad's incarceration: My uncles never again intentionally committed a crime. Sober and planned, that is.

Toodles and I didn't say much. Actually, we didn't say anything. Me, the wordsmith, had not one word in my head that I could think of to say. So tell me, Dad, what was it like to spend forty-three years in prison? Do you hate your brothers? Or maybe I should have asked if he had any of my favorite June bugs on his vest.

When Jackie called us in to dinner, Tessa ran into the kitchen. It was late and we were all hungry. I let my father go ahead of me into the house, but in the doorway, he paused. He didn't look at me, but stared at the sight of Noble and Jackie loading the table with food.

"You'll have me?" he asked in that thick accent that I hadn't heard in years.

For a moment it was as though the earth stood still. Even the fireflies seemed to pause as they waited for my answer.

What could I say? As Jackie had pointed out, the man had been put in jail because he was trying to get money to support his wife and son. Me.

I guess it was my turn to support him.

As Jackie said, I tended to get weepy, so I needed to say something that wouldn't put me there now. "Only if you show me how to make a cat's cradle."

It was at that moment that I found out where my weepiness came from. I was trying to be cool, but my dad made no effort toward restraint. Burying his face in my chest, he began to bawl. As he held on to my shirt for dear life, he cried loud enough to knock the plaster off the walls.

"What did you do to him?" Jackie yelled as she clutched Toodles's arms and tried to pull him away from big, bad me.

Part of me wanted to grab my father and hug him and cry with him, but another part was put off by his display. Toodles kept bawling, his face pressed hard against my chest. He started saying that he loved me and was glad I was his son, and that he was so proud of me and he knew men who'd read my books, and he loved me and wanted to be with me all his life, and—

Noble was clearly enjoying my discomfort, while Jackie was still trying to pull Toodles off. It was my guess that Jackie couldn't understand what my father was saying. I think you needed to grow up with an accent like his to be able to understand it, especially when a man was howling and his mouth was full of shirt.

The part of me that was affected by my father's copious tears seemed to be the part attached to my muscles because I couldn't get Toodles off. Jackie was pulling, but making no headway as he was a strong little guy. I had my arms on his shoulders, but every time he said he loved me, my arms turned to wet spaghetti and I couldn't push. "I love you" was not something I'd ever heard before from a blood kin. Heaven knows that my mother never said the words to anyone.

Noble finally took pity on me, pulled my father off, and got him seated at the table, where he hung his head and kept sobbing. Tessa moved her chair beside him, held his hand in hers, and got the hiccups as she tried not to cry with him. She kept looking at me in puzzlement. Had I done something good or bad to make her friend cry like that?

I was so weak I could hardly sit up.

We were a strange group. Toodles and Tessa sat on one side, him sobbing as though his heart was broken, her holding his hand and hiccuping. Jackie was at one end of the table looking

like she was going to cry too but not knowing
why. I was across from Toodles, feeling like a
deflated ball, and Noble was at the other end of
the table laughing at the lot of us.

Noble picked up a bowl of mashed potatoes
and slapped a mountain of them onto Toodles's
plate, then put an equal amount of meat loaf
and green beans beside the spuds. I saw where I
got my good appetite.

But Toodles didn't even look at the food.

"Did you know that Ford here can tell stories?" Noble said loudly, his words directed at
Toodles. "He never was good around the house,
hardly knows one end of a crowbar from the
other, but he can tell stories like nobody else.
My mom used to say that meals were never the
same after Ford left home."

"Yeah?" I said.

"Yeah," Noble answered. "My dad said that
all the lying of the Newcombes had gone into
you so that you could tell the biggest, best lies of
anybody on earth."

"Yeah?" I said again. This was high praise
indeed. I turned to look at Jackie to see if she
was taking note of this, but she was looking as
though she couldn't tell if this was good or
bad.

Toodles gave a big sniff, so Jackie got up to
get him a tissue. After he'd blown his nose so
loud that Tessa started to giggle, he winked at

her, picked up his spoon, and said, "Tell me a story."

I obliged.

It was after dinner that I told Noble I wanted to talk to him. I wanted the truth about what was going on. I'd known him too long and too well not to suspect he was up to something. We took a six-pack and went up to my office where we could talk man to man.

"Okay, so why are you here and what do you want?" I asked. "And think about who you're talking to before you make up any lies."

"I'll leave the lies to you," he said, his voice humble so he wouldn't offend me.

I wasn't fooled. Noble was a grown man and able-bodied. Even if he had been in prison a few times, he could find work, so why was he here? Why to me? Noble was well named. He had a great deal of pride, so I knew it would take some doing to find out what was in his mind.

It took me a while to get him to talk, but when he started, I thought he might never shut up.

He got off the couch and stood over me, glaring.

"I'm here because you ruined my life so I figure you owe me."

"And how did I do that?" I asked calmly,

keeping my own anger under control. What ingratitude! I'd never added up the amount of money I'd spent in giving free education to all the nieces and nephews, Noble's kids, legitimate and otherwise, included, but it was a lot.

He was still glaring at me. "I used to be happy. I loved bein' a kid near all my uncles, and I was crazy about my father. And you know something? When I look back at you and me, I thought **we** had a good time. Yeah, I know we all gave you a hard time, but you were such a snob you deserved it. You always looked down on us."

Pausing, he waited for me to say something, but what could I say? To deny that I'd looked down on them? To feel that I was superior was the only defense I had.

"When you left for college, I was glad to see the last of you—but you know what? I missed you. You always made us laugh. The rest of us, we could do things with trucks and a pock-etknife, but you could do things with words."

Pausing for a moment, he took a drink of his beer and smiled in memory. "I was pretty mad when you left for college. You remember how I ran over your suitcase with the tractor? You were goin' off to see the world, while I had a pregnant girlfriend and her dad was threatenin' to shoot me if I didn't marry her. Did you know that by the time I was twenty-one I'd been married and divorced two times and I had three kids to support? And all this happened while you were off at college meetin' town girls."

Noble drank some more beer, then sat down on the other end of the couch. His anger was gone now. We were just two men heading toward middle age, reminiscing. "Then you got a book published and all the aunts read it and said it was all about **us.** Only they said you'd made us look like we ate roadkill for dinner. Uncle Clyde's wife said, 'I don't know who he's talkin' about but it ain't us.' So after that, we all pretty much decided that you didn't remember any of us and you'd made up people to write about."

Noble gave a little smile. "I can't tell you how many times I was asked if I was kin to that 'writer feller' and you know what I said?"

He didn't wait for me to answer, but I don't think he wanted one. I think he'd waited a long time to tell me what he was saying now. In fact, maybe he'd driven all this way just to tell me what he thought of me.

"No. I told 'em no. Ever' time somebody asked if I was kin to Ford Newcombe, I told 'em no."

I tried to be philosophical about what he was saying, but I felt some hurt. Everyone wanted his relatives to be proud of him, didn't he?

"You humiliated us to the world, but you

know what was the worst thing you did to us? You changed the kids. My daughter, Vanessa, the one that was born right after you left for college, is just like you. She even looked like you, too, until she had her nose fixed. She read your book when she was just a kid, and after that she didn't want nothin' to do with us Newcombes."

Noble opened another beer. "You can't imagine all the ribbin' I got over that kid. People said she was yours, not mine." He looked at me over the top of his beer. "You remember her mother? That little Sue Ann Hawkins? You didn't . . . ?"

Of course I remembered Sue Ann Hawkins. Every young man and a few old ones within twenty miles of her house had been to bed with her. Of course no one dared tell Noble that. Not then and not now. Back then, we kept our mouths shut and wished them luck on their wedding day. Later, half the county breathed a sigh of relief when the little girl was born with the Newcombe nose. Whether the nose had come from Noble, me or one of our other relatives had never been discussed even in private for fear of Noble's legendary right hook.

Noble put up his hand. "No, don't answer that one. That girl swore she'd only been to bed with me in her whole life, and if I hadn't believed her, I wouldn't have married her, her daddy's shotgun or not. But if she was so damned pure, then why did she later take up with every—"

He stopped himself. "Naw, I won't go into that. Let's just say that her mother was so bad that Vanessa ended up livin' with me from the time she was four. But after she read your book, she was livin' with **you** in her mind. It was always, 'My uncle Ford this' and 'my uncle Ford that' until I wished I'd never saved you that time you fell into the creek and hit your head. You remember that? You remember how I carried you a mile and a half to get you home? I wasn't an ounce bigger than you, but I carried you. Then Uncle Simon drove his old pickup across the fields and through the fences to get you to the hospital as fast as he could. When you didn't wake up for two whole days, we thought you were a goner. You remember that?"

I did remember it. But, oddly, I hadn't remembered it when I was writing my books.

"You know what?" Noble said, looking at me. "My daughter didn't believe me when I told her about savin' you. She said that if it'd really happened, you would have put it in your book, 'cause you put everything in there. And since it wasn't in there, it didn't happen. How come you didn't put **that** story in there?"

I had to look away because I had no answer to that question.

"Well, anyway, you sent all four of my kids to college. Hell, you even sent my third wife money so she could go back to school and become a grade school teacher. She divorced me after her first year teachin'. Said I wasn't educated enough for her. And now my college-educated kids don't want anything to do with me. They want to see you, who they've laid eyes on maybe twice in their lives, but they don't want to see their own dad. But you don't have anything to do with any of us, do you? Except to write about us."

While he took a deep drink from his beer, I waited in silence for him to continue. I must admit that I was fascinated at this look at how I'd "ruined" his life. I was also busy speculating if smart little Vanessa could be **my** daughter.

"So, anyway, when we got word that they was gonna let Toodles out, I thought it was time for you to pay up for what you'd done to us, and to me, especially. 'King'? Did you have to name me **'King'** in your books? Ain't 'Noble' bad enough?"

"What do you want from me?" I asked. "You didn't come here to cry in your beer, so what do you want?"

Noble took a while to answer. "I got into trouble at home. I don't mean the jail time. It wasn't the first time I'd seen the inside of a jail, as you well know. But this time I got into trouble with the family."

I wasn't about to tell him that Vanessa had already told me her version of the "family trouble."

"After I got out of jail this last time, I had nothin'. My three ex-wives had cleaned me out, and nobody wants to give an ex-con a job, so all I could do was go back home. Uncle Zeb offered me a place at his house, said I could stay in the back room that he turns the heat off in—you know what an old skinflint he is. So I'm out there, freezin' cold, and here comes Uncle Zeb's new wife. You should see her. She's about twenty-five and a dead ringer for Joey Heatherton. Remember her? Lord only knows why she agreed to marry an old coot like Uncle Zeb. So I wake up and she's in bed with me. I'm a man and I hadn't had a woman in a long time, so there was no way I wasn't gonna give her what she wanted. The next mornin' she didn't say nothin' and I didn't say nothin', so I thought maybe things would be all right. But three months later, she's over at Uncle Cal's house and she's cryin' her eyes out, and she's sayin' that she's a faithful wife, but I sneaked into her bed one afternoon while she was takin' a nap, and now she's gonna have my baby."

I wanted to say that such a story wasn't new in our family, but Noble barreled on ahead.

"Back when I was a kid, people would have been more understandin' if somethin' like this had happened. But you destroyed our family. When we was kids, the uncles would have laughed somethin' like that off. And the girl wouldn't have told in the first place. She was married to an old man who couldn't give her what she wanted, and I did, so what was she upset about?"

He took a deep breath to calm his anger. "But that day she was cryin' to the uncles, one of the kids you sent to college was there, and he said that what I did 'is no longer done in our family.' That's exactly what he said, 'cause that's how they talk now. All hell broke loose and it was my own daughter, the oldest one, the one you ruined the first and the most, that told me I had to get out. She said she was ashamed of me and I had to leave. You know what they have now? 'Family councils.' Sounds like somethin' off **The Godfather** movie, don't it?"

Noble shook his head in disbelief. "You sent all the kids to college and what'd we get? They've 'upgraded' as they call it, so that now we're like the Mafia. Some 'upgradin' huh?"

I had to work to keep from laughing, but I figured if I did laugh, Noble might take a swing at me. Not that I didn't think I couldn't take him, but, well, sitting behind a computer day after day . . .

"And you know what else you done to us? You ruined our land. There ain't no more trailers. One of the kids—they're all so clean now I can't tell one from another—become an architect and he designed a bunch of little houses on Newcombe Land. Cute little places with garages to hide the cars in. The kid even designed matching doghouses and he bought each house somethin' called a 'pooper scooper.' You know what that is? He said we had to use it to clean up all the dog 'do-do.' That's what he called it. A grown man! So all the trailers were hauled away, and the old swimmin' hole was filled up just because it had a few leeches livin' in it, and they built those little houses. All of them are alike except just an itty bit different. They look like they fell out of a box of cereal. And rules! Those houses come with rules. No tires left outside. Not even if you fill 'em full of flowers. No cars that don't work. No weeds anywhere. We didn't have as many rules in jail."

Noble narrowed his eyes at me. "And you know what's **really** bad? The whole place won awards. One of the nephews named the place and entered it in a contest and it won. You know what they named it? 'Newcombe Manor Estates.' Can you beat that?"

Speaking of awards, I should have been given one for containing my laughter. To hide my mirth, I held the beer can in front of my mouth until my lip began to freeze.

"So, anyway, they had a 'family council' and decided that I'd done 'somethin' unforgivable' so I had to leave. Not one of the uncles stood up for me. They've got rich, college-educated kids to support 'em and make 'investments' for 'em, so they don't have to do nothin' but watch TV all day long and clean up the dog do-do before one of the kids arrives with those prissy little grandkids. Those kids told me I was a 'throwback to a darker age.' Can you believe anybody says things like that? When we were kids, what would one of the uncles have done if we'd said somethin' like that? We would have had our behinds blistered until we wouldn't be able to sit down even today.

"So, anyway, after they said I had to leave because I was 'soilin' the family name,' I said, 'What about Toodles?' One of the kids—maybe one of mine, I can't tell—said that Toodles was a criminal so he'd have to make it on his own. There's no sense of family in those kids. None at all. So I said that if I was leavin' I was gonna pick up Toodles and take him with me. See, I thought I'd get to their pride at that and they'd at least say they'd pay to send Toodles to some real nice old-age home. But nobody said nothin', so I took one of Uncle Cal's old cars and headed out. And all the way to the Fed where they had him, I kept wonderin' what I was gonna do with him when I got him. I didn't have no place to live and no way to support myself, much less a way to take care of an old man with a bruised brain. But just before I got there, I thought, 'Ford ruined our family so he owes us.' When I got to the prison I asked Cousin Fanner—You remember him? He works in the warden's office now. Lifer.—if he knew where you was livin' and he said that if you owned anything in the world, he'd be able to find you. So by the time Toodles was ready to leave, I had your address and we set out. And here we are."

And, I thought, here to stay. I've said a lot of bad about my relatives—and all of it deserved—but I knew, in spite of what Noble had told me about current circumstances, that they had a sense of family. They tended to travel around a bit—my relatives discussed the pros and cons (no pun intended) of prisons like businessmen compared airports—but they always returned "home." In fact, "home" was an important word to Newcombes.

As I sat there in silence with my cousin and went over his story in my mind, I knew what he was actually saying. He needed a home base. We might wake up tomorrow morning and find him gone, but he would leave some possession behind, a shirt, a pocketknife, something that would mean that my house was now his home.

His long story had been to tell me that right now he had no home base, no place to tie the far end of his leash.

All too well, I knew how that felt. After Pat died, I'd had no home base for years.

My problem in saying yes was that I was making a big commitment. We'd owned what we called "Newcombe Land" for a century. It was 146.8 acres of land that was owned jointly by all the adult Newcombes. When a boy or girl reached twenty-one, his/her name was put on the deed. The catch was that the land couldn't be divided or sold without the written consent of every person on the deed. Since there were now over a hundred names on the deed, that didn't seem likely to happen.

If I said Noble and my father could stay, I was making a sort of Newcombe vow. I'd have to stay here in this house in Cole Creek. If I moved, it would have to be done with the consent of Noble and my father.

Yeah, I knew it was ridiculous. I owned the house and I could sell it any time I wanted, but the rules that were taught to me when I was a kid were as strong in my mind as taboos against incest (something that wasn't done in my family) and turning blood kin over to the law.

I took a deep breath. "There're two unused bedrooms and a bath on the second floor. You and . . ." What did I call him? "Uh, Dad, can take those."

When Noble nodded, then looked away, I knew he didn't want me to see his smile of relief. When he looked back at me, he said, "This place is fallin' down, but I ain't got no tools to fix it."

After a moment's hesitation, I said, "Use the ones I have. The tools in the oak box."

Noble looked shocked. "I can't use them—not on my own anyway. Vanessa told me about those tools. She said they were famous. Said they were . . ." He thought. "She said they were a 'symbol of a great love.' They were a . . ." He frowned in concentration. "She said those tools were a meta . . . Meta something."

"Metaphor," I said, also frowning. As Jackie said, gag me with a spoon. If my sending Vanessa to college had made her talk like that, I wished I'd not sent the money.

The truth was, I didn't like to think of Newcombe Land being turned into some award-winning subdivision. I'd never thought of it consciously, but if I'd had kids—legal ones, that is—I'd have wanted them to swing out on a rope tied to a tree branch and jump into the Newcombe Pond. And what the hell did a few leeches matter? When I was in the second grade my teacher said, "We have a Newcombe in our class so let's have him tell us all about leeches." At the time I'd been bursting with pride, having no idea the teacher was being snide. But the laugh was on her because I went to the chalkboard and drew not only the exterior but the interior (don't ask) of a leech. When I sat down, the whole class and the teacher were looking at me oddly. I didn't know it until years later, but that afternoon in the teachers' lounge I was christened "The Smart Newcombe."

Smart is one thing, but pretentious is another. And my niece—daughter?—Vanessa was just too full of herself. "They're tools," I snapped. "Use them."

From the way Noble grinned, I saw that he understood. Maybe he didn't have the education to be able to reply to his uppity daughter, but **I** did.

"Yeah, tools," Noble said as he left the room, still grinning.

Three minutes after I was finally alone, I was on the Internet and had typed in Russell Dunne's name. It seemed like an eternity before the message came up saying that he wasn't known. At least not the Russell Dunne who fit Jackie's description.

At midnight, I went to bed. No Russell Dunne taught anything at any university in

North Carolina. Darn, I thought, I was going to have to tell Jackie that her paragon of virtue was a liar. Darn, darn, darn. I smiled happily to myself and wondered if I should tell her over champagne and candlelight. Break it to her gently.

I went to sleep with a big smile on my face.

CHAPTER SIXTEEN

Jackie

I couldn't begin to figure out all that was going on around me. There seemed to be issues between Ford and his dad, and Ford and his cousin, that were beyond my ability to comprehend.

Having read all of Ford's books, I figured I knew all about him, but he surprised me with the story about why his father had been sent to jail. Ford told me with his usual angst, with that poor-little-me face he always put on when he talked about his family, but I ignored it. I couldn't help but see Ford's father as a man who epitomized every virtue of a true hero.

While Ford told the story, my mind whirled.

I'm sure that Toodles—I hated the name but it fit him—knew Ford's mother didn't love him, but, in spite of that, he'd married her. Then he'd done everything he could to support his wife and give his child a good start in life. That a criminal act was the basis of that start didn't matter. Toodles had tried to do what was right. He'd risked everything for his wife, for his unborn child—and for his slimy brothers who'd wanted to use Toodles to save their own worthless hides.

I didn't agree with what Ford's mother did when she turned her son over to the guilty uncles, but I certainly understood why she'd done it.

In spite of knowing some of what was in that family, I was unprepared for Toodles's breakdown. First of all, I couldn't understand what was being said. Toodles said something I didn't understand, then Ford said he wanted to learn how to play cat's cradle, and the next second all hell broke loose. Toodles was crying—howling really—so loud that I had to shout over him. I think he was saying something important, but between the crying and his face being buried in Ford's beer belly, I couldn't make out his exact words.

But I could see that whatever he was saying was making Ford cry, too. Under my breath, I said, "Get a mop, there's **two** of them," but

Noble heard me and laughed. I tried to pull Toodles off Ford, but he hung on like a koala to a eucalyptus tree.

Noble finally put both his arms around Toodles's barrel chest and pulled him away. The scene had made everyone at the table weepy— except for Noble. He was the only one who seemed to think that what had just happened was "normal." If that was normal, then Ford's family was weirder than he'd made them out to be in his books. Was that possible?

Finally, Noble suggested that Ford tell a story and I must say that the idea intrigued me. **Could** Ford make up stories? He seemed only able to write roman à clefs about his bizarre family.

Taking his audience into consideration— namely, a nine-year-old and an adult child— Ford started telling about two little boys and the jams they got themselves into. From the way Noble was quietly laughing into his plate, I could see that Ford was keeping to his pattern and telling of the true misadventures of himself and his cousin.

I listened with half an ear because I was thinking about something that had happened earlier. That afternoon Noble had climbed in a window of my studio and removed the portfolio containing my photos of Tessa—the pictures I was saving to show Russell. It amazed me that, after having trespassed, Noble brought the photos into the garden and showed them to everyone. As though he had the right to intrude on a person's private property!

I was seething at his invasion and let him know it. What I wanted to say was that I had a great deal of influence with Ford and if I said something bad, there was a strong possibility that Ford wouldn't let Noble stay. But since Ford was right there (pouting in a hammock, but there) I didn't say any of this for fear it might backfire.

I did let Noble know of my extreme displeasure by giving him such a hard look I expected his eyebrows to burst into flame. However, I had to let up pretty quickly, because, after all, he was my employer's cousin, so I pretended I was interested in his praise. I was quite reserved, though, about what he was saying so he'd know to never again invade my privacy. I listened to what he had to say for a minute or two, then I took the photos to Ford. I wanted to let Noble know that Ford was the master of the household. Besides, now that my pictures had been exposed, I wanted to know what Ford thought of them.

Ford looked at the pictures slowly, one by one, but he didn't say a word. Nothing. For somebody who could maneuver words as he could, his silence was hurtful. I was at the point where I wanted to grab my pictures away from him when he did the oddest thing.

He kissed me.

He leaned over in that hammock—and that he didn't tip it over showed he'd spent a **lot** of time in one—and planted his lips on mine.

I wanted to say, "Ooooh," in that Valley Girl way of disgust, but, uh, well, it was, well, actually, the kiss to end all kisses. It was a real kiss. With feeling. Emotion.

At first it was as though Ford was saying that he thought my photos were really, really great. But, then, something happened a few seconds into the kiss and I began to see little stars. Okay, maybe they weren't little star-shaped stars, but they were tiny multicolored dots of light. It was like when your sleep-deadened leg begins to wake up and you feel hundreds of thousands of tiny points of pain. During my kiss with Ford, I felt those little dots—not of pain, nosirree bob, no pain at all—but they were dots of brilliant color. I saw them behind my closed eyelids as well as felt them.

After a while, Ford broke away. He looked a little startled, but he didn't seem to have felt anything like what I had, so I played it cool. However, I couldn't seem to take my eyes off Ford and I took a tiny step toward him. I don't know what would have happened if I hadn't slipped on something. Dazed, I looked down at the ground. Scattered on the grass were about a hundred or so little black rings of olives. Obviously, Ford had picked them off the miniature quiches Noble had made— enough to feed twenty-eight men, the number in his cell block, he'd told me. But I didn't understand. The night of my second vision, Ford and I had picked up pizzas and he'd asked for triple black olives, saying that he loved them. Knowing that, I'd bought lots of them, and told Noble to put the olives on the quiches with a heavy hand. So why had Ford picked them off?

I didn't ask because Noble said he was hungry and of course that meant **me.** I, the literary assistant had to, yet again, go to the kitchen.

After dinner, I got to continue being the high prestige assistant of a famous writer by making beds for everyone. Ford hadn't bothered himself to make a decision about where everyone was to sleep and, knowing him, he hadn't even thought about it, so it was left to me. Yet another crucial, executive decision I had to make. When I found out there weren't enough sheets in the house to make up the beds and I had to go shopping at eight P.M., and when Toodles and Tessa wanted to go with me so I knew a one hour job was going to turn into three, I started planning how big my raise was going to be.

I finally got us back to the house at ten-thirty, Toodles and Tessa loaded down with four-teen cartons of ice cream because they couldn't bear to leave any flavor behind, and I trudged up the stairs to make beds.

Noble and Ford had finally broken up from whatever they were doing in his office—play-ing with the train set?—and Noble helped me with the beds. I was feeling pretty over-whelmed by it all, but Noble made me laugh. He saw that I'd sort of taken my annoyance out on the credit card Ford had given me. And, well, maybe I'd had a little fun with Toodles and Tessa as we'd filled four shopping carts full of bed and bath accessories. As Noble carried everything upstairs, he told me that building contractors couldn't pack as much in the back of a pickup as I had. It was silly of me, but the way he said it made me feel as though I'd been complimented—which I didn't like. If I started thinking like one of the Newcombes, I was going to leave town immediately.

He got the electric drill I'd bought (in a case, complete with bits) and put up curtain rods while I used the new iron (deluxe, most expen-sive one they had) to press the curtains before he hung them. I must say that when we fin-ished, Toodles's room looked great. I'd bought him bug-printed sheets, curtains, rugs, and bath accessories. Well, actually, he and Tessa had chosen them, and Ford had paid for them—was going to pay for them—but I'd okayed it all. The bug fabric was relieved by a blue and green plaid comforter, and the curtains were white sheers with little pockets. They came with six embroidered bugs to slip into the pockets, and Tessa and Toodles had spent forty minutes discussing the other bugs they were going to embroider and put into the empty pockets.

Tessa chose colors for her room. No patterns, no prints, but every sheet and curtain was a different color. In the store I'd been dubious about her choices, but after Noble and I got the curtains up and the bed made, we looked at the room in awe. The kid had talent. Somehow, all her shades of green, purple, blue and yellow worked together. In the cart, the packages had been jumbled together with Toodles's bug prints, so Tessa's colors had looked like a mess, like bits of Play-Doh all mixed up—at least that's what I came up with so I could forgive myself for telling Tessa that her colors were all wrong. But when her linens were all together in one room, they were fabulous. And what I'd not realized was that she'd coordinated all the colors with the old, flowered wallpaper.

"Wow," I said, looking around. Under torture I couldn't have remembered what the wallpaper in that particular room was, but Tessa seemed to have memorized all the colors and repeated them in the curtains and linens.

"Wow," I repeated.

Noble was looking at the room in silence, the electric drill still in his hand, like a modern-day six-shooter. He cocked his head at me. "So who picked the stuff for **my** room?"

"Tessa," I said. He said, "Good," then we laughed together. The truth was, at the store, I'd grown so bored with the lengthy discussions Toodles and Tessa were having about the linens that I'd gone to the picture frame department and pre-spent the raise I was going to get from Ford. By the time I returned, they'd filled up two big carts, so I didn't see what they'd chosen for Noble's room.

Suddenly, we were both curious. He and I looked at each other, then we ran for the doorway at the same time. When he discourteously didn't allow me, a female, to go first, we ended up pushing through the opening together, and going nowhere. Had I not been told he was Ford's cousin, I would have known it then.

I won the first round. In disgust, I stepped back and said, "After you." Noble looked a little sheepish and when he stepped back, I ran through the doorway and down the stairs. But he wasn't carrying the extra weight Ford did, so he ended up beating me down the stairs and into the bedroom next to Ford's.

We looked at each other warily, not sure whether to laugh or not about our little one-upmanship escapade, but then we saw that Toodles and Tessa had dumped Noble's packages of linens on the bed before the two of them had disappeared, presumably to sample each of the fourteen ice cream flavors.

They'd chosen brown and white for Noble's room. The dust ruffle was white with a brown toile design of ovals of Roman coins, laurel-wreath-clad men's profiles in the ovals. The comforter and sheets were dark brown, the curtains brown and white striped. In the bathroom he'd be sharing with Toodles, there were no bugs, just brown towels and soap dishes of crudely-carved, masculine-looking alabaster.

When we finished Noble's room, it was nearly midnight, and we were yawning, but we took time to stand back and admire our work.

"I've never lived in a place like this," Noble said softly, and I thought that if he got weepy on me like Ford and his dad, I'd kick him.

"Now all it needs is a naked redhead between the sheets and the room would be perfect."

I was so relieved I wanted to laugh, but I said, "If she's for **you** she'd be red above but gray below."

Noble gave me a look that made me blink a couple of times, then said he'd show me how old he was any time I liked.

I was sure he was kidding. Maybe. Anyway, I went to my room rather quickly and locked the door. Ten minutes later I heard Ford lumbering down the stairs and I wondered what he'd been doing up there alone all evening. I'd told him that I hoped he'd write down that story he told at dinner. Based on the success of the Harry Potter books, I thought Ford might do well to branch out into children's fiction. Or, in his case, quasi-fiction.

The next morning at breakfast, there were a lot of us, and Noble made pancakes. Great stacks of pancakes. It was my guess that Noble had mixed up enough batter to feed twenty-eight men, but I didn't ask.

I'm not sure how it came up or who started it—although I think it was Tessa—but by the end of the meal, everyone was planning a party to be given on Saturday night.

Truthfully, I was torn by the idea of a party. What if Russell called and asked me out for that night? I'd have to say no, then I'd be miserable. I imagined myself being in such a bad mood that I'd dump a full bowl of punch over Ford Newcombe's head.

I knew it would be his head I'd dump anything on because I was only halfway down the

stairs that morning when Ford ran up them—
yes, **ran**—to tell me that no Russell Dunne
taught at the University of North Carolina.

Of course I defended Russell. How could I
do otherwise when confronted with Ford's I-
told-you-so attitude? No drug addict ever
enjoyed a fix like Ford Newcombe enjoyed
telling me that Russell Dunne had lied to me.

I wanted to push Newcombe down the
stairs, but, knowing him, he'd grab me as he fell
and probably land on top of me. And with his
ever-increasing girth, I'd be flat enough to be
pinned onto Toodles's vest.

So I didn't do anything physical. I just put on
my haughtiest manner and told him that I
knew all about everything, that Russell had
explained it all to me. Which, of course, he
hadn't.

So, at breakfast I was torn. Half of me didn't
want a party because I knew I'd have to attend
it and then I couldn't go out with Russell,
while the other half desperately wanted a
party so if Russell did ask me out I could say
I was busy. I wanted him to know that he'd
have to plan ahead to get a date with Jackie
Maxwell.

But I didn't have much time to think about
Russell because the Newcombes—and I was
beginning to think of Tessa as one, too—were
planning to put on a Party. Capital letter. No

hors d'oeuvres and drinks, but a major Party.

And you know what? They made me feel useless. Between Noble's ability to cook for twenty-eight people, Toodles's and Tessa's ability to make decorations, Nate's ability to set up, and Ford's ability to pay for everything, there wasn't much for me to do. Except to photograph it all, that is. I popped around with my camera in everyone's face and snapped, then retired to my studio to develop. I got some good shots, but nothing like the ones I'd taken of Tessa. I took a couple of Toodles sitting up and sleeping with his eyes open, but when I developed them, he looked dead. The pictures were too creepy for my taste. I pinned them on the wall, but I didn't really like them.

I tried to make a guest list, but soon realized we didn't know twenty-eight people in Cole Creek. "I could call some of the uncles to come up," Noble said. I guess I must have looked horrified at that idea because when I glanced up, both Noble and Ford were laughing at me.

When Allie came by that afternoon to pick up Tessa, I told her our problem. Allie said, "Serve food and the whole town will come." I said I didn't think that some people—I mentioned no names—liked us so they wouldn't be there, but that made Allie laugh. "You want me to invite people?" she asked. "Just so the total is twenty-eight," I answered, but didn't explain.

Allie left without Tessa. This time, Tessa and Toodles didn't have to repeat their tragedy act, as Allie was glad for some respite from the constancy of motherhood.

By the afternoon of the party, I still hadn't heard from Russell and I was beginning to be glad. In fact, I'd almost talked myself out of being attracted to him. I remembered that he was handsome, but so what? Obviously, he wasn't a good person or he would have called as he said he would. And, besides, he'd lied to me about UNC. He wasn't a man I wanted anything to do with.

And, too, there was Ford's kiss. I found myself glancing at him now and then and wondering about things. He'd never told me what happened the night he went to Dessie's house—and I certainly wasn't going to ask—but, as far as I knew, he hadn't seen her or even talked to her since.

As Saturday night grew closer, I was looking forward to it—and the reason for my excitement was that Dessie was going to be there. I was dying for Noble and Dessie to meet because I knew in my heart that those two were going to be a love match. And if Noble took Dessie away, then Ford and I . . .

I told myself not to think. Besides, just hours before the party I was sent away in Ford's pickup to get ice and more of everything that might possibly be needed, so that occupied my mind.

While I was out, I bought thirty-one rolls of film. Unfortunately, Ford saw the bag and gave a low whistle. "What in the world are you planning to photograph?" he asked. I grabbed the bag away from him and didn't answer. But blast it! My face turned red.

And of course Ford saw it. He was the snoopingest person in the entire world. I busied myself around the kitchen while Ford stood there and stared at me, and I could see the little wheels in his head working. Would smoke come out of his ears?

Finally, he gave a smug little smile and said, "The mayor and my dad."

I could have smacked him with a skillet. I wanted to tell him that he was wrong, but since he was right on, my dratted face turned purple. Ripe eggplant purple.

Laughing, Ford tossed a handful of peanuts in his mouth, and as he was leaving the room, he said, "Look out Diane Arbus."

Somehow, my face got redder. Diane Arbus had photographed circus people. She loved the weird and strange.

When I heard people's voices outside, I left

the kitchen (it now seemed to be Noble's territory anyway—which proved that God answered
prayers) and went outside. At about seven-fif-
teen the garden gate opened and in walked Miss
Essie Lee and Dessie. It was amazing that the
human body could take such disparate forms.
Dessie was all lush woman, while Miss Essie Lee
was as thin as a three-day-old stalk of wheat, and
about as juicy.

I couldn't help staring at the emaciated
woman and remembering what Russell had
told me. Had this woman helped pile rocks on
someone? Had Miss Essie Lee really helped
commit a murder?

Toodles and Tessa had been hanging some of
the origami insects they'd made on the trees
when I saw Toodles stop and stare at Dessie. His
arm was extended, a red paper giraffe hanging
from his fingertips, when he halted.

No, no, no, I thought. Toodles had the mind
of a child, but he was actually a full-grown man.
Was he going to be like his son and fall madly in
love with the over-endowed Dessie?

For a moment, I was frozen in my tracks.
What in the world could I do to stop this? As I
walked toward Toodles, I tried to compose
myself and think about what I could say to end
it before it started. That his son was already
having an affair with Dessie? That Toodles
would have to get in line? That if Dessie

Mason had any interest in a man like Toodles it would be so she could make a sculpture of him and sell it?

By the time I'd taken the three steps to reach Toodles, I'd come up with nothing I could say. He was still staring, his arm still extended, the little giraffe still swaying in the breeze—and his tongue was hanging out. No subtlety in him!

"She is the most beautiful woman I have ever seen," he said, and I let out a groan. Why was it that when I wanted to understand him, I couldn't, but now that he was saying something I didn't want to hear, his speech was perfectly clear?

When he started walking toward Dessie, I put out my hand to stop him, but he just brushed past me. I was contemplating finding Ford and seeing if he could do something with his father, when the most extraordinary thing happened: Toodles walked past Dessie as though he didn't see her. As I watched, my mouth open in disbelief, Toodles kept walking until he came to Miss Essie Lee. Looking up, since she was taller than he was, he gifted her with his paper giraffe.

I wanted to run to Toodles and protect him. What would that stiff-backed, dried-up old woman do to him? I'd taken one step forward when I saw Miss Essie Lee's face soften, and she became a wholly different person.

Toodles crooked his arm, Miss Essie Lee slipped hers into it, and the two of them walked toward the food table. As far as I knew, they hadn't exchanged a word with each other.

Feeling as though I'd just witnessed something out of a science fiction movie, I wandered back into the house. It was said that like attracted like. Ford's stories about his family made it clear that they knew all about various and sundry criminal behavior. Was Toodles subliminally attracted to Miss Essie Lee because the woman had participated in a murder?

The kitchen table and the countertops were covered with huge bowls full of food. I was standing there, munching and thinking about what I'd just seen, when Ford yelled, "What the hell is wrong with you?"

I jumped half a foot. "Nothing," I said. "Why are you yelling at me?"

Walking across the kitchen in two strides, he took a bowl of potato chips off the table. I had a potato chip—one of those thick, crinkly kind—on the way to my mouth. I looked at the thing as the nutritional poison it was and dropped it on the table.

Ford was frowning at me as though my eating a potato chip was immoral. I spent three seconds thinking about defending myself and starting a fight with him, but, instead, I stretched out my hand. Taking it as though he were a toddler, he followed me outside.

I hadn't been wrong in what I thought I saw. Miss Essie Lee was standing on a bench, Tessa was handing her origami creatures, and the thin woman was hanging them in the high branches. When Miss Essie Lee started to get down, Toodles took her by her narrow waist and swung her down. As she put her hands on his shoulders, she giggled like a teenager.

"Your father's in love," I said, but Ford was staring just as I had been a few moments earlier, so he couldn't make a sound.

It was sometime later when I finally saw Miss Essie Lee alone. By that time the party was in full swing and very loud. Earlier in the week, Ford and Noble had gone shopping and bought some serious speakers. The good news was that if the speakers ever broke, we could rent them out as condos.

Finally, there came a moment when I saw Miss Essie Lee standing by the fence by herself, drink in hand. As always, she was wearing one of her antique blouses, but her hair had come down a bit from its usual tight style, so she looked kind of good. I nearly ran over to her before Toodles returned and I lost my chance.

It took me a moment to get myself under control enough not to stare at her. Of course I wanted to know if she was a murderer, but that happened long ago, and right now there was something more urgent that needed attention. "So what do you think of Ford's father?" I yelled over the music.

"He is as pure as a sonnet," she said, her voice carrying better than mine. "Did you know that he doesn't know how to read? Isn't that refreshing?"

That set me back a bit. "Yeah, well, I guess it is," I managed to say.

"You don't know how tired I get of literacy. Everyone talks to me about nothing but what's inside books."

"But I thought—"

"That because I'm a librarian that I want my entire life to be about books? Not quite. We all want a **life.**"

Suddenly I thought of how Russell had lied to me about himself, or at least omitted some basic facts. Miss Essie Lee might possibly have a dubious past, but I still didn't want her, or any woman, to get hurt. "Did you know that Mr. Newcombe has . . . Well, that he's . . ."

"Spent his entire life in prison?" Leaning toward me, she whispered loudly, "I find that fascinating, don't you?" The next second her face changed. She was a girl seeing her first boyfriend. "There he is," she said as she ran toward Toodles, leaving me to stare after her in shock.

It was about a half hour later that I saw Russell. I was closing the garden gate—why, I don't know because everyone within hearing distance, invited or not, and far more than my original twenty-eight, had shown up—when an arm reached out and grabbed me. As the arm spun me out of the garden and toward the alley, I let out a little scream, but it was stopped by a man's lips on mine.

It took me a few seconds to realize that it was Russell, but his body next to mine made me forget that I'd decided I no longer found him attractive. Plus, I'd had three of some fruity drink that Ford had been making in a blender and telling me that he'd fortified with six essential vitamins.

Still, I could pretend to be furious. I pulled my mouth away from Russell's and said petulantly, "You didn't call me."

Still holding me, he nuzzled my neck. How did we go from two encounters to this? I wondered, but I didn't push my body away from his—his hard, lean, muscular body. Damn Ford and his vitamin drink. Was the thing half rum or two-thirds?

"I'm sorry, Jackie," Russell said in that divine voice of his. "I couldn't call. My father's been ill, but he's all right now. We thought it was a heart attack, so I went running back to Raleigh, but it was just anxiety. I was angry about the whole thing, but relieved. Can you forgive me?"

"They have telephones in Raleigh," I said even more petulantly. Are there degrees of petulance? Could I go from medium to high? "You don't teach at the University of North Carolina," I shot at him.

Smiling, Russell pulled me closer. "Not anymore. Not as of this spring. I quit because I'm working on a personal project and because I've had two other job offers."

He started to kiss my neck again, but I turned my head away. His arms were around my lower back, my hips against his. "Why didn't you tell me that?" I asked.

When Russell dropped his arms from around me, I wanted to take the question back. I wanted to be the injured party so he'd coax me into forgiving him. As he looked up at the stars, some wonderful person turned the music down. "I can't figure out what you've done to me," he said softly. "I've thought of nothing but you since I met you."

I tried to make my heart stop racing, but I couldn't. He was describing the way I felt about him.

Turning, he looked at me. "Promise you won't laugh, but for three days after I met you, I was like a cartoon character. I was walking into walls."

I tried to focus my rum-laden mind so I didn't blurt out that that's just how I'd reacted to meeting him, too.

"I'm just a boring college teacher who took some time off to do some research, but I can't think about my work because I keep seeing your face." Reaching out, he ran the back of his fingers along my cheek, and I could feel his touch all the way to my toes. "I don't usually reveal things about myself to people but to you . . . I told you more in an hour than I told the woman I almost married over the course of three years."

I forgave him. Damn, damn, and double damn, but I forgave him. Maybe he was lying. Maybe he never had been a teacher at UNC, but then maybe he had secrets he couldn't tell anyone. And didn't we all have secrets? Wasn't I sitting on some pretty big ones myself?

I slipped my arm into his. "Come to the party and meet everyone. Ford's father and his cousin are here, and I want to show you some photos I took."

Backing away, Russell glanced at the fence as though he were afraid of something. "They wouldn't like for me to show up in there," he said.

Why?! I wanted to scream, but my head was so fuzzy that it was difficult to think. I took a deep breath. "I told Ford about you." I stiffened my shoulders as I prepared for his anger. After all, I'd promised him I wouldn't.

But Russell didn't get angry. Instead, he gave a little one-sided grin and said, "What did he say?"

"He was jealous."

Russell laughed and the sound made me feel warm all over. "Does he have reason to be?"

He was reaching for me again, but I stepped back. "Ford has doubts that the whole town would dislike you merely because you gave Dessie Mason a bad review."

Russell smiled, his eyes bright even in the dark. "I've been caught." He looked at me for a moment, as though trying to decide whether or not to tell me the truth. "The research project I'm working on?"

"Yes," I said, and, somehow, I knew what he was going to say.

And Russell could see that I knew. Shrugging, he turned away. "Since I was in my twenties, I've been angry about what happened with my mother. Can you understand that?"

Oh, yeah, I thought, and nodded.

"All I've wanted to know is what happened. What really and truly happened. Does that make sense?"

So many words crowded my brain that none of them would come out, so again I nodded.

"I've asked too many questions in this town. People don't want to see me."

I didn't say so, but Ford and I had been in the same situation. "Miss Essie Lee," I said.

"She's just one of them."

"One of the main ones since she helped put rocks on that poor woman."

Russell looked startled. "No, her sister did that."

"But you said—"

Russell's eyes flashed in a way that made me take a step back. "No, her sister did that. You must have misheard me."

I put my hand on the gate latch. He was beginning to frighten me.

"I'm sorry," Russell said as he put his hand over his face.

Please don't weep, I thought. There was enough crying around me as it was. But when Russell looked up, the anger was gone.

"I really am sorry. I'm so tired that I'm short tempered. I may have said that Miss Essie Lee was directly involved because . . ."

I stood there in silence, waiting for him to continue.

When Russell looked at me, his eyes were those of someone who had known great pain. "Can I trust you? I mean really, really trust you? I need someone to confide in."

Part of me wanted to throw open the gate

and run back inside. I knew that he wanted to tell me something about the crushing, but I didn't want to hear it. I agreed with Ford that we should stop working on the crushing story because it looked as though I was involved. I did not, under any circumstances, want to hear or see something that would make me remember what I might have seen.

But there was that age-old man-woman thing, so I heard myself whisper, "Yes, you can trust me."

"I think my father may have . . . have taken what happened into his own hands. I think he may have—" Russell took a breath. "I think my father may have killed some or all of those people who put stones on that woman."

It was good that Russell's pain was getting through to me, or I would have been tempted to tell him that Ford had found out about the deaths. But I said nothing. I really and truly didn't want to become any more deeply involved in this.

I guess Russell could see that my silence meant something. Reaching out, he took my hand in his. "I've told you so much. You . . ." He paused for a moment while caressing my fingers. "May I see you again? This week sometime?"

I nodded. He and I needed to talk. With no

lies and no secrets—if that was possible, that is.

"Come Wednesday," I said. "At two. And, Russell, if you're too busy to show up, don't ever contact me again. Got it?" Amazing at how good that felt!

He nodded in understanding, his eyes twinkling. Then, smiling, he leaned over, kissed me on the neck, and slipped away into the darkness.

I went back into the garden and there was Ford, a CD in his hand, and he was looking at me curiously. "You okay?"

"Sure," I said, and tried to change my face from serious to party. "If your father marries Miss Essie Lee, does that mean you'll have to call her Mom? Will you have to speak at the garden club once a month?" I widened my eyes. **"Will she move in with you?"**

When Ford gave a groan of true fear, I went away smiling.

After that, I danced and had a good time. But in the back of my mind I was thinking about Russell. And Ford. At times what the two men had told me seemed contradictory, but Russell always seemed to have a glib explanation.

You know what was really in my mind? When he was a child, Russell had been bundled away in the night, and now he suspected that his father had murdered the people who'd crushed that woman. What kept going around my head, no matter how loud the music or how frantically I danced, was that maybe my dad had helped Russell's dad kill those people and that's the real reason my father and I had spent our lives running.

CHAPTER SEVENTEEN

Ford

On Sunday we all did some heavy-duty sleeping. Except for Jackie, of course. She was up and about before the sun was, and doing whatever she did all day. I'd roll over in bed, hear her outside, then inside, then out again. At one point, the words "cleaning up" came to me, and just the thought of expending that much energy made me even sleepier.

Somewhere around noon I got up, pulled on my old gray sweat pants and a T-shirt, and went downstairs to see if Noble had baked anything. I was hungry enough to eat all twenty-eight portions.

The kitchen was impressively spic and span, and although there weren't any home baked goods, there was a bag full of bagels. Since there were no doughnuts, I knew Jackie had been the one to go to the store. I ate one or two bagels before I went outside where I could hear voices.

Outside was as clean as in, and sitting in the shade were Noble, Tessa, and my father. Jackie was nowhere to be seen. On the little round table in front of them were three white bakery boxes full of doughnuts and four big cartons of orange juice. Ah, I thought, a real Newcombe breakfast. I took a seat and grabbed a jelly, surprised Noble hadn't eaten all of them, as jelly was his favorite.

"Right over there," Noble said, continuing what he'd been saying and pretending he hadn't seen me. I doubt if "good morning" had ever crossed a Newcombe's lips.

Of course I knew that his partial sentence was meant to intrigue me, but I'd die before I'd ask him what he'd been saying.

But Tessa wasn't a Newcombe. She was sitting on Toodles's knee, leaning back against his chest, and licking the powdered sugar off a cake doughnut—my least favorite kind. "Noble's going to open a bakery with my mom."

"Yeah?" I couldn't help saying as I looked at his profile. There was an edge of pink along his jaw, so I knew he was excited about this, but of course he was pretending to be cool.

Shrugging like it was nothing, Noble said,

"Maybe. It's somethin' to think about. Tessa's mother—what was her name?"

"Persephone," I said instantly.

Noble shot me a look that made me smile. As I picked up the quart carton of OJ, I glanced about to see if Jackie was in view. Between Pat and Jackie, it had been years since I'd drunk out of a carton.

"Allie," Noble said, "owns one of those Victorians across the street."

Since my office window looked toward those houses, I knew them well. Actually, not too well because of course I spent most of my time working and not staring out the window. "The yellow one or the one with the tarp over the hole in the roof?"

"Guess," Noble said, and I gave a snort. No guessing there.

"It's a great house," Tessa said, "but Mom won't let me go inside because the floors aren't safe." Leaning forward, she picked up a bear claw, broke it in half, gave half to my father, then leaned back against him. I wasn't jealous anymore. My dad and Tessa seemed to need each other.

Noble raised his eyebrows above the juice carton as he drank out of it. "Only habit," he said, meaning that only habit was holding the building upright.

"So what's the plan?"

Toodles smiled. "Allie says she can make coffee and Noble can bake so they're gonna open a bakery café."

When I looked at Noble, that pink line along his jaw was there again, only this time it was brighter. Well, well, well, I thought. This was serious. Last night I'd seen Noble chatting up Dessie, so I knew he was trying to get her in bed, but I hadn't seen Noble and Allie together at all. But if Noble was thinking of opening a bakery with a woman who could cook only enough to make coffee, then he was thinking of marriage. Would this be his third or fourth marriage? Or fifth? Vanessa said her father bought marriage rings by the gross—and she wasn't making a joke.

After a while Noble stopped trying to impress me with his coolness and started telling me what he and Allie had talked about. Toodles and Tessa got bored so they went to the big porch to make a kite. Noble told me that when they'd gone out to buy doughnuts, they'd stopped somewhere and bought some craft supplies.

"For the life of me," Noble said, "I can't understand bagels. Hard ol' things. What'd'ya think Yankees like about them?"

"Beats me," I said as I took the last cream puff. As always, I squashed the cream onto my extended tongue, and only when the pastry was empty did I eat the doughnut in two bites. "So tell me more."

I don't know exactly when they'd done all their talking, but from the red rim around Noble's eyes, I could believe he and Allie had talked on the phone after everyone went home. It seemed that Allie and her ex-husband had bought the rotten old house across the street from mine, intending to fix it up and live in it. But he'd received a job offer in another state and had accepted it.

"So why didn't she go with him?" I asked.

"Damned if I know," Noble said. "I didn't want to horn in on another man's territory so—"

He broke off at a look from me, as I silently reminded him that I didn't want to hear his B.S. If Noble wanted to know about a woman's ex, it was to see if he was going to, yet again, wake up with a shotgun under his chin.

But Noble shrugged in genuine puzzlement. "I don't know why she didn't go with him. She just said she 'couldn't.' "

"That's odd," I said. "That's just what Nate said. He 'couldn't' leave." I was looking at the doughnuts. There were six of them still in the boxes. Shame to waste them. "So what's the plan?" I asked again.

Noble told me he'd gone through Allie's house that morning and it was a mess, but he could fix it. He grabbed one of the napkins no one had used—**wipe** glazed sugar off fingertips? a sacrilege!—and looked about for a pencil. I pulled a little aluminum ballpoint out of my pants pocket. A person never knew when he was going to get an idea.

Quickly, Noble sketched the plan to the ground floor of the house. I'd never before seen him do that and I was impressed. I'd be willing to bet that his drawing was as close to scale as it could be without using a ruler.

As I looked at the drawing, I considered what Noble had told me about the next generation of Newcombes. One of the brats had had enough brains and talent as an architect to win awards. Judging from Noble's drawing, had circumstances been different, he could have gone to school and ... Well ...

I tried to concentrate on Noble's drawing and his talk, but there was something in the back of my mind that I couldn't seem to bring to the forefront. Noble showed how he could move this wall and that one, enlarge a door, and if he merged the kitchen with the butler's pantry, he could make a commercial kitchen.

My mind perked up when he started talking about "living quarters" upstairs. Those weren't Newcombe words, so Noble had picked them up from someone else, and I assumed it was

Allie. As far as I could tell, he was going to renovate the upstairs so Allie and Tessa could move
in there, then Allie and Noble would run a bakery on the ground floor.

Of course I was to pay for it all; that went
without saying. But I didn't mind. Having Tessa
across the street, and my dad playing ping-pong
back and forth between the two houses, suited
me. Of course with the way Noble cooked in
quantity, we'd all eat together.

As I listened to Noble, I kept trying to figure
out what was bothering me. It was an idea
about something, but I still couldn't pinpoint
what it was.

"Where's Jackie?" I asked after a while.

"Deep in acid," Noble said, nodding toward
her studio.

Last night I'd seen her camera flash go off
about a hundred times as she photographed
everyone and everything. I knew she was trying
to cover the fact that what she really wanted was
some knockout photos of Toodles and the
mayor together. A Munchkin and a gnome.

"So who was the man?" Noble asked, nodding toward the garden gate.

I grimaced. My cousin didn't miss much.
About halfway through the party, Jackie had disappeared through the gate and returned a few
minutes later with **that** look on her face. It was
the look I'd had to put up with for days after

she'd picked up that man in the forest. I hated to think of it as the "Russell Dunne look" but that's what it was.

But at least last night I'd been able to get her back to normal quickly. All it took was a joke or two from me about Miss Essie Lee and she was fine, dancing with everyone.

Noble was looking at me hard and waiting for a reply, but I had none, so I just shrugged.

Looking away, disgust on his face, Noble shook his head. "What'd they do to you up there in New York? Cut it off? What's wrong with you that you're lettin' another man take what's yours?"

I sat up straighter in my seat. "Jackie is my assistant. She's—"

"Hell! She's your wife except in bed. I never saw two people meaner to each other than you two are. Either of you gets in a bad mood, you just say somethin' nasty to the other one and you're all cheered up again. If that ain't true love, I don't know what is."

I couldn't believe what came out of my mouth next. "Love is mutual respect. It's caring about—"

Noble didn't even reply. He just got up from the table and went to help Toodles and Tessa with their kite.

Damn, but I knew what Noble was talking about. I knew very well that I was crazy about

Jackie. Yeah, she bossed me around and she sometimes cut me to shreds with that tongue of hers, but I sure did enjoy her company.

I sat at the table by myself, finished off the doughnuts and the OJ, and tried to think of something besides Jackie sneaking through the garden gate to meet some guy she'd known less time than she'd known me—but seemed to like more.

How could I tell Noble that I just didn't feel confident with Jackie? She was quite a bit younger than I was. And she was about half my weight. She should have some guy who got up at five and ran six miles.

Just days ago I'd kissed her and it had knocked me for a loop, but all Jackie did was start moving all those olive rings I'd pulled off my food with her toe. She was more interested in cleaning up than in me.

I sat there for a while, wallowing in self-pity, but also trying to figure out what was eating at the back of my mind. It had something to do with Noble. I went over all he'd told me about the family and Newcombe Land, but I couldn't pin down what I was thinking about.

For the rest of the day, I sat around in the garden or stretched out in the hammock, and at one point, I began pacing, but I still couldn't grasp what was so clearly in the back of my mind. It was as though there was a tiny nugget of gold buried in my brain, hidden under layers of debris, but, try as I might, I could **not** find it.

Jackie came out of her studio at about four and showed us her pictures from the party. The best ones were of Dad and Miss Essie Lee looking starry-eyed at each other. When Jackie looked at me, I knew she was thinking about who my stepmother was going to be.

But I was thinking so hard that I didn't so much as smile.

"What's wrong with him?" I heard Jackie ask Noble.

"Always been like that," Noble answered. "He's thinkin' on somethin' big, and when he gets it, he'll rejoin the livin'. And it's no use tryin' to talk to him now, 'cause he don't see you."

I wanted to refute that, wanted to tell Noble that that was absurd, but I was too busy trying to find the idea that was somewhere in my head.

On Monday morning I awoke at six A.M. and the single word "kids" was in my head. It was in huge letters inside my brain, and everything I'd been trying to find was in that word.

I pulled on whatever clothes I'd dropped on the floor the night before and went upstairs to my office. I didn't bother with a computer. This needed the intimacy of handwriting. I picked up a clipboard and one of the twenty-five unlined writing pads I'd bought, as well as one of my beloved rolling ball pens, and started writing.

It was Noble's presence and his story about saving me when we were kids that had planted that little nugget of gold in my head. And the story I'd told at dinner. And Jackie's remark about the Harry Potter books. Actually, I guess my idea had come from every word I'd heard since Noble and my father had arrived.

Noble had made me remember that there are two sides to every story. He and I'd been through, more or less, the same childhood. But he remembered our childhood as wonderful, while I remembered it as hell.

At the same time, when he'd told me what had been done to Newcombe Land, to the pond, to the trailers, and about the removal of the old cars and the truck tires, the hairs on my neck rose. What gave those snooty kids the right to try to homogenize America? Who said that all of America needed to have perfect little houses with "foundation plantings"? Who said that every inch of America needed to be "land-scaped"? In the Newcombe mind, plants and people were at war. If plants didn't produce food, they were treated to a Newcombe chain saw.

The tiny piece of gold inside my brain was to tell the same stories I'd already told, but from a different point of view. Stories, not about Pat's family because that was mine alone, but about the Newcombes. But instead of writing about them with angst—as Jackie persisted in calling my feelings about my past—I'd write about my family as though they were what's left of real Americans. Not homogenized non-people, but individuals.

My first thought was of Harley. In my fourth novel, I'd mentioned this young woman who'd been born while her mother was propped against a motorcycle and thus her name. I'd written that she'd died as she'd lived, at twenty-four, hit by a ninety-five-year-old man driving a thirty-year-old car, Harley's motorcycle flying across a ravine before crashing and breaking her neck.

I'd done a good job with that story because many readers had written me that I'd made them cry. I'd portrayed Harley as a wild girl who lived by her own rules, a girl who was doomed to failure because she couldn't conform to society's rules.

That story was mostly lies. Her real name was Janet and she looked exactly like her twin brother Ambrose. At least they were identical in all the parts we could see, and none of us wanted to look under the clothes of either one of them to see what was down there.

Their mother was my father's only sister, and she'd run off to Louisiana when she was fifteen and married a Cajun who spoke little English. They would come up to visit us every other year and we thought they were the strangest people in the world. One of the uncles told us that Cajuns ate crawdads, so Noble and I went around stuffing cherry bombs down all the crawdad holes so our Louisiana cousins couldn't eat ours.

Looking alike meant that Janet was an ugly girl and Ambrose was a pretty boy. Besides their faces being switched, so was their masculinity. Ambrose was afraid of everything and Janet—who Noble dubbed "Jake"—was afraid of nothing.

Jake climbed higher than any Newcombe boy dared climb. And she did **anything** on a dare.

She walked across a twelve foot long 2 x 4 stretched over a ravine, nothing but rocks a hundred feet below. She walked across the two inch side, not the four.

She climbed into Mr. Barner's bedroom window—while he was sleeping—and stole his false teeth, then hung them from a string inside his outhouse.

One evening, she sneaked into the elementary school kitchen and dumped the two jars of ants we'd collected into the baked beans that were about to be served to the PTA. School was closed for three days while they fumigated.

Jake stole the preacher's sermon from out of his Bible and inserted a copy of the Gettysburg Address. It was a sweltering hot day, no airconditioning, and since everyone was sleepy, including the preacher, he was halfway through reading the speech before he noticed. He looked right at Jake, Noble, and me, and said, "As our late, great president, Abraham Lincoln said . . ." then read the rest of Lincoln's speech.

After church the preacher took my right hand and Jake's left in his and told us he truly hoped we prayed every night that we weren't setting out to a path of evil that would see us end up in the flames of hell.

While he was telling us this, he squeezed our hands so tightly that I let out a whimper. I wanted to go to my knees and beg for mercy, but I looked at Jake and, even though there were tears of pain at the corners of her eyes, I could see that her hand could have been crushed and she would never ask for mercy. So of course I couldn't either.

As I began to sketch out stories of my relatives in rough form, and it seemed that a thousand ideas came to me, I began to develop a plot, a conflict between good and evil. In my previous books my relatives had been, if not bad, certainly looked down on. But in my new outline, I showed their heroic side. I excluded the stories about the way they dedicated their lives to suffering and were jealous of anyone who had the gumption to actually **do** something. I began to think of them as lazy, but lovable. And as every writer knows, what the writer feels, the reader feels.

Keeping to what I knew how to do, I based my story on truth. I made some of the second generation go to college and return educated and pompous, know-it-alls who were determined to make the family into some sanitized ideal. And I showed my fictional family fighting for a way of life that was fast disappearing.

As I was outlining ideas, I came up with making Jake grow up to be Vanessa. How did a devious, underhanded, fearless girl grow up to be a devious, underhanded, fearless woman? I'd have to **show** that.

I came up with a husband for Jake/Vanessa who I named Borden—so of course the Newcombe kids called him Ice Cream. He was from a rich Yankee family and Jake was trying to live up to his ideals of respectability.

I gave Jake the child some deep poverty so it would be understandable why she'd hunger for a stiff-necked husband like Borden, and why she'd try so hard to clean up her own family.

I rearranged my family tree so Jake and my hero—me—were cousins-by-marriage and not blood related. He was a widower, deep in depression—something I knew I could describe well—and he'd returned home the same summer Jake went back. Her intent was to remove the trailers and use an endowment from her husband's family to build cute little houses with no dog do-do showing. She didn't know that her husband's family was footing the bill so they could go to their Connecticut country club and show slides of the poor, downtrodden rednecks they'd enlightened—and show that their son's marriage to one of those "unfortunates" was actually a philanthropic act.

Of course Jake and my hero clashed, but in the end they fell in love and rode off into the sunset together.

The plot wasn't the big part of the novel. The characters and what they were and what they became was the story.

As I wrote down story after story from my childhood, I tried to figure out how to fit them into the overall plot.

I tried really hard to incorporate my father into the main story, but when I couldn't, I sketched out something about him on its own. "A short story!" I said aloud, then wrote down some things about a few of my other relatives. When I finished I had eight pieces, enough for a book of short stories, something I'd always wanted to write.

When a knock came on the door, I was quite

annoyed. How could I get any work done with interruptions every hour and a half?

Angrily, I yelled, "Come in!" and set my face to make whoever it was regret the intrusion.

My father and Noble came into the room, both of them wearing deeply serious expressions.

I wanted to say, hand me my checkbook and I'll sign it if you'll leave me alone.

Noble seemed to read my mind. "This ain't about money," he said as he and Toodles sat down, side by side, on the couch.

When I saw that they were sitting very close together, as though for safety—or reassurance— I thought, this is **big.** And time consuming.

"Look," I said, "couldn't this wait until dinner?"

"You ain't been to dinner in two days," Noble said, narrowing his eyes at me.

"Ah," I said. "Uh, what day is this?"

"Wednesday," Noble answered.

I'd entered my office on Monday at about six A.M. and it was now Wednesday at—I looked outside. Afternoon. Had I slept during those days? Eaten? There was a tray full of dirty dishes by the door so I guess I had.

If it was Wednesday I guess I could afford to take a break. A short one. "So what's up?"

When Toodles and Noble looked at each other, it seemed that Noble was designated to tell me. "You didn't tell us Jackie was crazy."

I suppressed a yawn. "She's more unusual than crazy. She's—"

"Crazy!" my father said. "I seen crazy people before."

What now? I thought. Couldn't these children settle their own disputes? "So what happened?"

"You know that man your woman's been seein'?" Noble asked.

"Jackie isn't my 'woman.' She's— Never mind. Yes, she's been seeing Russell Dunne. She told me about him."

"He ain't real," Noble said. "He ain't even **there.**"

The urge to yawn left me. "Tell me," I said.

"This afternoon at lunch—where you ain't been for three days now—Jackie said she had somebody she wanted us to meet. She said he was gonna visit her in her studio at two o'clock and could we come down."

When I looked at Dad, he nodded in agreement.

"Toodles and I didn't want to P.O. Jackie 'cause she runs everythin' around here, so we were in her little buildin' at five minutes to two."

Again Toodles nodded.

"We were lookin' at the pictures Jackie took when she looked up and said, 'Oh! There he is,' and we turned to look."

When Noble stopped, I said, "And?"

"And there wasn't nobody there."

"That doesn't make sense. Maybe she—" But I couldn't think of an explanation.

"You tell him," Noble said to Toodles.

And that's when I found out what a good mimic my father was. He got off the couch, put his hand on his hip in a way I'd seen Jackie do many times, and said, "I'm **busy.** Very, very **busy."** He swished about the room looking for dirt and cobwebs, then used an imaginary duster to eliminate them. When I laughed, Dad seemed to turn on, and he began to really put on a show. Pausing at one of the invisible cobwebs, he looked at it from different angles, then began to photograph it.

It was such a perfect pantomime of Jackie that I was laughing hard. The only word my father said was "busy," which described Jackie perfectly.

In my hilarity, I glanced at Noble, but he was sitting on the couch stone-faced, not even looking at Toodles.

Eventually, my father quit cleaning and photographing, and looked toward a door. "Oh! There he is," he said in a good imitation of Jackie's voice.

He opened the imaginary door, then introduced Russell Dunne to Toodles and Noble. Taking turns, Toodles portrayed himself and

Noble as they looked for, but didn't see, Jackie's guest.

It took me a few moments to stop laughing, but when I did, I wasn't sure I could believe that my father was doing such an excellent job of imitating.

Jackie had introduced Noble and Toodles to a man who wasn't there. She'd had a conversation with all of them, but when Toodles and Noble didn't reply to the invisible man's questions and comments, Jackie began to get angry. Toodles showed Jackie's anger, then stepped aside and mimed his own consternation. He showed how Noble had banged on the side of his head and said water had got in his ears in the shower that morning and he couldn't hear a thing. And Noble had put his arm around Toodles's shoulders, saying he was shy with strangers so that's why he wasn't speaking.

Toodles acted out Jackie's relaxing and smiling, then shouting to a deaf Noble that Russell said he liked Toodles's vest and did he have any rhinoceros beetles on there? Toodles showed himself displaying the horned beetle, his eyes wide.

Toodles showed Jackie listening to the man, then shouting that Russell had to go, so could Noble please move so Russell could get out the door? Toodles demonstrated Noble stepping in front of the door, blocking the exit, and pleading with Jackie to let Ford meet Russell.

"Would you?" Jackie asked, looking at empty space and waiting for an answer. "Sorry," she said, turning back to Noble. "Russell doesn't have time to meet Ford right now. So, Noble . . ." She motioned for him to move aside.

Toodles showed how he and Noble had held their breaths, watching the door to see if it would open by itself. But when the door didn't open, Jackie said, "It sticks sometimes," and she opened it, then went outside—after stepping aside for Russell.

Toodles and Noble got wedged into the door as they both tried to crowd through it. Toodles pinched Noble and when Noble yelped, Toodles went through first.

Once they were outside, to my disbelief—and no little repugnance—my father pantomimed Jackie in an imaginary embrace and kissing—complete with tongue—her invisible friend.

After the kiss, my father and Noble looked at me as though I was supposed to know what was going on and to explain it to them. As a kid, I'd seen that look often. From about the time I was nine, whenever anything filtered in from the outside world, I was supposed to explain it. Legal papers and anything from a doctor were handed to me, and I was to read and translate it into English.

Of course I knew that this imaginary friend of Jackie's had nothing to do with her being

crazy. If it did and she was, that would be an easy
matter to deal with. A few hundred milligrams
of some drug and she'd be fine. No more meeting men in the garden and we could all get back
to what we were doing.

I should be so lucky. I looked at Toodles and
Noble, once again sitting on the couch close
together. They looked like old first graders waiting for their teacher to explain why the sky was
falling.

"Well, you see . . ." I began. You're a wordsmith, I told myself, so start smithing those
words. "Jackie is . . . Well, actually, I think
maybe . . . I mean, **we** think maybe Jackie is,
uh—"

Praise the Lord, but the door to my office
flew open, distracting the three of us. Tessa stood
there, her eyes wide. "Jackie's having an epileptic
fit," she said.

I jumped up, Noble and Dad behind me.

"Get a spoon," Noble said.

"Join the twenty-first century," I shot back at
him as I ran down the stairs behind Tessa,
Toodles and Noble close behind me.

Jackie was sitting on the chair in the entrance
hall, her face buried in her hands and she was
crying. I knew she'd had another vision and I
wondered how much time we had.

Kneeling before her, I took her wrists and
pulled her hands away from her face. She looked

awful so I knew that what she'd seen this time was really bad.

I picked up all of what felt like twenty pounds of her, carried her into the living room, and put her on the couch. Noble, Toodles, and Tessa followed me so closely they were stepping on my heels, and after I put Jackie down, I sat on an ottoman in front of her, the Three Stooges sitting behind me.

"Where and what?" I asked.

If Jackie even saw the faces behind me, she didn't let on. She just put her hands back over her face and started crying again. "It's happened," she said. "Just what Russell said would happen, has." When she looked up at me, her eyes were full of fear. "I saw something bad inside someone's head."

I took her hands in mine. "Calm down and tell me about it."

She took a couple of deep breaths, calmed herself, then looked behind me. By this time Toodles's head was on my left shoulder, Tessa on his shoulder, and Noble had his head on my right shoulder. I must have looked like a four-headed monster.

I gave a couple of shrugs and for a second they pulled away, but they were back as fast as flies on watermelon. All I could do was try to convey to Jackie that it was okay to talk in front of them.

"Rebecca Cutshaw is planning to burn the town down," Jackie said, tears running down her cheeks. "I was inside her head and what I saw is horrible. She's full of anger. Rage like I've never seen before. She wants to leave here, leave Cole Creek, but she can't. Does that make any sense to you?"

"None at all," I said. "But a lot of things in this town don't make sense to me."

Tessa pulled her head off Toodles's shoulder and sighed noisily. It was the sound of kid-boredom. I guess that when she saw Jackie wasn't really having an exciting seizure, she wasn't interested. "The devil won't let us leave," Tessa said.

We all turned to look at the child. "What do you mean?" I asked as casually as I could manage.

Tessa shrugged. More boredom. "My dad has to come here to visit us because my mom is one of the people who can't go more than fifty miles outside Cole Creek. When she dies, I'll be the one, so I have to leave before she dies and I can never come back."

All four of us adults sat there blinking, opening our mouths like the proverbial fish. I think all of us wanted to ask a billion questions, but nothing would come out. After several seconds of silence it dawned on me that the urgency now was Jackie's vision. I looked back at her.

Her tears were gone and she was gaping at Tessa.

"How much time do we have?" I asked.

It took Jackie a moment to remember what we were talking about. "I don't know," she said. "It was night."

"Time for what?" Noble asked, turning away from Tessa, his head no longer on my shoulder. If I knew my cousin, he was thinking about changing the oil in his truck. Newcombes didn't like anything "ghosty" as they called it. They were superstitious to a medieval degree.

"Before some woman sets fire to the town," I said impatiently. Better to think of a fire than the devil.

Again Jackie put her hands over her face. "What I saw was catastrophic. People died because they **couldn't** get away, couldn't leave town. And, Ford"—she grabbed my hand in hers—"the fire trucks couldn't get here. They couldn't get into Cole Creek. Something wouldn't let them enter the town."

Tessa had wandered over to the little glass cabinet beside the door and was looking at some porcelain birds. "That's because the devil hates this town and wants it to die," she said.

My first thought was to find my Patsy Cline CD and listen to her sing "Crazy." My second thought was to raid the refrigerator and take six days' worth of food upstairs to my office and bolt the door. What had possessed me to ever want to write something about the occult? If I hadn't wanted to find a way to contact Pat I wouldn't have been interested in Jackie's devil story, so I wouldn't have—

Jackie was looking at me as though to say everyone except the two of us was insane. It was hard for me to meet her eyes because I knew, sooner or later, that someone—meaning me— was going to have to tell her that Russell Dunne didn't exist. And I deeply and sincerely hoped that the problem was that Jackie was a paranoid schizophrenic and/or had multiple personalities.

Maybe because my father had what Noble called a "bruised brain" he didn't see the shades of a problem. He got off the ottoman, went to sit beside Jackie, slipped his arm around her shoulders, and said, "Next time you see him, ask him to let them leave."

Pulling back, Jackie looked at my father in bewilderment. "Tell who what?" she asked.

"The devil," my dad said. "Next time you see the devil, ask him to let the people leave this town."

Jackie looked at all of us, seeming for the first time to see the way we were staring at her. "And what gives you the idea that **I** see the devil?" she asked calmly, but her eyes were flashing.

We adults, even my father, heard the edge in Jackie's voice, so we were quiet.

"The man you talk to," Tessa said. "The man

in the studio. The one who isn't there. The man you can see but no one else can see. He's the devil."

"Russell?" Jackie asked, incredulous. "You people think that Russell Dunne is . . . is the **devil?**"

All of us looked at Tessa in wonder. It looked as though she too had seen—or not seen, I guess—Jackie's nonexistent friend. When I turned back to Jackie, I saw that her face was turning red with anger. I'd seen her anger on the day she was to have been married, so I didn't want to bring it to the surface.

I gave a little smile and a shrug. "It's just a theory," I said, hoping she'd laugh.

But she didn't laugh. Instead, she threw up her hands and said, "I'm outta here," then stalked out of the room. I heard the keys jangle as she grabbed them off the hall table, and seconds later I heard my car start. I didn't try to stop her because she was putting into action what I wanted to do. But I wasn't free as she was. I had relatives to support and a house that I'd have to dispose of. I couldn't just walk away.

The truth was, I **wanted** her to get away. I didn't think I or my kin were in any danger, but for a long time now I'd felt that Jackie was in jeopardy. Whether the danger was from someone who'd murdered others, from a man who didn't exist in solid form, or the danger was to

Jackie's sanity, I didn't know. All I was sure of was that it was good for her to get away. Now. Immediately.

We didn't say much after Jackie ran out of the house, and I'd lost my desire to go back to my office. I went to the library to stare sightlessly at the pages of a book, while Noble went outside, opened the hood of my pickup and buried himself inside. Toodles went to the garden with Tessa, but whenever I saw him, he wasn't talking and there was a look of fear in his eyes. Only Tessa seemed normal. But then she had— maybe—possibly?—lived with the devil all her life.

Less than an hour after Jackie left, my cell phone rang. It was Jackie and she'd run out of gas. Exactly fifty miles south of Cole Creek, she'd run out of gas.

I'd filled the tank the night before.

CHAPTER EIGHTEEN

Jackie

I rode back to Cole Creek in the pickup with Ford in silence. Silence was the best I could do under the circumstances because I knew he and Noble had played a trick on me. Oh, yes, the two of them had shown up in the truck with a gas can in the back, but I wasn't "dumb female" so much that I couldn't see that the can was empty. They'd put it in the truck just for show, to make me feel better, because they knew they weren't going to have to put gas in a car that had a nearly full tank.

When I got in the truck with Ford he turned on the radio—something he never did because his writer's brain was so full he couldn't hear much else—so I knew he wanted to distract me.

Sure enough, as soon as I turned off the radio, I heard the car engine start.

I didn't look back but I knew that an hour ago, that car had been dead. So maybe Noble had done some boy-thing under the hood and made it start. Tapped on a spark plug. Put gin in the generator.

But I knew he hadn't. The car was dead for me, but alive for Noble. Just as Tessa had said, there were some people who "couldn't" get more than fifty miles outside of Cole Creek.

I leaned my head back against the seat and closed my eyes. I did **not** want this to be happening.

But curiosity got the better of me. Opening my eyes, I punched buttons on my cell phone. Random numbers with a New York area code. When I got someone's machine, I hung up. A few minutes ago the only number I could call on my phone was Ford's. Not even emergency numbers had worked.

Ford was silent, so I knew he was letting me have some time to sort things out in my mind. But how can one figure something like that out? Had I really seen and talked—and lusted after—the devil? Or was I—I hoped—merely insane?

I could believe that Noble and Toodles were "mistaken" about not seeing Russell. Or even lying. Noble could be angry that I was "steppin' out" on his cousin, and he'd be able to make Toodles believe whatever he wanted. But Tessa? She was the kid who told the emperor he had no clothes on.

I thought about how rude Noble and Toodles had been to Russell when they'd met him. At the time, I'd figured Noble didn't like the idea that I was seeing another man, so that was why he was snubbing Russell. Even when Noble pretended he couldn't hear Russell, I played along and shouted every word. I didn't get to tell Noble what I thought of him, but at least I got to use my preferred volume.

Russell had been wonderful. He'd smiled at Noble and Toodles, and had been gracious when they didn't answer his questions. He'd even smiled when they'd ignored his outstretched hand.

I'd been so angry at the two men that when I went outside with Russell, I'd given him a super kiss. I wanted those two to go to Ford and tell him that Jackie Maxwell didn't "belong" to him as everyone seemed to think I did.

Besides, I was sick of Ford's not being there. It was pretty boring around the house when he wasn't there. During Ford's three-day absence, Noble and Allie had spent quite a bit of time together in the rotting old house across the street, and a couple of times their laughter had drifted all the way back to me.

On Tuesday night Allie hung around so long we had to ask her to stay for dinner. Afterward, she got me alone outside and asked if Noble was impotent. When I asked her how she thought **I** would know that, I said it much more sharply than I'd meant to. It wasn't that I was jealous, but damn it! I had **two** men in my life, but both of them were weird enough to be aliens. Gorgeous Russell came and went like some migrating bird, and Ford had gone into hibernation like the bear he resembled. Result? I was manless.

"I just wondered," Allie said, oblivious to my bad mood. "I thought maybe Ford had said something about Noble's ability to . . . you know."

"That's the one subject we haven't discussed," I said, but she missed my sarcasm. It was odd, but I'd really liked Allie until she and Noble had become an item. Now Allie seemed a bit frivolous to me. It wasn't that she had a man paying attention to her and I didn't. I was bigger than that. It was just that I was more observant now.

Anyway, it seemed that Allie was worried about Noble's virility because he hadn't made a pass at her, not even to try to kiss her. They'd been spending many hours a day together and Allie had been lusting over him—making a spectacle of herself, actually—but Noble hadn't so much as held her hand.

I was disgusted with Allie's giggles but, to show her I was a nice person, I helped her out. Earlier, when she'd been stretching up on one foot to pick grapes, I'd seen Noble look at her from across the barbeque grill with red-hot lust in his eyes. So, obviously, he was playing some male game if he was making Allie believe he wasn't burning up for her.

I told Allie that at nine she should tell everyone she had to leave because she was expecting a call from her ex and didn't want to miss it. She protested but she agreed to do it. So Tessa had another sleepover, Noble volunteered to drive Allie home, and I called Allie at nine thirty, ready to pretend to be her ex's secretary, but no one answered.

When I got up the next morning, Noble was already in the kitchen, smiling and whistling, and when he saw me, he kissed my cheek. Minutes later my cell phone rang and it was Allie. She wanted to reassure me that Noble was **not** impotent. "Not, not, not, not, not—" she said. I hung up in the middle of what had to be the twelfth "not."

When I went back to the kitchen, I had to endure Toodles, Tessa, and Noble dancing around to some C-and-W tune on the radio. I stayed to one side and prepared a breakfast tray for Ford. I'd taken advantage of his continued, self-imposed isolation to fill him with nutritious food. I gave him cereal that was heavy on the fiber (oak sawdust would have been lighter) with soy milk, juice run through an extractor so it contained masses of pulp, and dry toast with whole seeds protruding from the dark brown surface.

So, okay, maybe I was trying to agitate him enough that he'd come out of his room and liven up the place, but I didn't succeed. At noon I delivered a vegetarian sandwich (plus veggie chips with an artichoke dip on the side) and picked up his empty breakfast tray. Right. **Empty.**

I didn't say a word when I delivered his food and sometimes I thought he never even saw me. Actually, a couple of times I was sure he didn't know I was there. I would have made myself known, but one day he was pacing and reading something out loud, so I stayed and listened. It was about Toodles and Tessa, and it was a combination of funny and so heartwarming that I wanted to sit down and listen to every word he was writing. But I didn't. Whatever it took to allow him to write a story like that, I was going to give it to him.

I closed the door and tiptoed away. Sometimes, between his grumpiness and having to feed him every two hours, I forgot that he was Ford Newcombe, the writer whose books had captured America's heart.

And, if I were honest, there was ego in my feeding him and keeping things quiet so he could write. I knew he hadn't written anything since his wife had died. So if he was writing now, maybe I'd had something to do with removing the block. Maybe plain ol' Jackie Maxwell had done something that had enabled this man to give yet more happiness to the millions of people who'd read his beautiful books.

By the time I was to meet Russell on Wednesday, I was feeling pretty good. I was getting some good food into Ford and I was doing what he'd hired me to do: help him write.

On the other hand, I didn't think it would hurt anything if when Ford did emerge from his den he was told that I was being courted by a divinely handsome man. So that's why I invited Toodles and Noble to meet Russell.

But the meeting was a disaster. Well, actually, half a disaster.

Part of me had been angry at the attitude Toodles and Noble had taken with Russell, but another part had been pleased by it. Did they see Ford and me as a couple so strongly that they couldn't bear to see another man near me? Is that why they'd been so rude?

Maybe I'd overdone it when, in front of them, I'd thrown my arms around Russell and kissed him with so much enthusiasm, but I'd really wanted to show them that I belonged to no one.

Just as I knew they would—okay, **hoped** they would—immediately after Russell left, Noble and Toodles ran straight up to Ford's office. I went to the kitchen and busied myself chopping vegetables for dinner. When Ford came down, I wanted to look busy and unconcerned. I entertained myself by rehearsing acting surprised at why he was so upset just because I was seeing another man.

But the clock ticked and Ford didn't come downstairs. In fact, the three of them stayed upstairs. What now? I thought. Do I have to haul three trays upstairs?

I got enough veggies chopped for fourteen people (Noble was cutting down by halves; next week he was going to try to go down to seven) and put them in the refrigerator. I went to the foot of the stairs and looked up. No sounds were coming from upstairs.

I fiddled with the dragon for a few minutes, watching the flame shoot out of its mouth, and wondered if anyone had shown Toodles the little creature. He'd probably really like it. Maybe I should call him. Or maybe I should go upstairs to Ford's office and ask if they were hungry.

But in the next second pain shot through my head and I collapsed on the rug at the foot of the stairs. Suddenly, I was inside Rebecca Cutshaw's head. I don't know how I knew whose mind I was inside, but I knew. I saw the interior of a house that I knew was hers, and I felt her boozy, unclear thoughts.

But most of all, I felt her rage. She drank to deaden the anger inside her. I couldn't tell exactly what she was angry about, but her rage was such that I felt as though I'd been tied to a stake and flames were eating me up.

I've never understood alcoholism, but in that moment I did. If I were being burned alive as Rebecca was and alcohol calmed the flames, I'd drink anything I could.

I was only in her head for seconds, which was almost more than I could bear, but I saw what she wanted to do. For some reason, the town of Cole Creek seemed to be the object of her rage, and she truly believed that the only way to get rid of the anger permanently was to burn it down. The vision inside her mind was so realistic that I knew she'd been planning it for a long time. And, worse, she didn't care if she died in the flames. She just felt as though she **must** remove Cole Creek from the face of the earth. And there was something I couldn't understand: She thought that there were people who could not get away from the flames—and people, like firemen, who could not get to the fire to put it out.

When I came to from the vision, I staggered

over to the hall chair, and moments later Ford was there—as he always was when I desperately needed him.

After carrying me into the living room, he asked me to tell him about my vision. I was so upset that I hardly noticed the other people in the room. It seemed to be just Ford and me.

Somewhere in my telling, Noble got involved, then Toodles and Tessa, and they started telling me that Russell Dunne didn't exist and that I'd been talking to a ghost. Only they didn't say he was a ghost. They said he was a devil. No, sorry. **The** devil. The one who's nearly as powerful as God. **That** devil.

It was all so ridiculous. I mean, if they wanted to break Russell and me up, couldn't they have come up with something less dramatic? They could have said he was gay. Or that he had a criminal record—and wouldn't Ford's family be in a position to know **that?** But no, they had to go for the gold and tell me I was seeing **the** devil.

Right. Sure. Why in the world would someone so important waste his time on a secretary-slash-cook-slash-amateur photographer? What was in it for the devil? Didn't he have his hands full with what was going on out in the world?

The whole thing was too absurd for me to take, so I left. I don't think I meant to leave forever, but I needed some time to get away from anyone named Newcombe—and that included Tessa and her devil-hating-Cole Creek story.

On the other hand, I'm sure that in the back of my mind was my deep desire to **know.** For weeks now Ford and I had danced around the idea that I was involved in what had happened to that woman years ago. But we had no solid proof of my involvement. By silent agreement, Ford and I had pretty much dropped the original reason for our coming to Cole Creek. And why not? He was writing again, and heaven knew I was happy since I now had my own photography studio. So why pursue something that seemed to alienate us from the residents?

The only problem seemed to be this Russell Dunne thing. And the fifty mile limit, of course. How absurd was that?

When I grabbed the car keys, I didn't consciously think of it, but I think I was determined to show them all that what Tessa had said was something the kid had made up. When I got into the car, I pushed the button to start counting the miles. I drove south in Ford's fast little Bimmer, so agitated that I straightened out curves. Twice I had to make myself slow down before I met an oncoming car and caused a wreck. If I got myself killed, no doubt they'd say the devil did it.

I watched the mile counter turn forty-eight, then forty-nine. As it started to roll over to fifty,

I smiled. Idiots! I thought. How could they make up a story like that? How could—?

When the counter hit fifty, the car engine stopped. No red light on the gas gauge. No warnings of any kind on the screen in that expensive little car. Just dead. And it wouldn't start again no matter how many times I turned the key.

Coincidence, I told myself as I got out of the car. I was glad I'd had the sense to grab my cell phone along with the car keys, but the phone wouldn't work. The ID panel said I had a signal, but when I called a number I got no sound. I couldn't call the police or a tow service. I went through every phone number in my directory but got only silence.

Finally, I called Ford's cell number and he answered. He and Noble got there faster than I had, which meant that they'd straightened out **all** the curves.

When I saw Ford I refrained from running to him and clinging. Yes, of course the fact that the car had died at exactly fifty miles was just a coincidence, but at the same time I was feeling decidedly unsafe.

Ford seemed to understand what I was feeling because he was quiet so I could think all the way back to the house. But then maybe he wanted to think, too.

When we got back, Ford pulled into the driveway, turned off the engine, and we sat there for a few moments in the truck cab.

Then, suddenly, Ford put a big hand on the back of my head and kissed me hard. "Whatever happens, Jackie Maxwell," he said, "remember that I'm on **your** side." With that, he got out of the truck and went into the house.

I sat in the truck and felt myself sigh—then I looked around to make sure no one had heard me. What is wrong with us women that we're such suckers for that strong, masculine crap?

I got out of the truck, shut the door, and stood for a few moments looking up at the beautiful house. If a person were trapped—and of course I wasn't—I could think of worse places to be than in this town in this house with this man.

As I went up the front steps I felt a great deal better than I had when I left.

CHAPTER NINETEEN

Ford

I don't think life prepares a person for meeting the devil. Or even for being just one person away from Old Scratch.

On the drive back to Cole Creek with Jackie, I knew that what I really wanted to do was hide in my room and disassociate myself from all of it. No one can explain how a writer feels when he/she has a great idea for a book, then the world steps in and won't let you write. I think it was Eudora Welty who said something like, "If you look outside and think, 'Oh, damn! It's a beautiful day so now people will come visit me,' then you're a **real** writer."

But you know what was odd? For the first time in years, I didn't think of Pat. I didn't think of how this wouldn't have happened if she'd lived.

Yeah, I wished I'd never started the whole thing about the devil story, but I certainly didn't wish I'd never met Jackie. And I didn't wish I'd not moved to Cole Creek. Sure, the house was creaky and it needed constant work, but I didn't mind it anymore. Jackie had replaced nearly all the wallpaper so there were no more thorns looming over me. I'd even come to enjoy one or two of the little porches. What she'd done in the garden was great, and—

And there was what she'd done with my family. Maybe I'd never feel about them the same way I'd felt about Pat's family, but, through Jackie, I'd been reconnected with my relatives.

All in all, I was happy with my life for the first time in years. And I figured that, maybe, eventually, Jackie and I would get around to my little fantasy with the olives. I knew she thought she was torn between me and some other man, but I didn't see it. I hadn't seen her sitting by the phone waiting for this Russell Dunne to call, and since that first meeting, she hadn't talked about the man in a way that made me think she was pining for him. In fact, at the

party when she'd sneaked outside the gate to
see him, she'd returned looking more angry
than anything else. She certainly hadn't looked
like a woman who'd just seen the love of her
life. Maybe it was my own ego, but I was beginning to come to the conclusion that her real
interest in Russell Dunne was in trying to make
me jealous.

Of course I deduced all this before I found
out the man couldn't be seen and was the devil.

How I wanted to ask Jackie questions! I
wanted her to describe his looks in detail. I
wanted her to repeat every word he'd said. I
racked my brain to remember what she'd told
me about him. He'd had a bag so full of things
she'd said it was like "magic." He'd made a
printer that wasn't battery powered work while
they were in the forest. Had he bought the
printer? What credit card did the devil use? Or
did he pay in cash? Maybe he paid with gold.
Doubloons, maybe.

I told myself to stop thinking like a writer
and start thinking like . . . Well, think like a
what? A ghost-buster? A psychic researcher? A
devil hunter?

When I glanced at Jackie, I could see that
she'd been pretty shaken up by all this, and I
knew that there was only one thing we could
do to end it all: find out the truth. We needed to

find out what had happened back in 1979, so we could figure out how to break the spell. Or could we? **Could** the spell be broken?

And then there was Jackie's last vision, the one that showed Rebecca burning down the town. When would she strike her first match? Where?

By the time we got back to the house, I had the beginning of a plan in my head. I tried to pep Jackie up because she was looking as forlorn as an abandoned puppy, then I ran into the house to enlist Noble's help. He and I had a few moments of a rather loud discussion because he was scared out of his mind by all of it. Noble would have taken on twelve lumberjacks in a barroom brawl by himself, but the mention of anything supernatural made him turn coward.

I pointed out some facts of life to Noble. He wanted to settle down in Cole Creek, but he couldn't with the devil running around and making people set fire to the town. When that had no effect, I wondered out loud if the devil would be kissing Allie next. The idea of **any** man, even the devil, touching "his" woman put steel in Noble's spine.

I called Dessie and asked her if she knew where Rebecca was. Dessie said Rebecca hadn't been to work in two days, which wasn't unusual, as she usually stayed at home to do her benders. But Dessie had been to Rebecca's house twice and she wasn't there, nor was she anywhere that Dessie had searched. "This time I'm worried about her."

I remembered the photo in Dessie's studio of the two high school girls together. They'd been friends for a long time, and I hoped they lived long enough to continue being friends.

I asked Dessie who in town knew the most about the devil's spell over Cole Creek.

When there was a long pause, I told her I didn't have time to play games. I needed to know **now!**

"Miss Essie Lee," came the answer, an answer I should have known.

After I hung up, I told Noble to get Tessa and to sit down with Jackie to go over every second of her vision, searching for details concerning places and times.

After I got them settled, Dad and I went to see Miss Essie Lee at her home.

Her house was a perfect little English chocolate-box cottage. I don't think it had started out that way but she'd made it so. In lieu of a thatched roof—who could find thatchers in the U.S.?—she had vines growing across the roof. The walls were white plaster, with inset, mullioned windows. The acre around the house was a perfect cottage garden, with vegetables and flowers all mixed up.

As we approached the door, down a quaint little stone path heavy with moss, pink flower petals fluttered down around us. While we waited for an answer to our knock (a lady's hand in brass) I looked at my father against the backdrop of that house and garden. They suited each other perfectly.

On impulse, I kissed my dad's forehead. Instinctively, I knew that he would soon move out of my house and into this one.

Miss Essie Lee opened the door, and in the seconds while Dad and she stared at each other in frozen rapture, I looked at her. Her at-home attire was as perfect as the house. She wore a cotton dress that had to be from the forties, and on her feet were pink, high-heeled mules with marabou feathers on the open toes. Some fifties bombshell would have worn those.

Without a question, Miss Essie Lee opened the door wider and we went inside.

If I looked hard, I could see that the place had once been a tract house, but Miss Essie Lee had transformed it into a movie set of an English cottage. The walls were plastered, the ceiling had beams cleverly painted to make them look ancient, and the furniture was all soft and comfortable-looking, covered with that

English mixture of a dozen patterns that some-how looked good together.

Oh, yes, I thought, my father would be living here. In fact, he looked like the perfect accessory for the house. It was as though Miss Essie Lee had said, "Now all I need to complete the decor is a funny-looking little man," and then ordered him off the Internet.

Or conjured him. And that thought reminded me of why we were there.

But before I could speak, my father did.

"Jackie talks to the devil," he said.

When Miss Essie Lee looked at me in ques-tion, I nodded.

"I'll change," she said. "There's no time to waste."

Minutes later she returned to the living room dressed in a suit from the 1930s, and black, stout shoes. I wanted to ask her if she too couldn't go past fifty miles outside Cole Creek.

I also wanted to ask her about all the people who had been crushed in various ways follow-ing the pressing.

But we didn't have time for that. Right now Rebecca might be striking matches.

As I pulled into my driveway, I said to Miss Essie Lee, "Jackie's name is Jacque**lane.**"

The face she turned to me was one of shock.

Then the next second she was crying. I was so surprised I couldn't move.

My dad jumped out of the backseat, flung open the front door, pulled Miss Essie Lee into his arms—and proceeded to bawl me out. According to him, I had a real talent for making women cry. And if being as smart as I was meant making women miserable, then he was glad he was stupid.

My dad said more, but I didn't have time to listen. As I ran into the house to find Jackie, my father's voice followed me. I didn't have time to stop and contemplate why I or anyone else hungered for a family.

Jackie was in the kitchen eating chocolate cream pie. Out of the pan. With her fingers. And the table was littered with empty cartons, bottles, and boxes: ice cream, cookies, maraschino cherries. The word "chocolate" was everywhere.

"Hi," she said cheerfully, with a **lot** of energy.

If I'd had a syringe full of a sedative, I would have given it to her.

Quietly, cautiously, I removed the nearly empty pie plate from in front of her.

"Mmmmm," she said, sucking chocolate from her fingers while reaching for the pie plate.

I half picked her up by her elbows and directed her toward the living room where I hoped Miss Essie Lee had calmed down by now.

Jackie grabbed a box of chocolate covered doughnuts—which I hadn't seen—on the way out of the kitchen.

Miss Essie Lee was resting her head on my father's shoulder. Considering that she was half a foot taller than he was and half his weight, this was an odd sight.

Plopping down on the couch, Jackie began eating the doughnuts.

When Miss Essie Lee looked up and saw Jackie, she moved to a chair across from her. "I should have seen it," she said. "I should have seen the resemblance. You look a lot like your father, you know."

"Thanks," Jackie said brightly, grinning, her mouth full.

I took the doughnut box away from her, and reached inside for one, but she'd eaten all of them.

Incongruously, I thought, I'll be damned if I'm going to live with a woman who I have to fight for the doughnuts!! If for no other reason, we have to get this thing solved.

"Orchids," Miss Essie Lee said. "Did you meet him at a place with wild orchids?"

"Yes," Jackie said, grinning and looking at me. "You saw the photo of the roses. There were orchids there, too."

"Yes," I said, "I did see them." I didn't like Jackie's perky attitude. I would have felt better if she were crying. Which reminded me. Why had Miss Essie Lee burst into tears when I'd told her Jackie's name?

"Can you walk?" Miss Essie Lee asked, looking me up and down.

So maybe I wasn't devilishly thin—every pun intended—but I wasn't past **walking.**

An hour later, I wished we'd had time to stop and buy a Jeep. Miss Essie Lee and Jackie, my father on their heels, were hotfooting it down an old trail that was all rocks and plants that I was sure were poisonous.

Jackie, leading the pack, was chattering away at ninety miles an hour about the time she and I had gone hiking together and, according to her, I'd complained "incessantly" about the cobwebs across the trail. I would have defended my honor, but I was too busy defending my life against tree branches, loose rocks, and a couple of kamikaze insects that looked lethal.

Every now and then, Miss Essie Lee asked Jackie a quiet question about her father and what she remembered about her mother. Jackie answered with a carefree air that made me want to give her pills to knock her out. Her attitude was proof that no one on earth should give up sugar. You needed to build up a tolerance so that when you did have it, you wouldn't go into some insulin shock and start acting like a toy with a broken wind-up spring as Jackie was doing.

After a long time we came to a clearing in the woods. It was a ghastly place. There was a rotting bench under a wall of dense trees, and a falling-down fence nearby. Few plants were growing, as though there was something wrong with the earth. Radiation, maybe. It was dark and gloomy inside the circle of tall, dark trees, but when I looked up, there wasn't a cloud. Behind me, I could see sunlight, but this place, open as it was, had none.

The worst thing was that it felt creepy. It was like the forest Hansel and Gretel had been lost in. It was like all the forests in all the scary movies. As I looked around, I expected big gray birds with long talons to swoop down out of the trees.

Miss Essie Lee, my brave father, and Jackie walked to the middle of the desolate spot. I stayed on the trail. There was light there and air.

"What do you see, dear?" Miss Essie Lee asked softly. Behind her back, she was holding my father's hand.

Jackie whirled around like Cinderella wearing a ball gown. "It's beautiful," she said. "It's the most beautiful place I've ever seen. The roses . . ." Closing her eyes, she inhaled. "Can you smell them?"

"Why don't you pick some?" Miss Essie Lee said, and it was the voice of a psychiatrist to a crazy, and probably violent, patient.

"Oh, yes," Jackie said as she sprinted over to the rotting old fence and began to break off bits of dying vine. When she had her arms full, she buried her face in the ugly mess. "Aren't they divine?" she said. "I've never smelled roses like these before."

When we were kids we used to catch bugs in jars, screw the lids on tight, and leave them there for days to turn into black juice. This place smelled almost exactly like that bug juice.

"What's on the ground?" Miss Essie Lee asked, and I saw my father step closer to her. He was as creeped out by the place as I was.

"Orchids," Jackie said. "Wild orchids. Lady's slippers. They're everywhere. Oh! I wish I had my camera."

"And when do lady's slippers bloom?"

"June," Jackie said, smiling, looking around the place, clutching her "roses" to her.

"And what month is this?"

"It's August," Jackie said, then she raised her head from the vines. "It's August," she repeated quietly.

I wish I could say that this bit of logic made Jackie see the place as it truly was, but it didn't.

Slowly, she walked over to the old bench and put the vines down, treating them as though they were precious.

Miss Essie Lee went to the bench, my father attached to her, and put her hand on Jackie's arm. She nodded toward the trees behind the bench, which were as dense as a rock wall. "Your grandmother lives in the house up there. She's been waiting for you for a long time." She smiled at Jackie. "When you played in this garden when you were a child, it looked as you see it now."

I saw Miss Essie Lee's hand tighten on Jackie's arm. "I hope you can forgive us."

This last sentence seemed to catch in her throat, and she turned away to the comfort of my father's arms.

Jackie looked up the hill and, for a moment, seemed to consider whether or not she wanted to visit this newly-found grandmother.

Personally, I wanted to get the hell out of there. If Jackie was seeing dying vines as fragrant roses, what was she going to see in her grandmother? Was the woman the witch from every fairy tale? Or was she the devil's handmaiden? Was she even **alive?**

I looked at Miss Essie Lee in question. "I can't go," she said softly. "Jacquelane must go alone."

Alone, I thought and looked at Jackie. She seemed to have made a decision because she took two steps toward the wall of trees.

Alone, hell! I thought.

By the third step, I was by her side. I slipped her arm into mine, and even though I wasn't Catholic, I crossed myself, and we started walking up the hill together.

CHAPTER TWENTY

Jackie

I know they all thought I was on the verge of insanity. It had never occurred to me before, but a person is the way she's treated. In the last twenty-four hours people had started seeing me as a person who was, maybe, losing her marbles, so I was beginning to see myself that way, too.

Ford had spoiled me. From the first, he'd acted as though my visions were normal, no big deal. He'd listened to my first "dream" and when he'd seen it in reality, he'd acted on it. Afterward, he'd not quizzed me or even once looked at me as though I was a freak. And we'd even had fun with my second vision.

While Ford was at Miss Essie Lee's, Noble

had grilled me until I felt like a cross between a witch and a spy. He made me feel as though burning-at-the-stake should be brought back as a legal punishment. He hinted that I'd moved to Cole Creek so I could find out everyone's dirty little secrets and use them to— What devious purpose I was to use my knowledge for wasn't clear.

I don't know how **I** came out to be the bad guy. If anyone was to be blamed, shouldn't it be Ford? I'd started this whole thing with a fiancé who'd stolen my life's savings, so I'd been pretty desperate for a job, preferably in another country. All I did was accept Ford's job offer and move to Cole Creek. Okay, so maybe it was my story that had set Ford off, but if he weren't so nosy, the story would have stayed buried inside me to my grave. So why was **I** being blamed? Because I'd had a vision or two? Me and half the world. Didn't these people watch cable TV?

As for Tessa, she was as bad as Noble. She didn't say much out loud, but she'd whisper something to Noble, then he'd ask one of his worst questions. After a while, I stopped thinking of her as an innocent child and started asking her questions in return. It didn't take long to figure out that she didn't know much. All I could piece together was that a

member of each of the founding families of
Cole Creek had helped kill the woman, and
as a result, the oldest descendant of each family couldn't leave town.

"So how do you break the spell and get out
of here?" I asked.

Tessa shrugged. "I don't know. My mom
won't tell me. All she says is that I have to
leave here before she dies."

"Then you never see her again?" I asked.
"Or if you do return and she happens to die
while you're here, do you get stuck here?
Forever?"

Tessa set her jaw in a way that let me know
that she wasn't telling me anything—or didn't
know any more to tell, I wasn't sure which.

In between questions, Noble offered me
iced tea-size glasses full of whiskey—such as
he was drinking—and kept glancing at the
door as though he were fantasizing about
escaping. Since I knew from Ford's books how
afraid of the supernatural his family was, I
could guess what he was thinking.

Afraid or not, Noble kept us on my vision
of Rebecca. I went over and over it in detail to
try to pinpoint where Rebecca would start
the fire. But we could figure out nothing. I'd
seen high, dry grass and the corner of a
wooden building. Nothing was identifiable.

Eventually, Noble decided to call Allie and get her to drive them around town to see if they could find Rebecca. I couldn't resist a remark about the nearly empty bottle of whiskey. I said Noble had made himself into a human compass and could now probably home in on any alcoholic.

I thought my comment was pretty funny, but Tessa turned traitor on me and, looking very adult, said, "You know what this town did to the last woman who loved the devil." Then, with her nose in the air, she took Noble's hand and pulled him out of the room.

After they left, the image that "child" had put into my head made me decide to see if some of my problems could be forgotten with alcohol. But when I picked up Noble's glass I couldn't get past the smell, so I set it down and went to the kitchen. Maybe I could find some cooking sherry.

But there was no sherry so I looked inside the refrigerator. Before Noble arrived, I'd had complete control of the food that entered the house. Except for Ford's ham, the most non-nutritious item I'd purchased was yoghurt with that high-sugar jam in the bottom of the carton.

But with the arrival of Noble and Toodles, I'd lost control of the refrigerator's contents.

As a result, there was sugar and fat, and fat and sugar inside that white box. Jam would have seemed healthy. I started to shut the door in disdain, but something snapped in me. I saw myself as one person—sane, hardworking, sensible—but the world was seeing me as someone else—flaky, semi-psychotic, and scary. Women who saw visions didn't eat healthy food. Women who saw visions wore purple shawls, big hoop earrings, and ate fried things.

By the time Ford returned, I'd pretty much emptied the house of its sugar content, and I was feeling **much** better.

In fact, I was feeling so good that I was quite agreeable to going for a hike with Miss Essie Lee, Toodles, and Ford. We walked through the lush North Carolina forest to where I'd met Russell, and the place was as beautiful as it had been the day I'd met him. But the others stared at me as though I were a madwoman. I figured that if they couldn't lighten up and enjoy the beauty, it was their loss. Ford wouldn't even step out of the forest. All this because this was the place where I'd met another man. His attitude gave new dimension to the word "jealousy."

Miss Essie Lee threw me a couple of times. She pointed out that the particular species of wild orchids that I saw so clearly bloomed in

June, not in August. I was a little shaken by
that, but then I thought that weirder things
have happened than some flower blooming off
schedule. Environmental conditions differ. If
there were snowstorms in June, couldn't there
be wild orchids blooming in August?

The second time Miss Essie Lee threw me
was when she told me my grandmother was
alive—and they all seemed to expect me to
walk into the dark forest to go to her.

Okay, so maybe "threw me" was a little
mild. Ran over me with a dump truck, backed
up, and did it again would have been more
correct.

I wanted to say, Couldn't we backtrack on
this a bit? First of all, didn't I need some more
information before I leaped ahead to "grandmother?" Maybe we should wait until we'd
established "who" I was. I had some ideas, but
I wasn't really sure. But Miss Essie Lee seemed
to know, and when I looked at Ford, he
seemed to know, too. Only Toodles and I
looked bewildered.

When confronted with the idea of entering
that forest, my first impulse was to suggest to
Ford that he and I go have a lunch of doughnuts and talk about this. Didn't I hear once
that some doughnuts came with cherry jelly
inside them? I'd always been partial to cherries.

I looked at the dark, dense, forbidding shadows of the trees, knowing they all expected me to walk into them to meet my grandmother. But my feet weren't moving. My sugar high was gone, and like an addict, I wanted it back. I turned to Ford. Surely, **he** would understand if I didn't do this.

But Ford was looking at me with his hero face. It was the face I'd seen in the seconds before he leaped out of the car and saved a bunch of teenagers from being blown up. I'd seen it when he'd kept me from going into hypothermia after my second vision. And I'd seen it when he carried me into the living room after my third vision.

Why, oh, why did I have to get hooked up with the only writer on earth who was a true-blue, dyed-in-the-wool hero? Didn't modern writers observe and not participate? Hemingways died out long ago. Now best-selling authors coached Little League. They didn't run with the bulls. They wrote eBooks.

I turned away from Ford and looked into the blackness under those trees. If I lived through this and Ford wrote about our experiences, he'd have to name it **Reluctant Heroine.** Reluctant to be; reluctant to go.

Taking a deep breath, I stamped down the urge to ask Ford if he had a candy bar, then took a step forward.

I wasn't surprised when Ford appeared beside me, caught my arm in his, held on tight, and started walking with me.

I thought of several things I wanted to say, such as begging him not to let me do this, but I didn't say any of them. Instead, I said, "If you write about all this, I want fifty percent."

Ford chuckled, but I didn't look at him. The forest seemed to grow darker, and the silence was maddening. No bugs or birds were making sounds.

I held on to Ford's arm and kept my eyes straight ahead. "Maybe you could write a story and I could illustrate it with my photographs," I said. "Or maybe you could write about your dad and Tessa." Words might help dispel my fear.

"Yeah, good idea," he said, not taking my hint and telling me he'd already written a story about them.

Ahead of us was pure blackness: a wall of dark so deep it looked solid. I'd been doing quite well in the bravery department, but that velvety blackness just about did me in. Maybe I should rethink my goals in life. Was staying within fifty miles of Cole Creek all that bad? I liked it here. I—

"Wish I'd brought the truck," Ford said, and for the first time since we'd started walking through that forest, I looked at him.

"Break a leg, kid," he said, then he kissed me on the forehead, and we looked ahead at the wall of darkness.

In the next second we let out a yell and held it as we started running directly into the void.

CHAPTER TWENTY-ONE

Ford

It was over.

Maybe not **over** over, but finished enough that we could all have lives and stop with the devil-story. I hadn't yet decided if I was going to write about what had happened. I think I'd have to discuss that with Jackie.

We were home now, and I'd managed to carry Jackie upstairs and put her in bed. I would have liked to undress her and snuggle down beside her while she slept, then, when she awoke, I'd let what happen, happen.

But I didn't do that. I pulled off her shoes and her jeans, but I left the rest of her clothed, then I sat on the chair beside her bed and looked at her. It had been a tough day and she slept like an infant.

At that thought, a little thrill ran through me. Kids. While I'd been with Pat, I hadn't thought much one way or the other about children. But since I'd met Tessa, I'd wondered, What if ? What if Pat and I had had children? What would they look like? Whose talents would they inherit? Whose mechanical abilities? Would the child be able to spell?

All sorts of things went through my mind, and I knew that I was toying with the idea that maybe Jackie would have me and we could . . .

Oh, well, I thought. That would come later.

Last night we'd burst through that forest onto a dirt road and seen a small, run-down house on the opposite side. For a moment, Jackie and I had stood there looking at each other in silence. The road and the house were so ordinary, reachable by an automobile.

I looked back at the forest, dark, gloomy, silent. "So what the hell was **that** about?" I asked.

Jackie looked as bewildered as me. "A short-cut through hell?" she said, making me smile.

Still holding her arm, I started across the road, but when Jackie stayed where she was, I looked at her in question.

"What did you see back there?" she asked. "You know, where I met . . . him?"

As we slowly walked across the road, I described the place, sparing no details.

Jackie didn't say anything, just nodded. I think she had the same thoughts as I did: Why? Over and over I'd asked that. Why? Why had the devil chosen Cole Creek? Why the woman Amarisa? Why Jackie?

By the time we were standing before the front door of the little house, I could feel Jackie trembling. I squeezed her hand, then knocked. A large woman in a white nurse's uniform answered the door and let us in. And inside, sitting up in a bed, was Jackie's grandmother.

Mary Hatalene Cole was in her eighties and, to my eyes, she looked as though she'd been wanting to die for a long time. There was loneliness, pain, and longing in those watery old blue eyes. She seemed to recognize Jackie instantly because she held out her hands, tears running down her wrinkled old face.

As I watched the two of them hugging each other—and Jackie had no reluctance or shyness—I couldn't imagine what it would feel like not to have relatives. I had so many of them that I got on planes just to get away from them. But Jackie'd had her father and no one else.

Neither Mrs. Cole nor Jackie seemed to want to talk about the devil or a woman who had been crushed by the townspeople. I knew that this woman had not participated in the crushing

or she would be dead. And as a Cole by marriage, I guessed she'd been spared the can't-
leave-town hex.

All Jackie and Mrs. Cole wanted to do was sit
close to each other and talk about their mutual
ancestors. Mrs. Cole had a two-foot-tall stack of
photo albums, and Jackie wanted to see every
picture and talk about every aspect of every one
of her relatives.

I looked at the dates on the spines of the
albums, chose one, and flipped through it until I
found a photo of the woman whose face had
been re-created by the forensic lab in Charlotte.
"Who is she?" I asked.

Mrs. Cole gave me such a hard look that I
turned red. She might be old but her mind was
certainly intact. Obviously, she knew that I
knew—

Holding the photo, Jackie studied it. I was
sure she also knew who the woman in the
photo was and, unfortunately, I could see that
she was struggling hard not to remember what
she seemed to be seeing.

I was eaten up with questions that I wanted
to ask, but I couldn't make myself voice them.
Jackie seemed to think she had all the time in
the world, but from the look of her grandmother and the machines by the bed, I didn't
think they had much time at all.

Was it true? I wanted to ask. Did Amarisa see

the devil? Had Jackie seen him? Why did the devil choose that woman? Who killed all the people who had been at the crushing?

When I looked outside, I saw that it was full dark around the house and not just in the surrounding forest. My imagination went into overdrive. Had the devil put up a protective force field around this house? Was this house like Brigadoon and only existed at certain times for a certain length of time?

To quieten my mind, I went into the living room and used my cell phone to call Noble. When they told me that he and Allie had found Rebecca in a bar **before** she set any fires, I offered up a prayer of thanks. And it seemed that Allie'd had to search for Rebecca before so she'd asked no questions.

I went back into the bedroom and told Jackie the good news. She and her grandmother listened politely, but I could see that neither of them was interested. They were talking about the store that Jackie's father had run after he married her mother.

"How can we break the curse?" I blurted out, making both women pause to stare at me.

"I would have thought Essie would have told you that," Mrs. Cole said. Looking at her granddaughter, she smiled, and I could see a world of pain in her eyes. There was a wheelchair poking out of a closet in the old house and I remembered the newspaper saying that she'd been in the car when her daughter had crashed. And I remembered that her daughter had taken two days to die. This woman must have had to lie there, trapped, and watch her daughter die.

"No one in town has told us anything," I managed to say, the images in my head making my throat swell. It occurred to me that my books appealed to so many people because so many had experienced as much pain as I had. To love someone so much then lose them . . . What was worse on the earth?

"It's time that you know everything," Mrs. Cole said, then waved her nurse away when she started to say that her patient was too tired. Mary Hattalene told us the story her daughter had told her during the days they'd both been trapped under the wrecked car. The rescuers arrived just minutes after Harriet died.

We'd pieced together much of the story in our time in Cole Creek. Harriet Cole, who Jackie's grandmother admitted had been spoiled and cosseted all her life, had snagged the handsome young man—Jackie's father—who'd come to town to open a pottery business. But after the marriage, the pottery had closed and Reece Landreth—Jackie's father's real name—had wanted to leave town, but Harriet refused. Over the next few years the couple had come to despise each other, with only their love of their young daughter holding them together. Reece spent his days running a small grocery, while Harriet, her daughter in tow, spent her days with Edward Belcher—which explained why Jackie knew my house so well. She'd spent endless hours playing there as a child.

When Jackie was about two and a half, her father's older sister, Amarisa, had been widowed and Reece had invited her to live with them. Mary Hattalene said that while it was true Reece loved his sister, he also desperately needed her help financially as his salary at the store was minuscule.

Amarisa gladly came to Cole Creek. She was a quiet person, as gentle and kind as Harriet was turbulent. The problem started because Jackie adored her aunt. It was understandable that Jackie would want to be with her aunt who took her for long walks, and let her use her camera to photograph the flowers, rather than with her mother who spent her days with pompous old Edward Belcher. It wasn't long before Harriet began to hate Amarisa, blaming her for all her problems.

Mary Hattalene said that as the months passed, Amarisa's life became difficult to bear. Harriet's anger and jealousy of the love that her husband

and daughter, and even the town residents, bore for the sweet-tempered woman increased daily. It was when Jackie, just learning to talk, came home from a walk with her aunt full of words about the man they'd met, that Harriet went over the edge. When questioned, Amarisa, blushing shyly, told of having met a man who had a lovely summer cabin in the mountains. No, she said, the man wasn't married.

Harriet was terrified that if Amarisa got married and moved away that Reece would go with her and take Jackie. Harriet began a campaign to keep Amarisa from getting married, but when she extended an invitation to the man, she was puzzled as to why he wouldn't accept.

Curious, Harriet decided to secretly follow Amarisa and Jackie and see the man for herself.

What Harriet saw was not the lovely cabin that Amarisa had described, but a pile of rubble from collapsed stone walls. Yet, as Harriet hid and watched, she saw her daughter and Amarisa laughing and talking as though there was another person there. She even saw them making the motions of eating and drinking.

Later, Harriet told her mother that, had it just been Amarisa, she would have thought the woman was insane, but that her daughter also "saw" this person horrified her.

Harriet ran down the trail to the minister's

house and told him what she'd seen. It was he who said that Amarisa had been talking with the devil. That night he called a meeting of the town council, which consisted of a member of each of the seven founding families, and two from the Cole family, Harriet and her father. They concocted a plan.

The next day Harriet told Amarisa that Jackie wasn't well so she couldn't go with her aunt on her daily walk. Smiling graciously, Amarisa set off on the trail, while Harriet left Jackie with a neighbor. What Harriet didn't know was that minutes after she started to follow Amarisa, Jackie slipped through a loose board in the neighbor's fence and followed her mother and aunt.

Eight adults and one child were hiding in the bushes in front of the fallen cabin that day. When Amarisa started laughing with a person they couldn't see, the adults stepped forward, but little Jackie crouched down and stayed still.

Mary Hattalene said that when the people confronted Amarisa and accused her of consorting with the devil, they angered him.

"For a moment," Mary Hattalene said, "he appeared. One second they were standing in that fallen-down house, then the next, the house was beautiful and there was a man there, a very handsome man. He was smiling at them in a way that my daughter said tempted her to smile back at him. It was a jealous Edward Belcher who picked up a stone and threw it at the man—and when he did, for a second, they saw the devil as people believed him to look: red, with horns and cloven feet. In the next second, he disappeared in smoke, and the house was again rubble and charred wood.

"My daughter said that after that she wasn't sure what order things happened in. When Amarisa backed away from the people, she fell, then someone dropped a stone on her, then another. Within seconds they were all in a frenzy and minutes later Amarisa was buried under hundreds of rocks. When she was covered, the people followed the preacher down the mountain and all of them spent the afternoon in the church on their knees praying."

It wasn't until late that night that an exhausted Harriet returned home. Reece wanted to know where his daughter and sister were. Harriet told him the lie she and the others had concocted, that Amarisa had been called away to an emergency in her late husband's family. One of the murderers had sneaked back and packed Amarisa's clothes and stored the suitcase in Harriet's father's attic. As for Jackie, Harriet said she was with a neighbor. But when they went to the neighbor's house to get Jackie, the woman said she'd seen the child go up the trail right behind her mother so the neighbor thought Harriet had changed her mind and taken her. Frightened, shaking, Harriet realized what had happened, but she kept calm long enough to tell her husband that Jackie had probably gone to find her aunt in the woods. Reece found his little daughter sitting in the dark forest next to a pile of stones in an almost catatonic state. It was two days later, when Jackie still had not spoken and Amarisa had not reached her late husband's family, that Reece got his wife to tell him what had happened.

Reece was enraged. He wanted to call the police, but he knew that to do so would further traumatize his daughter. She would lose her mother and grandfather as well as her aunt if Reece went to the police. Besides, he thought, who would believe him? It was his word against that of several people, one of whom was a minister. In the end, Reece's only concern was for the recovery of his daughter.

But not long after Amarisa died, the minister was killed when the marble altar in his church fell on him. Before he died—a slow, agonizing death while men tried and failed to get the massive marble altar off of him—he told Edward Belcher that the devil had appeared to him. The minister said that two days earlier, in the midst of the snow, he'd seen a beautiful garden, with wild orchids growing everywhere. Minutes later, the devil, the handsome form of him, had appeared. He'd said that the seven families must stay in Cole Creek until they had been forgiven by "the innocent one."

They didn't know who "the innocent one" was until Harriet told them that her daughter had seen everything. But Jackie had regressed to babyhood. She was back in diapers and was no longer trying to speak. The child wasn't capable of saying that she forgave them.

The night the minister died, the people who had crushed Amarisa, including Harriet, tried to leave town, but they couldn't. No matter what mode of transportation they used, they never got farther than fifty miles away.

It was after Mary Hattalene's husband, Harriet's father, told his wife that he'd seen wild orchids growing out of season, and two days later he was buried under a load of gravel, that the participants saw how each of them was going to die.

For months, Reece stayed in Cole Creek and tried to act as though everything was normal. He spent as much time as possible with his daughter. But just when Jackie was beginning to talk again, beginning to again be able to go outside without crying in fear, Harriet told her daughter that "people who love the devil must die."

When Reece was told this, he realized that his wife had no remorse for what she'd done. That night, he put his daughter in a car and took her away. Because he feared the people who'd killed his sister, feared that they'd use the Belcher money to take his daughter away from him, Reece changed his name and for the rest of his life, he moved often. From the time he left Cole Creek with his daughter, he was a man on the run. Every six months he'd hire a private detective to go to Cole Creek and snoop around. If the man heard anything, he'd call Reece and, often, the information he received would make him gather his daughter and move to another town.

When Amarisa's body was found in 1992, old man Belcher, who employed most of the residents, told the few people who had been living in Cole Creek when Amarisa was murdered that if anyone identified the picture the police were passing around, they'd no longer have a job. In those days, Belcher's word was law.

What Reece didn't know, and wouldn't have believed, is that the people of Cole Creek were looking for him and Jackie so she could forgive them and release the curse put on them by the devil.

Even though within two years after Amarisa's death, all the people who'd put rocks on her were dead, the curse was still in effect. The oldest descendants of the murderers couldn't leave Cole Creek. Allie'd had to stay behind when her

husband left to take a job in another state.
Dessie, returning to Cole Creek for her friend's
wedding, had been trapped there when her aunt
had unexpectedly died the day before the wedding. Rebecca had started drinking when her
husband, who refused to believe Rebecca's devil
story, had left her to travel the world. Nate had
been trapped when his young mother died in a
car wreck.

When Mrs. Cole finished, she looked at
Jackie. "The only way this can end is if you, who
saw it all, will forgive them for what they did to
your aunt. Can you do that?"

"Yes," Jackie said and I knew that she meant
it. Some people might want revenge but not my
Jackie. That thought made me smile. "My"
Jackie.

Mrs. Cole took Jackie's young hand in her
old one, tears sparkling in her eyes. I couldn't
imagine how she must feel to be able to at last
see the end of this horror.

It was late when the nurse, who'd listened to
every word, said that Jackie and I had to leave. I
felt frustrated because there were still thousands
of questions I wanted to ask, but we'd run out of
time. I told myself I was being ridiculous, but I
felt as though we might never see this woman
alive again.

When I'd called Noble, I'd told him where I

was and he'd asked Allie how to get there. I'd heard Allie ask why we were at Mary Hatalene's—as everyone seemed to call her— and when Noble said that she was Jackie's grandmother, Allie had gone into such hysterics of crying that he hung up on me.

When Noble called back he said he couldn't figure out what Allie was saying. The only sentence he could understand was, "We've been looking for her for years."

I knew I'd have to explain everything to my cousin and father later—and that thought surprised me. When had my relatives gone from being my enemies to being my confidantes?

When the nurse finally made us leave, I wasn't surprised when we walked outside and, standing in the moonlit yard, were the descendants of the seven founding families of Cole Creek. Allie had called them all together. Some of them we knew and some we didn't.

In spite of her fatigue, Mary Hattalene insisted that I help her into her wheelchair and we all went outside for the impromptu ceremony. One by one, Jackie forgave each of them for what they'd done to her aunt. It was a quiet group, but if the emotion could have been heard, it would have rivaled the trumpets of the angels.

It was late when the people began to leave, all of them too drained to be happy—or maybe they didn't yet believe their imprisonment was over.

Noble had left my truck, so I had transportation to take Jackie home. I wasn't surprised when she fell asleep beside me. With all that she'd been through in one day, I knew she was exhausted.

But she fooled me. As we got near home, she opened her eyes and said, "I want to see the place."

She didn't have to elaborate. I knew she meant she wanted to see the place where she'd met Russell Dunne.

Part of me wanted to say that it was late and we were both tired and we could do it tomorrow, but the larger part of me knew that I was being a coward. I was afraid of that awful place.

Jackie's courage fueled me. If she could take it, so could I. I turned the truck on a dime and went back to where I knew the trailhead was, but when I started to turn the engine off, Jackie gave me a wicked look and said, "You can't drive us into there?"

I couldn't help smiling. Years fell away; I was a Newcombe after all and I had a town girl beside me. I was sure there were several places on the trail that were too narrow for the truck to pass between the trees, but I was going to give it my best shot.

It was one hell of a ride! I'd gone with Noble and some of my other cousins over what I'd thought of as rough terrain, but it was nothing compared to what I went down with Jackie that night. If it'd been daylight and I could have seen what I was narrowly missing, I'm sure I wouldn't have continued. On the other hand, there was a giggle from Jackie now and then, and there was the thrill of seeing her bounce so high on the seat that she hit the ceiling, so I went on.

When we reached the clearing, I put the truck in park and we sat there looking at that awful place. It wasn't possible, but it looked even creepier in the headlights.

I didn't look at Jackie. Was she seeing roses? Wild orchids?

"It's horrible," she said at last, and I was so relieved that I wanted to shout and sing.

Instead, I turned on the radio and out came acid rock. Old-fashioned and mean. I glanced at Jackie, sending her a mental message, then raised my eyebrows in question.

She gave me a little smile, grabbed the handle above the door, braced her feet against the glove box, and nodded. She had read my mind, and she was ready!

I used the truck to tear up that place in the woods. Jackie whooped in delight as I ran over the fence and that odious bench. I felt a tire give, and I was pretty sure I'd done some major damage to the undercarriage, but as long as the truck went, I was going to keep smashing.

When everything in the area was flat, I backed down the hill and pointed the headlights toward the blackness that was the forest, toward what Jackie and I had earlier walked through. Again, I looked at her in question and she nodded a resounding yes!

I drove up the hill, dodging trees and rocks and unidentifiable shadows. And when we made it to the top and saw Mary Hatalene's house, with all the lights out, so peaceful and still, Jackie and I shouted in triumph.

The poor truck limped back to my house, sputtering, one tire flat, black smoke pouring from under the hood. I knew I was going to catch it from Noble tomorrow. Newcombes didn't say a word when a woman or a kid showed up with a couple of bruises, but you didn't do to a truck what I'd done to that one.

By the time we got back to the house, I was on top of the world and I was wondering if there were any olives around. I still had my little fantasy about Jackie, and I thought that tonight might be the time to enact it.

But when I turned off the engine, I saw that Jackie was sound asleep, and when I tried to wake her, I couldn't.

I was going to have to wait to get my hands and mouth on Jackie's sweet little body.

I opened the passenger side, caught her before she fell out, and ended up carrying her into the empty house and all the way up the stairs. To keep my mind off the way my heart was pounding from the exertion, I chanted, "I am Rhett Butler and you are Scarlett," all the way up. Of course I was hoping that Jackie would wake up, laugh, and we'd end up in bed together.

But that didn't happen. Instead, I pulled off her jeans, gave a couple of ferocious sighs full of self-pity, then went downstairs.

No one was in the house. I was sure that Noble and Allie were together somewhere, and no doubt Toodles was with Miss Essie Lee, and both thoughts made me feel even lonelier.

I went into the kitchen, poured myself some bourbon, and walked back into the living room.

There was a man sitting there. A tall, slim man who was devastatingly handsome.

Russell Dunne.

Maybe I'm flattering myself, but right away, I noticed things that weren't right. The scene was like a drawing in a kid's magazine: Find six things that are wrong in this picture.

For one thing, everything was too perfect. The flowers that Jackie had put in the room three days ago and that were ready to be thrown out, were fresh again—and they were perfect. There were no leaves half eaten by bugs, no brown spots on the petals. The faded chintz on the secondhand couch that Jackie had bought was now bright and new.

And, oh, yeah, even though it was about three A.M., the room was full of sunlight. And the sunlight was not coming from the windows.

I wanted to run away and hide, but I couldn't. I don't know if it was him pulling me to him or my own curious nature, but I couldn't stop myself from entering that room.

He lit a cigarette, one of those little gold-tipped black ones that look like elegant cigars, and gazed at me through a haze of smoke.

"I think you have some questions for me," he said in a beautiful voice.

God help me, but I could see why Jackie had believed herself to be in love with him. And I could even understand why she'd spent three days in a daze after she'd met him.

"A few," I said, then cleared my throat because my voice was breaking. Surely he hadn't shown up just to answer my questions about a murder?

"Why," he said. "You always want to know why." He smiled, letting me know that he knew all there was to know about me. "I liked that woman, that Amarisa," he said after a while. "Did anyone tell you that she had visions? Just now and then, nothing of importance, but she did manage to stop a few of my projects. But what really made Jackie's mother angry was the fact that her husband helped Amarisa when she had visions."

"Like Jackie and me," I said.

I was scared, true, but also, inside, I was jumping up and down. I was talking to the devil. The real, honest-to-gosh devil. Fumbling about as though I were blind, I found a chair and sat down facing him. I didn't want to blink. I might not live through tonight, but if I did, I wanted to be able to record every word, every look, every nuance of what I was seeing, hearing, feeling.

Instead of answering me, he smiled. "Amarisa could see me and she saw me as handsome. And little Jackie saw me as Santa Claus. You can't imagine how tired I get of being depicted as red with a tail. How banal."

The chapter heading flashed across my mind: "The Angst of the Devil." Or should it be "Life from the Devil's Point of View"?

"Amarisa used to talk with me. Did they tell you that the preacher put the first stone on her? He's in my house now." He smiled sweetly. "I have many so-called holy men with me."

I quit being flippant, because what he was saying sent a little shiver down my spine.

"But Amarisa was different. She wasn't afraid of me. She—"

"You were in love with her," I heard myself say, astonished at my bravery—or stupidity—for saying it.

That smile again. "Love? Perhaps, for even I have feelings. Let's just say that there are some people I want more than others."

That gave me more chills and I wanted to ask what my rank was on his "want" list. Top? Bottom?

"Her mother"—he nodded upward toward Jackie's room—"was jealous of Amarisa because she was good. She was . . . inside good. I don't see that much."

While he was talking, behind him, beautiful colored smoke floated up from the floor to the ceiling. I couldn't seem to look away from it as it wove in and out, around and about. It was only gradually that I realized the smoke was forming itself into a scene.

Slowly, I began to see scenes of my life with Pat. I saw Pat with her parents. The three of them were laughing together, glancing at each other now and then. Then, I saw Pat's father fishing. The scene changed, and I saw him on his front porch with his tools, with Pat's mother in the kitchen cooking.

She was baking her special cookies, the ones that were made of a combination of spices and raisins that used to fill the house with fragrance. Right now, yet again, I could smell them. For a moment I closed my eyes and inhaled. When I opened my eyes, Pat's mother was in front of me and she was holding out a plate full of them.

Instinctively, I reached for one. But it was just a vision and my hand went through the plate.

"Sure?" he said to me, as he took a cookie off the plate and began to nibble at it. "Very good. Now where was I?"

I guess he was used to people being too dumbfounded to answer him, because he continued without my saying a word. But I wasn't thinking about him. I was remembering Pat. The smell of the cookies hung in the air, and as he talked, he was waving one of those precious cookies around. One bite, I thought. Let me have one bite and let me remember clearly. **Truly** remember.

"Ah, yes," he said, "you want more information. Let's see. Where should I begin?" He got up from his chair and walked about the room. He was a very elegant man, beautifully dressed. "I was surprised you never guessed that I was the one who threw the rock over the wall. You were becoming much too complacent for my taste and I was a little concerned that you might stop searching altogether. And if that had happened, well ..." He shrugged to let me know that he and I were here now because of his planning.

He pointed the cookie at me, then looked at

it in surprise. "Does this bother you?" In an instant the cookie was gone and he gave me that winning smile of his. "I want to make it clear that I have a very, very easy job. People think I go around whispering in their ears, enticing them to do evil. But I don't. I just leave them to their own devices and they do all the evil that I could never even think of. Humans are much more imaginative than I am. You've heard of the people who get their ideas for their crimes from novels, haven't you?"

I nodded but since I don't write horror novels, I knew he wasn't talking about me.

He read my mind.

"You think your books haven't caused anything bad because they're so sweet? Back in . . . oh, well, I'm not good with years. 1283, 1501, they're all the same to me. But you remember how you wrote about your cousin Ronny drowning and how all of you were glad?"

He didn't wait for me to answer.

"A boy in California killed his cousin. He drowned him because he didn't like the kid. Got the idea from your book."

I slumped back against the chair at that one.

"So, now, where was I? Oh, yes, Amarisa. She didn't have an affair with me like people later said. I find it interesting what people make up to justify their actions, don't you? You see, what only two people on earth knew was that Amarisa was going to have a baby. Remember the preacher?"

Wide-eyed, I stared at him. "Was it his child?"

"Yes. But it wasn't a so-called 'love child.' The man met her on the trail late one afternoon and he raped her. Amarisa never told anyone because she knew that the information would hurt people, such as the minister's wife. When Amarisa found out she was pregnant, you know what she did? She thanked . . ."

He didn't say the word, just pointed upward, smiled at me in conspiracy, then continued. "Of course that guy had nothing to do with it, but I find that people often tend to give Him credit for whatever good happens to them. You see, Amarisa thought she was barren. Silly woman, she'd been totally faithful to her late husband, and he'd told her that their not having children was her fault." Again he smiled in a way that made the hairs on the back of my neck rise. "Her husband came straight to me from his deathbed."

Behind him, the smoke video began to play again. But this time it was just Pat, and she was sitting at our dining table blue penciling one of my manuscripts. I used to stand in the doorway and watch her, partly out of vanity, but partly just for the joy of looking at her.

The sight of Pat was making me remember her so vividly that I could think of nothing else. I needed to distract myself. Don't look at it, I told myself. "The minister was afraid of exposure for what he'd done so he placed the first stone and the others followed him."

Russell Dunne—for want of a better name—got up again and for a few moments he looked at the scene of Pat. She was in the kitchen now, pouring canned soup into a pan. Such ordinary scenes, but they pulled at my heart until I was sure it was bleeding.

Turning, he smiled at me again, and behind him, the scene changed. But this time there was a young man at a party. I was confused. Who was he?

"When Harriet saw Amarisa talking to no one, she was delighted because she saw a way to get rid of the woman. She didn't think of murder then; that came later. Of course I knew all of them were hiding in the bushes when Amarisa arrived that day, but I didn't let on. I wanted to see what they'd do. I know I'm not supposed to have a sense of humor, but I do. It's just that my humor is . . ."

"Black?" I asked.

"Exactly. Things that don't make other people laugh, amuse me to no end."

"They saw you." When I realized who the

boy in the vision behind him was, I thought I was going to be sick. It was the boy who'd killed Pat's mother. In the smoke-surrounded scene, the boy was drinking and partying, having a good time, but I knew that in just minutes he was going to end the lives of several people. One life he'd take with his vehicle, but he'd destroy others with grief.

"Yes," Mr. Dunne went on. "They rushed out of their hiding places and told Amarisa that she was talking to no one. And you know what? She didn't care. She really wasn't a bigot. Most of the time when someone finds out they've been talking to me, they panic. Or they"—he smiled—"start thinking how they can use me. Can you imagine that? They think they can use me to get them what they want, which is **always** one of those seven deadlies." He rolled his eyes as though trying to express his extreme boredom at people's lack of imagination.

The seven deadly sins, I thought. I was listening to him, but I couldn't take my eyes off the scene behind him. The boy was about to get into his car. It was an expensive car, paid for by his father.

"But Amarisa didn't do what other people have done," I said. The scene changed and I saw Pat's mother getting into her car. I wanted to jump into the vision and stop her. Please don't, I wanted to scream. Please, please don't go.

"No," he said, as though there was nothing going on in the room besides our very civilized conversation. "Amarisa believed that everyone deserved kindness."

"Even the devil," I said, trying to pull my eyes away from the sight of Pat's mother starting her car. The last time, I thought. The last time she'll go anywhere. Had I said goodbye to her? How long had it been since I'd told her I loved her?

"Yes. She was kind even to me. But they wouldn't listen to her. Instead, they acted like those people in . . . where was that in your country? Those little girls? Made into plays and movies?"

"Salem," I said.

"Right. Salem. They told her she was a witch. Of course Jackie's mother and the preacher had ulterior motives."

Pat's mother was sitting at a stoplight. When it turned green, I knew that she was going to die. The scene changed to show the kid in his car drinking a beer, and taking a deep drag on a joint. Marijuana hadn't been in the police report. How much had it cost the kid's father to keep that hidden?

"So I showed myself to them. Not in the way the books love to depict me but as I am. As you see me now. When that didn't work, for an instant, I let them see what they expected to see."

I watched as Pat's mother took her foot off

the brake, and the car moved forward. The kid didn't so much as glance at the traffic light. He was looking in the back for another beer.

As I watched Pat's mother approach the center of the intersection, my heart nearly stopped. I put my hand out as though I could stop her.

In the next second, I saw Pat's mother's face in the instant before the crash. She knew she was going to be hit, knew she was going to die.

He freeze-framed it. He stopped the scene on Pat's mother's face, then enlarged it. That look of horror on the face of a woman I had loved so much was frozen there for me to see.

I used every ounce of willpower I had and pulled my eyes away to look at him, concentrating so that I didn't see her face. "And how is that?" I asked.

"Oh, the usual. Lots of red. Forked tail. Shall I show you?"

"No, thank you."

Laughing, he waved his hand and Pat's mother's face was gone. I had to blink to keep from crying in relief. "So they knew then that she was talking to . . ."

"You can say it. The devil. Although I have a few other names. They were afraid and would have run away, but two of the people believed that Amarisa was the cause of their problems, so they didn't run. When Amarisa saw murder in their eyes, she backed away from them. But she caught her foot on one\of the stones that had been used for the chimney of the old cabin." He shrugged in a way that made me sure that he'd made her fall—and he had pinned her foot so she couldn't move. "I was still there and I could have stopped them but I didn't. You know why?"

"No," I said. My heart was pounding in my throat. I was looking into the beautiful face of pure evil.

"Come on, you're a writer. Make a guess."

"I have no idea."

His handsome face lost its humor. "If you ever want to write again, I would suggest that you make an effort."

I swallowed. "You wanted her."

The smile was back, encouraging me.

Maybe he was putting things into my head because, suddenly, I knew the answer. "If Amarisa had died in hatred, she would have been yours."

"You are good. Very good. Yes, exactly. I hoped she'd denounce them, hate them, and if she did, I could have her. She could live with me."

Behind him, the smoky visions had returned, and this time they were again of everyday things. Pat and her parents were at the dining table, laughing. They're waiting for me to come home, I thought. I could see that Pat's mother had baked a cake and it had my name on it. Which birthday was it for? I wondered. Which precious birthday was it?

"Don't you have enough people with you?" I asked, trying to sound—dare I say it?—devil-may-care.

"No. I'll tell you a little secret. I'd like to have everyone. I'd like for every person on earth to come live with me."

"Based on the news reports, you're making a lot of headway with that."

"Oh, yes, I am," he said proudly. "Large scale and small. The Internet is helping me a lot. People can do bad in private now. Evil likes privacy."

Pat and her mother were wrapping a gift for me. It was an expensive piece of software. Something to help me write The Great American Novel. But I wouldn't be able to do that as long as I had all of them. It would take death before I could write. I cleared my throat. "Did you get Amarisa?"

"No, I didn't." He sighed. "She didn't denounce them. Not even at the end when she was in great pain did she curse them. Her true feeling was regret about her child. She wanted that child, no matter who the father was." He said this with wonder in his voice.

"But you had your revenge on them."

"Oh, yes. That I did. One by one, I took her killers off the earth. They're all with me now. Every one of them. I get to keep them forever."

I drew in my breath, trying to calm myself. "And what about Jackie?"

"Oh, she was there, hiding in the bushes, and she saw it all. At the end, she even tried to save her aunt. You see, I gave Amarisa lots of time to hate the people who'd killed her. Jackie loved her aunt, really loved her. Which is what caused all of it. Harriet couldn't stand that her daughter loved her aunt much more than she loved her, so she looked for a way to get rid of Amarisa, and she found it."

"You didn't get Amarisa so you killed her murderers and wouldn't let their descendants leave Cole Creek. You . . ." I trailed off because the screen had changed again. Only this time I could see myself—younger, thinner, but me. I was in bed with Pat. She ran her hand down my naked thigh and, oh, Lord, I could feel it. I could feel her touch. When I closed my eyes, I could smell her breath, her hair. I had forgotten so much.

". . . have it back . . ."

I didn't hear the first or the last part of his sentence. Pat was sliding down under the sheet now. In all the years since I'd lost Pat, I'd not allowed myself to remember how fabulous the sex with her had been. It was "complete" sex.

Not just physical, but mental and emotional as well. Not just my body but also my mind. "What?" I said through a closed throat.

"You can have them back," he said softly.

It took all my strength of will to pull my mind away from what I was feeling and seeing on the screen to be able to listen to him. I looked at him, blinking. Even if I wasn't looking at Pat and me, I could feel her. Her mouth was on my ear now. I concentrated hard, trying to give my attention back to him.

As he glanced behind him, the picture began to fade. And so did the sensation. Jackie, Jackie, Jackie, I thought, trying to concentrate. And as my mind went elsewhere, Pat faded from the screen.

"I'm impressed," he said. "But then you writers do have excellent powers of concentration." This time when he smiled at me, I felt warm and good all over. What a nice man, came to my mind.

"I can give it all back to you," he said. "I can put Pat's soul into Jackie's body—or into Dessie's, or into any movie star's body that you want. But she'll be Pat. I can give you all of them, the whole family. You'll have a long life with them, grow old together."

"I . . ." I began, then tried to draw a breath. "This isn't about me. It's about Jackie and a woman who cared about you." Could the devil be made to feel guilty?

"Ah, but there you're wrong. My visit this time has nothing to do with Jackie. This time in Cole Creek is about **you.** What do I care whether these people go to the local mall or to one a hundred miles away? Jackie didn't send me an invitation."

I guess I must have looked as blank as my mind felt.

"You act as though you don't remember. Wait, I have it right here." Reaching into the air, he removed a floating piece of paper and looked at it. "I want to get this exactly right. I'm so unjustly accused of things that I had nothing to do with that I want to be sure I have it right. Ah, yes. **Have you ever lost someone who meant more to you than your own soul?"** He put the paper on the table and looked at me. "Is that what you said?"

"Yes," I answered.

Getting up, he walked to the far side of the room. Across from him began a vision of Pat in a sundress. I was pushing her in a swing. She looked beautiful, but I made myself look away from her. "Nothing to do with Jackie." Is that what he'd said? And it is "about you." Me.

He looked at me. "You drew Jackie to you because you wanted your wife back so very much. You wanted her back enough that you were ready to sell your soul to get her. Do I have that right?"

Yes, he had it right.

"You realized early on that Jackie had a connection to me, and you wanted a way to contact me so you could make a bargain. Your soul told me that you'd do **anything** to get your wife back. You yearned for all of them so much that you called me to you."

I couldn't say anything. That **I** was the reason for his appearance made my mind spin.

"I'll tell you what," he said. "I don't usually do this, but I'll make you an even better offer. Instead of putting their souls into new bodies, I'll rewrite history."

At that he looked toward the far wall and I saw Pat's mother's face again, just before she was hit by a drunken, high kid and killed. But this time, I saw the kid look up in time to swerve the car and miss her. In the next second, Pat's mother was on the side of the road, scared, but safe.

I couldn't help the tears that came to my eyes. As I watched, I saw other scenes. I saw Pat's mother grow old beside her husband. He didn't die young because he hadn't had the grief that killed him. And he didn't go blind.

In the next second, I saw a little girl on her bicycle and at first I didn't know what the scene was about. But then I remembered. It was Pat as a child, and it was the day she'd fallen on a piece of rebar and had been rendered barren. But as I watched, I saw her young body twist just before she hit the piece of iron.

The next scene was me with a little girl on my lap. Our daughter, and she looked exactly like Pat.

"I can give it all to you," Russell Dunne said.

I could feel tears running down my cheeks, but I didn't have the strength to wipe them away. It wouldn't be just me affected, but them, too. Didn't they deserve a lifetime of happiness? A **full** lifetime?

"It's yours if you want it," he said. "And, by the way, I'll read the answer from your heart, not from your words. If a person says no to me, but his heart says yes, then I take the yes."

"No," I said, as Pat came back onto the screen. She was older than she'd been when she died, and she was picking up a child who I knew was our grandchild. "No," I said again. I saw myself, older, too, and I was rolling on the grass with the three most beautiful grandchildren the world had ever produced. I said "no" a third time, but even I could hear what my heart was really saying. Yes. I wanted what I was seeing enough to give up my soul to get it.

As I watched, Pat turned to me, smiling, and

said, "I love you, Ford. I want to be with you. Don't let me die again."

And that's when I released her. Pat wouldn't have said that. She didn't blame me for her death. She would never have insinuated that **I** had let her die. Whoever was in that vision wasn't Pat, not **my** Pat, not the woman I'd loved so much. I looked back at him. "No," I said softly, but firmly this time. "No."

When the screen went blank, I wasn't sure if I felt relief or deep emptiness.

"I tried," Russell Dunne said, smiling in that charming way he had. "You can't blame a guy for trying." He nodded toward the ceiling and Jackie's room. "She doesn't love you, you know. No one will ever love you as wholly as your wife did."

"Maybe not," I said, giving him the cockiest look I could manage. I was scared to death of him—literally—and I'm sure he knew it, but I didn't want him to see the pain his words caused me. I knew I'd come to love Jackie and I'd come to hope that she cared for me. But if not . . . I gave a little shrug, meant to say that I'd take what I could get out of life. "I'll tell Pat how much she meant to me when I see her again."

He gave me a little one-sided smile. "Right. In **that** place. I used to live there. Did you know that?" He didn't wait for my answer. "Maybe I'll try you again later."

"Yeah, you do that," I said.

And in the next second, he was gone.

I don't know how long I sat there in the dark. When he left, so did the sunshine. I sat down on one of the big leather chairs and tried to think about all I'd heard and seen. I wondered how long it would take me to stop shaking inside. Years?

The sun came up, but I didn't notice. In fact, I didn't come alive even when Jackie came into the room, yawning.

"Did you take my jeans off last night?" she asked.

"Yeah," I said, distracted.

To my surprise, Jackie sat down on my lap and began to kiss me. "Why don't you ever do that when I'm **awake?**"

It took me several moments to come back from the dark place in my mind, but I did it.

I needed Jackie at that moment, needed her warmth, her strength, and her laughter. I kissed her back and before long we were making love on the living room carpet. After an hour or so, we decided we'd better go upstairs in case anyone came home, but we only made it as far as the stairs. I bent Jackie's supple body across the treads and showed her how "old" I was.

It was hours before we finally made it into her bedroom.

Somewhere about noon, we paused for a while, and I ran downstairs to get us some lunch. I was smiling. Actually, I was smirking, because young Jackie was worn out. Ha ha. She had at last discovered what I conserve my energy **for.**

While I was in the kitchen making us sandwiches and getting myself some of a peach pie Noble had made—and thanking heaven that Jackie had said she never wanted to see sugar again—I picked up a can of black olives and an opener.

As I went back toward the staircase, I saw a piece of paper on the floor. Setting down the tray, I picked it up. **Have you ever lost someone who meant more to you than your own soul?** was printed on the paper.

Looking at the note made me shudder. Slowly, I turned the tip of the dragon's tail and burned the paper in the flame that shot from its mouth. Somehow, destroying that paper with fire seemed appropriate.

It was an hour later, after I'd eaten every olive in the can in a very interesting way, that Jackie told me she loved me. She was a little hurt at my initial reaction because I laughed. And it didn't help that the explanation for my laughter was that she'd just proven that the devil was a liar.

That statement made her look at me as though I was crazy. "Did you think he wasn't?"

she asked. "Did you think the devil was a good, kind, honest person?"

"**You** did," I said, pulling her on top of my naked body. "When you met him, you liked him a lot."

"Naw, I just wanted his camera equipment."

"Yeah?" I said. "It just so happens that I have some camera equipment to share with you."

"Let me guess," she said. "A tripod. Fully extended."

We laughed together.

But then, from the first, Jackie had been able to make me laugh.